THE RISE OF SCARLETT HEROUX

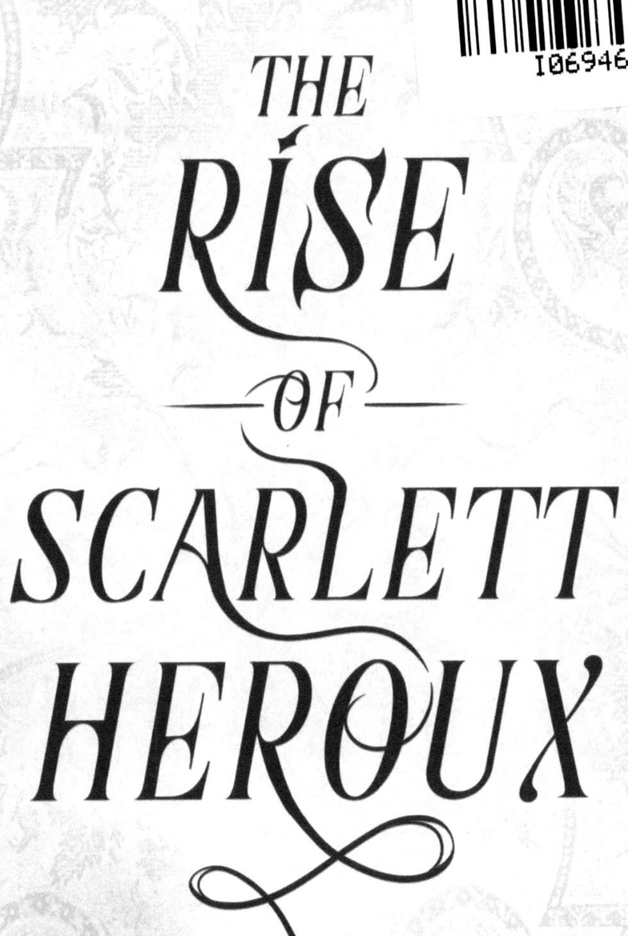

THE RISE OF SCARLETT HEROUX

The
NORTH STARS SAGA
BOOK ONE

ELIZABETH WATSON

First Edition
Published in the United States of America

Cover design by Story Wrappers
Interior design by Travis Hasenour
Map illustrations by Dewi Hargreaves
Edited by Ema Barnes
[illegible]
Copyedited by Bryony Leah Editorial
Proofread by Crystal Shelley/Rabbit with a Red Pen

ISBN 978-1-969389-00-9 (ebook)
ISBN 978-1-969389-01-6 (paperback)
ISBN 978-1-969389-02-3 (hardback)

For my husband, Marcus,
who loves me exactly as I am.
We're my favorite love story.

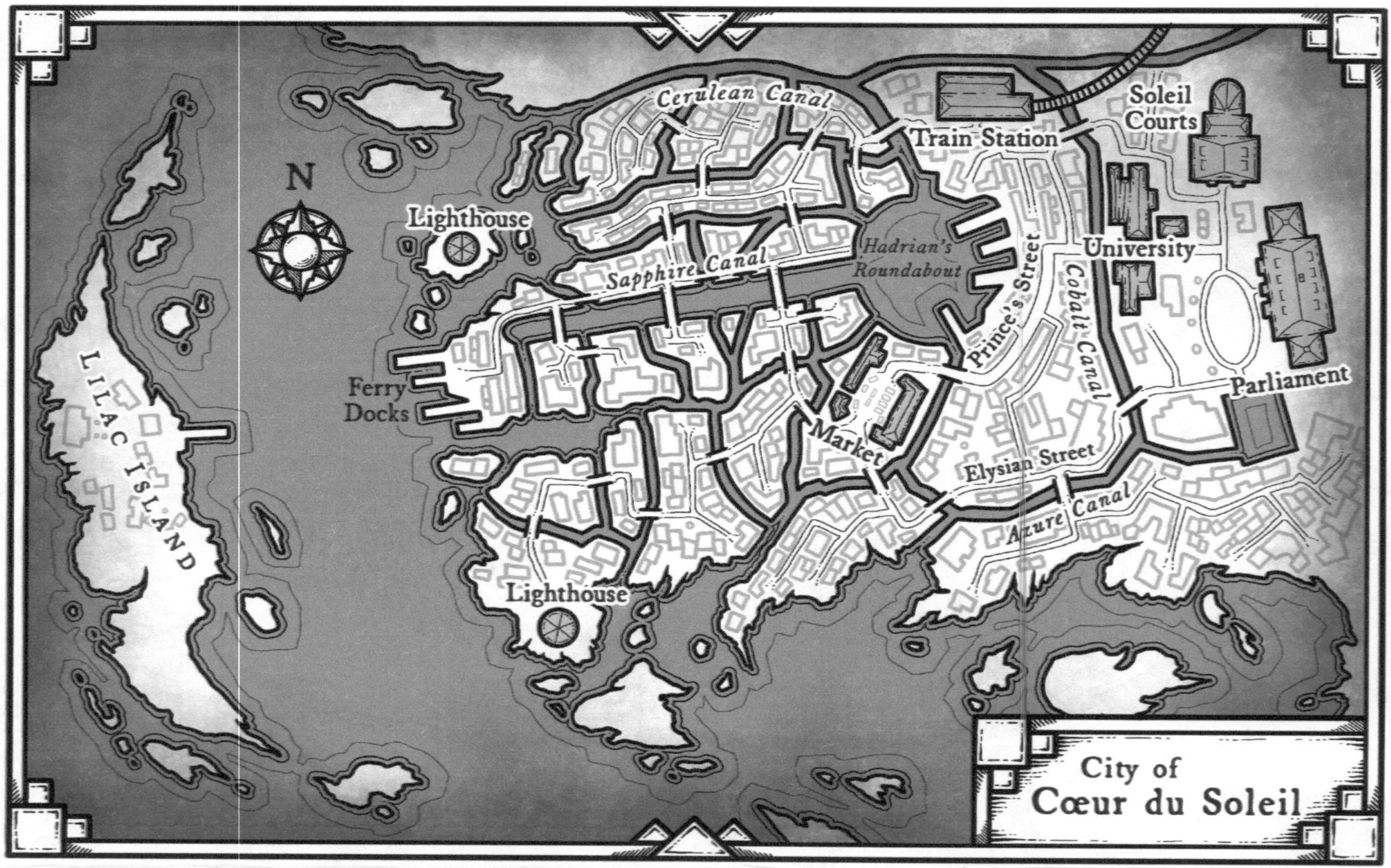

Cerulean Canal
Train Station
Soleil Courts
N
Lighthouse
Hadrian's Roundabout
Sapphire Canal
Prince's Street
University
Cobalt Canal
Ferry Docks
Parliament
Market
Elysian Street
Azure Canal
LILAC ISLAND
Lighthouse
City of
Cœur du Soleil

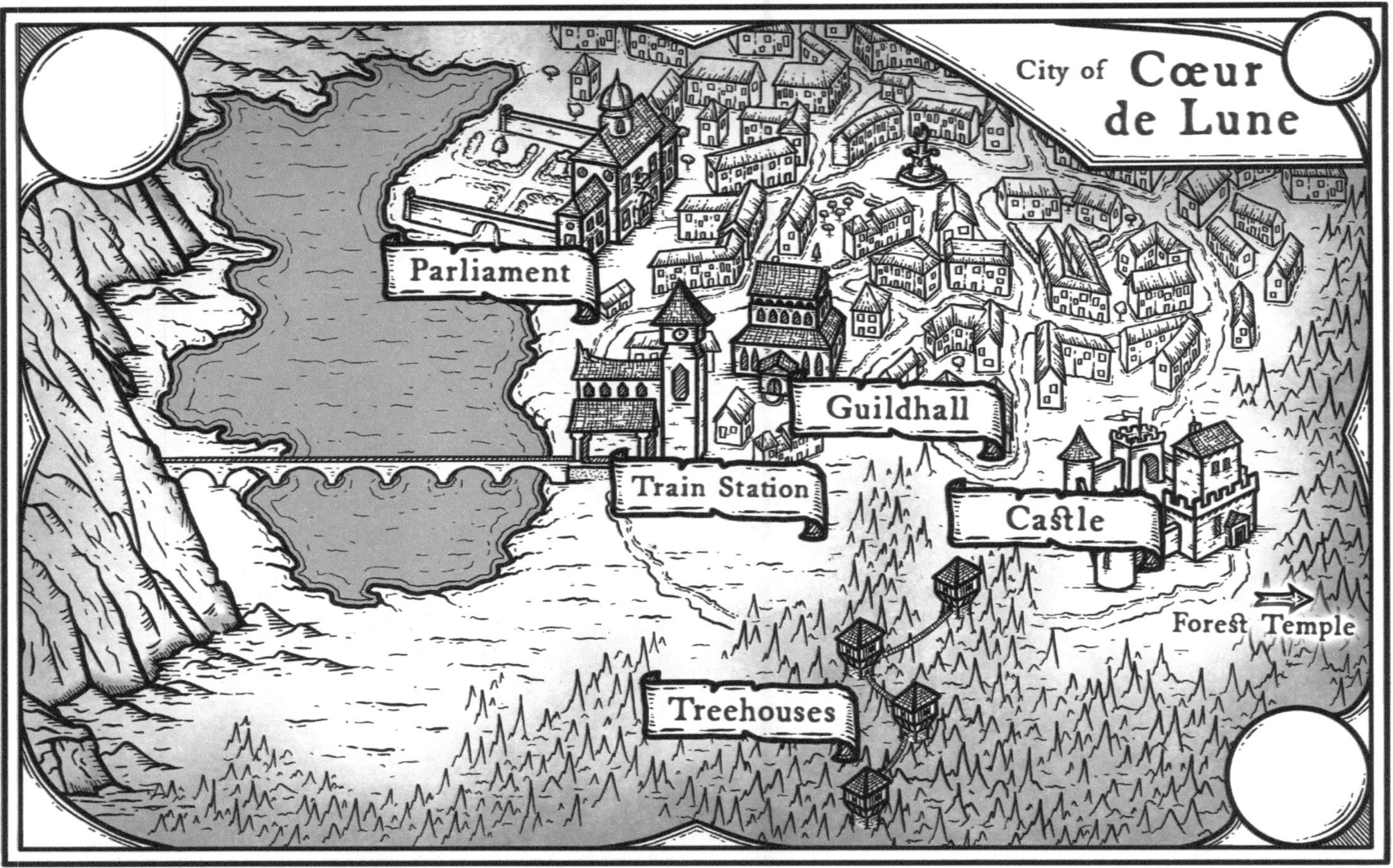

City of Cœur de Lune
Parliament
Guildhall
Train Station
Castle
Forest Temple
Treehouses

Sigur
Clair de Lune
Cœur du Soleil
Mont Noir
Cœur de Lune
Lilac Island
Soleil
The Brightness Isles

Vidur
N
Tovelo
Evory
Zahara
Utidi
HIERATIA

Welcome, reader, to *The Rise of Scarlett Heroux*, a fantasy romance set in a world brutalized by backstabbing politics. Within these pages you'll find intense violence (including gun violence), kidnapping, parental death, discussions of miscarriage, abusive medical malpractice, graphic language, depictions of war, and sexual activities that are shown on the page.

CHAPTER 1

The people of Soleil feared magic so much they'd banned it, but thrill-seekers and the desperate still found ways around the law. Scarlett Heroux couldn't believe she was about to become one of them. She hesitated at the end of the dark alleyway, suddenly aware she was about to go into an illegal magical boxing match undisguised. Pulling a black silk scarf out of her purse, she tied it over her platinum-blonde hair, which was twisted at the back of her neck.

"I don't want to be recognized," she said when her boyfriend, Alastair Spencer, stopped to give her an impatient stare.

"We'll miss the start."

He'd been rushing her all night, even though she'd been telling him for days it would be tough to make it on time.

"Does this look all right?" she asked.

"You look like a movie star. Now come on." He held out his hand, softening the demand with a charming smile. His perfectly

symmetrical face was so beautiful it was almost enough to make Scarlett forget she was mad at him.

Almost.

"I wish you hadn't insisted on leaving the charity ball for this." She took his hand, allowing herself to be pulled along. "I shouldn't have left. I've worked so hard to convince my dad to make the homeless shelter his charity of the year. It's important to me, and it should be important to you."

"It *is* important, but they'd already served dessert. The press got their picture of the prime minister and his daughter. It was practically over." His bright blue eyes begged her to agree, but this time it wasn't working. "Besides," he added, hitting her again with his flawless smile, "you go to a dozen charity dinners a year, but this is your first black-market boxing match. We never do anything this cool."

She fumed as she thought of all the times she'd planned dates and gone along to events he'd wanted to attend. Either oblivious or willfully ignorant to Scarlett's irritation, Alastair led her to a large steel door and knocked several times. A tank of a man stepped out to greet them. Alastair showed him their tickets, and they were admitted to a narrow hallway.

Curiosity overtook her anger as they emerged into a cavernous, damp-smelling space. The floors and the walls were made of concrete, and in the center of the room was a large, well-lit boxing ring. But it was the people who interested her the most. Who was so into watching a fight with magic that they'd risk getting arrested to be here? There were about a hundred bodies packed around the ring, so a fair few, to be sure. Several men puffed on cigarettes, and tendrils of smoke streamed through the air.

Scarlett wrinkled her nose at the stench. She tried to hang back near the door, but Alastair tugged at her hand impatiently.

"Can't we move closer to the front? I want to get a good look at these men." He craned his neck to see into the ring, where both fighters were limbering up. "If that's even what they are."

"No, we can't," hissed Scarlett. "My dad will kill me if we cause a scandal before the border vote."

The full weight of the risk they were taking had finally sunk in. Scarlett's father was Lord Jules Heroux, the Prime Minister of Soleil and Head of the Cerulean Party, and his dream of opening Soleil to trade with the magical world was just within reach. But the vote was expected to pass by the thinnest of margins. *Why* hadn't Scarlett flat-out refused to come here?

Oh, right, because she was a people-pleaser who hated to fight with her boyfriend. And right now she loathed herself for it.

Alastair linked his arm through hers and walked forward, forcing Scarlett to stumble across the sawdust-covered floor. "We've been through this. No one's going to tattle on you for being here. Rufus comes all the time and never gets caught, and his dad is a lord. And look over there—I know I've seen that old man in the fedora at one of my father's parties. Besides, you've got your hair up and under that scarf. No one will recognize you."

The old man turned toward them then, his gaze lingering. Scarlett turned away and pulled Alastair a few feet in the opposite direction. He took advantage and edged her directly up to the side of the ring, where two men stood ready to begin. One was lean but tough-looking; the other was packing an obscene amount of muscle and had a bent nose that looked like it had been broken and not set properly. They both seemed like they'd be hard to overpower.

To Scarlett's surprise, a woman stepped into the ring, positioning herself between the two fighters. Her presence heightened the energy in the room as the fighters greeted her like they knew her well. She was both attractive and fierce, with more muscle on her frame than Scarlett had ever seen on another woman. Her brown hair hung over her left shoulder in a practical braid, and she wore black trousers, sturdy black combat boots, and a white T-shirt tucked into her pants. Everything about her said she took no shit.

"Right, ladies and gents," said the woman in a faint accent Scarlett couldn't place. "I'm Cass, your master of ceremonies. Tonight we've got Brixton the Beast, the most fearsome dire wolf this side of Mont Noir." She gestured toward the leaner of the fighters and paused for a smattering of cheers from the crowd, which Brixton ignored. "And Mace the Menace, our favorite hydra you don't want to surprise ya!" She introduced the monolithic boxer with a twist of her hand, and he waved as the crowd applauded. "This is going to be a good one. Finish placing your bets—we're about to begin!" Flashing the crowd a devious grin, she added, "Reminder, if I catch anyone recording this fight, I'll break your kneecaps before I kick you out."

Scarlett couldn't look away from the badass woman totally dominating the underground boxing ring. Goddess, she wanted to be like her. Cass was so confident as she owned the room, and she'd clearly chosen this life for herself. She locked gazes with Cass, who smiled wider and raised her eyebrows as if she recognized Scarlett.

Before Scarlett could react, Cass turned back to the fighters. "Standard rules apply tonight, boys. Win a round by getting three hits in. First two rounds, magic. Round three, no magic. Win three rounds or knock the other fighter out, you win the fight. If you kill your opponent, you're banned for life."

A few boos came from the audience.

"Bloodlust," she said with amusement. "But you know how it goes—someone dies, then the law gets involved, then I have to start giving up names. We don't want that. Right, my lord?" She leaned over the rope and waved to a man whose face Scarlett couldn't see, but she saw him nodding in response. Cass looked to the boxers.

"And I know you fuckers won't break the golden rule, because you want your money."

Mace chuckled as he bounced on the balls of his feet. Brixton just stared at the ground.

"I find it disturbing she needs to clarify murder is off the table," said Scarlett, but Alastair ignored her. His piercing gaze was fixed on the ring.

The bell rang, and Scarlett's jaw dropped as both fighters began to shift. In a blink, Brixton's body had twisted and expanded until a seven-foot-long dire wolf was standing before them. Across from him, Mace's skin took on a serpentine texture and shone green in the dim light as his arms and his legs thickened and grew. In no time, he had the body of a four-legged dragon. Scarlett thought her brain would explode as his head began to split in two, and then those heads split, until there were six snake heads with slitted eyes weaving through the air around his body. He towered above the wolf.

In that moment, she felt a glimmer of understanding. This was why people came here. They came because magic was fucking *incredible*.

Her thoughts flickered to her best friend, Brayden Maddox. He lived in Clair de Lune, a country where magic was legal. Did he see things like this all the time? They didn't usually talk about magic, but she was dying to know what he'd think of this.

"Fucking hell," said Alastair as the hydra reared its heads in the air. The creature was easily fourteen feet tall when it stretched to its full height. Several members of the crowd took a few steps backward.

The wolf snapped its jaws, and the hydra leaped back with more speed than Scarlett thought possible for a creature of this size, especially considering it was seeing the room through six sets of eyes. Its heads strained high toward the ceiling, letting out the most earsplitting of screeches. While the dire wolf and most of the audience were looking up, several heads dropped to the ground and crashed into the wolf with a loud thump. It fell hard, stunned from the impact. The hydra gripped the wolf's skull and bashed it against the floor as the six heads attacked its body. After a couple of hits to the wolf's skull, the bell rang. The hydra leaped back to Mace's original corner of the ring.

"Round one to Mace," said Cass.

More than half the room yelled with approval. There were a couple of boos.

"If you hadn't made us late, I could have put money on the Menace," grumbled Alastair. "He's the favorite to win, and he was close to achieving a KO there before that bell."

Scarlett prickled but held back from reminding Alastair she'd encouraged him to come here alone. She'd let him have it after the match. For now, she wanted to watch the amazing shifters in front of them.

In spite of the blows to the head, the wolf was up off the floor after a few long seconds. It shook its head, bared its teeth, and growled at the hydra. When the bell sounded, the wolf lunged. This time its jaws closed around the hydra's scaly front-left ankle, and the crowd groaned as its teeth sank into the snakelike skin. Black blood spurted from the wound, and all the hydra's heads screeched as the dire wolf pulled it to the ground.

Scarlett's stomach turned, and she grimaced. She glanced toward Cass, hoping she'd ring the bell before the wolf ripped off the hydra's leg—but rather than watching the fight, Cass was staring at the only entry to the room. She looked straight at Scarlett, then back at the door. Scarlett followed her gaze.

Flashlights flickered against the walls.

Scarlett tugged at Alastair's hand. "Look!"

He kept his attention on the fight.

The hydra's screams assaulted Scarlett's eardrums as the bell failed to sound.

"We need to leave." She shook Alastair's arm.

He turned to her just as two police officers burst into the room, rushing toward the ring. More streamed in behind them.

"EVERYONE, GET ON THE FLOOR."

"Shit," Alastair muttered. He wrapped his arm around Scarlett's shoulders, but aside from that, he was frozen.

Cass and the two fighters climbed out of the ring as all the lights in the room, including the officer's flashlights, flickered and went out. The pitch-black room filled with screams.

Scarlett gripped Alastair's arm as panic rose in her chest. "There has to be another way out."

But if there was, she couldn't see it. Bodies slammed into her as people scattered around, a few choosing to lie on the grimy floor.

Why did I let this happen? I have to get out of here, or I'll go down in history as the dumbass who ruined everything for my dad.

Alastair's voice shook. "Maybe the police can be bribed . . ."

A hand clutched Scarlett's upper arm. "Scarlett Heroux?"

She tried to yank her arm away from the sudden touch. "Who are you?" She couldn't see a foot in front of her face.

"Follow me if you don't want to get arrested."

Then it clicked. The lightly accented voice belonged to Cass. Shocked as she was, Scarlett made a split-second decision.

"Lead the way."

"Take my hand." Fingers slid into Scarlett's free hand, and she stumbled but stayed on her feet as she was led through the pitch-black room, pulling Alastair behind her. All around were sounds of frantic people desperate to escape the dark, but somehow Cass avoided them all.

Then Scarlett walked into Cass's back as she came to an abrupt halt. Alastair stumbled into her, and she held his hand tighter to steady them both.

"There's a trapdoor right here," said Cass. "Feel for the ladder on the side closest to you. Scarlett, you go first. Mace and Brixton have gone ahead, so don't freak out if you hear them." She placed Scarlett's hand on the first rung of the ladder.

"I can't leave my boyfriend," said Scarlett. "You'll let him follow me, right?"

"Of course. He'll be right behind you." Cass was reassuring even under the circumstances.

"Thank you," Scarlett said, infusing gratitude into her voice. She tentatively descended through the darkness until her feet hit the ground. Seconds later, Alastair was beside her, and she reached for his hand. He took it, gripping it tightly in his.

Scarlett jumped as a thump sounded above them, and then again when Cass landed on the ground with a thud. She switched on a flashlight, illuminating their faces in a soft glow, and pointed the light toward an archway.

"That tunnel will lead us out of here. It'll take them a while to get the lights back on up there, but we'd best be on our way before they find the trapdoor."

Alastair started toward the archway without a word, Scarlett's hand still in his. Cass fell into step beside them.

They walked for a few minutes, gravel crunching under their feet in the cold tunnel. Drops of water occasionally hit Scarlett's face as she tried to pinpoint their location in her mind's eye.

"Are we walking under the Sapphire Canal?" asked Scarlett.

"Yep," said Cass.

Scarlett waited, hoping she'd go on, but Cass didn't elaborate as she walked the underground path in silence.

"Why are you helping us?" Scarlett asked, unable to resist.

"I support the prime minister's plans to open the border. Couldn't have his daughter's arrest on my conscience."

Scarlett couldn't see the other woman's face, but she sounded genuine. "I can't thank you enough for helping prevent a scandal."

Alastair snorted. "Won't the open borders shrink the profits you get from running illicit boxing matches? You won't be able to charge as much if it isn't underground."

Scarlett pulled her hand out of Alastair's grip for the first time since they'd started down the tunnel. "Not everyone's top priority is money."

"What?" he huffed. He stopped walking but then took several quick steps to catch up with them. "I was only asking."

They arrived at a fork in the path. Cass considered for a second and then led them down the path to the left. She cleared her throat.

"We pay exorbitant bribes. If we could go legitimate, the market would expand, and the crooked cops would truly be the only ones worse off. Besides, like your girlfriend said, some things are more important than money. I believe in freedom for Soleil, and it'd be nice if my family could visit me."

Scarlett was fascinated. All of Soleil knew about the magical black market, so of course the police must too. It made sense, even if she hated to hear about crooked cops.

"Apparently, your bribes aren't exorbitant enough," said Alastair.

"That has me concerned." There was venom in Cass's voice. She shone her flashlight on the curved wall of the tunnel, and metal glinted back. "This ladder leads to a side street not far from the Prince's Street Dock. Can you make your way home from there?"

"Yes." Scarlett nodded. "I can call my driver. Would you like a ride? We can drop you off anywhere you'd like."

Cass considered for a second. "Sure."

The three of them climbed onto the street. The moon shone high in the clear sky, giving them far more light to see by than they'd had in the tunnels. They moved to the closest alleyway for shelter from passersby, and Scarlett called Charlie, who'd been her family's driver her entire life.

He picked up on the first ring. "Hey, kid. Are you ready for a pickup?"

"That would be great. Thanks, Charlie. We're at the Prince's Street Dock. Alastair and another friend are with me. We'll drop them off before going home." She could've waited to tell him this, but she wanted it known she was going home alone tonight.

"No worries. I'll be there in about fifteen minutes."

Charlie hung up, and Scarlett turned to Alastair and Cass.

"It won't be long. Should we grab a coffee while we wait?"

Alastair shook his head. "Nah, it'll take too long." His gaze pierced Scarlett. "Why don't you have him drop Cass off first and come back to my place?"

Remembering the promise she'd made herself back at the match, Scarlett steeled herself. "You dragged me to that match even though you knew I didn't want to go, and we were *this* close to getting arrested. I want to be alone tonight."

"You could've chosen not to go," he protested.

Cass moved toward the street and put her back to them.

"You're right. I could have, but you kept hounding me. You pressured me." Scarlett was angry at him and at herself, because he was right. For three years she'd swallowed every negative thing she'd felt to make sure he was happy. And she shouldn't have done that.

He came closer, his expression softening, but he couldn't bring her back to him with a pleading look this time. "I thought it would be good for us. Things haven't been the same since you decided not to move in with me . . ." His expression was pinched as he reached for her.

Scarlett pulled away. "Yes, that's another thing you kept insisting on even though you knew I was thinking about going abroad. By the way, I'm not thinking about it anymore. I'm doing it, and I'm going to tell my dad tomorrow."

He closed his eyes for a long moment. "If you go, where does that leave us?"

She was so tired of him that her next words came easier than expected. "I think time apart will be good for us."

"Are you asking for a break?" His voice caught as a pain she'd never seen entered his gaze.

That *was* what she'd meant. She'd only wanted to express how mad she was at him, but suddenly, it wasn't enough. Alastair only loved her when she was playing the role he expected her to play. A role she no longer wanted. Now that she was tearing her life apart, she burned with the desire to level it to the ground and begin anew.

Scarlett swallowed and forced herself to tell the truth. "No, I don't want a break. I think we're done."

His hands fell away; his expression hardened. "Three years together, and you don't even want to *try* doing long-distance? Or going abroad together? I don't *want* to go, but I'd do it for you. Do all our years together mean nothing to you?"

"Of course they mean something to me. I've loved you all the years we've been together, but that doesn't mean we're meant to be together forever." She willed him to understand.

He scowled at her. "Beyond loving me, we're forever linked. I took your virginity."

"Wow . . ." Cass muttered from a few steps away.

How could he say something so outrageous, let alone in front of someone else? Scarlett rolled her eyes at Alastair's old-fashioned views.

He ignored her and went on in a lowered voice. "You've

practically been living with me. I've been *inside* you hundreds of times. Do you think I'd have done any of that if I didn't believe we'd marry one day?"

And not one of those hundreds of times did you give me an orgasm. Twenty-two and I've never had a single goddamn orgasm. She wanted to shout the words at him, but it was far too late to talk about that. He had no idea she never had. It also wasn't fair to fault him for something she'd never told the truth about. But as he stood there trying to make a sexual claim on her, she was tempted to throw it in his face anyway.

Scarlett glared at him. "We never spoke about marriage. It's not my fault if you made assumptions."

His expression shifted from hard to vacant. "What did I do to make you stop loving me?"

Her brief spike of anger faded, replaced by wavering heartache. She *had* slept in his bed so many nights for years. They'd been each other's worlds for so long. She still remembered when he'd asked her out on their first day at university. Scarlett had been nervous, hoping to make friends, and he'd stepped in and filled her life with inside jokes, study dates, nights out in dazzling places, and quiet nights in snuggled up in his bed. He'd done a good job of making her happy.

When *did* she stop loving him?

The truth was, she had a growing sense of disgust at how Alastair carried his privilege. Comments he made here and there that made her think their values were far from aligned. She wasn't sure if he'd always been that way and she'd been unwilling to see it or if he'd changed. But what was one more lie? One last lie to keep him from being unhappier than he already was.

"You didn't do anything. I don't know why it changed for me."

His gaze darted to hers before he looked up at the sky. "Is there someone else?" His voice sounded thick.

She grabbed his hand. "Of course not." It wasn't a lie, although for months her fantasies had featured a man with thick, dark hair and warm brown eyes . . .

"Scarlett, you're *mine*." He squeezed her hand so tight it hurt. "I bought a bloody engagement ring for you. I'd have proposed by now if you weren't acting like such a selfish shrew. You're *supposed* to marry me. We'd make the greatest political dynasty Soleil has ever seen. With you by my side, I could be prime minister after your father—our children would inherit *two* seats in Parliament." His voice was raised, and his handsome face twisted. "You'll *never* find this good of a match again. Do you understand that?"

Shock became fire as his arrogance erased Scarlett's guilt. Heat flooded through her body. He'd never sounded more entitled. Was this how he loved? It felt like the veil over her eyes had lifted, and without the sickness of her own love for him distorting her view, she didn't recognize him anymore.

Cass turned around then, but Scarlett waved to let her know no intervention was necessary.

"I'm now one hundred percent certain I don't want to be with you, so thanks for that. Do *you* understand *that*? Fuck off, Alastair."

He stared at her with wild eyes. "That's all you have to say? Fuck off? *You* fuck off, Scarlett. You'll regret this for the rest of your life, and don't think I'll take you back!"

Scarlett, filled with rage, strode toward Cass. "Let's wait on the dock."

Cass nodded and fell into step beside her. "That was intense. Are you all right?"

"Yes. I'll be fine." Scarlett kept her gaze ahead. "It's for the best."

It wasn't long before Charlie had pulled up in her family's sleek speedboat. Alastair didn't follow them, and Scarlett was glad. He could find his own way home.

"Sorry you had to listen to that," she said as they waited for Charlie to secure the boat.

"Don't be sorry," said Cass, amused. "He seems like a prick."

"He's *never* acted like that before. You saw the worst of him back there."

But deep down, Scarlett wasn't entirely sure that was true. It was why she felt relieved to be free, whatever that meant. Given their respective roles in Soleil, she feared she'd never be truly free of Alastair Spencer. She tried her best not to dwell on the thought as the boat sped off into the night.

CHAPTER 2

The next morning Scarlett sat in bed staring at the sunlight sparkling on the water outside her window, mulling over the events of the previous night. The police raid, the breakup—it all seemed like a dream. She'd been using magic in secret for years, but that was the first time she'd seen anything like those shifters. It was definitely the closest she'd come to being caught. All because of a magical spectator sport.

She nuzzled into her pillow as she wished for the thousandth time her country would change. Soleil's magic ban was in place to prevent darker kinds of magic, such as the mind control and possession her country had been subjected to centuries ago. That, Scarlett understood. But along with all the dark stuff, Soleil had also gotten rid of the good magic and closed itself off from the outside world. The country had developed incredible technology to make up for its magical disadvantages, but despite interest from foreign buyers eager to merge magic with the advanced tech, Soleil still hadn't legalized

cross-border trade. Other countries used magic to communicate across far distances. Soleil had to rely on letters for legal communication beyond the border. It was all so stupid.

Barely anyone foreign-born was allowed into Soleil, and anyone caught using magic in the country was arrested and shamed, though the black market was well-known. She'd never understood how a black market was allowed to exist. After last night, though, she wondered if its days were numbered.

She sighed, looking at the time. Normally, she'd be waking up in Alastair's bed. It was a relief to be alone in her room instead. The emotional hangover from her breakup had dissipated somewhat overnight, and she was ready to wreak new havoc on her life.

He should be awake by now . . .

Scarlett slid off her bed and padded into her dressing room. The expansive adjoining room between her room and her grandmother Manon's room was quiet when she entered. She looked to the huge gilt mirror hanging between two bureaus. The secret mirror that could get her and Manon arrested if it were ever discovered. The mirror that connected her to the outside world of magic even though she lived in Goddess-damned isolationist Soleil. Most importantly, it was the mirror that connected her to *him*.

At first, she simply saw herself at an angle as she approached the mirror. Only when she was standing directly in front of it did the image change to a room full of meticulously ordered bookshelves, a tweed couch, and a grand mahogany desk. The rest of her tension melted, and she smiled.

There he is.

On the other side of the mirror, Brayden Maddox was on the carpeted floor of his father's study, bent over as he stretched his hamstrings for his morning run. Though they'd never actually met in person, Brayden had been Scarlett's friend through the mirror since she moved into the room. She was eleven when she accidentally found the contraband magical mirror linking her home to his. Now she was twenty-two, and Brayden was one of the few people in her life who cared for her unconditionally. Their relationship was so precious to her. She'd never felt that kind of love from her father and had lost it from her relationship with her ex-boyfriend in recent months.

As he straightened, Brayden noticed her watching. "There she is. Good morning." He flashed her a charming smile that accentuated his prominent cheekbones. "You look a little keyed up. What has you so bright-eyed this early in the morning?"

Goddess, that deep voice of his. Brayden was from Clair de Lune, the country to the east of Soleil, and his accent always hit her hardest first thing in the morning. Even after all these years. She'd never get enough of the way he pronounced "you."

Focus.

"I have news," she said excitedly as she approached the mirror. "Alastair and I broke up yesterday, and today I'm telling my dad I'm going abroad to tour the embassies instead of working for him this year." Telling her dad counted as news, because he fully expected Scarlett to join his staff now that she'd graduated from university, to prepare her to one day inherit his seat in Parliament.

Scarlett scanned Brayden's face for a reaction. He pushed his messy dark brown hair out of his even darker eyes and blinked a couple of times. He definitely looked surprised. It might have been wishful thinking, but was that a glimmer of happiness in his expression? Tempered happiness?

He stood. "Are we playing that game where only one of those things is true and I have to guess which?"

She beamed at him. "Nope. Both things are true. I'll have to talk to my dad today if I'm going to get my plans together in time to leave in two weeks. That's when the Soleil Embassy in Sigur Viður has agreed to host me." Scarlett gathered her long hair and twisted it into a bun.

He stared at her. "That's huge, Scarlett. And you split with Alastair . . ." He was unnaturally still. "Are you all right? Was it your decision?"

She nodded. "Yes, it was my decision."

His shoulders relaxed, and Scarlett exhaled.

Somehow they'd both gotten closer to the mirror, and she could see the stubble coating his strong jaw as it often did first thing in the morning. When Brayden had first started growing facial hair, she'd wanted to reach out and touch it. She still wanted that. She could admit to that now that she was free of her relationship, even if she couldn't say it out loud.

He lowered his gaze. Was he looking at her chest, or was he looking at something on his side of the mirror? Scarlett was wearing a stretchy tank top with a built-in bra that was admittedly not the most substantial, but he'd seen her in her pajamas before without seeming fazed.

For a split second she imagined him pulling her shirt down and putting his mouth on her chest. The intensity of the ache that arose in response surprised her. What would it be like to sleep with him? She'd only ever been with Alastair.

The reminder of Alastair lessened the building heat inside her. She took a deep breath, willing herself to get a grip.

Brayden's eyes flicked back up to her face, and he gave her an expectant look. "And you're okay. Are you sad?"

She grimaced. "Does it make me coldhearted if I say I'm fine? I think I fell out of love with him a while ago and just didn't admit it until yesterday."

A flash of guilt squeezed her heart. But then his parting words rang in her head. *"You'll never find this good of a match again. Do you understand that?"* She was sure she'd done the right thing. But she didn't want to get into the details of that now.

He shook his head. "If it had run its course, then definitely not. If you feel fine, it was probably the right thing to do. Do you think you might change your mind though?" He grinned. "I don't want to move into my post-Alastair mindset today and then be in trouble with you tomorrow if you get back with him." His smile faltered as he studied her.

She laughed, her nose wrinkling as she imagined patching things up with Alastair when her gut was screaming at her for sweet, sweet freedom. "I ended it, then he burned the bridge and pissed on the ashes. There's no going back. Let post-Alastair life commence."

His smile returned. "And you're leaving Soleil in two weeks?"

"Yes. I'm planning on six weeks in Sigur Viður and then on to Evory. If I'm in Clair de Lune around winter solstice, will you be there? I could try to change my plans if you'll be gone then." They were the best of friends, but insecurity crept in. What if, after years of being long-distance friends, they missed their first chance to meet in person? What if he didn't want to meet?

Scoffing, he stretched his triceps, leaving his long torso on full display. "Of course. The only thing that could stop me from being here when you visit is if I get deployed, which is unlikely." Brayden was in the army, but thankfully, there hadn't been war on the continent for two hundred years. "I can't wait to see you without the mirror. We can actually go out together. And hug. We're about a thousand hugs overdue at this point."

She clapped her hands. "Yay!" *Oh Goddess, I can't wait to touch him. Please let it turn out to be way more than hugging. I want to feel him.* An image of his body hovering over hers popped into her head and made her shiver. She spun around in a circle to hide her giant smile. She was totally losing it.

"Did you just do a little dance over there?" he said with a laugh.

"Fuck yes, I did a dance. We're finally going to meet!"

A flush of color spread across his pale cheeks. "I'm excited too. Stay strong with your dad. Don't let him change your mind. I *need* those thousand hugs. And the deficit will only grow the longer you wait to visit."

"I'll stay strong. I want it too badly to cave." She worried her lip, noticing as she did that his dark eyes found her mouth. "I might go speak to him now, actually, before we leave for the Remembrance Day ceremony. Will you be around later tonight?" She wanted to see him again as soon as she could, so she could tell him how it went.

"Yeah, sure. I'm grabbing dinner with James, but I'll wait here for you afterward." James was his brother—and his best friend.

"Are you sure that's not inconvenient? I can always catch you tomorrow morning."

He shook his head. "Nah, I want to hear how it goes. James won't mind. Try not to burn any bridges or piss on them, if you can help it."

To her delight, his eyes were bright.

"I won't. See you tonight."

Scarlett flew downstairs hoping to find her father in his study. Instead her stepmother Laylani's raised voice reached her in the hallway.

"Why you thought it was appropriate to say this to a reporter is *completely* beyond me. You speak as if we don't love you, when every single decision I've made in my life was made with your well-being in mind. Nothing has aged me more than your birth!"

Scarlett's hackles went up. It put her on edge when her stepmother shouted—especially if it was at her younger brother, Beni. The urge to protect him from his mother's narcissistic bullshit overtook her desire to look for her father, and she followed the sound of yelling to the dining room.

There she found Beni sitting at the ample dining table in his pajamas, black hair still ruffled from sleep. His expression was shuttered, presumably a result of the verbal tongue-lashing Scarlett had overheard from the hallway. Laylani sat next to him, her face fully made-up, though she was still wearing a dressing gown.

Scarlett had long suspected Laylani's first act upon rising from her bed in vampiric fashion was to immediately put on enough makeup to be photogenic. The woman was so vain and frigid Scarlett had never understood why her father chose her out of all the women in Soleil.

"Happy Remembrance Day." Scarlett glanced down at the table, where a glossy magazine sat open. A page had been ripped out and crumpled into a ball—she could see it at the other end of the table. "Did something happen?"

"Beaufort was interviewed by *Soleil Citizen* magazine," said Laylani in a clipped voice.

Scarlett sighed. She'd tried to meet Laylani's expectations for frequency and perfection when it came to their presence in the media for years, but she'd given up on it long ago. She attempted to catch her brother's eye, but Beni stared down at his plate, looking way too defeated for this early in the morning. Knowing she couldn't abandon him to this, Scarlett lowered herself into the chair next to him and met her stepmother's stony gaze with narrowed eyes.

"What was so upsetting about the interview?"

Beni finally lifted his head, showing Scarlett the anger he'd been hiding. "The reporter asked me what it's like living with Mum and Dad, and I . . ." He trailed off with a shrug.

"I see," said Scarlett. He'd told the truth, which was that her parents were seldom around. Unfortunately for Beni, telling the truth to a reporter meant the whole country was privy to the truth, and Laylani valued her image as Lord Heroux's wife and Beaufort's mother above all things.

Laylani turned back to him. She picked up the magazine and threw it to the ground with such force that a curl came out of place and hung awkwardly down by her neck. "We're going to insist they retract this article, and if you ever embarrass me like this again, I'll throw your laptop into the canal and send you to a screen-free boarding school."

Beni's eyes filled with tears.

Scarlett leaned in closer to her brother and whispered, "I won't let that happen. Dad would never send you away, and if he tried, I wouldn't let him."

Before Laylani could react, Martin, their chef, strode into the room and put Scarlett's usual breakfast of two eggs and toast down in front of her, along with a cup of hot coffee. She thanked him quietly and waited for Martin to leave before turning toward Laylani, who had only a cup of coffee—*her* usual breakfast.

"None of that is Beni's fault. Maybe next time, you shouldn't let your twelve-year-old son give an interview without you. Better yet, maybe you shouldn't approve of *Citizen* featuring him at all."

"They took him to play tennis to get some pictures of him. It wasn't supposed to be an in-depth interview," said Laylani. The rage in her tone had been replaced by icy politeness. "We need Beaufort to get *some* media exposure, even if he isn't your father's heir." She sat back in her chair as she sipped her coffee, her gaze lingering on Scarlett. "Speaking of media exposure, you're getting quite busty, Scarlett. Be sure to wear something that doesn't show your cleavage today. Are you sure you should be eating eggs every morning? They're so full of fat."

Scarlett had to laugh. Laylani had been so judgmental all her life that the words intended to cut her down were only funny these days. "You think I'm gaining weight because of eggs? I thought it was the ten pints of ice cream I ate during exams," she said.

Laylani snorted, and Beni's face turned pink as he stared at his plate.

Scarlett took advantage of the lull in conversation by breathing in the grass-scented breeze. She stared out through the open glass doors to their lush garden, where the blossoming morning was so at odds with her stepmother's vitriol. Judging by Laylani's silence, she might have finished laying into Beni now. Scarlett spoke in an attempt to change the subject and spare her brother further attention.

"Alastair and I broke up yesterday."

Beni's expression shifted from subdued to shocked. "Wow. Are you all right?"

"I'm sad, but I'll be fine." Sad, but not too sad to eat. Scarlett shoved an egg onto a piece of toast and took a bite.

"I'm surprised to hear *that*," said Laylani. "Your father told me he was planning to propose."

Scarlett chewed and swallowed, scrutinizing her stepmother's moderate response. "He was."

"That's quite a bold move, alienating the Spencers. I'd have thought you'd marry for the political benefits alone. Does your father know yet?" Laylani asked with a glint in her eye.

If someone Scarlett cared about had reacted to her breakup this way—with political machinations and gleeful anticipation of a fallout with her father—she'd have been distraught, but from Laylani, it was totally on brand and didn't warrant an emotional response.

"I haven't spoken to him since it happened." Scarlett turned to Beni. "Should we go surfing this morning?"

"Need some surf therapy?" he asked with a knowing smile.

Scarlett nodded. They'd chased away many a bad run-in with his mother with the sun and the ocean ever since Scarlett taught Beni how to swim. "Yes. Exactly."

"Do we have enough time?" he asked.

"No, you don't," said Laylani loudly.

They both shot her dark looks.

"Don't look at me like that," she said. "Scarlett, you have to leave for Parliament in three hours. By the time you've taken the ferry all the way to Lilac Beach, you'll barely have time to surf before it's time to come back again. Beaufort, you're coming with me to the luncheon at the Bucklands' house, and we have to leave at eleven."

"Goddess, not that boring luncheon," he muttered. "Can't I go with Scarlett and Dad?"

Laylani's dark eyes flickered. "Absolutely not. I've already said you'll be there."

Though she was married to Scarlett's father, Laylani was also the sister of Lady Moira Ashworth, leader of the opposition: the Goldenrod Party. The luncheon at Lord Buckland's house would be full of Goldenrods.

Scarlett sympathized with her brother, but it was the politics of the attendees that would drive her mad more so than the dullness. Her own ideals were Cerulean, like her father's, and she found it impossible to avoid confrontation when surrounded by people who were such self-interested assholes. Putting in long hours surrounded by the press at Parliament was definitely a better use of her time. Time in the spotlight Laylani would usually vie for . . .

"Why are you going to the luncheon instead of Dad's speech?" Scarlett asked after a moment. Her stepmother had always supported her dad in public despite her ties to his opposition.

Laylani sighed theatrically. "I've spent quite enough Remembrance Days with your father—I feel I've earned a pass on this one. Beaufort, be ready at eleven. The dress code is smart casual." Without another word, she walked out of the room.

Scarlett's gaze met Beni's. With Laylani gone, the energy in the room had brightened. As if he also sensed the shift, Martin whistled a happy tune in the kitchen down the hall.

"I wish we could go to the beach," grumbled Beni.

"Let's go tomorrow."

"Sounds good." Her brother took a bite of a syrup-drenched pancake.

Scarlett smirked at his enthusiasm as she mopped up her creamy egg yolk with the rest of her toast.

When Beni was born, barely a year after her mother's death, Scarlett—then age ten—wasn't happy. After losing her mother, she didn't want to share her father with a stepmother, let alone a baby. From day one of her dad's second marriage, she'd been as rude to Laylani as a child her age could be. With Beni just a newborn lump in a cot, Scarlett was fully prepared to write him off as a nonentity. But sometime around his first birthday, the smiley little boy had begun to tail her around the house, shrieking, "Sca!" with glee. Before she knew it, he'd completely won her over. She'd taken the plump, sweet-faced toddler under her wing, deciding once and for all that her troubles weren't his fault. They'd been allies ever since.

"You know the year abroad I've been thinking about?" she asked him.

Beni nodded. "Yeah. Are you doing it?"

"Yes, and I'm telling Dad today." Her shoulders tensed as she waited for his reaction.

His eyebrows shot up. "Amazing. I think that's great. Get out of here for a bit while you still can. Before you have to be a workaholic like Dad."

She relaxed. He seemed genuinely happy for her. "You'll be okay here, right? While I'm gone."

He scoffed. "I'll be fine. I'll just stay in my room when she's home and spend the night at Blake's house on the weekends." Blake was Beni's best friend from school. "I'm excited for you."

She smiled. "Thanks, kid."

After breakfast, Scarlett approached her father's study wondering if she should talk to him about what she'd interrupted between Laylani and Beni, but she paused with her hand on the doorknob when she heard him rehearsing. Today was particularly important. Her father was on the verge of the biggest civic moment of his career. After about a hundred iterations of the proposal to get it into a passable state, his legislation to open the economic borders of Soleil was expected to pass by a razor-thin margin next week. Not wanting to interrupt his final run-throughs, she listened through the door.

Lord Jules Heroux's baritone voice was crisp, each word perfectly enunciated. "The impact of the border legislation goes beyond the massive boost our economy will receive by allowing the import and export of goods. Presently, only those with a visa for work or school are allowed into Soleil. Only one thousand visas are issued each year. Think about that for just a moment. And now consider the impact widespread tourism will have on Soleil's small businesses."

Scarlett's heart burst with pride. Many in the country were afraid of the outside world, but her father was brave enough to push the country beyond its comfort zone. She believed a lot of that was because of her mother, Sabina, who was from Clair de Lune, same as Brayden. Sabina had died thirteen years ago, at the age of thirty-six.

Aside from the clear economic benefits the legislation would bring about, if Parliament dropped the damn border, Brayden could finally visit her. She already knew a six-week stint in Clair de Lune wouldn't be enough time with him, and thus, Scarlett had a personal vested interest in her father's success—one she'd never vocalized publicly. Or privately. Even Brayden didn't know. A superstitious part of her worried speaking it aloud would make it not come true.

Her dad finished his run-through and began the speech again, so Scarlett went up to her room to get ready, leaving him to rehearse in peace.

When it was nearly time to go, she threw an opaque scarf over the mirror and changed into an off-white tweed skirt and blazer, tying a black bow at her neck. She pinned a tiny Soleil flag to the breast of her blazer and let her hair fall loose down her back. Laylani would approve of everything but the hair, which was why Scarlett left it loose.

She looked down at herself and liked the way her skin, tanned from surfing, contrasted with the off-white fabric. *Will he like this outfit? He never sees me dressed up.* She sighed. *The more things change, the more they stay the same.*

Not even twenty-four-hours single and she'd unwittingly gone back to her old teenage habit of wondering if Brayden would like the way she was dressed. That old misery of pining for a boy she could never have wasn't something she wanted to revisit. It was one of the reasons she had to convince her dad to let her go abroad. She needed to move forward—to see him—sooner than the border legislation would allow.

Scarlett was still putting her pearl drop earrings in as she descended the final few steps to find her father in the foyer, his phone to his ear. He waved at her and gestured to the front door.

They were seated in the cabin of the speedboat, heading toward Parliament, when her father wrapped up his call. Forcing herself to relax her clenched jaw, Scarlett straightened, gathering the words to tell her father her plans.

"That was Elestine," he said to Scarlett.

She sighed. Alastair's mother, Elestine Spencer. Why couldn't she have five minutes with her father without having to discuss Alastair?

Her father continued. "Alastair is devastated and refuses to leave the house. Why didn't you tell me you were thinking of breaking things off with him?"

His exasperated tone irked her almost as much as his guilt trip. She shouldn't be expected to check in with her father before making decisions in her own relationship. The idea was ridiculous.

"I didn't know I was going to do it until it happened."

"Are you all right?" asked her father after a moment, his irritation replaced by genuine concern. "You know my main priority is you, right?"

Scarlett shot him a sideways glance. "Not when you're jumping straight in with 'Alastair's devastated.'"

He blinked several times and nodded. "I apologize. You're right. I should have checked in with you before telling you about him. Now, how are you doing?" He moved across the cabin to sit next to her and pulled her into his arms.

She leaned into him, inhaling the familiar smell of his vanilla-and-leather-scented cologne, and the embrace melted away her irritation. After a few seconds she sat up and gave him a small smile. "I'll be fine." Hesitant to tell him her news so soon after their charged exchange, she asked instead, "Are you ready for your speech?"

"You know me—I'll probably run through it once more in my office. Mind listening and telling me what you think? Someday, it'll be you giving a Remembrance Day speech."

Scarlett smiled, deciding not to mention she'd already heard the bulk of it through his study door. "I'd love to listen. Did you know Beni wanted to come today? He wasn't happy to be dragged to the Buckland luncheon."

"Yes. It's a shame he and your stepmother aren't coming, but

Laylani insisted she had to be at that luncheon. Thankfully, I have you to keep me company. Once the speech is over and I can relax a little bit, I want to hear all about what you want to do now that you're not with Alastair. You might want a new flat closer to Parliament—that would be a livelier part of town for a single career woman. You need some excitement away from the family home." He was trying hard to be upbeat for her, and she appreciated it.

Before she could reply, his phone rang.

While her dad spoke to his chief of staff, Scarlett imagined herself a year from now moving into a new flat. Maybe by then, the border would be down and Brayden could come to see her in her new place. Her vision of the future wasn't incompatible with her dad's, if only they could agree on an adjusted timeline.

He'll say yes to the year abroad.

Wouldn't he?

CHAPTER 3

In her father's office at Parliament, Scarlett listened as Lord Jules Heroux rehearsed his Remembrance Day speech.

". . . let us also celebrate the future they gave us." He turned to Scarlett. "How did I do?"

"You sound great," she said. Her father was a born orator. "No notes from me."

"Excellent. We have about twenty minutes. Would you like a drink?"

Her dad kept his whiskey decanter and his crystal glasses inside an ornate globe in his office. He'd told Scarlett more than once that his best political partnerships were forged and fortified over drinks. She hoped booze would help put him in an amenable mood.

"Why not?" she said as her heart rate sped up. "While we're imbibing, there's something I wanted to talk to you about."

"Oh?" He handed her a glass filled with two fingers of amber liquid, and they sat in the leather armchairs on either side of the globe.

Scarlett forced herself to breathe. "I know you were hoping I'd join your staff now that I've finished university, but I've decided to spend a year abroad touring the embassies. It'll be great for me to build some political alliances, and if you think about it, now's the perfect time for me to go. It'll take some time to gear up for the border opening once your legislation passes, and I'll be back before the most intense work begins." She bit her lip and waited for his reaction.

Her father couldn't stop her, exactly, but his disapproval would settle in her stomach like a stone, dragging her under the surface until she drowned. Trying to please him by being like him was ingrained in her. If her dad put his foot down about her leaving, her relationship with him would be at risk.

Jules sighed as his demeanor changed from bright to resigned. "I had a feeling you'd go. Your ideas were too detailed to be theoretical. Are you still planning to begin in Sigur Viður?" When she nodded, he shook his head. "I wish you'd reconsider beginning your travels in a country we have such poor relations with. You don't know a soul there, and you have no idea how to live in a magic-using country."

She had more of an idea than he knew, from Brayden and her grandmother, but she couldn't tell him that.

Scarlett moved to the edge of her seat and turned to face her father, determined to make him understand how badly she wanted this. She looked directly into his eyes as she spoke. "I want to see more of the world before you retire and I take your seat."

Her father's brow furrowed as he took a long sip of his drink. "Is there no chance of you reconciling with Alastair and him going along with you?"

And there it was—what he really wanted for her. To get back with Alastair.

Scarlett took a deep breath, trying to rid herself of the desire to scream. Her father meant well and didn't know her relationship with Alastair had fit like a dress half a size too small. Her need for his approval had never been more at odds with her own desire. She *had* to be honest.

"No."

He frowned and cocked his head to one side. "I'm still not clear on what changed. You two seemed so solid. What made you change your mind about him?"

"It was time to admit the relationship had run its course. We weren't solid at all, and we definitely weren't well-suited for the long term."

Jules shook his head and held up a hand. "Tell me the truth, not the press release."

She continued eagerly. "I fell in love with him because the timing was right, not because he was right. He doesn't love me. He loves that I'm from a powerful family. I want real love, not an alliance." Scarlett took a couple more deep breaths and forced herself to pause. "I need to go have an experience alone—*any* experience that isn't this one. I'm dying to get out of Soleil."

Her father held up his hands like he was surrendering. "I had no idea. You need to see more of the world. Point made. I felt the same way when I was your age, actually, but I met your mother here, and she helped me settle. You do want to come back after your travels, though, right? I'm counting on you to join my staff eventually." His green eyes were warm with fondness.

Her chest tightened. The truth was, deep down, Scarlett dreaded joining Parliament, but that was a truth she'd never reveal to her father. If she gave up her place as his heir, their only tie to each other would be gone, as would his love for her.

So she lied.

"Of course I want to work with you. Eventually. But I need to do this first."

"We'll make it happen, then. If you agree to let me hire a body-guard to accompany you, I'll fully support your decision."

The corner of Scarlett's mouth twitched. It was just like her father to make her feel like she'd won and then make it conditional. Still, relief overrode her other feelings.

"I can agree to that."

"Then cheers to you and your adventures abroad." His smile was uncertain as he raised his glass, and she clinked hers against it. Excitement coursed through her anyway. He'd agreed.

Scarlett took a sip, grimaced as she swallowed the nasty drink, and beamed at him.

"I'll have my chief of staff make a few calls and start to flesh out your itinerary. You should meet with the Soleil ambassador in Zahara. She has a daughter near your age." His voice was brighter again.

Scarlett's world was considerably lighter now that her father had given his blessing. *One year of freedom. One beautiful year to be away and be me. And six weeks to be with Brayden.*

"How do I look?" asked her father. "Camera-ready?"

A man in his fifties, Jules was handsome, with thick salt-and-pepper hair, crow's feet around his eyes, and angular cheekbones. Not a hair on his head was out of place.

"Let me just straighten your tie a little." Scarlett loosened and resecured the knot. "There. Now you're perfect."

He smiled at her. "Thank you, darling."

After they'd finished their whiskey, Scarlett and her father made their way to the parliamentary chambers. She stood behind him while he gave his speech to the two hundred peers of Soleil's parliament, which included one hundred hereditary seats like the one she would take one day, as well as one hundred elected seats. She listened to Jules's well-rehearsed speech, clapping and smiling at the correct moments, but inside she was mentally packing for her trip.

Sigur Viður would be freezing, so she'd need her warmest coat. Zahara was mediterranean—would she be able to surf while she was there? She should research surfboard rentals. Her phone wouldn't work outside of Soleil right away, because the rest of the world used magic to power their technology, but someone at the Sigur Viður Embassy would help her set it up to work on their magical network, surely. Whatever that entailed. It had to be like joining a new phone network. Should she bring Brayden a gift? Would he like a new phone? Was that too much?

Her father's voice grew louder, drawing Scarlett's attention back to the speech. Lord Jules Heroux's voice rang with passion, and his words echoed throughout the chamber.

"The time has come to put the prejudices and fears of the past behind us as we open the borders of Soleil to magic-wielding countries. On this Remembrance Day, we honor the people who gave their lives in the Great War that ended nearly two hundred years ago, but let us also celebrate the future they gave us."

More than half the lords and ladies stood and broke out into thunderous applause. Even some of the Goldenrod Party clapped. Her dad was well-loved.

While reporters jostled each other in the standing room near the podium, each of them eager to snap a picture for tomorrow's papers, Scarlett struggled to hold her most photogenic smile and not blink at the flashing cameras. As relieved as she was to have revealed her plans to her father, she was also tired from the past twenty-four hours. The breakup with Alastair had taken it out of her.

As soon as the press feeding frenzy died down, Scarlett and Jules joined the stream of people heading to the back entrance of Parliament to prepare for the departure of the Remembrance Day motorcade, which would circle the drivable part of Soleil's downtown. They were walking the marble-filled hallways when a voice called out.

"Scarlett! Jules!" Lady Elestine Spencer, Jules's closest colleague, rushed to catch up with them.

Scarlett's stomach lurched at the sight of her ex-boyfriend's mother. With her golden-blonde hair and fine-boned features, she was a feminine version of her son and the second-to-last person Scarlett wanted to see today.

"Wonderful speech, Jules."

Her father beamed. "Thank you." He leaned in to kiss Elestine's cheek.

"Scarlett, good to see you," said Elestine, her tone overly bright.

Scarlett forced a smile as she wondered what version of the truth Alastair had told his mother about their breakup. "You too, Elestine," she lied. "Who are you riding with for the motorcade?" *Please not us.*

Elestine didn't respond. She had her phone out and scanned it as she walked.

"Is something wrong?" asked her father.

She sighed as her eyes darted to Scarlett. "Oh, it's Alastair. He says he regrets not coming to the parade. I'm worried about him."

It was as if Elestine were a vampire, the way her words drained Scarlett of her energy. Had Elestine caught up with them just to talk about her son? Was Alastair, who'd told her in the past he thought depression was a choice, struggling emotionally for the first time in his life? Or was Elestine just using this tactic to see if Scarlett could be brought around to console him, potentially—in her mind— leading to a reconciliation? Trickery would be less of a surprise than Alastair actually being devastated, but even so, Scarlett wanted him to be okay. Just not in the same time and space as her.

Her dad stopped and pulled them to the side to avoid blocking the procession of lords and ladies streaming through the hallway. "Is it too late for him to make his way here?"

Scarlett's eyes went wide, and her stomach dropped. *It would be better for* me *if he stayed home. Why can't you see that, Dad?* She tried to meet her father's gaze to convey some of her thoughts, but he was staring at Elestine.

Elestine shook her head. "With all the streets blocked for the motorcade? He'd have to take the northern canal all the way around."

Scarlett relaxed slightly.

Her dad furrowed his brow. "That's a shame. Perhaps we can all go visit him after the festivities." He gave Scarlett a pointed look.

She stared at him. *Is he serious?* It was as if he'd forgotten their conversation in his office. Even if he only wanted them to be friendly, he was prioritizing a political alliance over her feelings. How could he ask her to visit him when she'd told him only an hour before that every fiber of her being needed to be away from Alastair? The thought of going to the Spencer house after the parade filled her with dread. She bit her lip, fighting for diplomatic words, and blew out a breath.

"It'll be late by then."

"It won't take that long," said her father, a hard glint in his eye. "Not if we go straightaway." He wasn't backing down.

"We literally just spoke about this, Dad. What part of 'he doesn't really love me, and I'm dying to get out of Soleil' did you not understand? I don't want to see him right now. I'm sorry, Elestine, for having to say this in front of you."

Her father took a step backward as if her words were a physical blow.

Elestine looked between them uncomfortably. "Scarlett, I don't mean to overstep, but Alastair told me he regrets some of the things he said yesterday. I know he does love you *very* much, and he'd never have intentionally hurt you. I know he wants to apologize as soon as he can and make things up to you. There doesn't have to be an immediate engagement."

The corners of Scarlett's mouth turned down, and a tension

headache hit her out of nowhere—a result of all her repressed rage. Alastair had told his mother enough for Elestine to know he'd behaved badly, but Scarlett doubted he'd told her *how* badly he'd behaved. He'd tried to destroy her self-worth, spoken as if he owned her, and implied her only value was as a partner to him and his ambitions. No, she definitely didn't want to see him again today.

Her dad nodded. "Yes, it would be good to clear the air, dear. Relationships require work. Remember, you'll be working together for decades."

Their refusal to acknowledge her feelings pushed against her skull until the pressure exploded, scattering her thoughts like broken glass. It was time to move to a delay tactic.

"I'll consider it during the drive," she said finally. It was the best she could do with both of them staring at her. She could talk to her father while they rode in the car. She needed time before she was ready to see Alastair again.

"Excellent," said her father as if she'd just agreed.

She stared at him, full of disbelief. Had he always been this unyielding? She'd thought speaking her truth would be enough, but her father wasn't accepting her honesty. A dark part of Scarlett was gleeful as she imagined wordlessly leaving after the parade. That would be one way to avoid continuing their argument.

They made their way onto the circular driveway. A row of gnarled oaks surrounded the manicured lawn, but they didn't keep the sun from beating down on Scarlett's face, exacerbating her headache. A frazzled-looking woman with a clipboard led Scarlett and her father to the armored car they'd be riding in. Two soldiers in fatigues and sunglasses were already seated in the front. Scarlett climbed into the back seat, and her father slid in after her.

"Let's roll our windows down," said her dad. "I want to be able to wave at the crowd."

The eternal politician.

"It's absolutely boiling today." Scarlett pressed the button to lower her window and sighed as a hot breeze immediately kissed her face.

As they sat side by side waiting for the cars to begin moving, Scarlett contemplated how to tell her dad off for how he'd double-crossed her with Elestine. Before she could say anything, though, he grasped her hand from his side of the back seat.

"I don't think I've said this yet in the pre-speech frenzy, but you look lovely today, darling. You're the spitting image of your mother when I met her." He pulled his hand away and rested it in his lap.

"Thank you." The unexpected compliment dispelled some of her anger.

Scarlett was silent as they moved slowly around the circular driveway in front of Parliament, police on motorcycles flanking their vehicles. She went over their route in her mind. She'd ridden in the motorcade every year for as far back as she could remember. The route was always the same: The procession would move along Prince's Street, past the University of Soleil, and over the Cobalt Canal Bridge to the business district, as well as through the southern portion of the city via Elysian Street, where the army was based. There, they'd all lay wreaths on Soleil's Great War monument, the obelisk outside the army headquarters. All in all, she was trapped with her father for several more hours.

Scarlett's gaze lingered on Elestine alone in the car ahead, and she said a quick prayer of thanks to the Goddess that Alastair had stayed home. She was going to avoid seeing him today even if it meant running off into the night.

The citizens of Soleil waved flags and called out to the procession in excitement as the line of cars appeared. Today, Remembrance Day parties would be taking place all over the city. Many of them would begin right after the motorcade. People waved at their vehicle when they spotted the distinctive Soleil flags on its headlights, and Scarlett and her father smiled and waved back.

Scarlett turned toward her father. "I need space from Alastair for a while. I'm not going to his house today."

He didn't look away from the crowds, and his bland, public-facing demeanor didn't change. "I understand why you don't want to see him, but it's better to not let things deteriorate too much. You'll need to be able to work with him when you both join Parliament."

Scarlett's anger bubbled to the surface once more. "Isn't it okay to put my private life first sometimes? You married Mum for love, didn't you? Even though it wasn't advantageous." He'd once told her the story of how he'd defied his father to marry her mum, and she wanted him to tell her again.

He didn't hesitate. "I loved your mother completely. It caused a huge falling-out between me and my parents when I told them I wanted to be with her, but I was happy to fight for her. Of course your private life should ultimately come first, but I hardly think it's a big ask for you to be courteous to Alastair. You don't have the option of never speaking to him again."

"Dad, *he* said awful things to *me*. It's like he thinks he owns me because he took my—"

"WE LOVE YOU!" a young woman holding a baby shouted at them from behind the barrier. "Lord Heroux!"

Scarlett sighed. Maybe the universe was trying to prevent her from telling her father how she lost her V-card, even if it did illustrate her point.

"Scarlett, we love you too!" called an old woman.

Scarlett turned away from her father to smile brightly at her.

They both continued waving to all their well-wishers. Sweat beaded on Scarlett's forehead. The breeze had ceased, and her blazer was trapping the heat.

"Dad—"

"We'll finish this conversation later, okay?"

"Fine," said Scarlett. *But I'm going home—*

A whoosh of air sliced through the car, and wet warmth sprayed across the side of her face. Deafening bangs in quick succession assaulted Scarlett's eardrums as the car veered left and slammed to a stop. Her stomach tightened into a knot as her head whipped around, searching for the source of the sound. She touched her cheek. Red coated her fingertips.

Scarlett's window went up. The soldier in the passenger seat yelled at them as the driver hit the gas.

"Lord Heroux, Miss Heroux, get on the floor of the car!"

Dread overtook Scarlett as she reached for her father. He was slumped over, his face hidden. Her hands shook. Screams from the crowd grew louder, but Scarlett heard them as if from a distance as she stared at her father. Was he unconscious? She had to help him. They could get him to a doctor who could help. Her heart thudded in her chest. There was so much red covering the back seat of the car. Where had it all come from? Was it blood? It couldn't be. Was he shot? Her father had been shot. She looked down, and it was like staring at herself from some faraway place. She'd been thoroughly sprayed with red. It was stark across her white skirt.

With trembling hands, Scarlett tried to push her father into a sitting position, but his body was heavy and uncooperative. She pressed her hand into his shoulder, willing him to wake up.

"Dad!" she shouted. Then she burst into tears.

The side of his head was bloodied, but her eyes slid over it, not wanting to see how badly her father had been hurt. She took off her blazer, thinking numbly that she could use it to put pressure on the wound.

The screams and shouts around them continued outside, but Scarlett blocked it all out. Nothing existed outside of her father. She took his hand and squeezed it as she held her blazer to the side of his head. His big hand was warm in hers even though he was slumped forward and still. She sobbed as she buried her face in his arm. Why had they been fighting over stupid things? Alastair, going abroad—who cared about any of it, if he would only live? The tightness in her chest made it hard to breathe.

They sped through the streets until the car halted, and then Scarlett finally lifted her head. A flock of people in scrubs and white coats and numerous soldiers in fatigues surrounded the car. Arms pulled her away from her father, and two men carefully lifted him from the vehicle. Scarlett scooted out after him, desperate for someone around them to step in and save him. Her bloodied white blazer fell to the ground as he was moved onto the stretcher, and she let out a gasp that became a sob as she took in her father's gaping head wound.

The staff's urgency evaporated as soon as they got a good look at him. The way they stopped rushing. The careful, defeated way they lowered their hands. Scarlett knew before anyone said a word. Her world spun on its axis, her very sense of self crumbling as a hollow void opened up in her chest. She'd spoken her last words to him and not known it. Her dad was *dead*.

She didn't even feel it as she collapsed to the ground, breathing raggedly.

"Shit—is she hurt? Get her onto a stretcher!"

Arms lifted her. She opened her eyes enough to see she was being wheeled in behind her father. Two nurses stood off to the side crying as the stretchers were pushed into the hospital. Scarlett closed her eyes, not wanting to see any more. Unable to take in any more.

When she opened her eyes again, she was in a curtained-off space somewhere inside the hospital. *Where did they take Dad?* She sobbed and took a couple of jerky breaths.

"Lady Heroux, I know this is hard, but you need to take some deeper breaths," said a stern female voice. "Can you breathe with me? In for one, two, three, four . . . We need oxygen here, please—she's gonna pass out . . ."

When Scarlett came to, her head felt heavy. As she stirred, something on her arm pricked at her skin. She forced her eyelids open to find she'd been hooked up to an IV. She was in a different room—a private one—filled with beeping monitors. For a moment, she hoped it had all been the most realistic nightmare she'd ever had in her life. But then she looked down at herself. Someone had put a blanket over her legs. She lifted it and saw her skirt still had blood on it. She began to wail.

Her father's body.

The blazer falling away.

The gaping hole in his head.

Her body shook as she cried. Someone had murdered him. She hadn't even been looking at him when he was shot. She'd wasted the last moment she'd had with her father resenting him for pushing her to talk to Alastair. She wished she could go back and tell him she loved him one last time. Her sobs grew louder.

A nurse entered the room, followed closely by Laylani.

"Lady Heroux, are you in pain?"

"N-no. I mean, I don't know . . ." Her body wasn't in pain, but everything was horribly wrong. Scarlett couldn't be Lady Heroux yet. It was too soon.

"Your stepmother just arrived. Would you like some water? We gave you a relaxant after you passed out. You should feel calmer now," said the kindly nurse.

Scarlett shook her head before turning to Laylani. "Where's my dad?" Her voice wobbled.

Laylani's elegant face was blank. "He's in the hospital morgue. He was dead on arrival. You're Lady Heroux now."

Scarlett's vision blurred as fresh tears spilled over onto her cheeks, the massive well of pain inside flooding through her once more. She glared at Laylani through her tears. How could she be so cold?

"Pull yourself together, please," her stepmother hissed. "My husband is dead, and you don't see me collapsing on the floor wailing as if the world is ending."

Scarlett sniffed and shuddered, finding Laylani's lack of distress inhuman. "Is Beni here?"

"He's at home. Where we should be. Get up, and let's go."

The nurse, who'd been clicking away on the computer in the corner, returned to Scarlett's bedside. "Lady Heroux collapsed and lost consciousness. The doctor would like to keep her for a couple more hours to monitor her."

"Is that what you want, Scarlett—to stay and be monitored? Or do you want to go home to your brother and your grandmother?" asked Laylani. "Makes no difference to me."

Scarlett pushed herself up. She needed her brother and her grand-mother. She needed Brayden. "I want to go home."

CHAPTER (4)

The next morning, Scarlett awoke to pink and yellow light streaming in through her window, along with flickers from the shimmering water of the Sapphire Canal. Her body and her soul were raw.

How long was I asleep?

After an awful car ride home from the hospital, she'd stumbled into her grandmother's arms and been put to bed. *Beni.* The thought of her brother was enough to make her sit up. He'd been in his room when she got home, and she hadn't spoken to him since . . .

Scarlett put her face in her hands. She kept seeing the hole in her dad's head in her mind. Other memories intruded, bringing white-hot pain: a quiet dinner they'd enjoyed, just the two of them; the time he'd given her ten of his favorite novels for her sixteenth birthday; the day he'd taken her to visit the University of Soleil. Arguments they'd had. Times she'd said too much, or things she'd left unsaid. Shuddering, she forced herself to take several deep breaths.

She had to be strong. Falling apart wasn't an option.

Once the jagged feelings and memories were below the surface, she stood and took a few steps toward her dressing room, rubbing her eyes as she went. She needed to get dressed and check on Beni. He was her responsibility now that their father was gone.

The dressing-room door opened from the inside, and her grandmother Manon appeared, her eyebrows knitted tightly in concern.

"Oh, Scarlett, you're awake. Can I do anything for you?" Manon was already wearing a long-sleeve black dress for mourning, and her hair, the palest blonde with streaks of gray, was in an elegant bun. She looked nowhere near as wrecked as Scarlett felt, but then Jules wasn't her son—Manon was Scarlett's maternal grandmother.

Scarlett's face crumpled as it hit her she was now an orphan. She opened her arms. Her grandmother came closer and squeezed her tightly, rubbing her back as she held her. Scarlett breathed in the familiar smell of her peony-scented perfume as hot tears fell down her cheeks.

A minute or so passed, and then Scarlett pulled away.

Her grandmother's face was pinched with concern. "Oh, my darling girl. Let me do something for you. Anything. I was about to ask Martin for some coffee. Would you like some?"

Scarlett sniffed and pulled back. "I want to check on Beni." Her throat was thick, like she had a cold.

"He spent most of yesterday in bed, same as you. How about I check on him while I'm down there, and if he's awake, I'll see if he wants to come up?"

"Thank you."

"Dark roast coffee? Can I bring you breakfast?"

The image of her dad that was burned into Scarlett's brain appeared in her mind's eye again.

"I'm worried I'll puke if I try to eat."

Manon clasped her hand. "I understand, but you won't have much in your stomach to heave up, and food might make you feel better. I'll bring a tray so you can try to take a few bites."

Scarlett nodded. Her grandmother was probably right.

"Brayden and Lachlan are in the mirror, so don't go in there unless you want to say hello."

"Already? It's early."

"There's some disturbing news out about Sigur Viður and Evory, and they want to discuss it with me after I've finished checking on you and Beni."

Sigur Viður, the country she'd been planning to go to first on her embassy tour. What an idyllic alternate reality she'd been living in where her father was still alive and her biggest concern was convincing him to let her leave.

"Oh." It was all she could manage without risking tears.

Manon gave her hand a sympathetic squeeze. "I'll be back soon."

Her grandmother closed the bedroom door behind her.

Scarlett stood still in front of the door. She could handle seeing Brayden like this, but it would be awkward having Lachlan Maddox, his dad, see her in her current state. She'd known Lachlan for a long time, because he often talked to Manon through the mirror, but he was her father's age.

Still, the draw to see Brayden was strong whether his father was there or not, so she crossed her arms over her chest to hold herself together and strode through the dressing-room door. Scarlett lifted her gaze to the huge gilt mirror. She'd stood before Brayden a thousand times, but never like this.

Brayden rose to his feet when she came in. She'd never seen him look so serious. The hint of a smile she often saw on his lips was absent. As he took in her expression, worry was all she could see.

"Scarlett. I'm so sorry about your father. I wish I were there. I wish there was something I could do." His voice was deep and warm, but it barely reached her.

Lachlan stood too but remained behind his large mahogany desk. His dark eyes bore into her from a distance. "Yes, we're so sorry for your loss, Scarlett. It's a huge loss for the world, but most of all for you." Like Manon, he was already pristinely groomed and ready for the day in his freshly pressed Clair de Lune military uniform. His salt-and-pepper hair was parted on one side and combed. It was a normal day for him.

Scarlett swallowed thickly. "Thank you." She looked up at the ceiling, willing herself not to cry.

Brayden came close enough for her to see the depth of concern in his warm brown eyes, but *never* close enough to touch. She put her hand on the mirror anyway, and he put his hand up against it. She could almost imagine his body heat coming through the glass.

"I'd come stay with you if I could. I hate that I can't be there for you in person," he whispered.

"I know. I wish you could be here too," she said, tears spilling over onto her cheeks. If only. She stared at him, sure there was raw pain radiating out of her and not caring, because he was her closest friend. The only one she didn't have to censor herself for. Who never expected her to behave a certain way. He cared for her just as she was.

Of all the times she'd wished Brayden could come through the mirror into her dressing room, this moment topped them all. She wanted him to hold her. But it was impossible for him to be there, just like it always had been. She'd have to continue to live without him. The trip to Clair de Lune would be impossible now.

She dropped her hand as she heard two sets of footsteps coming into her bedroom.

"Scarlett, my love? Beni is here, and we have breakfast!"

This was her grandmother's warning to get out before Beni came inside and caught her using the magic mirror.

"I have to go," she told Brayden in a low voice.

"I'll be around later if you need me."

"Thank you. For everything."

She hurried away from the mirror.

In her room she found Beni. His angular face was her father's replica—although, unlike Jules Heroux, her brother wore his heart on his sleeve. His green eyes were puffy from crying, and his narrow shoulders were hunched. Her heart, already broken, split again at the sight of him. She pulled him into her arms, and they held each other and sobbed.

Three days passed in a blur of condolences, sleepless nights, and tears. Scarlett sat in the armchair in front of the mirror. It was nearly midnight, and her father's funeral was tomorrow morning. The moments she tried to fall asleep were the hardest, so she was resisting going to bed even though it was late.

Brayden was on the other side of the glass, like he had been every night since her dad's death. He'd stayed up with her while she sat in her armchair alternating between talking, crying, and dozing. Being near him helped. She could lean on him without having to be strong for him like she did with Beni.

On Brayden's side, Lachlan's couch was as close to the mirror as it could be. Brayden lay there staring at her, his face half in shadow, lit only by the dying fire. On her side of the mirror, a dim lamp on a nearby table fended off the darkness.

"What do you think it's like when we die? Do you think some part of us lives on?" she asked. The question came out of nowhere. They'd been sitting in comfortable silence for several minutes.

He shifted, adjusting the pillow resting under his head. "I believe we're more than some meat on a bunch of bones, so yes, I think some part of us lives on."

"Really?" she asked, her eyebrows lifting.

"Yeah. I mean, how could we not be? It would be ridiculous if all this were meaningless. If death was *it*. Art, music, my friends, my brother, you—all of it's too wonderful to be random."

His words brought her some relief, and she smiled softly. Her father had dismissed any belief in the unseen as foolish. Facing his death would be much harder if she chose to believe it was the true end of him. But she still thought his spirit was out there, and leaning into that made her feel better. It was still painful, but the pain wasn't as brutal. Knowing Brayden believed the same brought her even more comfort.

"I agree." Scarlett's throat was thick. "The world we've built, the love we have, the dreams we dream . . . it makes more sense to me that the souls who create such beautiful things live on somehow. I think we'll be together again." Her voice broke.

Brayden reached out and touched the glass. He reached for her often when she broke down, even though the glass was always there. "You'll see your father again. He'll be waiting for you when you die. Just like our mams will be waiting for us."

Tears streamed down her face as she sobbed quietly, and she lifted the blanket in her lap to wipe the tears away as they fell. Brayden had lost his mum at a young age too. They'd bonded over that as children, the loss of their mothers. Thinking of Brayden's mother always made her emotional, especially now. Probably because his pain was so similar to hers. They were both hurt in the same way, deep down. Scarlett wished she could climb through the mirror and lie in his arms.

"I'll be there waiting for you if I die first," he added. "I promise."

She cried harder, and each breath was an effort. "Don't make me think about *y-you* going first. You're not allowed to d-die before me." The loss of him would kill her.

"Sorry. I'll try not to. It's harder for the ones who get left behind." He smiled. "Maybe we can go at the same time. Maybe if we're lucky, we'll die in our sleep on the same night when we're old and ready to go. How cool would that be?"

His odd excitement over something so macabre soothed her somehow, and her breathing became smoother. "Yes, please. At the same time. But let me go, like, one minute before you do."

He smiled sadly. "Okay, but just one. I'll follow you into the dark."

The next day, Scarlett and her family made their way to the Tornaling National Cemetery, on the far eastern side of Soleil, for the funeral. She'd come to the cemetery plenty of times to visit her mother's grave, and now she'd be visiting her father here too.

Far from the canals that surrounded the heart of the city, rows and rows of white tombstones peppered the thick green grass. Rare cloud cover kept the summer sun from beating down on Scarlett's head as hundreds of dignitaries surrounded the casket, but her outfit still made her miserable even without the direct sun. The waistband of her tights dug into her stomach as she sat down, and the new black dress, delivered by Laylani that morning, made her skin itch. Scarlett's vision blurred as she stared at the Soleil flag covering the polished wood box that held what was left of her dad.

A large security detail hovered around Scarlett and her family, keeping away anyone who tried to approach. They'd escorted them to the ceremony and would be taking them home again afterward, as if anyone cared what happened to them now that her father was gone. An honor guard dressed in full ceremonial military attire stood at attention alongside the casket, waiting to bear it to her father's final resting place. Police and military swarmed the perimeter, probably trying to look useful to compensate for how they'd failed to protect their prime minister four days ago, but Scarlett ignored them. They were all trying to look important and busy, but none of them could do anything to make it better.

The investigation into who'd shot her father was the only thing being spoken about in the news, but all the coverage was pure speculation, because the Soleil Bureau of Investigation had no leads. The greatest country in the world, with the best technology, and there was not a single fucking lead.

Scarlett stood between her grandmother and Beni while the Chief Justice of Soleil gave the eulogy.

"Prime Minister Jules Heroux led a life of service, from his time in the navy to the day he died . . ."

The crowd was silent.

As Scarlett stared at the casket, images of her father flashed through her mind. She saw him across the dinner table at home, smiling at her; sitting on her bed and talking politics with her while she studied; holding her and gruffly patting her back when she cried as a child. Never again would she see him laugh or make him proud. He wouldn't be there if she ever got married.

Her father had held Scarlett's hand at her mother's funeral in this same cemetery. Now her father was gone too. Time had healed her grief over her mother's death, but her father's murder had sliced into that old scar, reopening it and deepening it.

They were both gone. Scarlett was alone.

The speaker's words didn't reach her.

But then Manon gripped her hand, and Scarlett looked down at where her arm was linked with Beni's. She wasn't really alone.

Manon, Beni, and Brayden. Her reasons to hold it together.

She stole a glance at her brother's face. His breathing was jagged as two tears slipped down his cheeks. She let go of her grandmother's hand and pulled him into her arms. Beni threaded his arms around her waist, and they held each other for a long moment.

Beyond him Laylani stood next to her sister, Lady Moira Ashworth. The women both wore black netting over their faces, but underneath it, they were stoic and composed.

Scarlett glared at her stepmother's profile. Since her father's death, Laylani had offered only frigid advice, such as "you'll get over it," even to her son. The most upset Laylani had been was when she'd learned Jules had asked to be buried next to his first wife in his will, but she'd seemed more angry than sad or hurt. The only other crack in her composure was the return of her secret cigarette habit. Scarlett never actually saw Laylani smoking, but the smell of smoke mixed with her expensive perfume whenever she passed Scarlett in the hallway. Scarlett couldn't believe a loving wife would react so minimally to her husband's violent murder.

Scarlett, on the other hand, had eyes that were swollen from crying.

The eulogy ended, and she turned to look at the rows and rows of chairs behind them while the next speaker approached the podium. Her gaze immediately locked on the Spencer family. They were in the second row, along with most of her father's peers from Parliament. Elestine looked far more devastated than Laylani and was dabbing her veiled face with a tissue while her shoulders shook. Alastair stared at her until she turned away to face forward.

He'd come to see her the day after her dad's death, but she was asleep after returning from the hospital, so Martin had turned him away. Their breakup seemed like such an insignificant thing in the wake of this tragedy, and yet it had tainted her final hours with her father.

Scarlett flinched as guns fired into the air in a salute. Manon grasped Scarlett's hand tighter. A bagpipe played, signaling the end of the funeral.

The past few hours—the past few *days*—had been utterly draining, and all Scarlett wanted was to be out of the public eye. She couldn't believe she still had to get through a funeral luncheon at the Navy Club. She'd rather go home and be alone with Beni and Manon, and later that night, with Brayden.

She stood and took a deep, steadying breath as their security team approached, ready to lead the family back to their vehicle. Laylani took Beni's hand and pulled him away from Scarlett, either ignoring or not noticing Scarlett's glare. In front of hundreds of onlookers, they all began the walk to the car. To Scarlett's surprise, Lady Moira Ashworth began to walk beside them, directly next to Scarlett. Her presence chafed. Her dad had privately hated his sister-in-law, and Scarlett had never liked her either.

Is she trying to be in the photographs of the funeral? To look patriotic?

"It goes without saying that I'm sorry for your loss," began Moira as they walked side by side toward the vehicles. "Your father and I didn't agree politically, but I respected him."

"Thank you." A bead of sweat trickled down Scarlett's back. The eyes of the crowd were weighing her down, and she hoped Lady Ashworth was done talking.

As her family got into the waiting SUV, Moira pulled her aside.

"Scarlett, could I have a quick word?"

Scarlett stiffened. "I shouldn't keep them waiting."

"I'll make it quick. I wanted to let you know you have options." She waved when Laylani looked at them, motioning to Scarlett.

To Scarlett's surprise, her stepmother waved back, seemingly fine with the delay.

Oh, here we go. What the hell could this be about? Unable to force a polite, attentive expression, she let her features relax without attempting to smile.

Moira looked as if it were any other day as she spoke. "Laylani mentioned you've postponed your tour abroad, which is wise, but you've got a couple of years before you'll inherit. You'll need to do *something*. If you'd consider it, I'd like you to join my staff. I could offer you opportunities you may have never considered."

Moira waited for a response, but Scarlett stared at her. Was she *serious*?

After a long pause, Moira went on. "Give it a think, and we can discuss it anytime you like."

Scarlett willed her bleary eyes to focus. Who did this woman think she was, trying to get Scarlett to abandon her father's beloved Cerulean Party the day of his funeral? She sucked in a breath and spoke.

"Lady Ashworth, my father was shot in front of me four days ago. I find it odd you're offering me a job under these circumstances. Don't you think, if I were going to work in Parliament, it would make more sense for me to take my father's seat early? With respect, why would I want to work for you?"

Before Moira had approached, Scarlett's only plan was to quietly make it from one day to the next until being alive wasn't nonstop pain. That was still her plan, if she were honest, but it was gratifying to piss off Lady Ashworth all the same. Her dad would have loved the way Moira's eyes flashed at Scarlett's words. She'd never looked more like Laylani. It had always confused Scarlett that Jules could love Laylani and hate her sister when, to Scarlett, they were a matched set.

Then Moira's calm demeanor returned. "There's no rush to take his seat, is there?" Her voice was soft enough that no one around them could overhear. "You'd benefit from a year or two of mentoring."

Does she think I'm stupid?

Scarlett stared pointedly at Moira. "If I take his seat, I could help pass my father's border legislation. I've been watching the news over the past few days. With my father dead, his legislation is in jeopardy. I could use whatever sympathy I have in the wake of his death to help. I know my vote is needed to preserve his legacy."

Moira's gaze darkened. "I'd hoped you might be more open-minded."

In a way, Scarlett's anger was a relief, because it took from the sea of grief filling the rest of her. Unlike the grief, her rage was a practical outlet. It burned through her apathy for the future and grew her desire to take her seat in Parliament. She wanted nothing more than to see the look on Moira Ashworth's face when the border legislation passed. It would make both of Scarlett's parents proud, wherever they were. Her father's death wouldn't have to mean the death of his dreams. She could end the isolationism of Soleil and thus reduce bigotry toward other countries like Clair de Lune in his honor. It was what her parents both would have wanted.

She shrugged, her barely-there patience wearing thinner by the second. "Like I said, you've caught me at a low moment." She waved her hand toward her father's casket. "Your timing is incredibly bad."

"I suppose I should have known you'd be like this, given your mother was forest trash from Clair de Lune."

The comment was so venomous it stunned Scarlett, and her lips parted.

Moira took two steps away, paused, and came back. Her glare was angry enough to startle Scarlett even in her current state. "Take care, Scarlett. I hope it's all worth it. I'd hate to see you end up like your father."

"I'd rather end up like him than end up like you," spat Scarlett, her voice raised.

"That can easily be arranged." Moira walked off without another word.

Scarlett's eyes widened. *Did she really just say that?* She was sleep-deprived, and her brain was full of fog, but Moira's parting threat pierced through her and shook her to the core.

CHAPTER (5)

Two days after the funeral, Scarlett stepped out of her palatial family home and onto the dock that extended out over the sparkling Sapphire Canal. One of their security guards was waiting on her family's speedboat with their driver, Charlie. Another guard followed Manon. Sick of watching the news, since there'd been no update in the investigation into her dad's death, Scarlett had decided to act on the feelings that had been simmering since the funeral. She was going to the Soleil courts to apply to join Parliament early.

Once she and Manon were seated in the boat's enclosed cabin, Charlie pulled out into the waterway. They sped down the canal and under the numerous footbridges connecting the northern and southern halves of the city. The view of the morning sun on the water in front of the palazzo-style residences was as dazzling as ever, and it was a relief to Scarlett to know she could still find the Sapphire Canal beautiful in spite of everything.

Her feelings were all over the place as they rode into town. There

was the ever-present omnipotent sorrow for her dad. She was also silently mourning the loss of her year abroad, which made her feel guilty. Because she shouldn't care. But she did. She'd give up the travel, though, for Soleil. For the greater good.

Hadrian's Roundabout came into view. The statue of the long-dead Emperor Hadrian at the center of the three-lane circular waterway towered over her, as it always had. Even through the lens of grief, these familiar sights remained the same. It made sense life would go on, but the change within Scarlett was so enormous she almost expected the world to look different too.

The traffic was as busy as ever as Charlie maneuvered the speedboat through it. Scarlett stared up at the lofty statue as they passed. She'd always loved the look of Hadrian's Roundabout. It marked the beginning of the grandiose buildings of the city center, where large plots of land that held the Soleil train station, Parliament, and the University of Soleil sat within a grid of canals. It also reminded her of Soleil's colorful past. Founded two hundred years ago, Soleil was one of seven countries created when the empire spanning the continent of Hieratia disbanded after the Great War. Soleil had the legacy of a thousand-year reign of emperors and the promise of a modern new beginning now that they were on the cusp of reintegrating with more of the world. Or at least it had seemed that way before her father died. Scarlett hoped Soleil's promising future wasn't lost with him. That was why she was going to the courts—to do everything she could to make the future bright.

Charlie pulled the boat up to Prince's Street Dock. It was almost always heaving with people, given the huge dock was the main access point to the city center from the residential canals on the western side.

Scarlett stepped out of the cabin. "Thanks for the ride, Charlie. It may be several hours. I'll call when we're done."

"Sounds good, kid."

The security guards made to follow her and Manon. Tired of the constant presence of near strangers, Scarlett spun toward them.

"I don't mean to be rude, but the Soleil Bureau told me yesterday there's now a low security risk for my family. I think we all know your days of being assigned to us are numbered. Would you mind giving me some privacy to run this errand?"

"Scarlett, anytime you begin a sentence with the phrase 'I don't mean to be rude,' it's common knowledge you're about to say something rude," said Manon.

The guards chuckled, and Scarlett's mouth quirked up in a half-grin as warmth crept across her cheeks.

"Sorry for being short," she said. "It's been a rough few days."

"It's fine. We understand," said one of the guards. He glanced at his partner, who shrugged, then turned back to Scarlett. "We're here for your safety until otherwise assigned, but we can follow from a distance if you'd prefer."

"We don't have to go inside a civic building with its own security," said the other.

"Great. Thank you." With a wave, Scarlett led Manon toward the courts.

Their security dipped into a café across from the courts, so Manon and Scarlett were blissfully alone as they walked up the steps into the Court of Soleil. The imposing gray limestone building sat just up the canal from Parliament. Recognition flickered across the face of the clerk who greeted them, and they were quickly shown to a private office and asked to wait.

"Are you sure about joining Parliament?" asked her grandmother for the third time. "You know it would be okay to still take a year off while you're mourning. You never know. Maybe Elestine Spencer will manage the border on her own."

"But I told you what Moira said. *She* clearly didn't want me to join now, which means the head of the Goldenrod Party thinks I can make a difference. I have to do this." She looked down at the table in front of them. Scarlett was resolved but still wished the responsibility wasn't hers. Then she glanced up and noticed a framed poster on the wall. It was old. Probably a hundred years old. The slogan read, "Stronger Without It! Magic Is a Blight!" The illustrated graphic showed a clean-cut-looking woman and her children—obviously Soleil citizens—turning away from a sinister-looking man whose clawlike hands shot bolts of lightning at them. The caricature made Scarlett wince, but her resolve also strengthened. Her country needed to move on, and she would help them do it.

A woman in a brown tweed suit greeted them warmly as she stepped into the small room. "Good morning, Lady Heroux. I'm Shannen, an officer of the court."

The use of her new title was a constant reminder of her dad. Unlike her seat in Parliament, the title and her father's money had passed to Scarlett immediately.

She shook Shannen's hand. "Good morning, Shannen."

Manon stood. "I'm Lady Heroux's grandmother. You may call me Manon. I'm here for moral support. I hope that's all right."

"That's perfectly fine," said Shannen. "I want to offer my condolences, Lady Heroux, on the passing of your father. It's a huge loss for the country."

"Thank you for the kind words," said Scarlett woodenly. Her oft-repeated response was becoming automatic.

They all took their places at the small table.

"I understand you want to file a petition for an exception to the age of inheritance," said Shannen.

Scarlett straightened in her chair. "Yes. I've read there's precedent for it. Is that right?"

Shannen gave her a small nod. "Yes, in several instances, particularly when the heir in question is over eighteen and the peer has passed away. I'm confident your application will be approved without issue."

Scarlett let out a relieved sigh. "Good."

"I've brought a few forms for you to fill out." Shannen placed a small pile of papers in front of Scarlett. "Once we've filed these, it'll take some time to process them. There is a special panel of judges who rule specifically on issues relating to the peers of Parliament, and I believe their next meeting takes place two weeks from today."

Scarlett's brow furrowed. Two weeks was ages. She shook her head, forcing herself to relax. She could use the two weeks to meet with her future colleagues and speak to the swing voters. She'd use any goodwill she had as the dead prime minister's daughter.

"I bet the Ceruleans will be elated to hear you're filing," said Shannen, snapping Scarlett out of her thoughts. Shannen handed her a pen.

Scarlett gave her a tired half-smile. At least someone would be happy. Her mind flashed to Brayden's face when she'd told him she had to stay in Soleil for now to focus on joining Parliament. He hadn't been able to hide his disappointment, but he'd understood her sense of duty and had been supportive. "I hope so." She turned her attention to the forms.

"They'll be over the moon," said Manon, sounding pleased. "I'm pretty sure there was a twenty-four-hour Cerulean prayer vigil for the rise of Scarlett Heroux. I hope they appreciate her stepping up so soon . . ."

Shannen smiled politely, but her eyes were on Scarlett as she passed back the first form. "While you're here, have you considered naming an heir? Now you're the head of household for House

Heroux. I brought this form as well, just in case." She pulled another sheet of paper out of a folder and slid it toward Scarlett.

"My brother, Beaufort, would be next in line—correct?" asked Scarlett.

"Yes, but if he's your explicit heir, you can act as his legal guardian. You'd have all the same rights as his mother. With the paperwork filed, it'd be in place should you need it down the line."

The idea of being Beni's legal guardian brought lightness to Scarlett's soul. Being able to protect him from his mother would be huge.

"That sounds prudent. Let's do it."

A short while later, the paperwork was filed, and Scarlett and Manon were standing on the breezy steps outside the courts. Their security guards were nowhere in sight, but they were probably close by.

Manon faced Scarlett. "We don't have to go straight home. Would you like to stop for a pastry somewhere, maybe walk along one of the quieter roads for a while? Then we can come back here and pretend we were inside the courts the whole time, so the guards don't get in trouble."

With a scarf over her hair and wearing a nondescript black dress and boots as she was, Scarlett knew she wouldn't be recognized. "That sounds lovely," she said. She'd end up regretting the decision if she were spotted, but it was such a beautiful day.

Things were looking up. She was Beni's legal guardian, Laylani and Moira couldn't touch her, and when she eventually passed the border legislation, Brayden could come visit. Or she'd visit him during a parliamentary recess. For the first time since her dad's death, she felt optimistic.

They were heading down a side street with croissants in hand when an arm encased Scarlett's waist and a large body pressed into her from behind. Scarlett breathed deeply, intending to scream, but a soft cloth was already over her mouth when she inhaled. Something sharp poked her neck as a sweet, medicinal smell flooded her senses. Her struggling ceased as she slipped quickly into unconsciousness.

CHAPTER (6)

Scarlett awoke in bed, disoriented. She didn't know where she was. Without the strength to open her eyes, she fell asleep again without fully waking.

Sometime later she edged back into consciousness and opened her eyes. The uneasiness of a half-remembered nightmare lingered in her. As she tried to wake up, she registered she was at home, in her own room. Tubes were in her nose. Something was lodged down the back of her throat, and as she shifted, she gained awareness of something foreign between her legs too. Blinking rapidly, she tried to make sense of the heaviness of her body, but her eyelids were weighed down by the need for sleep, and she gave in.

Sunlight was shining through the open curtains the next time she opened her eyes. Beni sat in a chair next to her bed, but she couldn't speak to him. The dreamless sleep beckoned her once more.

She drifted for hours or days or weeks. Beni's and Brayden's voices pulled her to the surface.

Her brother's voice grew louder in her dream. "Scarlett." More insistent. *"Scarlett."* A hand gripped her shoulder, shaking her lightly.

No one had ever shaken her in a dream.

Her eyes flew open. "Beni." Her lips were dry, and her voice was croaky with disuse. She glanced at the window as she cleared her throat. It was pitch-black outside.

Beni leaned over her. "Thank the Goddess." His green eyes were full of concern. "Hang on. I'll be right back." He ran to her closet and stuck his head in. "It worked—she's up."

She was more awake than she'd been since . . .

She tried to recall what had happened, but all she could remember was going to the courts and walking with Manon. Nothing to explain her current state. She had the haziest memory of being surprised and a sickly-sweet smell.

Beni returned to her bedside. "I'm going to take the tubes out of your nose."

He slid the oxygen tubes out gently and threw them to the floor.

Scarlett rubbed her nose, relieved to be breathing freely. "What happened to me?"

"You disappeared. Mum said you were in the hospital, but she wouldn't tell me where, and none of the press knew about it—it wasn't in any of the papers." As he spoke, he unplugged a machine and slipped a heart-rate monitor off her finger. "After a couple of days, an ambulance brought you home and put you here, with all these tubes in you."

Scarlett's lip trembled. "Wh-where's Manon?"

"She's been asleep too. She's in her room. Hopefully, she's waking up now."

She closed her eyes and said a quick prayer of thanks for her grandmother's life. "How long have I been in bed?"

Beni set down the cords he was holding and looked at her. "It's been a month since Dad died," he said, his voice thick.

A month asleep.

An entire month.

Scarlett blinked away her tears and mustered her rage. Anger was better—it helped her wake up.

"Mum told me you've both got sleeping sickness like your mum had, because you're so sad, but we think she's been lying about all of it," said Beni.

"Why do you think she's lying? And what do you mean, 'we'?"

He raised his eyebrows. "I met Brayden and Lachlan. They helped me figure out how to"—he gestured to the medical apparatus next to her bed—"get you to wake up."

Scarlett's mouth fell open as she looked down at her arm. Medical tape was in disarray, and there was bruising where her IV had been. "You pulled an IV out of my arm?" Her twelve-year-old brother. Why hadn't anyone else been here to help him?

"And a feeding tube out of your throat. Can you sit up and drink this?" He pulled out an energy drink, cracked it open, and then dumped a small sachet of white powder into it. "I'm adding extra caffeine," he said in response to her questioning stare.

Scarlett pushed herself up to sit. "I'm sorry I didn't tell you about Brayden."

He shook his head. "Don't be silly. I understand why you kept it a secret." Beni spoke fast as she took long gulps of the sugary drink, quickly downing it. "I was walking through your closet to check on Manon, and Brayden was all, 'Beni, don't be scared—I'm friends with your sister.' He scared the *piss* out of me, but they knew my name, and they knew you, so I talked to them, even though that mirror is clearly illegal and they could have been evil. I just *knew* they weren't, because they were worried about both of you. I told them I'd overheard Mum talking to your doctor. He wanted more money for keeping you and Manon asleep, and she agreed to pay him what he wanted."

She tugged Beni into her chest and hugged him tightly before pulling back to look at him. "Thank you, Beni. I'm pretty sure you saved me. Thank the Goddess you're so brave."

His eyebrows pinched together, and the shadows under his eyes deepened as he stared down at the floor. "She hasn't seemed sad at all that you've been in bed for weeks. My mum is . . ."

She grabbed his hand and squeezed it. "She must have given everything good in her to you." Scarlett's stomach clenched and her pulse raced as the full impact of his words hit her. Laylani had tried to kill her. "Where is your mum?"

"I checked on her before I came up here, and she was asleep, but we need to leave before she wakes up."

"Yes, we need to get out of here." Scarlett pulled the bedsheets off her body and tried to move her legs. She needed to get herself, Beni, and Manon somewhere safe. She needed to fix her body and figure out what was going on.

With Beni's help, she stood on shaky, weak legs. Her body didn't feel like her own. She'd lost all her strength.

"Let's check on Manon," she said. "Can you help me walk?"

"Yes." Beni linked his arm through hers.

Scarlett glanced at her bedroom door, her chest tightening as she imagined her stepmother walking in and forcing her back to sleep. With one hand, she grasped the stand that still held her bag of urine and held on to Beni with the other. The catheter stand had wheels, so she was able to use it for support as Beni walked her to the dressing room. He flipped on the light, and Scarlett was flooded with relief as she spotted Brayden in the mirror, with Lachlan beside him.

Brayden scrambled closer to the mirror. "Scarlett! Are you okay?" He had dark circles under his eyes and looked exhausted.

Scarlett had never been so happy to see him, and she smiled as tears sprang to her eyes.

"I feel like shit, but I'm alive." *The last time we spoke wasn't the last time I'll see you in this life.* She laughed—from sheer joy—and it sounded slightly hysterical to her own ears.

"Alive is all that matters," said Brayden as he examined her from head to toe. "We can fix everything else."

Lachlan came forward to stand just behind Brayden. "Thank heavens you're awake, Scarlett."

Beni eased her into an armchair. "Talk to them while I get Manon." He inclined his head to Brayden and Lachlan as he passed the mirror on his way to Manon's bedroom.

Scarlett wanted to see her grandmother, but her legs were so unsteady she was relieved to be sitting down. Her body was *frail.*

How can I do what needs to be done when I'm so weak?

She looked past Beni to Manon's bed and was relieved to see her grandmother stirring, although she wasn't yet sitting upright.

Scarlett turned her attention back to Brayden and Lachlan. "I don't remember things clearly, but I think someone may have drugged me on the street when I went to the courts. I somehow ended up back here, which makes no sense."

Brayden's eyes were overly bright. "You need to get out of there—*right now.*"

"If I were stronger, I'd go down there and . . ." Her rage and frustration boiled over, and she let out an actual growl.

"It's going to be all right," said Lachlan. "Save the revenge for later. We've helped Beni concoct a plan."

Beni pushed Manon through the doorway. She was in the wheelchair Beni had used after breaking his leg skateboarding last year. It was smaller than an adult wheelchair, but it worked nicely for her slight frame.

"Are we making a mad dash for it?" she asked in a hoarse voice.

Scarlett's shoulders sagged with relief at the sight of her grandmother. "Thank the Goddess you're all right."

"I found this for you, Scarlett." Beni held up the cane from their father's knee surgery several years ago. "Charlie has the boat ready, and he said he can carry Manon and Scarlett downstairs one at a time."

"I wasn't thrilled about involving your driver, but Beni swears the man is like family," said Lachlan.

"He is," said Manon. "We can trust him. He's been with the Heroux family for thirty years, and he loves Scarlett and Beni."

"Good." Lachlan sounded slightly mollified.

"Where should we go?" asked Scarlett, her eyes on Brayden.

"Clair de Lune." Brayden took a step closer to the mirror. "Come here."

"Yes, please come here," echoed Lachlan.

Manon's golden eyes flickered. "Going home sounds great right about now."

Scarlett's eyes went wide. *We're going to Clair de Lune.* After all these years, *this* was how she was leaving Soleil.

Beni started pulling clothes out of Manon's wardrobe and throwing them onto her lap. "I prepared for international travel. Your passports and your folder of important papers are already packed. And so are mine." He closed the wardrobe door and looked from Manon to Scarlett. "I'm coming with you," he said, his expression haunted.

How hard had the last month been for him?

"Of course you're coming," said Scarlett. She wanted to take his hand and squeeze it, but he'd moved to her wardrobe and was tossing more clothes onto Manon's lap.

"Beni, are you sure it's wise for you to leave your mother?" asked Manon, concern etched across her features. "I don't want to leave you somewhere you don't want to be, but won't she follow you?" Her tone was not unkind, merely questioning, but her words were a dagger through Scarlett's heart. She couldn't leave her baby brother here alone.

He faced Manon. "I can't stay here with her." His voice was pleading. "She's awful, and she treats me like . . ." He took a deep breath. "She'll know I helped you, and she'll be furious. Just let me come."

"I can't leave him here," Scarlett said. "He's coming. End of." There was no way she was leaving him to face Laylani alone.

"Beni is welcome to join you both," offered Lachlan.

"Fine," said Manon, looking resolute. "The three of us will go to Clair de Lune. We need to leave. Let's be off!"

Scarlett let out a sigh of relief.

"I'll send Brayden and James to collect you at the Clair de Lune train station," said Lachlan. "The only train out of Soleil leaves at 6:30 a.m. You should make it to the station with time to spare."

"Be careful," said Brayden.

Their gazes met. There was no trace of his usually carefree demeanor on his face. The moment reminded Scarlett of the morning after her father had died. She prayed this would be the last tragedy they endured together.

"I will," she said. There were so many other things she wanted to say to him, but there was no time.

Beni wheeled Manon into Scarlett's room, and Scarlett tore herself away from Brayden to follow slowly behind them.

"Good thing you named Beni your heir, Scarlett," said Manon as Scarlett closed the dressing-room door. "That guardianship paper-work should be in place by now."

Beni beamed. "You did?"

Scarlett smiled at his happiness. "Yes, of course I did." Her smile faltered. "But we have no proof . . ."

"Getting into Soleil is difficult," said Manon. "Getting out is not. They'll let him over the border. His passport shows he's Jules Heroux's son, and I still have your mother's marriage certificate to Jules—and her birth certificate—in my important documents. You said you'd packed the black folder, yes, Beni?"

Beni dipped his chin. "It's on the boat with the rest of our bags."

"Excellent," said Manon. "That should be enough. Now lie down on the bed, Scarlett. We need to get these catheter tubes out of us."

Scarlett eyed the bag of yellow urine on the stand she was using for support. She stood straighter in an attempt to support her own weight, but her body was weak. She'd lost so much muscle mass in the weeks she'd been asleep. It was a good thing she had the cane— and adrenaline pumping through her veins.

"Beni, wheel me to her bedside, then go tell Charlie we're ready to be carried downstairs. We need to be gone five minutes ago."

Scarlett tried not to think about what was happening as her grandmother gripped the tube that had been emptying her bladder for weeks.

"Try to relax," said Manon.

"Have you done this before?" Scarlett asked.

"No, but it can't be hard. Buck up, buttercup," she added with a light pat on Scarlett's bare leg. "You're going to have to return the favor in a moment."

Scarlett gritted her teeth and tried to relax her lower body as Manon pulled gently at the tube. She tried to go somewhere else in her mind, but to her surprise, the tube was out before she had any time to think.

Scarlett let out a huge breath. "Your turn," she sniffed as she sat up.

A minute later, they were both catheter-free.

Beni came back into the room.

"Beni, can you please bring me a bag?" asked Manon. "One of the gift bags in my largest desk drawer would do."

He did as she asked, and Scarlett grimaced as Manon wrapped up their urine bags and tucked them safely into the side pocket of her wheelchair.

Manon caught sight of Scarlett's expression and raised her eyebrows. "I don't know why you're looking at me like I'm packing this up for my own sick amusement. We might be able to use this as evidence."

Scarlett's disgust turned to admiration for her grandmother's resourcefulness. "That's smart. Sorry for making a face while you wrapped the bags of pee up like a solstice present."

Manon smiled crookedly. "No bother. Let's get ourselves dressed."

Scarlett somehow found the strength to pull on the dress, trench coat, and boots Beni had grabbed from her closet. She shoved her phone and her bank cards into her jacket pockets, then she helped Manon pull a loose dress over her head and slide loafers onto her feet. As an afterthought, Scarlett stuck a wide-brimmed hat in the second wheelchair pocket.

"Charlie's here," called Beni from the doorway.

Scarlett waited at the top of the staircase while Charlie carried her grandmother down. Every time his foot hit the steps, a loud thump reverberated through the space, making Scarlett's nerves jangle. She leaned against the wall worrying about everything that could go wrong until Charlie reappeared a few minutes later.

"Thank you for helping us," she whispered.

"Of course, kid," he said. "I've been so worried about you. I'm glad to see you awake."

Outside, Charlie sped down the dock and onto the boat with Scarlett in his arms, setting her down only when he reached the boat's cabin, where Manon and Beni were waiting.

The feeling of an imminent heart attack finally ceased once the boat had pulled away from House Heroux and was speeding down the Sapphire Canal toward the train station. The first signs of the sunrise appeared on the horizon, illuminating the city. Manon let out a loud sigh and looked up in a prayer of thanks.

CHAPTER (7)

Charlie parked the boat, and Beni unloaded their bags. Dawn-colored mist rolled off the canal as Scarlett pulled up the hood of her trench coat and slid on her sunglasses. Manon donned her hat, and Beni put on a cap and his sunglasses too. Once their basic disguises were in place, Charlie carried the bags, walking alongside Scarlett with her cane, and Beni pushed Manon's wheelchair through the near-empty train station. Whether it was due to nerves or shock or both, they spoke barely at all.

Scarlett's stomach knotted as they purchased tickets for the train, withdrew the maximum amount from the cashpoint, and bought a few things from the newsagent while they waited to board. She eyed the few others in the station, afraid they'd try to stop her, but everyone went about their business oblivious to their escape.

Once the train began to admit passengers, Scarlett gripped Charlie in a tight hug goodbye, and then they boarded the early-morning train to Clair de Lune. She was out of breath from boarding, but

inside the train she looked around with interest. She'd never been on one before. The interior was dark wood, and they found their way to an empty compartment with a table and four green tweed seats. Beni helped Manon and then Scarlett into their seats and stored their bags and Manon's wheelchair in the overhead luggage racks.

"There's almost no one on this train," said Beni.

Scarlett peered into the hallway. He was right. Only a few other passengers were on board. "It makes sense, right? There aren't many visa holders to begin with, and so few people from Soleil travel."

"Then why does it run every day?"

"Correspondence," said Manon. "The Soleil firewall prevents magical communications from going to and from the outside world, so they have to keep the physical mail delivery going regularly."

"But you have your mirror," said Beni. "You don't need the mail, do you?"

Scarlett put a finger to her lips. "Shh. Don't talk about that."

Beni snorted. "What you just said is *way* more suspicious than what I said."

Manon shifted in her seat, looking around the train car for anyone who could have overheard. "You're right, Beni, but still, best get used to never mentioning it in public." She lowered her voice to a whisper. "To answer your question, the mirror only connects me to the Maddoxes. I have to write letters to everyone else. And besides, most of the world does not have a mirror."

"Fair point." Beni sighed as he slumped lower in his seat across from them. "Goddess above, I can't believe we made it. You both were still dead asleep a few hours ago." He ran his hand through his dark hair and stared down at the table.

"Thank you, Beni. You did so well, helping us get out of there," said Manon.

"You saved us. Thank you for being brave," said Scarlett. "Are you all right?" Her brother's breathing was uneven.

"I thought you were going to die on me like Dad." His voice wavered. "I'll go get us some drinks from the canteen." He stood and left before they could reply.

"Poor kid. I think he's had it worse than we have," whispered Manon.

"Agreed." It killed her that he'd been so alone. "I need to figure out how to help him."

"We will," said Manon.

When Beni returned with two cups of coffee and a hot chocolate, he looked less upset.

Scarlett waited for him to sit down and then spoke. "Is there anything else I should know about what happened while we were asleep? Anything Laylani did that you want to get off your chest?" She reached across the table and grabbed Beni's hand.

"She was . . . the worst version of herself every day. Instead of being sad, she's been mean. She kept dragging me out with her and demanding I wear just the right black outfit. No matter what I did, though, she was never happy. I hated it. The idea of being alone with her forever. Having her as my only family." He shuddered.

Scarlett pushed herself to her feet and opened her arms to him. He stood and let her embrace him.

"I promise you," she said, "we'll do everything we can to make sure you're never left alone with her again."

Beni sighed in her arms, and she thought maybe some of the tension had left his body.

After a long moment, they sat back down. Beni fell asleep minutes later, but Scarlett wasn't sleepy. The extra caffeine in the energy drink Beni had given her had to be keeping her up. After weeks of unconsciousness, she hated the idea of sleep and embraced the added buzz from her coffee.

Staring out the window, she didn't register anything as they moved away from the waterways of Soleil and into the marshes on the outskirts of the city. Only when they passed Tornaling National Cemetery did a stabbing ache pierce through the numbness of their escape. She imagined her dad's casket in its final resting place next to her mother and her paternal grandparents, and the stabbing ache became sharper. In an attempt to forget about his body lying cold in a field it would never leave, she imagined him alive.

What would Dad say if he could see me now?

She wished he could see her. Although, if he were alive, they wouldn't be running for their lives.

Scarlett glanced from Beni to Manon. They looked normal. The three of them were running away from Laylani and whoever had abducted them, but to anyone looking at them now, Scarlett and Beni could simply be setting off on a weekend getaway with their grandmother. Their minimal disguises seemed to be working.

Next to her, Manon pored over the newspapers they'd bought. Her grandmother glanced up and caught Scarlett's attention.

"They still don't know who shot your father," she whispered. "All I see in the papers is mention of the ongoing investigation."

"How is that even possible?" It made Scarlett want to scream.

Manon continued. "There's nothing at all about our abduction, only some nonsense about you having sleeping sickness." She snorted. "There's nothing about me. Guess no one noticed I was gone."

Scarlett let out a sigh of frustration. "That's unbelievable. Can I see one of those?"

Manon slid one of the papers to Scarlett. It was the *Soleil Times*, the favorite paper of anyone who preferred the Cerulean Party's politics. An op-ed article on the second page caught her eye.

HEROUX'S DREAMS DEFERRED

The Cerulean Party is scrambling to reorient themselves after the assassination of Lord Jules Heroux. Some hoped Lady Elestine Spencer would be able to pass the border legislation, but the votes haven't materialized. The much-anticipated border vote has been delayed indefinitely, or at least until alliances with key members of the Goldenrod Party can be renegotiated.

Soleil was on the cusp of being a global citizen for the first time in two hundred years. Access to magic might have followed after, with all the benefits to health and quality of life that have not been enjoyed in Soleil in our lifetimes, but alas, that is not to be.

How can Lady Spencer wrangle more support? With Lady Scarlett Heroux bedridden with the hereditary sleeping sickness known to plague descendants of Clair de Lune, there's little hope of her stepping up near term to bridge the gap. That is a shame for the Ceruleans, given she's known to be of the same liberal stock as her father and has recently completed her first-class degree in politics at the prestigious University of Soleil. In the event of her death, the seat would pass to Beaufort Heroux, who is woefully underage at twelve years old.

The article filled Scarlett with longing to help the Ceruleans. Reading about Lady Spencer made her think of Alastair. She glanced toward Beni. She wanted to ask him if Alastair had come by or offered Beni his assistance while she was asleep, but she didn't want to wake her exhausted brother.

Brushing thoughts of Alastair aside, she focused instead on

Elestine struggling without her father there to help. Elestine was more to Scarlett than just Alastair's mother; she admired the woman and wanted to see her succeed. She wanted to help Elestine. Was Scarlett's influence being exaggerated? One more vote wouldn't be enough, surely. But could public sympathy for her family's tragedy change things? The public had such a short memory, and her father's death was weeks ago . . .

She mentally flicked through her father's Goldenrod colleagues. Who were the holdouts? They could be peers she knew well. If so, she *could* make a difference. It made Scarlett want to disembark from the train and go straight to Parliament, demand to take her father's seat, and resume his work. It broke her heart that everything he'd worked so hard for had fallen apart.

I'm going to fix things. I'll go back as soon as I'm well and I've figured out how to stay safe. I'll try to help, no matter the cost.

Although, her life was one hell of a price. Even as they sped away from the dangers of Soleil, Scarlett's death felt near. She'd been abducted, and her father had been shot. Then there was Moira's threat at the funeral. It was too suspicious of a coincidence that she'd been abducted shortly after and ended up in a medically induced coma under her stepmother's care. The two points had to be related, and what if it all tied in with her father's death? Her throat was thick as she flashed back to the last time she'd seen him—as he was wheeled away on a stretcher.

That could be her if she was too bold. Moira had said so herself.

Shaking off that worry, Scarlett returned her attention to the newspaper. An article about her father's murder caught her eye. The journalist gave the Soleil Bureau a severe dressing down for their failure to pinpoint the shooter. It pleased Scarlett to see someone else was angry about that. The reporter went on to note the popular opinion that magic users from abroad must have done it, perhaps even sanctioned by a foreign government. There was also a conspiracy theory—found only on message boards used by members of Soleil's magical black market—that the prime minister's death was an inside job. Intrigued, Scarlett read the article twice. The anonymous posts claimed that a cut of profits from the black market was being used to pay out officers as high up as Aaron Fox, who was second-in-command of the Soleil Bureau, and suggested that a stream of substantial income was the reason they'd allowed the prime minister to be shot.

Scarlett set the paper down. The black-market angle was interesting, but she wanted to parse through her immediate experience. "What's the last thing you remember before we were abducted?" she whispered to her grandmother.

Manon looked up from her paper. "We were walking along the bridge. Next thing I knew, Beni was getting me out of bed. You?"

"Similar memories. Nothing in between the bridge and waking up at home. Who do you reckon was behind it all? It can't have been only Laylani." Scarlett filled Manon in on what Beni had told her about Laylani's conversation with their doctor and then described the dark moment with Moira Ashworth at the funeral. "Do you think it could all be related?"

Manon's eyes grew cloudy. "Moira and Laylani working together to kill Jules? Goddess above. If that's true . . ."

"Could Laylani have been involved in Dad's death? They were having a rough patch, but I thought she still loved him," said Scarlett. "They were together for so long, and they had Beni."

Manon lowered her voice to the quietest whisper as she looked at Beni, who was asleep. "I don't think she loves anyone. Not even—" She inclined her head toward him. "She likes the wealth and prestige of being a Heroux, but I don't think she loved your father. She's a narcissist, possibly a psychopath, and I'm bloody glad to be getting away from her."

"Before today I might have said your views were extreme, but given what she did to both of us, I'm inclined to agree. Why do you think my dad married her?"

"Politics," said Manon. "Goldenrod votes. He thought you needed a mother. She was charming in the beginning."

Scarlett regretted asking. Manon's answer depressed her so. "I never asked . . ."

"What is it?"

Scarlett's voice was quiet. "You and Dad got along, but you weren't warm and fuzzy with him. You've always hated Laylani. Why didn't you go back to Clair de Lune after my mum died? You could have been free of them, and maybe . . ."

Manon gave her a small smile. "Maybe Jules would have let you come for long visits? His beloved daughter and heir away to Clair de Lune while he was too busy with work to accompany her?"

Scarlett frowned. "Still, if I couldn't have visited, you could have come back to Soleil to visit me. You didn't have to stay full-time, right?"

Manon shook her head. "No. It wouldn't have been enough. When your mother died, I promised myself I'd watch over you as closely as she would have. That's why I stayed."

Tears pricked Scarlett's eyes as she reached over and squeezed her grandmother's hand. Manon had lived a life she hadn't wanted and had almost *died* just to be close to Scarlett. "I feel bad you sacrificed so much for me, but I'm grateful."

"Now, don't feel bad about it! I don't. It's been one of the greatest joys of my life to watch you grow up. You look so much like your mother. She's still here when I'm with you. And now we're going to Clair de Lune *together*—a beautiful silver lining to this whole shitty experience." Manon grinned.

Scarlett choked out a laugh and leaned in to hug her grandmother, resting her head on the older woman's shoulder.

When she pulled away, Manon patted Scarlett's thigh and returned to her reading. Time flew by as Scarlett studied every section of the newspaper, wishing she had a notebook to write down her racing, jumbled thoughts as she tried to come to grips with everything she'd missed.

Hours later, Scarlett blinked and looked up from her reading. Beni's eyes were still closed, but he stirred like he might soon wake. Scarlett peered out the window at the much-changed landscape. Clouds cloaked the sky. The marshes on the outskirts of Soleil were now giving way to rocky terrain as they approached an enormous mountain range. Scarlett's eyes grew wide, and she pressed her face against the glass to look up at Mont Noir. It was bigger in real life. The cursed black ice that had inspired its name glittered on the bits of the peak visible through the clouds.

Scarlett glanced away from the window in time to see a young man in a University of Soleil sweatshirt walk by their table in the direction of the dining car. The smattering of passengers she'd seen were probably the few visa holders allowed in Soleil or people visiting family abroad.

Manon peered out the window. "We're about to go under the mountain. That's where the firewall takes effect. You're going to lose phone service."

Beni blinked awake and leaned toward the window. "Whoa, look—there's a staircase going up into the mountain."

The steps looked wide enough for two lean adults to stand side by side.

"Those steps are ancient," said Manon. "Before the Hieratian Empire built the tunnel through Mont Noir, that stairway was the only way in or out of Clair de Lune from the Soleil side for anyone without a magical means of travel."

"I learned at school that people used to die on that staircase all the time," said Beni.

"I read that's why the Soleil accent is so different from the Clair de Lune accent even though we're not that far from each other," said Scarlett. She didn't add that daydreaming about Brayden's accent had caused her to do an internet search on its origins. Better to let her grandmother assume it was general interest—or an interest in Manon's accent, which was lighter than Brayden's but still cute— that had inspired the deep dive.

The train whooshed into darkness as they passed through the mountain. Little lights along the aisles of the train lit up as they were immersed in blackness, and Scarlett shivered as the temperature dropped. She reached for her coat, jammed under her seat, and handed Beni his jacket as well. He put it on without argument. Manon had never taken hers off.

A full forty minutes later, they finally emerged on the other side, and Scarlett gasped as she glimpsed Clair de Lune for the first time. The train sped across an expansive dark lake. There was nothing but water on either side of the train, giving the illusion they were floating. The blustery sky hinted at rain. Beni and Scarlett were glued to the windows as Manon looked on from her aisle seat. The train flew over the lake's edge, passing massive hills covered in mossy green bracken and trees. The trees became thicker the farther they went; the closer they got to the city. And the closer she got to Brayden.

CHAPTER (8)

As she stared out at the foreign landscape where Brayden had grown up, an undercurrent of excitement raced through Scarlett. Though the circumstances were dire, butterflies in her stomach fluttered at the idea of finally seeing him. She ran her fingers through her dirty hair. It was obvious she hadn't had more than a sponge bath for weeks. If only she could've met him on a normal day. She could freshen up in the train bathroom, but she'd have to ask Beni for help getting her toiletries out of her bag, and even if she did make it there on her dad's cane, it wasn't like she'd be able to wash her hair. She'd seen the bathroom on the way in, and it was tiny, with a minuscule sink.

It is what it is.

Tears pricked at her eyes, and she blinked them away in frustration.

Of all the things to cry about, my appearance is at the bottom of the list. We're alive. Be grateful.

When the trees became so thick they were all she could see, the

train slowed and pulled into a small station. After this, it would continue to Evory, Clair de Lune's eastern neighbor. It would've been one of Scarlett's stops on her trip abroad. Maybe someday she'd make it there.

"Right." Beni stood. "I'll put the bags on the platform and come back to help you."

"Thank you, Beni," said Manon.

Rising, Scarlett helped Manon out of her seat and into her wheelchair. She leaned heavily on Manon's chair as they made their way to the door. Tapping her foot impatiently, Scarlett waited with Manon as a staff member lowered the wheelchair ramp onto the platform while Beni stood next to him.

Scarlett searched the platform for border control. "He'll get through with us, right?" she whispered.

Manon hesitated, then she nodded. Her hesitation was enough to make Scarlett tense.

When the ramp was down, Beni helped them disembark, distracting Scarlett from her momentary anxiety. Then she was hit with the beautiful scent of the trees. Soleil smelled like summer year-round. The sometimes sweaty heat could be too much, though she enjoyed it when they were at the beach. This smell was better, fresher. The damp soil, the dewy raindrops coating all the plants, and the oxygen flooded her lungs.

Scarlett looked around, enthralled.

For a train station, it was quite ornate, built with old stonework. The arched windows were made of stained glass, and an enormous vintage clock was fixed to the wall, near the platform's high ceiling. One clerk at the turnstile glanced at tickets and passports. Manon handed him all their documents, and to Scarlett's surprise, he didn't even ask about Beni, the only one without a Clair de Lune passport.

Scarlett smiled as they exited. "That wasn't hard at all." She'd seen the walled-off space for passport checks in the Soleil train station, and it was a lot more intense than what they'd just passed through.

"I told you, getting into Soleil is much harder than getting into any of the other countries on the continent," said Manon, her tone confident again now they'd gotten Beni through. "No one else is as obsessed with keeping people out."

They went through the turnstile, and Scarlett's heart leaped when she spotted Brayden and James waiting for them farther down the platform. She waved, catching James's attention. He pointed, and Brayden's head swiveled, finding her. His face came alive at the sight of her, and she beamed at him.

"You're here!" he said, crossing the platform.

"I'm here." She hobbled toward him.

The pull to him was unlike anything she'd ever experienced. She'd barely formed the thought when Brayden closed the distance between them and wrapped her in an all-consuming hug. Scarlett dropped her cane and threw her arms around his neck, breathing him in. He smelled fresh, like the forest. His hard body pressed against hers, warming her. The scratchy stubble of his face rubbed against her cheek. She never wanted to let him go.

But then the contact was over.

He set her down, his hands lingering at her waist before dropping to his sides. He picked up her cane and handed it to her, giving her a smile that was familiar and yet devastatingly different.

Scarlett drank him in. There was a little bit of dissonance as her brain replaced some imagined aspects of him with reality. They'd been viewing each other through a mirror for over ten years, and now he was right here in front of her.

"Look at you," she said.

Brayden was bloody huge in person and at least six feet tall. She realized with a jolt he'd seemed shorter because of the way the mirror was hung in Lachlan's office. His fitted T-shirt showed off the body he worked so hard to maintain.

She was dying to run her hands over his chest, but *that* urge was wildly inappropriate. In her mind they'd done everything together, but in real life they were still just friends. For now.

Brayden's eyes glimmered with amusement as she pored over him until, with an embarrassed grin, she forced herself to turn away and greet James.

"Thank you for coming to get us." She gave James an arms-only hug.

"Of course," he said, his voice bright. He resembled Brayden, but his lighter brown hair was shorter. He had a narrower—albeit still quite handsome—face that was dominated by thick, dark brown eyebrows. Scarlett had glimpsed him many times in passing over the years, but they hadn't spoken much. He had a runner's build, whereas Brayden, despite all the running Scarlett knew he did, looked like he spent all his time lifting heavy weights, wrestling, and maybe even throwing big rocks around a field for fun.

Scarlett reached for Beni, who hung back. "Beni, you already know Brayden. This is his brother, James."

James waved. "Welcome to Clair."

"Nice to meet you, James," said Beni. Then he approached Brayden. "Thanks for helping me save my sister."

Brayden squeezed Beni's shoulder, looking down at him fondly. "You saved her, dude. Thank *you*."

"Aww," said James.

Beni looked between the brothers, seemingly taking them in. He didn't know many adult men—especially now, Scarlett realized with a pang. Maybe some time with the Maddoxes would be good for him.

"Since we're introducing ourselves, how'd you get the nickname, Beni?" asked Brayden. "Scarlett told me your real name is Beaufort."

Beni glared at Scarlett.

She held up her hand. "Sorry!"

Beni turned back to Brayden. "I couldn't pronounce Beaufort when I was little," he explained. "Normally, Beaux would be the nickname for Beaufort, but with my last name . . ."

"You would have been Beaux Heroux," chortled James.

"Exactly," said Beni. "A rhyming name is not cool. Scarlett came up with Beni. It's a little random, but it suits me fine."

"I named him after a cartoon cat," Scarlett admitted. "I was young."

"Love it." Brayden patted him on the back.

"Beaux Heroux," chuckled Manon.

"Anyhow, Beaux Heroux, should we get out of here?" asked James.

Beni scrunched his nose, feigning annoyance, but he was laughing.

Scarlett looked eagerly at the exit. "That'd be great. I'm desperate for a shower. Manon, can we stay at your house? Is it far from here?"

Manon frowned. "We could, but there's no food or anything. And in our current state, we might struggle."

"Is there a hotel nearby?" Scarlett asked Brayden.

"Don't be silly," said Brayden. "You're staying with me. Us." He handed Manon's suitcase to James, who began to wheel it toward the exit. Then he looped his arm around Scarlett's waist, giving her extra support. "We're taking you home to the castle."

"Castle?" she managed, but almost all her attention was on his arm around her.

His grip tightened, warm and strong. "You'll see."

Outside the station, Brayden and James led them to a massive forest-green SUV and carefully helped Manon into the front passenger seat. James slid into the driver's seat, while Beni scrambled into the very back, leaving Brayden and Scarlett together in the middle row.

For a few minutes James drove them through tree-packed forest, until gradually the trees thinned out, though they were still surrounded by plenty of *enormous* trees.

"It's good to be home," Manon said from the front seat.

"What's that?" Beni pointed to a network of bridges high up.

"There are tree houses up there," said James. "A lot of folks live in the city center, where you'll find mostly townhouses and such, but a good number live here in the woods. The houses are all twenty feet off the ground and connected by bridges."

"Why do you have tree houses instead of regular houses?" asked Beni.

"Erm, there used to be dangerous creatures that roamed at night," said James. "They were unfortunately very good at breaking into buildings, but they couldn't climb. So tree houses were the solution for the people living further out. It also allowed us to preserve most of the trees instead of clearing the forest for housing."

"*Used to be* creatures?" asked Scarlett. "Where'd they go?"

"They've been banished to the western woods," said Brayden. "The magical wards that used to protect only the city have been extended to the tree houses now. You don't have to worry about anything coming for you here. We'll keep you safe."

Dangerous creatures capable of breaking into ground-level houses gave her pause, but her worry quickly dissipated. It was impossible to be scared sitting next to Brayden. He'd never let anything hurt her.

James continued playing tour guide as he drove, pointing out plant life native to Clair de Lune and various landmarks, but his overview wasn't enough to distract Scarlett from her friend, who was sitting close enough for her to touch. Brayden caught her looking at him and leaned over to wrap his arm around her shoulders, beaming down at her like it was solstice morning as he let her go. In the excitement of seeing him for the first time, she'd somehow forgotten how gross she was. She resisted the urge to mess with her hair again. At least her clothes were fresh from that morning.

He leaned in again and pointed out her window, his eyes bright with excitement. "One of my friends lives right there. She's having a party tonight and would love to meet you."

Scarlett's heart thudded as she took in his smell and his heat while simultaneously trying to forget how her hair smelled. "I'd love to, but I need to get Manon to a doctor before I do anything else. There are a few things I need to do, actually."

His eyebrows rose. "Oh, yeah, of course—you've been through so much. A party is probably a stupid idea for tonight." He searched her face.

"No, it's not stupid. I really want to go if I can." Scarlett grabbed his hand and squeezed.

Before long, a massive stone building came into view.

"And there's home sweet home," said James.

"Why do you live in a castle?" asked Beni.

"The castle was built when we were still part of the Hieratian Empire, but now it's where the military is based," said Brayden. "Since Dad has been head of the army for the past twenty years, it's where we've lived most of my life."

"It looks huge." The castle was smaller than Soleil's parliament, but it looked like it had hundreds of rooms. "Is it just your family that lives there?"

Brayden chuckled. "No. Anyone working for the military or the government can reside there, and given Manon's work for Dad, it totally makes sense for you to stay with us. It's nice. There's always food when you're hungry, and because of the military, there's tons of cool stuff—like the archery field and the shooting range."

Manon's work for Lachlan?

Before Scarlett could ask what Brayden meant, Beni perked up. "Archery?"

With a glance at Scarlett, Brayden leaned toward him. "Yeah. Have you ever tried it?"

"Only in video games," said her brother.

"We'll change that while you're here." He grabbed Beni by his shoulder and ruffled his hair, making Beni laugh as he tried to bat his hand away.

James drove through open steel gates onto a circular driveway within the castle's massive courtyard and parked behind several other vehicles.

As Brayden helped Scarlett out of the SUV, Lachlan strode through the enormous wooden doors, his presence more commanding than it had been through the mirror. He approached Manon first and pressed light kisses on both of her cheeks.

"Back where you belong, eh?"

Manon chortled. "It's nice to be home."

Lachlan turned to Scarlett and Beni, who stood shoulder to shoulder. Scarlett had met Lachlan countless times, but his in-person presence was making her a touch nervous.

"Welcome to Clair de Lune." His dark eyes twinkled. He was handsome. He looked like Brayden, if Brayden had graying hair, a square jaw, and bushier eyebrows.

"Thank you for helping us," said Scarlett.

"Yeah, thanks," said Beni.

Lachlan squeezed Beni's shoulder. "You did well, son."

Beni hadn't been slouching, exactly, but he stood taller in response to Lachlan's words.

"And you," he said, turning a mischievous smile on Scarlett. "You're even lovelier in real life."

Scarlett smiled broadly, half-embarrassed and half-soothed, given her current self-consciousness over her unkempt state.

"Dad," said Brayden reprovingly.

Lachlan ignored him. "You gave us quite a scare, my dear. I'm so glad you're safe."

To Scarlett's surprise, he leaned in and wrapped her in a warm hug. The starchy feel of his uniform and his spicy cologne were new, and his fatherly presence made her heart ache as Lachlan pulled back and smiled at her.

"Come inside." He led them through the halls of the castle, taking a pace that allowed Scarlett to keep up. "Did you hear from Laylani before you left Soleil? Do you think anyone knows where you've gone?"

Scarlett pulled her phone out of her pocket and glanced at it. As expected, it didn't have service. "My phone stopped working when we went through Mont Noir. Before that, no."

"Same here," said Beni.

As they made their way down a hallway, they passed a giant oil painting of a knight on a horse, maybe an ancestor of Lachlan's.

"Manon, has she contacted you? Your phone is working, correct?" asked Lachlan.

"Why would her phone work if mine doesn't?" Scarlett stared at her grandmother.

"I can't talk to Soleil either, Scarlett, but my phone works, yes," said Manon, looking up at Lachlan from her wheelchair. "I checked it in the car. I haven't heard from Laylani either."

James smirked. "We're going to have to take Scarlett to the Forest Temple."

Brayden looked amused, like Scarlett was doing something unintentionally funny. "One thing at a time."

She frowned at James's know-it-all smirk, but before she could demand to know what they meant, she was diverted again as Lachlan opened a set of double doors to reveal an expansive sitting room. Fine-looking tapestries depicting more medieval scenes covered the walls.

Beni parked Manon's wheelchair near two long couches. Scarlett sat closest to her grandmother, relaxing back into the soft velvet couch with a sigh of relief. Brayden glanced at the empty space next to her just as Beni plopped into the seat. After a moment's hesitation, he sat across the antique coffee table from her, next to his brother and his father.

A middle-aged woman appeared, dressed in slacks and a tucked-in button-down shirt. "You must be the visitors General Maddox warned us about. My name's Flora. I'm part of the castle staff," she said in a heavy Clair de Lune accent.

Scarlett, Manon, and Beni each introduced themselves to the smiling woman.

"Please let me know if you need anything at all," said Flora. "For now, can I bring you anything to eat or drink? We make lovely cinnamon hot chocolate here."

"Yes, please!" said Beni.

Scarlett studied her grandmother, who looked rather peaked even though she was smiling softly. "Do you think we can get Manon some medical attention today?" she asked, directing the question at the Maddoxes.

Lachlan spoke. "Not to worry. I've already contacted the doctor. She'll be here soon—to look after both of you. She's a fantastic magical healer."

"That's great. Thank you." But even as she thanked Lachlan, Scarlett's stomach jolted at the idea of someone using magic to heal her. She was all for healing magic in theory, but to her surprise, she was suddenly nervous. She could hear Alastair in her head. If he were here, he'd tell her she'd be a fool to let them try it on her.

But then again, can it be any worse than what the non-magical doctors did to me in Soleil? She snorted softly. No, probably not. And it would be amazing not to need her dad's cane anymore.

Manon's expression was full of understanding. "We'll be healed as soon as we see a doctor."

Scarlett nodded. She trusted her grandmother, and if she met the doctor and didn't trust her, she could always back out.

"Oh, if you need anything, let one of us know, and we'll sort it," said Lachlan.

The way he said it suggested they'd be staying awhile.

"We won't be here long, right?" she asked Manon. Her mind swirled with a thousand more questions, but the pressure to get back to where she was desperately needed trumped them all. Looking toward Lachlan, she continued. "I'm supposed to join Parliament." She paused to collect herself as she glanced over at Brayden.

Beni scooted closer to her, brushing his hand against her arm in a soothing gesture, and she took a deep breath.

Lachlan leaned forward, his bushy eyebrows dominating his heavy eyes. "I understand, but we need to make sure you're healthy and then figure out how to ensure your safety in Soleil before you go back. But let's save the detailed strategy talk for once you're healed."

"Are you planning to join Parliament now? Isn't the age of inheritance in Soleil twenty-five?" asked James. "That's our minimum age for Parliament."

The question threw her for a moment. She'd forgotten James had just joined the Clair de Lune Department of Commerce. "I applied for an exception the day I was abducted." The thought made her dizzy. "The courts probably ruled on my case already. I'll contact them and make sure." Grasping the handle of her cane, she stood— although to go where, exactly, she didn't know.

"Wait, Scarlett. You won't find the answer right now." Manon gestured for her to sit.

Flora arrived with drinks as Scarlett sank back into the velvet couch, and she took a cup of hot tea with a grateful smile, centering herself again with a small sip. The tea was milky but bold, and it tasted better than the tea in Soleil.

"Is there anyone in Soleil whom you'd trust to check your petition with the government?" asked Lachlan. "Unfortunately, we'll be stuck writing them a letter, but we can get a note out on tomorrow's train."

"Can't she—?" James began, but Lachlan shushed him.

"Lady Elestine Spencer could check for me," said Scarlett. "Or one of her staff."

Lachlan's bushy eyebrows shot up. "The new prime minister?"

"That's right." She glanced at Brayden, who was frowning. "She was my father's collaborator. They cowrote the legislation that likely got him . . . killed." Her body ached, and a wave of exhaustion overcame her. "I can't believe I'm dealing with this right now. I still can't believe my dad . . ." Tears spilled onto her cheeks. She wiped them away, embarrassed.

Beni wrapped his arms around Scarlett, and Scarlett leaned into her brother's comforting touch, grasping him to her protectively.

Then she pulled herself together and released him. "Elestine will help."

"Let's contact her when you're able," said Lachlan.

"But Scarlett, we shouldn't rush home. It's important you stay here for a while," Manon said.

When Scarlett looked up, she and Lachlan were having some kind of private conversation with their eyes.

Lachlan made a sympathetic noise. "Why don't you rest while you wait for the doctor? Worry about Parliament when you're healed."

"Too right," Manon agreed.

Scarlett bristled, wanting to argue. Soleil's fate was more important than her health or her grief. But then Brayden looked at her imploringly.

"Please, Scar? Take it easy."

"Yeah. You need rest," added Beni.

"You're right." She had to take care of herself before she could take care of Beni or anyone else. She breathed deep to push her emotions further under the surface.

"Should I take you to your rooms in the north wing?" offered James.

"No—I'll do it," said Brayden.

"Go ahead, Beni and Scarlett," said Manon. "I want to speak to Lachlan briefly."

"Yes, I'll wheel your grandmother to her room in a bit," added Lachlan.

It was still early, but the energy drinks and coffee that had propelled her through the day had worn off, and Scarlett was dead on her feet. Brayden offered her his arm, which she took with grateful relief. Beni and James walked alongside them.

"Beni, you want to get some food and come to archery practice?" asked James.

"Yes!" exclaimed Beni. "What kind of food do you have here?"

"Oh, you know, all the usual kinds." James ruffled Beni's hair.

Beni waved goodbye to Scarlett and followed him through a set of double doors.

"Alone at last," said Brayden as he led Scarlett out of the sitting room.

She huffed out a laugh, stopping at the bottom of a staircase to catch her breath. "Alone at last, and I'm disgusting," she said.

"What do you mean?"

She gave him a look like, *Really?* "I've been bedridden for weeks, and I don't think they did a great job of keeping me clean."

He studied her. "I mean, your hair is usually fluffier, I guess, but you still look beautiful to me."

"You're sweet."

He offered her his arm again, and she took it.

Upstairs, Brayden led her down a carpeted hallway filled with closed doors. Halting in front of one, he pointed to it. "This is you." He pointed next door. "That's Manon, and that's Beni." He gestured to the room across the way.

"How do you know?" Scarlett asked.

"I helped the housekeeper open up the rooms earlier today. There are hundreds of rooms here, so they're not always kept ready."

Scarlett unwound her arm from his and put her hand on the door-knob. "Thank you for doing that. Thanks for everything."

He brushed his thumb over her cheek, lingering near her, and for a moment she thought he might . . . But then he took a step back. "Anything for my best friend. I'll see you later. Rest up, Scar." He winked at her and walked away before she could reply.

Best friend? Why did the title she'd once held so dear now make her sad?

CHAPTER (9)

*B*rayden's face inches from hers, the brush of his touch on her cheek . . . Scarlett ran through the moment over and over again. That parting shot. *Anything for my best friend.* Something had been in the air between them—she was sure of it. But his farewell . . .

She collapsed into an armchair. The awkward moment with Brayden, paired with her list of things to do, made her chest tight. *Self-care first, then I'll be in better shape to take action. I'll take a bath, see the doctor, and then write to Elestine.*

With her eyes closed, she took several deep breaths.

When she opened them again, she was calm enough to appreciate the space around her. For an old castle, Scarlett's room appeared fresh and modern. The walls were bright with peach-colored wallpaper, and several elegant oil paintings of landscapes adorned the walls. She was sitting in one of two inviting armchairs opposite a fireplace with a crackling fire, and there was a comfortable-looking four-poster bed a few feet away.

Feeling slightly more grounded, Scarlett hobbled to the bathroom. The plumbing was the same as Soleil's. She drew a bath in a large clawfoot tub.

Immersed in the warm water, she scrubbed the scummy tape marks from her arm where the IV had been and did a full-body check. Aside from general weakness, she didn't find anything *wrong*. All the hair on her body had grown longer during the weeks she'd been unconscious. She supposed it'd be more disconcerting if it hadn't. The mental image of a nurse shaving her legs while she was in bed made Scarlett snort. She grabbed a razor from her toiletry bag. Once she was done shaving she felt more like her normal self. A tired, weakened version of herself.

She lingered in the tub. How surreal had it been to see Brayden in real life? He was more magnetic than she'd dreamed, which was something, because he'd always been handsome. There was an uncomfortable niggling in her stomach she didn't understand though. Was she *afraid* of being around him? She'd expected to be nervous, but this was closer to dread.

Scarlett dug deeper, and the dread became a thought. *What if he doesn't like me anymore now that I'm here?* He'd had no expectations of her through the mirror—how could he? What would he expect now? What if he preferred the fantasy of her to the reality?

Scarlett sighed. *Stop catastrophizing.* She'd be here for a couple of days. The friendship wouldn't be ruined if she was nice and didn't reveal she fell asleep imagining having sex with him.

Just keep it in a box, Scarlett. It'll be fine.

Then she remembered all the quiet lies she'd told Alastair over the years, and a wave of nausea rolled through her. She didn't want to lie anymore. At that thought, her stomach settled immediately.

I am a certified mess.

Feeling both better and worse, Scarlett climbed out of the tub.

She rifled through the limited clothing options in her suitcase, selecting a black silk dress with a fitted corset bodice and the same black leather ankle boots she'd worn for traveling. Dressed, she went to Manon's room and found Flora helping her onto her bed. Her grandmother was now in her dressing gown.

Flora came closer, her expression kind as she spoke to Scarlett in a hushed voice. "I've just helped her with her bath. I expect the doctor will be here shortly."

"That's above and beyond. Thank you," whispered Scarlett.

With a smile and a wave, Flora left, closing the door softly behind her.

"Come sit," said Manon, patting the bed beside her. She leaned back against several pillows. Her eyes looked like they didn't want to stay open.

Scarlett climbed onto the bed and settled in next to her. "That was nice of Flora to help you take a bath."

"Mmm. Yes, it was. She's very kind."

"I'll let you sleep in a minute, but can you quickly tell me how phones work here? I know I can't call Soleil, but how do I charge my phone? There are no electrical outlets."

Manon rubbed her eyes. "Soul-light magic powers electronics here. It'll work once you charge it with magic. I'll show you after we see the doctor."

"You told me about your soul light. It's a little ball of light, right? But you didn't tell me it charged cell phones."

Manon scoffed. "Soul lights are more than that. They're our connection to the divine—the energy we're all a part of."

"Remind me, how did you meet your soul light? Isn't it a ritual or something?"

Yawning, Manon closed her eyes once more. "I don't know if 'ritual' is the word I'd use. It's more a rite of passage."

Scarlett spread a soft, woolen blanket over her grandmother's body. "Is it too late for me to meet my soul light?"

"No. You could go to the Forest Temple while we're here." Her voice grew quieter. "Beni could too." Seconds later, Manon let out a soft snore.

Resolving to let her sleep, Scarlett sat there silently contemplating the soul light concept. The Forest Temple intrigued her, but then she recalled all she needed to do: contact Elestine and investigate their abduction.

Her thoughts raced until they were interrupted by a soft knock at the door. A petite woman with short black hair entered the room, bringing a new level of calm with a cheerful smile and a soft-spoken greeting. Scarlett rose to shake her hand, and the woman introduced herself as Dr. Bowen.

Scarlett glanced at Manon. "My grandmother is exhausted. Does she need to be awake for this?"

Dr. Bowen shook her head. "No, it's fine to let her sleep."

"Before we begin, I have a question," said Scarlett, struggling to remain calm knowing this woman was about to use magic on her body. Magic she didn't understand well enough to trust.

"Go on."

"Did Lachlan mention why we're here?" Scarlett looked at her grandmother's sleeping form.

Dr. Bowen nodded. "He said you were attacked and sedated."

"Both of us were sedated when it wasn't medically necessary. We brought urine samples with us. Can you test them to see if we can prove malpractice? The samples are from early this morning." Scarlett retrieved the bag from where Manon had hidden it in the side pocket of the wheelchair.

Dr. Bowen took it from her. "I'll get these to a lab and see what comes up. Given the nature of your situation, I'll ask for a rush job."

"Thank you."

Dr. Bowen's response made Scarlett trust her more.

"Now, why don't you tell me what happened to you? Do you mind if we take a seat?" She gestured to the armchairs by the fire.

As she relayed everything—murder, sedation, abduction, death threats—Scarlett was conscious of how impossible it all sounded. But Dr. Bowen listened receptively, only interjecting with a few clarifying questions about her symptoms.

When they were finished, the doctor looked from Manon to Scarlett, her eyebrows drawn together. "I'm so sorry for all you went through. I think I have enough information to begin with. Is it all right if I start with Manon? I can tell from her aura she's worse for wear."

"Of course," said Scarlett, although her chest tightened in anticipation.

Dr. Bowen moved to the bedside. "In Clair de Lune we assess the body by examining the energy field. With my magic, I can see overall vitality on sight, but I have to get in closer to know the specifics."

"Oh, interesting" was all Scarlett could think to say. She stared, mesmerized, as Dr. Bowen's hands hovered over Manon's body, moving in slow, deliberate passes up and down her extremities.

"Her energy field is very weak," said the doctor after a couple of minutes. "I'll do some energy healing on her muscles and prescribe her a course of antibiotics. The catheter gave her an infection. She should be walking again in a day or two, but I want her to take it slow. If she's laid low again too quickly, her weakened energetic system might not be able to cope."

Scarlett's eyebrows rose. Walking tomorrow? She'd assumed Manon would take much longer to heal. In Soleil, it would've taken her weeks of physical therapy to recover, so it was a pleasant surprise to hear that wasn't the case here. The depleted energetic system was a concern though.

"Thank you, Doctor," she said.

Dr. Bowen resumed her work. Scarlett stared at the woman's hands, where a faint white light radiated out of her palms into Manon's body.

"Does your soul light help you heal people?" She was so curious she had to ask, even though the question was childlike in its ignorance.

Dr. Bowen glanced up at Scarlett and paused her work. "Well, yes, it does. But healing isn't everyone's gift. Do you know what valors are?"

Scarlett shook her head.

"A valor is a kind of magical specialization. Like most doctors, I'm a medicus. That's my valor. Even with that, it still takes years of training to heal people."

"Oh," said Scarlett. So many questions came to mind. Magical specialization? How many were there? But she wanted Dr. Bowen to focus on her grandmother, so she stayed silent.

The doctor glanced at Manon, then at Scarlett. "Your room is next door, right?"

"Yes."

"The energy healing for Manon will take an hour or so. If you like, you can wait there. I'll come to you afterward."

Back in her room, Scarlett lay on her bed thinking. Her life had been turned upside down since the night of the fight and her breakup with Alastair. Had he reached out while she was asleep? She didn't want his help, didn't want to see him, but it was horrible to think he didn't care whether she lived or died after all their years together.

Her mind wandered to the beginning of their relationship—a more soothing, if bittersweet, set of memories. He'd been so charming, making her feel chosen, showering her with gifts, and welcoming her wholeheartedly into his life, his friendships, and his family. Then he'd *changed*, wanting her to exist only for him. He'd been controlling and unwilling to compromise on the things most important to her. The life he'd wanted with her . . . it wasn't what she wanted.

Maybe it was for the best he'd been honest, even if it wasn't what she'd wanted to hear. She had no desire to go back to him. All she wanted was to heal and go home.

The lie sat heavy in her stomach, and she sighed. There was something else she wanted.

Him.

She pictured Brayden's face when he'd spotted her across the train station, and her skin tingled as she remembered the all-encompassing hug he'd wrapped her in. She wanted to deepen their friendship in any way she could now that they were finally face-to-face. She wanted more, but she only had days here. It wasn't enough.

I should have zero expectations of romance, and I just broke up with Alastair.

Somehow, though, her longing for Brayden was undeniable. Scarlett shook her head. She was a lost cause. Thankfully, no one else had to know about it.

Dr. Bowen's knock snapped her out of her thoughts. She let the doctor in and lay down for the same assessment she'd performed on her grandmother.

Once she'd gone over Scarlett's body, Dr. Bowen sat in a chair next to the bed. "The good news is your atrophy is mild. You'd heal fine in a short time without me, but with energy healing, it'll be even faster. In the emotional space, however . . ." Dr. Bowen patted Scarlett's hand. "I heard about your father's death. And how you were there. Under the circumstances, the blockages you have around your heart are normal, but it's not healthy to live like this long term. Is there anything you'd like to tell me?"

The simple inquiry broke Scarlett. The grief she'd buried rose like a tidal wave. She saw it clearly in her mind—the bullet hole in her father's head, his hair matted with blood, and the chunks of his skull and brain that were missing. It was the sight that haunted her whether she was asleep or awake.

Her pent-up emotions broke through her wafer-thin emotional armor, and Scarlett burst into tears. "N-no. I just feel s-sad and overwhelmed."

"It's all right to feel overwhelmed, Scarlett. Talk with your loved ones. A burden shared is easier to bear." Dr. Bowen held Scarlett's hand and patted it while she cried. She didn't try to calm her or ask her any more questions.

When the tears stopped of their own accord, the doctor stood. "Now that you've cleared some of that out, shall we begin?"

Throat still raw, Scarlett nodded.

Dr. Bowen moved her hands over Scarlett's body. "Try to relax. You may have more feelings come up. That's normal. If it becomes overwhelming, we can stop."

"All right," said Scarlett from where she was reclining on the bed.

Dr. Bowen's hands emitted faint white light. After her tears, Scarlett was too exhausted to fear the magic entering her body. The energy healing nipped at the hollowness in her soul, and her body pulsed with a warm, fuzzy sensation. Scarlett fixated on the doctor's glowing hands, but the healing was so pleasant her eyes eventually closed. Gradually, she felt lighter.

Memories did come up as Dr. Bowen worked on her. At first, they were all unpleasant—the breakup with Alastair, her father's funeral. But by the time the energy healing was over, she was recalling mornings spent talking to Brayden in front of the mirror with her favorite coffee and happy days surfing at the beach with Beni.

She opened her eyes for a moment when Dr. Bowen said a hushed goodbye, but as soon as she was gone, Scarlett fell into a deep sleep and began to look for Brayden in her dreams.

CHAPTER (10)

*A*lastair's lips are so familiar and sweet, but I shouldn't be here. Why is that?

I run my fingers through his blond hair as he pushes my dress up my thighs and moves my panties aside. His head is between my legs. I want to stop him, but all I can do is close my eyes.

When I look again, it's Brayden's messy brown hair. He kisses my inner thigh, his brown eyes glancing up to meet mine as my uneasiness fades. Now I'm aching. His tongue. His fingers. I want to see his face.

I reach for him . . .

Knocking pulled her out of the dream. *Alastair and Brayden—Goddess above, what the hell was that about?* The already dark day had shifted into true twilight. Disoriented, Scarlett startled at her unfamiliar surroundings before remembering she wasn't in her room at home in Soleil, but rather in Brayden's castle in Clair de Lune.

More knocking at the door. "Scarlett, are you in there? It's me, Brayden."

Longing pulsed in her still. Scarlett rubbed her face to clear the dream from her head. "Come in."

"Were you sleeping?" He stood by the doorway looking unsure.

She stared at him, her cheeks burning hot. She couldn't stop picturing his head between her legs. "I'm up now." She pushed herself upright.

"Should I come back later?" He stepped backward.

She shook her head. "No. I should stay up unless I want to be awake all night. Have you seen Beni and Manon? Are they all right?"

"They're fine. Manon is talking to Lachlan. Beni made friends on the archery field and was out all afternoon. He's in the dining room with them now."

"Oh, good." Scarlett tried to look anywhere but at him.

Brayden sat at the foot of her bed, smiling gently. Her face grew hotter. She'd been so turned on in the dream, and he was right here—

Stop it.

She tried to clear her mind, but it didn't help when Brayden asked, "Feeling better?"

"Yes." She swung her legs over the edge of the bed and stood with surprising ease. She looked at Brayden as she smoothed her black silk dress and fluffed her clean hair. It was nice to be clean in front of him, if nothing else, but the way he was watching her reassured her she looked better than just freshly showered.

Scarlett walked around the room testing her balance without the cane. Everything seemed back to normal. "I still feel . . ."

Her dad's face flashed into her mind, and she let out a shuddering breath. It was still all too much. Everything she'd processed during the energy healing had helped, but there was so much grief left— grief so potent it forced itself out of her without her permission.

Brayden enveloped her in his arms. She leaned into him, inhaling his woodsy scent. A spark of joy lit in her chest from being near him, but mixed with her grief, it confused her. Was that what the dream had been about—jumping from Alastair to Brayden in her imagination just to stay distracted from the pain? She was too tired to make sense of it.

"Is there anything I can do?" he asked.

"This." She held him tighter, so grateful there wasn't glass between them.

"All right." He rubbed her back.

As she took a few deep breaths, the heaviness in her heart eased somewhat. Scarlett looked at him. He smiled at her, his gaze soft with affection. She'd never been able to see all of that in the mirror.

"There is one other thing you could do for me," she said, her voice hesitant, because she didn't want their closeness to end.

His fingers stilled on her back. "Name it."

She wanted to ask for lots of things, but the fate of her country hung in the balance, and she couldn't afford to be distracted. Scarlett pulled out of his grip and took a step back.

"I need paper and a pen to start writing letters to people in Soleil."

He tilted his head to one side as his fingers brushed his lips. She could practically hear him thinking she should relax, not write letters. But then his easygoing smile returned a second later.

"Psh. That's easy. Let's get some food and then go to Lachlan's study. You can write your letters there."

Being on the other side of the mirror was surreal. Scarlett had seen the brown tweed couch and the mahogany desk through the glass so often that the details were familiar, yet it was her first time being immersed in the room. Like the hug with Brayden, it was more vivid being here in real life.

She went to the mirror. An opaque black covering hid it from view.

"We'll keep it covered as long as you're here, and there's a silencing spell on it," said Brayden.

"Can I peek through it quickly? Just to see what it's like from this end."

"Sure."

He peeled back the cover. Her dressing room was there on the other side, still in disarray from their hasty departure that morning. Seeing it made her heart race as if she were still there. She backed away, not wanting to relive their escape, and Brayden replaced the cover.

"It must be a trip seeing it from this side." He strode over to Lachlan's desk, Scarlett trailing behind him, and pulled some paper out of a drawer. "I wonder if I'll ever see this room through your mirror."

She liked the hopeful way he said that. "I hope so. I want you to visit when all this settles down. I'll get Laylani thrown in jail and get the border legislation passed so you can come anytime. With her gone, I'll have my house all to myself. Plenty of space for you." She said it with a touch of humor knowing she was making it sound easy, when, in fact, she'd listed enough tasks to potentially fill a lifetime.

He chuckled. "I love the confidence. You reckon it'll be hard to prove what she did?"

"I'll find a way." Scarlett sat at Lachlan's desk and picked up a pen.

Brayden stretched out on the tweed couch and started tossing a ball he'd taken from the desk into the air above him. "Who are you writing to first?"

"Elestine Spencer." She pondered what to say for a moment. Then she wrote a letter conveying the essentials of the abduction and what Beni had overheard Laylani saying to the doctor. She closed it by asking Elestine to keep everything to herself for the time being. Scarlett signed the letter and walked to the couch to hand it to Brayden. "How's that?"

He skimmed the page. "This isn't the whole truth, right?"

She shook her head. "Dad always said, 'Never write anything down that you don't want on the front page of the paper.'"

Brayden nodded in approval. "Good advice. Tell me the whole story front to back."

Scarlett paced the office as she talked him through the chain of events, beginning with her dad's death, continuing with the ominous threat from Moira Ashworth and her abduction, and ending with Laylani putting her into a medically induced coma in her own home.

She came to a halt in front of him. "Do I sound paranoid?"

He shook his head, eyes full of worry. "No. The chain of events is suspicious."

"What if I'm wrong? What other explanation is there?" she asked. "If it's not Moira, how did I end up unconscious for almost a month?"

Brayden's brow furrowed as he considered this. "It's possible Laylani acted on her own. Maybe Moira wasn't involved and your dad's death was someone else. Who were his enemies?"

"Plenty of people don't like his politics, but most of them aren't public figures."

"What do you mean?"

"Well, if you believe—like many do—that opening the border to tourism and trade is the first step toward legalizing magic, there are people who'd be impacted negatively by that. Namely, those who profit from Soleil's black market."

"Are any of those people well-known?" asked Brayden.

"No. Although I did meet someone before my dad died. Alastair dragged me to an illegal boxing match between a hydra and a dire wolf." She told him all she could remember about the night, including Cass saving them from being arrested. "As we were walking through the tunnels, Cass mentioned she bribes the police for immunity from raids." Scarlett ran the tip of her finger over her bottom lip as she pondered it all.

"*That's* interesting. So the police stand to lose bribes if the black market is legalized. How high up does that money go? Beyond the head of police, up into the Soleil Bureau and the government? That could be a motive for Moira or one of her sidekicks. If Cass is any indication, perhaps the black market itself wouldn't have gone after your father."

Scarlett stared sightlessly, considering all the possibilities. "I need to look into it more, but I agree. Cass said they'd make more money if the matches were legal, and the police's cut from the fights is bigger than what the house keeps. Their audience could be much larger if the fights were legal. The black market is way more than boxing matches, so I don't have any idea if that motivation would extend to people selling other magical things, but it's possible."

"So now we have two suspects. The police and Loira."

"Loira?"

"You know, Moira plus Laylani. Loira. Or we could use Maylani if you like that better."

Scarlett shook her head, but she was smiling as she sat back down at Lachlan's desk. She put the letter to Elestine to the side. "Who else should I write to? Probably Alastair. We haven't spoken since the breakup. He'd be pissed off to only hear about me from his mother."

Brayden's face went blank. "I don't know if you owe him that courtesy, but I'd appreciate a letter from you if I were him." After a moment he asked, "Do you miss him at all?"

She huffed. "No. Breaking up was the right thing to do."

Although it *was* confusing that her dad had died the day after their breakup. Her life had been split in two, the before and the after, and Alastair was firmly part of the before—a time she longed for. But returning to him wouldn't fix what was broken. He'd make things worse, not better.

She sighed. "I keep thinking how he's the last boyfriend I'll ever have who knew my father. Like, *really* knew him. Is that a strange thing to be sad about?"

"Not at all." Brayden's fathomless brown eyes were full of sorrow.

She cleared her throat, trying to refocus on the task at hand. "None of that's going in this letter, of course."

He searched her face, but all he said was "Good."

She penned a few lines to Alastair explaining the same things she'd mentioned to Elestine. She apologized for missing him when he stopped by after her father's funeral. The letter read awkwardly when she skimmed over it, but she couldn't be bothered to try again. Scarlett set it on top of the letter to Elestine.

"Where do I take these to be mailed?"

"I'll take them after morning drills. The mail goes to Soleil on the afternoon train."

"Thank you."

She leaned back in Lachlan's chair. "I suppose I should write to the Sigur Viður ambassador to apologize for not turning up for my visit."

Brayden shook his head. "I think you've officially reached the non-urgent portion of your to-do list. Why don't we go do something relaxing, or fun, to take your mind off things?"

She put down her pen. What she really longed for was the before times. "I have a weird request."

He looked at her curiously. "Anything for you."

"Can we pretend my dad didn't die and I'm here just to visit?"

He stilled at first, his eyes flickering with sadness or pity, but then he grinned and pushed his hair out of his face. "That, I can do." He patted the couch beside him.

She plopped down next to him. Brayden stretched out his long legs, while her feet barely reached the floor. He took her hand in his and rubbed her wrist, sending jolts of pleasure down Scarlett's arm.

"Tell me about the energy healing with Dr. Bowen."

Her body relaxed into the sensation of his fingers kneading into her. She'd never known how tactile he was, and it was making it hard to remember he was just her friend.

"It was good but weird. I had a lot of memories come up."

"Uh-oh," he said.

"Not *that* memory, thankfully." She couldn't have handled reliving her dad's death. "Only my breakup with Alastair."

Brayden groaned. "It's everywhere we turn."

"I know, right? I can't wait for it to be further behind me."

His expression lightened. "Me too. I was trying to be neutral when you first told me, in case you *did* get back together, but I'm a huge fan of you ending it with him. I'm selfishly excited to say whatever I like again without worrying about what Alastair will think."

"What kinds of stuff have you been holding back?"

"Stuff like . . . someone told me yesterday doing it doggy-style is banned in Soleil. Is that true?" His grin was wicked.

She frowned in confusion. "What? Where did you hear that?"

"Well, I assumed it's not allowed since it's totally magic." His expression was comically earnest. "And, you know, magic is banned where you're from. So sad for you."

She stared at him for a beat and then shook with silent laughter. "You're ridiculous."

"You love it."

She did. Scarlett stared wordlessly at his hands as he worked the rough pads of his fingers over her skin. His muscular arms flexed as he shifted to grab her other hand, which was bad enough, but when he dropped her right hand, it landed on his thigh. And she left it there.

And so did he.

When he kneaded the muscle below her thumb, she groaned with pleasure, the fingers of her other hand pressing into his leg. "Are you doing this because you're *so* happy to see me? Or do you do this for all the girls?"

He smirked at her, a twinkle in his eyes. "What do *you* think?"

That old delicious tension she remembered so well from their talks through the mirror was back like it had never left.

"I don't know," she mumbled, not wanting to guess. "James and your dad are the only other people here that I know."

Brayden squeezed her hand. "Oh, I meant to ask—did you get your phone working?"

She pulled it out, grateful he'd asked. "Not yet. Manon said she'd fix it, but we both fell asleep before she had a chance."

"Give it here." Brayden held Scarlett's phone in his open palm. She watched wide-eyed as his palm and the phone glowed with a white light.

Scarlett leaned closer and touched his glowing hand. Her fingertips tingled. "That is fucking freaky. What's making it glow?"

Brayden chuckled. "Magic, baby."

"What happens when the phone dies?"

He looked at her like she was being thick. "You charge it again."

"And you never run out of soul-light juice?"

Brayden raised one eyebrow. "You won't run out of *juice* doing normal things like charging a phone as long as you're taking care of yourself. Only sick people can't use their soul light connection. Or the very drunk."

He gave her back the phone.

"Thank you," she said, pressing the power button. Her phone was lightweight, with a touch screen bigger than her hand.

"That thing is slick." He eyed it as it lit up. "Show me how it works. I want to put my number in it so you can reach me now that you're outside the Soleil firewall."

She pulled up the screen for entering in a new contact, and Brayden typed out his number. Taking the phone back, she sent him a quick text.

"There—now you have mine." She smiled at him. "Let's see . . . What else can I show you? I'm not totally sure what will work without being on the Soleil network, but I can at least show you what I've got downloaded." She opened up a movie. Then she pulled up a hologram of her favorite singer in 3D. The pop star stood like a live doll on-screen as she belted out a song.

"Incredible." Brayden stuck his fingers in the hologram, laughing. He was in awe of her phone the way she was in awe of his magic.

"What does yours look like?" she asked.

He held out his phone.

Scarlett took it, examining the clunky thing. "A black-and-white screen?"

He shrugged. "Yeah, no color. No video. But it calls people."

Scarlett shook her head. "The rest of the world needs our tech."

"Yes, please. I want a cool phone."

Her heart lifted—that was something she could give him. "I'll get you one for winter solstice. I'll sneak it into the country for you."

Brayden laughed. "Don't break any rules for me. You wanting to come back is enough of a gift. It's nice to know you don't feel the same as the rest of Soleil seems to. Most of your friends probably think we're a bunch of nasty magic worshippers."

"Not everyone thinks that. *I* certainly don't. After the energy healing I received today, I'll go back to Soleil and campaign hard to legalize magic. Half my family is from Clair de Lune, and you make life here sound so fun."

"It *is* fun here. So fun." He released her hand. "Speaking of fun— what else should we do tonight?"

Scarlett stared at him. She knew what she wanted to do. *What would he do if I reached up and . . . ?*

He continued. "We could watch a movie if you want?"

Fuck it.

"You know what I want?" Her heart rate sped up as she got on her knees so her face was on the same level as his. "Kiss me." So much for not rocking the boat while she was here. But seriously, fuck it.

You only live once, right?

Brayden's face was unreadable as his gaze dipped to her mouth. Was that a green light? She moved closer, desperately hoping he'd reach for her and pull her onto his lap. She put her hand on the nape of his neck, threading her fingers into his hair so she could pull him closer. But before she could press her lips to his, he put his hand up.

"Wait."

Wait?

Wait?

She fell back on her heels, and her heart dropped. "I'm sorry."

"Scarlett," he whispered, reaching for her, but she pulled away.

He lifted her chin, forcing her to look him in the eye. It took all her willpower not to cry.

"I want you, but you're grieving, and I don't want to be your rebound. You mean more to me than that."

She forced a smile. "Sure. Of course."

He frowned at her short answer and her obvious hurt. "I just want you to wait until you're running toward me, not away from something else."

"I get it." She stood. "I'm going back to my room."

He grabbed her hand, unwilling to let her go so easily. "Are we okay?"

"Of course." *Why did I do this to us?* She smiled as tears hit her cheeks. "I'm fine." She pulled her hand out of his and hurried out of the study, but instead of heading toward her room, she made her way downstairs.

Scarlett prayed to not run into anyone, but luck wasn't on her side. James was lingering in the foyer by the door to the courtyard, dressed like he was going out.

"Hey—" Concern etched across his features when he saw her expression. "Are you all right?"

"Hey," she said with false brightness. "Don't worry—I'm just sad about my dad. I'm going out for some air."

"Don't go into the woods. You know it's dangerous, right?" he called out after her.

"I won't," she replied, striding off into the dark Clair de Lune night.

CHAPTER (II)

Scarlett ran from the castle's courtyard onto the gravel road they'd driven in on. There were only two directions she could go, so she chose the familiar route along the tree houses. Out in the inky night, the lit tree houses provided the only illumination. A nice walk around the countryside sounded like just the thing while she wallowed in thoughts of Brayden.

Crickets chirped around her, and she shivered as a huge gust of wind blew straight through her clothes. Summer in Clair de Lune was colder than Soleil's winter.

I'll warm up if I keep moving.

Her chest tightened as she heard a car leaving the castle courtyard behind her. Was it paranoid to think James would've immediately narced on her to Brayden? The idea of him chasing after her like a naughty child was unbearable. As headlights flashed on the road, she ran toward the forest to hide.

From behind the thick trunk of an enormous redwood, she peeked

out at the SUV, letting out an exasperated sigh when it pulled over where she'd left the road.

Fuck my life.

They probably knew she'd run into the woods to avoid them, which only increased her desire not to be caught.

A chill that had nothing to do with the cold washed over Scarlett as she stared at the wild forest. No moonlight streamed down through the trees. If she went fifteen feet into the woods and crouched down, they wouldn't see her. James had said it was dangerous, but how dangerous could it be this close to the road?

Before she could lose her nerve, Scarlett scrambled through the trees with her hands out in front of her to make sure she didn't hit anything. She winced as a low branch scraped her leg. Grasping the nearest tree trunk, she turned to see if she was still being pursued. To her shock, she couldn't see the road through the trees. She'd only come a short way—hadn't she?

"Scarlett?" Brayden's voice reached her from somewhere nearby. "It's dangerous out here. Please don't hide from me."

She crouched down on the forest floor, touching the mossy base of the tree to steady herself.

I don't want to see you right now.

It sounded like he was to her left. Maybe if she stayed in place he wouldn't spot her. The sounds of unseen animals—or other things—washed over her. A wolf howled, and it didn't sound far away. She whirled around when a human scream pierced the night air and leaves rustled nearby.

Okay, time to go back to the road.

Scarlett had just risen when a rotten, wrinkled form came into sight a mere twenty feet away. She screamed, stumbling backward. The thing emitted a faint glow, and the mummified human corpse with black holes for eyes shrieked again as it came toward her, taking halting steps in her direction. Another corpse emerged from the trees, marching forward in the same labored way.

Footsteps came at her. Brayden and James appeared.

"Scarlett!" Brayden yelled, and all desire to hide from them disappeared in the face of whatever these disgusting things were. Thank the Goddess they'd found her.

"Brayden," she called in a shaky voice.

James said, "Don't look at the wraiths!"

But it was too late. Those black holes had looked into her eyes, and she was paralyzed by them. Everything around her faded as she stared back—until Brayden came into view, grabbing her by the shoulders and breaking her eye contact with the creatures.

He shoved her into James's arms. "Protect her." Then Brayden spun around, hands up, looking down at the forest floor with his palms facing the corpses. A stream of fire emerged from his hands, illuminating the forest around them as he targeted the creatures.

Scarlett's jaw dropped. How was he doing that? She remembered the hydra and the dire wolf from the boxing match. Was he some kind of dragon shifter? And he'd never told her?

His blaze surrounded the creatures, and, shrieking, they tried to protect their leathery faces. In seconds, they were piles of ash, the ground around them scorched black.

Brayden's flames went out, plunging them into darkness once more. He rushed back toward her and James and reached for her with hands that had just been covered in fire.

Scarlett jerked back, afraid he might burn her. "What are you?"

The hurt in his eyes snapped her out of her fear and shock. He'd never harm her.

She grabbed his hand. It didn't burn, but it was unusually warm. "That was wild. Your fire is incredible," she said in a shaky voice.

He sagged with relief as he wrapped her in his arms. "Thank

the Goddess you're all right," he whispered.

His breath caressed her ear, and warmth pooled deep in her core. The heat of his arms around her . . . Goddess. She almost forgot about his rejection. His smell was so similar to the forest, but with a distinctly male undertone that made her want to rub herself on him like a cat.

James cleared his throat. "You didn't tell her about your power?"

Brayden released her. "I'm a phoenix."

"And I want a full description of what that entails as soon as we're out of here." Scarlett turned to James and hugged him briefly. "Thank you for coming after me."

"Of course. I told you not to come out here—the woods are full of wraiths." He shuddered.

"*That* was a wraith?" Scarlett looked at the burned piles of ash. "How are people living so close to a forest with wraiths?"

A wolf howled, far too close, and Scarlett's whole body shuddered.

"Yep. We're leaving. Now." Brayden's tone left no room for argument. He and James walked on either side of Scarlett as they hurried back to the road.

Brayden didn't stop scanning the trees as they moved. Scarlett relaxed when the SUV came into sight, but her mind was still reeling from what she'd just seen.

Back on the road, Brayden ran a hand through his hair as he stood with his back to the forest. "For future reference, don't look wraiths in the eyes. They'll literally eat you if they get close enough."

Her eyes went wide as she pictured those puckered mouths tearing into her flesh. "I will *never* go into the woods alone again. What the hell are wraiths though?"

"They're lost souls trapped in the woods for a thousand years as a punishment for abuse of magic. The government stopped punishing people that way when the Hieratian Empire fell, but there are still a ton in the woods," said Brayden. "Are you sure you're okay? I've never looked them in the eye. It's supposed to be really strange."

"It *was* strange, like I couldn't focus on anything but its eyes. I'm fine now though. Thanks to you. Thank you for saving me." Then she smacked him on the shoulder. "Why didn't you ever tell me you could do that? And what's a phoenix?" Scarlett shivered again. It was freezing out here.

Brayden's focus was all on her as he wrapped an arm around her and steered her toward the SUV. "Let's get in the car, and I'll tell you."

Scarlett sat in the front seat. James made to get into the driver's seat, but Brayden elbowed him aside. Scarlett raised an eyebrow as he climbed in and started the engine, pointing the vents so the hot air warmed her. Touched by the kind gesture, she gave him a grateful smile as she held her hands up to the vents.

The engine idled as Brayden shifted to face her. "All adults in Clair de Lune receive a magical gift we call a valor. My valor is the phoenix. I wield fire, and I'm really hard to kill."

"Valor . . . Dr. Bowen mentioned that term. Are you a shifter? Like the people at that boxing match I told you about?"

"No. I don't shift into a literal phoenix—I can just create fire. Lots and lots of fire."

She cocked her head to one side. "Why'd you keep that a secret from me?"

He gave her some serious side-eye. "I didn't think you'd want to hear it. You got nervous every time I brought up anything to do with magic, so I kept that part of my life to myself."

Had she come across that way? She'd always viewed magic with a fascinated respect. She had none, and that made her feel deficient. She asked her grandmother whenever she was curious about something magical, because she didn't want to highlight her deficiencies to Brayden.

"I didn't mean to be like that," she said. "I'm jealous you can do magic." She turned around to look at James as it dawned on her he probably had a magic power too. "What's your valor? Can you do anything cool?" Inside the warm car, the horrors of the night faded from her mind. It was so easy to feel safe with Brayden and James.

"I'm a vox. I'm good at giving great speeches." He gave her two thumbs up.

"Do you shift or do anything like what Brayden can do?"

Brayden huffed in amusement beside her.

"Nope. I'm a lover, not a fighter." James winked.

She debated how to ask her burning question with tact. "Do you like being a vox?"

He raised his eyebrows. "You mean, do I wish I had a flashy, impressive valor like Brayden instead?"

"I was trying to ask that nicely." Scarlett gave him a crooked half-smile.

"Honestly, being a vox suits me. I'm a civil servant, and a vox is more useful in politics than a phoenix." He leaned closer. "I could show you—"

"Remember that party I mentioned earlier?" interjected Brayden. "My friend Minnie's house is three minutes away from here. We could continue this valor discussion with drinks, if you're up for it."

Scarlett shifted in her seat and smoothed the skirt of her dress. Miraculously, her silk corset dress had come out of the encounter with the wraiths with only a few wrinkles, and her appearance wouldn't embarrass her at a party. Did she want to go? It sounded like a lot after the long, emotional day, but she was wired from the encounter in the woods and had tons of questions.

As for what had led her out to the woods . . . A drink did sound like a great distraction from her failed attempt to kiss Brayden.

"Sure. Let's do it."

CHAPTER (12)

A chill breeze and the sounds of crickets surrounded them as they climbed up the precarious wooden staircase to a full-sized tree house nestled in the branches of an enormous tree. Scarlett gripped the smooth wooden banister, but the steps were steep. A fall from any point would be disastrous. She wished she'd worn something warmer. Brayden and James were both dressed in trousers with hooded sweatshirts, so at least she wasn't underdressed.

Finally, they emerged onto a circular wooden platform. Minnie's door stood before them, and an adjacent wooden bridge went off toward the neighboring homes. The view was gorgeous, with the flickering lights in most of the homes cheery and welcoming amidst the night-drenched forest. Scarlett inhaled the earthy, fresh scent of the lush plant life. Everything around her was so gorgeous and so different from home. It felt like she'd come to another planet instead of the country next door.

James opened the front door without knocking and stepped into

a cozy living room. Bookcases lined the walls, and plants grew in all corners. It was a surprisingly normal living room for a tree house, and Scarlett sighed in relief, her tension easing in the warmth of the room.

A pretty, raven-haired woman with piercing blue eyes stood at the end of a long, thin table, surrounded by several onlookers. She glanced over as they entered but kept her attention on the table. "You three had better be my new good-luck charms," she muttered. "I'm on the verge of disgrace or glory here." She held a little golden ball and was focusing on two cups at the other end of the wooden table, where a lanky redhead with her hair in double buns stood with her arms crossed.

"Woo! Go, Minnie, go!" shouted Brayden. There were some hoots and claps from the rest of the observers.

Minnie bounced the ball off one cup and into another. Scarlett grinned as she whooped and did a high kick into the air. The redhead picked up both the cups the ball had touched and downed one of them. It wasn't a game Scarlett was familiar with, but it looked simple enough. And fun.

Minnie approached them. "Good evening, friends!" She gave James, who was closest to her, a side-hug. "Who is this fair creature?" She cocked her head toward Scarlett. Her purple feathered earrings exaggerated the movement. "You have the most elegant bone structure I've ever seen. I'm Minnie, and this is Keeley." Minnie held out a hand. The redhead gave Scarlett a friendly wave.

"I'm Scarlett. Nice shot, by the way," she said with her friendliest smile as she took Minnie's hand in hers. She glanced toward Brayden, who was hugging Keeley. She wanted to finish their valor discussion, but they could do that later. After the party, maybe.

"Where are you from?" asked Keeley, her eyes lighting with interest.

"Soleil," said Scarlett.

"Scar's grandmother is from Clair de Lune," Brayden said.

"Oh, Scar—I love the nickname," said Minnie.

James took a couple of steps toward the hallway. "Minnie, I'm heading outside, if that's all right?"

Minnie waved him on.

James locked eyes with Brayden, a wicked smirk on his face before he disappeared.

The room emptied as the rest of the people who'd been watching the game followed him.

Before Scarlett could guess at what James's deal was, Minnie asked, "Keeley, can you please give this woman a drink?"

"Thanks," Scarlett said as Keeley handed her one of the cups from their game.

Scarlett studied Minnie. Her short white dress showed off a large tattoo of a cluster of leaves and flowers covering most of her outer right thigh. Scarlett envied her—the girl looked like her life was her own and she had no cares in the world. She'd probably been drinking for a while, judging by the look of the room, which had random cups and bottles sitting on many of the available surfaces. Scarlett glanced inside the cup Keeley had handed her. It looked like beer, so she took a sip. Lukewarm. Yuck. She set it down, hoping Minnie wouldn't notice.

"Scar, how'd you meet the Maddox brothers?" Keeley's white T-shirt was covered in cartoon mushrooms and tucked into a hot-pink miniskirt. She also wore white fishnet tights. These girls were possibly the coolest people Scarlett had ever met.

Brayden put his arm around Scarlett. "What you should be asking is, how did she meet *me*?"

Scarlett fought to contain her grin as she leaned into him. He was just trying to cheer her up after the awkwardness earlier, but she was grateful things weren't weird.

"Ooh, she's *mine*, he says." Minnie arranged the cups back into a triangle formation. Then she froze. "Wait, is this the girl you've been talking to for years? The one you'd never actually met?"

Brayden's arm tightened around her. "Yep. This is her."

Scarlett felt the rumble of his answer in his rib cage and thrilled at the closeness.

"Bray, fancy a game?" Keeley was halfway through refilling the empty cups with beer.

Scarlett looked up at Brayden, hoping he'd stay with her. But he kissed the top of her head and moved to stand opposite Keeley. She felt the kiss like a brand as he walked away. He was back to touching her every chance he got, even after rejecting her earlier. What did it mean? She was eager to observe him with Minnie and Keeley to see if he touched them as much as he did her.

Minnie handed Scarlett another cup of beer. "Here—this one is actually cold."

"Thanks."

"So how'd you meet Brayden?"

"He scared the shit out of me through my grandma's magic mirror." Scarlett smiled fondly at Brayden, who was making his first shot.

Minnie choked on her drink. "Elaborate, please."

Scarlett remembered the night as if it were yesterday. "One night when I was eleven, I woke up from a nightmare and was scared, so I headed to my grandma's room. Her magic mirror is in the room that joins our bedrooms together. The mirror is illegal in Soleil, obviously, but all my grandma did to hide it was cover it with a thin scarf."

"Hilarious." Minnie's eyes danced.

Scarlett's mouth twitched, fighting back a grin. "Yes. Anyway, I was walking past when I thought I saw something move in the mirror, beneath the scarf. I went a bit closer and wasn't sure if it was my reflection, because it moved when I did. As soon as I got close enough to touch the scarf, Brayden screamed, and I nearly pissed myself I was so scared."

Brayden flashed her a smile and then sank his ball into a cup. Keeley pulled the ball out and downed the cup of beer.

"I pulled the scarf off the mirror, and this weirdo was there, laughing his arse off." Scarlett grinned at the memory. "Then my grandma rushed in and explained who he was and that his father was her friend. That was the first time she'd really talked to me about magic. She swore me to secrecy and told me I could use the mirror to talk to Brayden if I fancied it. Which was really incredible, looking back, because she could've been sent to jail if I'd been caught. Obviously, I took her up on the offer." Her gaze locked with Brayden's.

"After that, you were friends?" asked Minnie.

"I wouldn't leave him alone after I found out where he was from," said Scarlett. "My mother grew up in Clair de Lune. She died when I was nine, so meeting someone from her country was special to me. He was the first person from Clair I'd met outside of my family."

Minnie gave her a sympathetic look. "I'm sorry about your mother. That sucks."

"Thanks," said Scarlett.

"Scarlett couldn't get enough of my accent," said Brayden between shots, lightening the mood immediately. He'd already sunk the ball into several cups, but Keeley hadn't made any shots. "She used to always ask me to say 'power' and 'film.'"

"I love the way you all say certain words," admitted Scarlett.

"Aww, you like our accent!" said Keeley as she missed another shot.

"I do." Scarlett laughed.

"Then, when we were thirteen, we started playing Verity or Gauntlet," said Brayden. "That's when I learned she has balls of steel. She always picked gauntlet."

Minnie waggled her eyebrows. "Oh, do tell."

Scarlett waved her hand dismissively. "Ah, it wasn't that wild. Just teenager stuff. Once, Brayden dared me to run naked through my stepmother's dinner party."

Minnie's eyes lit up. "And you did?"

Scarlett's shoulders shook with laughter. "I convinced him to let me do it in a swimsuit and a devil mask. I've never seen my stepmother try so hard to keep from screaming at me in front of company. The Zaharan ambassador was there!"

Keeley snorted, and Minnie gasped.

Scarlett winced. "I was grounded for a month that summer—no phone, no computer."

"Which was great, because you were around whenever I wanted to talk." Brayden sank a game-winning shot.

Keeley happily downed her beer in one long gulp. Brayden returned to Scarlett's side, and she handed him her half-empty cup. He raised it in her direction before finishing it.

"You made being grounded more fun."

They'd talked late into the night so many times she'd often fallen asleep in the chair opposite the mirror and awoke to see him asleep on his father's couch. She'd definitely been crushing on him by the end of that summer. He was the first boy she'd had feelings for, although she'd never admitted it out loud. She assumed he knew she adored him.

He definitely did now.

She needed to change the subject fast before her train of thought became obvious on her heating face. "How do you all know each other?"

"We all grew up together," said Minnie, ruffling Keeley's hair.

"Now Minnie and Keeley go to university in Evory." Brayden's arm brushed against hers.

Scarlett's eyes lit up. She'd been looking forward to visiting Evory on her tour. "Oh, cool. Do you like Evory? What are you studying?"

"It's incredible. I just finished medical school. They have a top-notch course in plant medicine," said Minnie. "Dear Keeley went to veterinary school."

"Wow, you're a doctor?" asked Scarlett in awe. Politicians claimed to want to help people, but doctors actually did. "And you're a veterinarian?"

"There are limited choices available if you want to stay in Clair de Lune," Keeley said as she wiped the table clean. "The options are soldier, farmer, doctor, or shop owner. I chose vet."

"You're exaggerating," said Scarlett.

"She's exaggerating," agreed Brayden. "There's also teacher, politician, and dentist. We have all the normal jobs."

Scarlett laughed. At least he'd included politician in the list, like there was room for her here if she wanted there to be.

Minnie glanced down at their empty hands. "Oh shit, we need more drinks. Would you like a moon cider? It's made with special apples that only grow here. There's mead as well, but it's quite strong."

"Moon cider sounds delicious. Thank you." Anything other than warm beer.

"Moon cider for me too, please," said Brayden. His body was so close to hers he kept brushing up against her, but he was still so far. She wanted to put her hand in his back pocket, but there was no way she was going to after his rejection earlier on.

"Could I try the mead as well?" Scarlett wanted three drinks, max. Enough to get a nice buzz.

Brayden tilted his head, looking at her appraisingly, but he said nothing.

"Of course. Double-fisting is my favorite pastime," said Minnie.

"You'll fit in here nicely," said Keeley. "Let's head outside—we'll get the drinks on the way."

Keeley and Minnie led them through a crowded kitchen, and Brayden put his hand on her lower back, sticking close to her, while Minnie poured their drinks. Everyone knew Brayden—several people shouted drunken greetings at him. He nodded at them but never took his hand off her, and he didn't stop to talk or introduce her to anyone. She hoped that was because he didn't want to share her and not for some other reason.

As they stepped outside onto the back veranda, Scarlett sipped the cider, and the cold, crisp apple drink went down easy. It tasted more like an actual apple than the cider in Soleil, and it was delicious.

It was much warmer outside than it had been in the forest. Was this magic? The porch had a vine-covered trellis over the top of it, and it twinkled with fairy lights. She spotted James at a long table grazing on a large charcuterie platter while talking to the girl next to him. Several people sat around a lit firepit. One of them was smoking out of a hookah pipe. Scarlett had only seen pictures of one before, although she'd read they were popular in the desert country of Utidi.

Minnie's home was cosmopolitan, and this openness to Evory, Utidi, and the rest of the continent was exactly what Scarlett wanted for Soleil.

Brayden moved toward an open seat around the firepit, but before Scarlett could follow, Minnie grabbed her elbow.

"Do you want a shot of peanut butter whiskey?" She gestured to the table, where Keeley was lining up a row of shot glasses next to a glass bottle of brown liquid.

Scarlett was already moving toward it. "Absolutely." The shot would be her third and final drink. She made eye contact with Brayden and pointed to the glasses. He gave her a thumbs-up from where he was talking to the guy next to him—an athletic-looking redhead who was nearly as large as Brayden. Maybe they were gym buddies.

Minnie steered Scarlett toward the table, and Keeley handed her a shot.

"To science and friendship," said Minnie.

The corners of Scarlett's mouth turned up. This woman had nonstop banter. They all threw back their shots. The nutty-flavored liquid burned as it slid down her throat. The warmth of the alcohol hit her stomach, followed by a buzz.

Is it bad to drink when you've just had energy healing? She shrugged. *Too late now.*

"That was yummy," said Keeley. She and Minnie sat in some chairs next to the charcuterie. After a glance toward Brayden, who was happily conversing with ginger gym man, Scarlett joined them.

"So, Scarlett, what are your interests? Do you have a boyfriend? Girlfriend?" asked Minnie.

"Erm, I like surfing, and this might sound sad, but I genuinely like politics. I *had* a boyfriend, but we broke up right before my dad died. He passed away last month." Everything led her back to her dad's death. Scarlett took a cracker and a piece of yellow cheese off the charcuterie plate and munched on it as she tried not to let her mood get dark.

"Oh wow, a breakup and a death in your family. I'm so sorry," said Keeley, her eyes full of sympathy.

"Thanks," said Scarlett. "I've barely processed any of it. I'm not sure where to begin, you know?"

And I've ruined the chat with my depressing life.

"Have either of you ever been through a big breakup?" she asked, hoping to move the conversation on. "He was my first boyfriend, so I don't really know what to expect."

"Getting over a breakup can take ages," said Minnie. "I read in the *Evory Journal of Medicine* that for every orgasm you have with your partner, you should be single for a day before you date again."

Scarlett stared at her. How was she supposed to react to *that*? "Really?"

"*Evory Journal of Medicine*—? Very funny," said Keeley, scrunching her nose. "What if you're a two-a-day kind of girl and you're together for a year? You're supposed to live the celibate life for two years?"

Scarlett laughed. "What if I've never had an orgasm but my last relationship was three years long? Am I allowed to get a new boyfriend right away?" Her hand flew to her mouth. That was literally the most embarrassing thing she'd ever said out loud. *Thank you, alcohol.* She glanced at Brayden again, relieved he was too far away to hear.

Minnie chuckled. "Good one, Scarlett. Can you imagine?"

"Wait . . . I think she's serious," said Keeley. "That was way too specific to be a joke. You never had one with your boyfriend? Or you've never had one at all?"

"Never had one at all," mumbled Scarlett, feeling exposed as she stared at her hands in her lap.

"Girl, please tell me that's not true," said Minnie, her expression horrified.

Scarlett shrugged. She downed the remainder of her moon cider in one gulp. She hadn't told a soul about her orgasm problems, and now she'd gotten buzzed and spilled her guts within twenty minutes of meeting Minnie and Keeley. Might as well go all the way. "It's true."

"That's terrible!" Keeley took Scarlett's hand in hers, giving it a sympathetic squeeze.

Minnie leaned in closer to Scarlett. "All right, my medical training is kicking in. I need to triage you. Have you *tried* to get yourself off?"

From his seat by the fire, Brayden stood and took a couple of steps toward them.

"No!" Minnie put her hand up. "Sit down, please, and don't interrupt until we're finished."

"Scar, you all right?" he asked.

She nodded rapidly, smiling at him to let him know she appreciated him checking on her. "I'm good. We're just having girl talk."

"Okay." After one last lingering glance at Scarlett, Brayden sat and took the hookah pipe from his amused neighbor.

"Answer the question, Scarlett," said Minnie.

"I've tried a few times, and it never goes anywhere." Scarlett's face grew hot. "I've tried with my fingers a few times, and I've tried with a shower head." *That* had felt good, but the feeling hadn't escalated anywhere new, and after a few minutes she'd given up.

"Have you tried any sex toys?" asked Minnie.

Scarlett choked out a laugh. She didn't know anyone who used sex toys.

"What's funny? I'm dead serious," said Minnie, incredulous.

"Sorry. No, I haven't tried any. I'm not against them, but I've never come across one."

"It's so Soleil, isn't it?" said Keeley to Minnie. "No offense, Scarlett. It's just funny—Soleil is technologically advanced, but fuck me, if you aren't the most emotionally, sexually repressed people in all Hieratia."

"It's so Soleil," Minnie agreed. "I don't want to paint the entire country with a brush of sexual repression, as generalities aren't always true, but a *three-year relationship* and you had not a single orgasm? What did your boyfriend think about his abject failure?"

"He didn't know."

Minnie and Keeley stared at her.

Suddenly, the floodgates opened, and the whole truth came

spilling out, helped along by the alcohol. "It's not all his fault. When we first started dating, I didn't want it to be a weird thing that I'd never had one before. So the first time we ever slept together . . . I faked it."

"Not ideal, but understandable," said Minnie.

"And then?" asked Keeley.

"After that, I couldn't exactly reveal the lie, so I kept faking it, until suddenly, we were years into the relationship."

"Yikes." Keeley leaned closer and wrapped her arms around Scarlett. "That is *tragic*."

"It *was*. It weighed on me quite a lot, especially toward the end. I'll never do that again." Scarlett took a couple of deep breaths. Despite everything, a new sense of lightness came over her.

"Goddess," said Keeley. "So much repression."

"I think I can help," said Minnie. She stood. "We'll be right back."

Before Scarlett could protest, the two of them went inside, leaving her to wonder nervously what Minnie's idea of help would entail.

Scarlett sipped her mead and looked toward the firepit. Brayden was in the same spot, laughing with his friend. He looked up at her and made a come-hither motion with his head. She stood, feeling the effects of the alcohol. He watched her with an eager smile as she made her way toward him, and she couldn't wait to be near him again.

She'd just seated herself in the chair next to Brayden when Minnie reappeared. She stood in front of him, blocking his view, as she handed Scarlett a nondescript cloth bag.

"Thanks. What is it?" she asked as she accepted the bundle.

Minnie leaned in. "It's a magic wand." She winked.

Scarlett cocked her head. "Don't you need it for yourself? I don't want to inconvenience you or anything. I also don't know how to use it." She offered the bag back to Minnie.

Minnie smirked, holding her hands up in clear refusal. She spoke in a low voice, with her back to Brayden. "You'll figure it out. It's self-explanatory. And I actually have two of these, so it's no bother. I won this in a game at a bachelorette party last month, and I already had one." She shrugged. "It's meant for you."

This at least made Scarlett comfortable enough to accept the gift. She set the bag down in her lap, feeling touched that this near-stranger was gifting her a wand. "That's so nice. Thank you."

Minnie's eyes darted to the bag. "I charged it with magic, but you'll need someone with a soul light to recharge it when the magic runs out. Maybe Brayden?" Her smile turned devious.

"Don't open it until you're alone," Keeley chortled next to her. "And let us know how you get on after you've given it a bash."

"Thank you," she said, too embarrassed to ask how a wand was supposed to end her struggle to have an orgasm. Hopefully, Minnie was right about it being self-explanatory.

"Of course! Fate brought us together so I could help you thus," said Minnie.

"What are you talking about?" Brayden poked his head around Minnie to see inside the small circle she and Keeley had formed.

"I'm sure Scarlett will fill you in." Minnie shoved him away. "We'll let you have some quality time with Bray," she said to Scarlett. "Let's have coffee while you're in town, yes?"

"Yes!" said Keeley, jumping up and down.

"I'd love that," said Scarlett. Then her face fell. "I actually don't know how long I'll be here. I have to get back to Soleil, but it might take a few days. I'll get your number from Brayden though. It was so nice to meet both of you!"

Scarlett waved to them as they walked over to a group on the far side of the veranda.

"What's going on with Minnie and Keeley? I hope they were

nice to you." Brayden glanced curiously at the bag in Scarlett's lap. It felt like it might burst into flames at any moment she was so aware of it.

"They were so nice," she said warmly.

"I'm glad." He bumped his knee against hers. "Are you tired?"

"I am. Can we leave? Is that all right?" Her buzz was tinged with excitement to find out what the hell was in the bag.

"I have to be on base at 6 a.m., so that's fine by me," said Brayden.

Scarlett caught sight of James, who was engrossed in conversation. "Should we tell your brother we're going?"

"Nah. He's a big boy."

Outside, away from the shelter of the tree house, the already cold night had grown colder. Scarlett shivered, goose bumps all over her skin as they climbed down to the gravel road.

She headed for the SUV. "Are we taking the car?"

"I'll come get it in the morning. I know we're five feet from home, but I had four drinks, so I'd rather not drive. Can you manage the walk? Or I could carry you."

He was so responsible. Duh, they couldn't drive.

She set off in the direction of the castle. "I can walk, no worries. As long as you stay between me and that forest full of ghouls."

He grabbed her elbow, forcing her to stop. "Wait. Take this." Brayden pulled off his gray hoodie and held it out to her. "I should've given this to you earlier."

"That's sweet of you." As she took the sweatshirt, she fought the urge to bury her face in it. It was warm from his body heat, and once she had it on, she could smell him.

Fresh pine.

"So, Minnie and Keeley—what did you talk about?" asked Brayden as they began the walk back to the castle.

"Mostly my breakup with Alastair and some . . . issues I had with him." She couldn't look at him, even though she could feel him staring. Hopefully, he wouldn't press her.

"What issues?" asked Brayden. "Something you've told me?"

"Not exactly." She'd revealed the truth to strangers, but she couldn't tell *Brayden*. Any attraction he might have for her would wither and die if she did. She also didn't want to lie to him. "They gave me some advice about issues I've had physically."

He grabbed her hand and threaded his fingers through hers. "Are you all right? Did you tell Dr. Bowen?"

"It's not like that." Her embarrassment bubbled over. His concern was touching, but the last thing she wanted to do was alert him to the fact she had a magic wand that was supposed to get her off.

"What's in that bag?" He gestured to the cloth sack.

"None of your business." She knocked their linked hands into him.

"Why won't you tell me?" he whined.

She sighed, exasperated. "It's a magic masturbation wand. Are you happy now?"

Chuckling, he dropped her hand and raised his own in supplication. "All right, all right. Keep your secret. I don't have to know."

Brayden walked her to her door. She would've been thinking about a good-night kiss if he hadn't rejected her. Good thing she had a bag of reasons to spend the night alone.

"Good night." Brayden leaned in and wrapped his arms around her. She closed her eyes, basking in the feel of him. It would be so hard to go back to looking at him through glass.

She forced herself to pull away. "Good night," she said with a wave.

He blew a kiss at her as she closed her door.

Goddess above. They were a mess of crossed wires and mixed messages.

Alone in her room, Scarlett opened the bag and pulled out two boxes. Her brow furrowed as she stared at the larger one. It wasn't a magic wand; it was a . . . vibrator?

She started to giggle. *I thought Minnie was giving me a literal magic wand, and it was actually a sex toy.* How funny it would be if she could have figured this out herself all along.

She opened the box and pulled it out. The toy was purple and penis-shaped, with a funny-looking pointy piece that jutted out on one side. Scarlett pressed the button, and it vibrated wickedly in her hand, which only made her laugh harder. The second box held a bottle of lube.

When she was done laughing, she undressed and got under the covers. Lying on her back, she took the vibrator in hand and started to explore. It was cold at first, but the lube created a nice slickness. She pressed a button, and her eyes opened wide as the shorter piece hit her clit. The sensation as it vibrated was like nothing she'd ever experienced.

An idea struck her. Pausing her exploration, she grabbed Brayden's hoodie off the nightstand, put it on her pillow, and lay down again, closing her eyes.

Alone in her room, with Brayden's fresh cedar scent surrounding her, she pretended he hadn't rejected her earlier or said good night at her door. He'd followed her into the room, joined her on the bed, and kissed her.

She pulled him onto her and undressed him, surprising them both. He slid into her, and Scarlett pictured his cock moving inside as she moved the vibrator, gasping when it grazed her sensitive clit. Then he picked up the pace, burying himself in her, and a wave of something completely new arose within. A deep heat pulsed as she pleasured herself, and her clit throbbed from the stimulation.

Brayden over her.

Inside her.

Losing himself with her.

Ahhhh.

Scarlett's hips jerked as a burst of pleasure flooded her body. She gripped Brayden's sweater with her free hand as she came for the first time. While she lay there in the afterglow, happiness radiated through her. Her life was pretty fucked up, but at least this one thing was going right. She'd finally had her first orgasm.

CHAPTER 13

The next morning Scarlett stared at the thick fog outside her window. Brayden was probably outside doing drills. Would their paths cross today? They'd never have enough time together, but especially not on this short visit.

Forcing herself out of bed, she pulled on a black camisole, a sweater, and a pair of black pants—without underwear, because she had none. She'd just finished dressing when there was a knock at the door.

Scarlett opened it to find her smiling grandmother standing with the help of a cane. Next to her, Flora stood holding a tray with a pot of tea, fresh fruit, and toast.

"Oh, good. You're awake." Manon's hair was in its typical neat bun, and she was wearing a purple velvet dress.

"Good morning." Scarlett stepped aside for them to enter.

"Morning." Flora set the tray down on a small table between two armchairs.

"Thank you, Flora," said Scarlett. "You seem to be here every time we need help. Do you live here in the castle?"

"Yes, I do," Flora answered cheerily. "It's quite a good gig. Five days on, two days off, and I never have to worry about buying milk."

"I appreciated your help yesterday. I'm not sure I thanked you properly for the bath. I was so tired. I'm not sure bathing people is part of your job description, is it?" Manon sounded apologetic.

Flora waved a hand in dismissal. "Don't worry yourself. You'd been through it, and I was happy to help. I hope someone would help my granny if she were in a state and far from home."

"You're very gracious," said Scarlett.

"No bother. Anyway, I'd best get on with it. Enjoy your breakfast."

"How are you?" asked Manon once Flora had gone.

"Much better after a good night's sleep. I need to find somewhere to buy underwear and pajamas. Beni forgot those two essentials."

Manon chuckled as she used the cane to hobble toward the fireplace. "He didn't pack any socks for me, bless him. We'll sort that out today. Not to worry. They've got wonderful boutiques here. I'll pick up some pajamas and maybe get you a couple of extra dresses."

"That would be great. Thanks. *You* look well. I can't believe you're out of the wheelchair already. Energy healing is incredible."

"It's great to be walking, although I'll admit I'm not one hundred percent. It doesn't work as well when you're old." Manon lowered herself into an armchair. "But still, no wheelchair is a definite win."

"It's criminal that the healing they have here is unavailable in Soleil. Think of the lives that could be saved."

"Yes. It could've saved your mother." Manon looked out into the fog, her eyes distant, before returning her attention to Scarlett. "Everyone here thinks it's absolute madness medical magic was ever made illegal in Soleil."

Scarlett sat down in the chair opposite Manon. "Yes, the government banned the good magic along with the bad after the war crimes all those years ago. I'll be trying to correct that once I'm back in Soleil. Anyway, have you seen the news yet? I'm dying to know what the papers are saying about us."

"Today's papers will come in on the afternoon train."

"Good to know." Scarlett poured out two cups of steaming tea.

"I'd wager there won't be anything. Laylani's in a tricky spot. She told the country we were bedridden. If she calls the police or the media, what will she say? That we're dead? That the two people who were comatose for weeks woke up and stole her son?" Manon sipped her tea.

"I wrote to Alastair and Elestine last night," said Scarlett. "Brayden has the letters. He'll mail them today." She filled Manon in on the details of what she'd written.

Her grandmother pressed her lips into a thin line. "I'm not thrilled about advertising we're in Clair de Lune. What if Elestine tells the press?"

"We won't be here long anyway," said Scarlett, thinking. "I need to get back. Should we contact the Soleil media ourselves? We could use the press to get ahead of Laylani's lies."

"Give me a moment," said Manon. She got that faraway look in her eye Scarlett associated with her decision-making process. A good thirty seconds later, she snapped out of her trance and spoke. "We need to gather as much hard evidence as possible before we act. Right now, we have a couple of piss bags and your brother's testimony, which isn't enough to take down your stepmother, let alone Moira."

"Then we wait to get the results from the urine and confirmation my petition with the courts was approved before we return, preferably with some serious protection," Scarlett said with a shrug. "In

Soleil, with me in Parliament, we'll find a way to incriminate her and Moira."

Manon's brow furrowed—with worry or confusion, Scarlett wasn't sure.

"What's wrong?" she asked.

"We should remain here longer than that," said her grandmother. "You're not ready to go back."

Scarlett's gut clenched. The idea of waiting here longer than necessary made her nauseous. "Why? Don't you care about what's happening in Soleil?"

"I do, but it's not my top priority. You're here." She held her hand high above her head. "Then comes everyone else we care about." She lowered her hand just a bit. "And Soleil is somewhere down here." She hovered her hand as low as she could without stooping.

Scarlett sighed. She was desperate to return to Soleil in a fiery blaze of revenge, but she could save this argument for after the urine tests came through. "We're waiting either way for now. While I wait, I want to go to your house and see where my mother used to live. And the Forest Temple with Beni, if he's up for it. Brayden used his fire magic in front of me last night, and I want whatever magic I can get. A soul light, a valor—I want it all."

Manon gave her a long look. "Are you sure? You'll forever be more of Clair de Lune than you are of Soleil if you seek your magic."

The note of warning in Manon's voice made Scarlett tense. "You said no one in Soleil would be able to tell, right?"

"Right."

"Then I'm sure. Being here without magic is showing me how much I'm missing out on. And I already feel *other* in Soleil, so I don't think I'm giving much up. I want to explore these things myself and potentially spread them to others who might have better lives with magic."

"Well, let's get to it, then." Her grandmother's cheeks rounded as she smiled. She was still beautiful, even at seventy. "Let's go to my house first."

"I'll check in with Beni and meet you back here. Then we can go."

"Sounds like a plan."

Scarlett slipped out of her room and crossed the hallway to knock on her brother's door. Beni answered half-dressed, with wet hair.

"Hey," he said as he made way for her to come inside.

Scarlett sat on his bed, eyeing the mess of clothes and shoes he'd scattered across the floor. "How are you? We haven't had time to talk about everything since we got here."

He started towel-drying his hair. "I'm all right."

"Do you miss your mum?"

He kept drying his hair and said nothing.

"It's okay if you do. She *is* your mum."

He stared at her. "As far as I'm concerned, you're the only family I have."

Scarlett searched his face. If only she could take away his pain. She wrapped her arms around her baby brother, who was nearly as tall as her, and made a mental note to look into counseling for him when they were back home. Hell, she needed some counseling herself. Maybe they could go together.

"I'll always be here for you, Beni. Manon loves you too. Don't forget that."

"Thanks." He took a couple of deep breaths before pulling away.

Scarlett sat back down on the bed. "I wanted to ask, did Alastair come by while I was asleep?"

Beni looked at her as he brushed his hair. "Yeah, he did."

"Was he helpful?" asked Scarlett.

Beni went to his suitcase, selected a shirt, and pulled it on over his head. "He asked me if I needed help. I didn't know what to ask him for though. He brought his mum over once, but my mum sent them away." Now fully clothed, he sat down in a chair by the door, facing Scarlett. "Then I met Brayden, and he helped me figure things out."

Scarlett sighed with small relief that Alastair had been decent enough to try.

"You shouldn't get back with him because of that though," said Beni, his brow furrowed. "Brayden helped way more than he did."

Heat spread across Scarlett's face. "Don't worry, I won't. I just . . . wanted to know he hadn't abandoned me. And you."

Beni stared at the ground. "I get that."

Scarlett stretched. "Enough about Alastair. Has anyone mentioned soul lights to you? Or valors?"

"At archery yesterday, Tommy and Patrick asked why I don't have a light. They thought it was weird. Why?"

Scarlett went over the concept of the soul light with him, the same way Manon had for her. Then she told him of her experience in the forest. She left out the part about her running into danger like a fool, focusing mainly on Brayden's fire magic. Then she asked, "I want to meet my light today and get my valor. Do you want to come check out the Forest Temple with me?"

His eyes lit up for the first time that morning. "Of course. I want magic powers too! Charging my phone with my hand? Hell yeah."

Scarlett chuckled. "We're going to my mum's house first, but we'll come back in a couple of hours and head to the temple then. You gonna be okay here for a while?"

"Oh yeah. I'll go to the gym." He flexed his skinny arms. "I need to work on these guns."

A rush of fondness for her kid brother swept through Scarlett. Part of her wanted him to stay young and innocent like this forever. "I'll see you later."

Manon opened the door to her tree house with a set of keys Scarlett had never seen. The tree house looked similar to Minnie's on the outside. On the inside though . . .

"It's good to be home." Manon let out a contented sigh.

Vivid fabrics and oil paintings of flowers dominated the living room. Scarlett was immediately reminded of Manon's room in Soleil, although this place was homier. She peered at a cross-stitch hung next to a doorway. *Ad Astra et Ultra.* Under it was a constellation surrounded by shooting stars.

"That's interesting," said Scarlett. "What constellation is that?"

Manon came to stand next to her. "It's the Fortuna constellation with the Bedivere family motto. It means 'to the stars and beyond.'" She leaned into Scarlett. "Your mother made that when she was grounded for a week as a teenager. That constellation is part of our family crest, so that's what inspired her."

Scarlett wanted that cross-stitch. Would Manon let her take it home?

"Is there more of my mum's stuff here?"

"Oh, sure," said Manon. "I had all her things moved here after she passed. It made your dad too sad, so he gave them to me. I saved it all for you. It's all in her old room."

She led Scarlett through the kitchen and down another hallway, stopping in front of a closed door. "Do you want to have a look?"

Scarlett vibrated with excitement. She had so few of her mother's belongings. She'd wondered where they'd all gone. Now she knew her father had erased her mother from their home. "Are you sure you don't mind?"

"I don't mind at all. Go in there and take anything you want. She was *your* mother." Manon squeezed Scarlett's hand. "I'll go make some tea. No milk, obviously, but there's still some black tea in the cupboard, if I remember right." She left Scarlett standing at the doorway to her mother's childhood bedroom.

A big bed with a cream-colored tufted headboard took up much of the room, along with a simple wooden desk. A large poster of a surfer girl on a beach at sunset hung above the bed—it could have been a beach in Soleil. Scarlett's eyes welled up at the sight of it. Maybe it was just a poster, but imagine if her mother had, on some level, dreamed of Scarlett's life while she'd been growing up in Clair de Lune . . . Was her life her mother's dreams made manifest? She wished she could ask her about the poster.

There were two bookshelves crammed with books and decorative boxes. Scarlett ran her fingers over the titles, finding a few she'd read. A love of reading was one of the things her parents had liked about each other. Her dad had told her that much.

There were a few dresses pushed to the far left of the closet, but most of the space was filled with boxes. Scarlett opened the closest one and found a stack of notebooks. She picked one up and opened it, finding it stuffed with concert tickets and photographs.

"Have you read any of these journals?" she called to Manon.

Manon appeared in the doorway. "No. She wouldn't have wanted me to. You, though—you should. She'd want you to know her."

Scarlett put the diary down. Reading them could reveal weirdness she wouldn't like, but she ached to know more about her mother. She opened another box, filled with scarves. She pulled out a red tartan scarf and put it on.

Manon dragged a garment bag out of a closet. "Here's her wedding dress." She set the bag down on the bed, unzipped it, and lifted out the dress. It was a simple yet elegant white dress: long sleeves, mid-thigh length, with a square neckline lined with pearls. Time had left it untouched all these years.

Scarlett gasped. "I've never seen this before. Not even in pictures."

"She was so beautiful." Manon's breath hitched. "They got married here, you know. At the courthouse."

Scarlett was touched by the happiness that shone on Manon's face. She missed Sabina, but it seemed like the good memories were still good.

The kettle whistled in the kitchen. Manon, whose eyes were suspiciously shiny, hobbled to the door.

"Back in a moment."

Alone once more, Scarlett touched the wedding dress reverently. She'd kill for a wedding photo of her parents. Turning back to the journal, she flicked through the pages until she found what she was hoping for: a photo of Sabina.

The picture was of her and several friends. Scarlett didn't recognize any of them other than her mother. They all beamed at the camera. Sabina looked a little younger than Scarlett was now, but not by a lot, and Scarlett was struck by how much she really did look like her mum. Her dad had always told her that, but she'd never felt it more than she did now, standing in her room, looking at a picture of this very real girl who once had a happy life before she died and was erased from Scarlett's life.

Manon reappeared with two cups of tea. "Scarlett, there's something I need to talk to you about." She sat on an empty part of the bed and patted the space next to her.

Scarlett sat. "What is it?"

"It's about my valor."

"Go on."

"So Brayden showed you his valor and told you he's a phoenix."

"Yes. I saw the fire." *Please don't ask more.* She didn't want to tell Manon the embarrassing story of how she'd ended up in the woods.

"When valors manifest, they appear on your physical body as a tattoo. Your soul light can help you make the tattoo invisible, which is why you've never seen mine, but one will appear on you during the ceremony. Mine's on the back of my neck." Her grandmother's hair was already up in a neat bun, so all she had to do was turn her head for Scarlett to see.

Scarlett gasped. A tattoo of an eye stared at her—it was open wide and had long black lashes.

"I'm an oculus. This is my valor tattoo. Together, the valor tattoo and the soul light give me the oculus power to see glimmers of the future. My unusually good intuition comes from being an oculus."

Scarlett reeled as she lifted a finger to touch the tattoo. "This tattoo gave you magic?" She stared at the eye, transfixed.

Manon faced Scarlett. "Yes. The powers manifest through the valor ceremony."

"What does it mean to be an oculus?" When Scarlett was a kid, Manon had always swooped in—seemingly out of nowhere—to stop her from doing something she wasn't supposed to, like sneaking off to the beach alone.

"Wait . . . Is this how you always caught me when I tried to sneak out?"

Manon chuckled. "Not *really*. That was my sixth sense as a grandmother. My intuition was strong even before my valor manifested. The oculus power just enhances what's already there. Sometimes, being an oculus means you get exceptional psychic abilities. Other times, it means you're simply intuitive. I'm somewhere in the middle. I wouldn't call myself a psychic, but I have excellent instincts."

Scarlett's mouth fell open. Those mentions of her grandmother and Lachlan . . . A new understanding dawned. "You use your abilities to help Lachlan, don't you?" *My grandmother is a spy.* "That's why you talked in the mirror so often."

Manon's smile was apologetic. "My specialty is assessing strategic decisions, which is helpful for the military and the government."

"Could you have seen Dad was going to die?" It was an awful

question, but Scarlett had to ask. "I'm not accusing you of anything. I just want to understand."

Manon's eyes watered, and she grasped for Scarlett. "From the bottom of my heart, I wish I could've saved him. And your mother. I can't see the things I don't know to look for."

Squeezing her grandmother's hand, Scarlett gave her a reassuring smile. She knew deep in her heart Manon would have saved them if she could have, and she wished she'd framed the question differently so as not to upset her.

Manon continued. "Take Lachlan, for example. He'll come to me with a decision he's trying to make and ask me what I see. I'll usually give him good advice. However, if someone were planning to kill him, I wouldn't know unless he asked the right question. It's far from a perfect power." She pinched the bridge of her nose. "I couldn't save us from Laylani either, which was irritating as hell."

Scarlett huffed out a laugh, satisfied by the explanation. "Yes, I wish you could have seen that in advance. How do you get *that* label—oculus? Why do different people have different valors? What was my mum's valor?"

Manon crossed her legs and leaned back on the bed, looking around at her daughter's old room. "She was a scientia. She was always brilliant in school, specifically in science, and her valor enhanced that, which is why she went to Soleil for university, where she met Jules."

Soleil, where she'd died. It was a wonder Manon didn't hate the whole country.

Manon sniffed. "As for why we get what we get, sometimes valors run in families, but it's often a total surprise. I have no idea what you'll be."

"I guess I'll find out soon enough. Is that all you wanted to tell me?" Scarlett glanced at the boxes in the closet. She wanted to sort through more of her mum's things before it was time to go.

Manon looked at the ceiling. "I also wanted to tell you I spent yesterday evening searching for our best path. Unfortunately, Scarlett, when I see myself returning to Soleil, I die. Every time. No matter how I change the path, the outcome remains the same. Laylani gets me, and I weaken and die. But if I stay here, I live." Her stare was empty as she let out a heavy sigh.

Scarlett's heart grew heavy as it sank in that her grandmother wasn't coming back with her. "Then of course you'll stay. Will you move back here?"

"Yes, dear. As soon as I'm able."

Scarlett ran her fingers over the worn duvet on her mother's bed. "Can we take some of Mum's journals back to the castle? I'm losing the will to go on, and I want to go to the Forest Temple before I'm emotionally and physically exhausted."

"Of course. Let's head back."

Scarlett rushed to load a box of journals into their borrowed car before returning to help Manon. She tried not to catastrophize as she imagined what it would be like to take Beni back to Soleil alone.

CHAPTER (14)

Heading out of the castle courtyard on foot, Scarlett and Beni followed Manon to a path at the edge of the tree line that marked the beginning of the forest beyond the castle walls. As they walked, Scarlett marveled at how well Manon was getting along with her cane. She seemed to grow stronger by the hour.

"I can't tell you how much it has weighed on me over the years that you two were unable to experience this," said Manon. "I'm over the moon you're meeting your lights. And I mean both of you, Beni."

"I know." Beni smiled at Manon. "Thank you."

"Are there wraiths in these woods?" asked Scarlett, too distracted by nerves to respond to the heartfelt sentiment.

Manon frowned. "Wraiths? How'd you hear about those?"

"Um, Brayden mentioned them." Scarlett avoided her grandmother's gaze.

"Oh, don't worry," said Manon, missing her evasiveness. "The

path is charmed. Besides, they don't come out in the daylight, typically."

Scarlett sighed in relief. "That's good."

The ever-present clouds cloaked the Clair de Lune sky, as usual. The air was crisp with the smell of fresh pine and wet dirt as they walked. The trees and bushes surrounding them grew so close together it would have been a struggle to leave the path.

After about twenty minutes of walking, the path abruptly ended in an enormous clearing, revealing a stunning building that had been hidden from view by the forest. Scarlett was in awe as she glimpsed the Forest Temple for the first time. It looked ancient—far older than anything else she'd seen so far in Clair de Lune. A worn-looking set of stone steps led to the entrance. Six columns dominated the building's façade. Illegible words were carved into the entablature lying horizontally across the six off-white columns.

"Who built this?" she asked.

"It was here before Clair de Lune became a proper country," said Manon. "The priestesses believe it was built by the Goddess herself or her ancient disciples."

Scarlett stared at the temple. "This is the first building ever erected in Clair de Lune?"

"Strong start, wasn't it?" Manon stared up at the building too. "It hasn't changed at all since I was young."

Manon led the way up the steps. The double doors at the top of the staircase were painted a deep blue and stood open, but there was no one in sight.

They walked into the main chamber, which was illuminated by ensconced torches lining the walls. The stone floor was pristine, and the white walls looked freshly plastered. A marble statue of a woman peering into a pewter cauldron dominated the room.

"Who is that?" asked Beni, pointing toward the statue.

"Cerridwen, the Goddess of Rebirth," said Manon. "When someone from Clair de Lune thanks the Goddess, this is typically who they're thanking."

In Soleil, "thank the Goddess" was more of a colloquial expression than a saying with religious undertones. At least, that was the case with the people Scarlett knew personally.

"Why is she in front of a cauldron?" asked Scarlett. Witch imagery was exactly the kind of thing people from Soleil found strange about Clair de Lune. Cerridwen could be making a potion to steal children's souls or something equally awful.

"That's her mirror of the soul," said Manon.

A mirror of the soul sounded slightly less sinister than what she'd imagined, but the cauldron was definitely a bit weird to Scarlett. Pushing her trepidation aside, she decided to trust her grandmother, but she couldn't help but ask, "What's a mirror of the soul?"

"It's where the soul lights come from. There's a longer myth about her and her children, but I forget the details of it."

As Manon spoke, a woman in a green dress emerged from one of the doorways, her brown hair swaying behind her back as she walked toward them. Manon pivoted toward her.

"Hello. I don't think we've met before. I'm Manon Bedivere."

The woman smiled. "My name is Gwen. Lovely to meet you."

Manon took the priestess's outstretched hand and then gestured to Scarlett and Beni. "These are my grandchildren, visiting from Soleil. As you can see, these two haven't yet met their soul lights, and we're hoping to remedy that today."

Scarlett shook Gwen's hand next. "I'm Scarlett Heroux. This is my brother, Beaufort. We call him Beni."

"Please don't call me Beaufort," grumbled Beni, and the woman laughed.

"Welcome to the Forest Temple," said Gwen. "I'd be delighted to help you meet your soul lights."

Manon's eyes lit with excitement as she rested a hand on Gwen's arm. "If it's not too much, Scarlett would like to manifest her valor today as well."

Gwen patted Manon's hand. "Of course. What an exciting day for you, Scarlett."

"Why is the valor only for Scarlett?" asked Beni.

Gwen gave him an apologetic smile. "Young people are too changeable for valor magic, so you have to be eighteen to receive your valor."

"Oh." Beni's brow furrowed.

"Manon, unless you have any questions, you can leave us to it for now and come back in a couple of hours."

"I'll go back to the castle in the meantime," Manon said to Gwen. "Good luck, you two." With a wave, she was gone.

Gwen's eyes were luminous. She had the air of an excited teacher about to chaperone a school trip, but her enthusiasm put Scarlett on edge. "Ready?"

They both nodded.

"Wonderful."

She led them down a long hallway, speaking to them as they walked. "We typically do a soul-light ceremony once a month for all the children in Clair de Lune and Evory who've recently turned ten, kind of like a birthday party. The young ones enjoy coming together."

"Sounds fun," said Beni.

"I feel better knowing most people are ten when they do this," said Scarlett.

Gwen came to a halt and shot Scarlett a dubious look over her shoulder. "Sometimes adults have a tougher time, but you never know until you try."

Scarlett stared at her, annoyed at the vague answer. "Why is it harder for adults?"

"Emotional baggage," said Gwen in a singsong voice.

Scarlett frowned but left it at that. She had so many questions, but she didn't want to ask Gwen any of them if she was going to get cryptic responses back. Had anyone ever walked away from the temple empty-handed?

Her internal worries were silenced as they came to an ancient-looking staircase at the end of the hallway. They descended behind Gwen to a circular door, which Gwen yanked open. On the other side was a torchlit room. Several large oil paintings were on the far wall, and a balustrade lined a ramp up to another doorway on the left side of the room. It looked harmless, yet the windowless room gave off an ominous feeling.

Gwen stood to the side. "Good luck, you two!"

"Thanks, Gwen." Beni walked through the door without a backward glance.

"On you go," said Gwen to Scarlett, who was still hesitating as she worried about all the things that could go wrong.

Scarlett steeled herself. She could do this. She jogged to catch up to Beni, who'd already stopped to look at a painting. The air was colder inside, and an old, earthy smell hit her as she halted next to her brother, her jaw dropping as she looked at the painting. It wasn't just a striking image of the Forest Temple and Mont Noir; there were people in the paintings who appeared to be moving as if they were alive. The little figures glowed like they were exuding moonlight. The people in the largest painting of the Forest Temple were dressed in tunics and laurels similar to what Scarlett had worn for her graduation months ago.

"These must be ancient," Scarlett said, full of awe.

"Hello," said Beni. He stood as close as he could to the Forest

Temple painting without actually touching it. Several of the figures turned to look at him. A couple of them moved toward Beni and Scarlett, and to Scarlett's shock, they became clearer and larger as they approached.

The painting unsettled her. "Come on, Beni. Let's keep moving." She grabbed Beni's arm. "Let's get to the mirror."

"Sorry—I have to go." Beni waved farewell to the painting as Scarlett hurried them up the ramp toward the door. The figures ceased their approach and waved back at him.

Scarlett let out a bemused laugh at the ease with which Beni moved through the ancient space. She was glad he didn't seem nervous. Was this what Gwen had meant about this being harder for adults? But her laughter faded as they moved into the next room.

The only way forward appeared to be through an archway hung with streamers of tattered beige cloth—so many she wouldn't be able to avoid touching them. The fabric moved as if there were a breeze coming from the other side, but of course there couldn't be a breeze. They were underground.

She only had to walk a few feet forward to get beyond the archway, but Scarlett was overcome with dread. Beni didn't hesitate before stepping into the arch. His footsteps slowed, and Scarlett began to panic as he halted halfway through the passageway.

"Are you all right?" she asked.

"I'm fine . . . but I can hear a voice," said Beni.

Concern for her brother overcame her fear, and Scarlett hurried forward. The air around her was electric as she joined him in the arch.

"True love is unconditional. Don't lie, even for love. Serve me through your love. I choose your desires for you."

She halted as the words touched a nerve. Her mind flashed to her father. Her father and Alastair. The two most important men from her past whose love had always seemed entirely conditional.

"*Stop striving for love that is conditional and give love unconditionally,*" the voice replied. "*Unconditional love is your birthright. To give and to receive.*"

Scarlett forced herself forward as her mind raced. Whose voice was that? And how had it—or they—cut right to the darkest fears of her heart?

"*Can you let go of your own insecurities, or will you forever serve the happiness of others? You've lied for years, to yourself and to those closest to you.*" The accusatory voice jabbed right at the most sensitive part of her soul. "*How can you connect with the divine if you can't be honest?*"

Scarlett tried to follow Beni, but she was frozen in place as if the voice had taken control of her body. She began to panic. Beni had moved out of sight. He was alone. *She* was totally alone.

"*Answer me.*"

"I want to be honest," she said out loud, terror coursing through her. "I regret lying to make other people comfortable."

"*Really? Then speak the truth. Or I'll not let you go forward.*"

She could hear the pounding of her own blood in her ears. "I . . . I don't want to go back to Soleil, but I'm obligated to return and finish what my father started. Is it lying if I return to help others?"

"*Self-sacrifice for the good of others is holy, but you must not lie to yourself. That was a good truth. Speak another one.*"

"I'm afraid my love for Brayden is unrequited." She'd never used the word "love." In the context of friendship, sure, but never like *that*. Not even in her own mind. It terrified her to cross that line, but deep down it was true.

He hadn't even wanted to kiss her, and she was in love with him.

"*Remember, unconditional love expects nothing in return.*" The voice had softened again.

Scarlett fell forward as she regained movement, landing on her hands and knees. *What the actual fuck was that?* She scrambled to her feet and ran out of the archway, looking for Beni.

She found him in the next room, standing in front of an enormous gilt mirror covering the far wall. The room was the grandest of them all, with a domed ceiling covered in filigree and frescoes. Scarlett halted when she saw a man with dark hair in the mirror. Two balls of blue light orbited his head.

Scarlett stood there uncertain she wanted to go on, her heart racing. She squinted, and her breath caught. The man in the mirror was . . . Brayden? She took a couple of steps forward. He looked different from the Brayden she'd seen earlier. Older, maybe? The man in the mirror beamed at her, and—yep, it was Brayden. She'd know that smile anywhere.

For the first time since entering the catacombs, fear and anxiety left Scarlett as she hurried toward him.

Was this what Beni was seeing? She tore her gaze from Brayden and looked at her brother. He'd approached another part of the mirror, to the right of Brayden, and had both hands pressed to the glass as he stared, transfixed, but Scarlett couldn't see anyone there.

Halting in front of the mirror, she stared at Brayden. Longing to touch him unfurled deep inside her, and her breaths became shallow. She took one last step forward, and when her foot hit the bottom of the mirror, her shoulders slumped as she touched the glass. She couldn't go any further, no matter how badly she wanted to. It reminded her of all the years she'd spent talking to Brayden through the glass. This Brayden gave her a crooked grin and stepped as close to her as he could. He put his palm up against hers. His messy brown hair and his warm brown eyes made her ache. This Brayden had a scar splitting his left eyebrow and laughter lines around his eyes. His eyes raked over her, the hunger in his expression mirroring hers.

"My beautiful Scarlett," he said, his deep voice full of adoration.

She searched his face for answers. "Are you real? You can't be. I know you're back at the castle, but you look . . ." She sighed as she took in his broad chest, covered in a black cotton shirt that emphasized how deliciously defined his arms and his chest were. But it was the way he looked at her that made her desperate. He looked at her like she was his love. Scarlett wanted to travel to whatever multiverse this version of Brayden existed in and run into his arms.

He grinned at her in that cocky way she knew so well. "I'm real. I don't live in this mirror—I'm just visiting from a different moment in time. I don't want to get metaphysical with you, because that's not why you're here, but time isn't linear, you know. I'm here because the universe knows we belong together, and so we are."

"That's . . ." whispered Scarlett, her cheeks heating. "How do you know? We've never even . . ."

He let out a throaty chuckle. "We will, Scar. We have, like, thousands of times in my timeline. Never doubt that I want you as much as you want me."

His words thrilled her. She was overcome with the desire to run back to the castle—to the Brayden she could touch. She wanted to give and receive the unconditional love the voice had promised.

"How do I make sure I'm on your timeline?" If she didn't end up in this version of the future, she'd be so disappointed.

"Bet on us, and you'll win every time. Always choose us. Not every path ends happily, but if you do that, we'll find our way." He looked over his shoulder at something she couldn't see. "Now, it's an honor to introduce you to your soul light. Scarlett, this is Nori."

One of the balls of blue-white light that had been fluttering around his head passed through the glass and floated toward Scarlett. She took a step backward as the light hovered in front of her face.

"Nori?"

"I've been waiting for you."

Scarlett jumped as the light spoke. Nori's musical voice was distinct from Scarlett's own inner voice.

"It's wonderful to meet you," Scarlett said. She had no idea whether she was supposed to talk to Nori out loud or in her mind. She turned back to the mirror, wanting to share her delight with Brayden. But he was gone.

Beni let out a loud laugh, distracting her. Was he brushing away tears? A light identical to her own floated beside him.

Noticing his sister's attention, Beni pointed to his light. "His name is Riley."

Sensing he might need comfort, Scarlett wrapped her arm around her brother's shoulders. "Mine's called Nori. Who did you see in the mirror?"

Beni's face crumpled, and he leaned into her. "It was Daddy." He hadn't called Jules that in years.

Scarlett's eyes filled with tears. She held Beni for a long moment, until he eventually pulled away.

"Was it nice to see him again?"

Beni wiped his eyes. "He seemed happy. It was . . . it was good."

Longing for her father stirred in her chest, but she was happy for her brother. "I'm so glad you have a new happy memory of him."

Beni sniffed as he ran his hand through his shaggy hair, but his eyes were filled with wonder as he stared at his light. "Yeah, me too. Who did you see?"

Scarlett hesitated, but Beni had just told her about seeing their dead father. "Brayden."

Beni's brow furrowed in confusion. "But he's not dead. How does that work?"

"It was a future version of him, I think. A possible future version, anyway. It was surreal." She wasn't ready to share all the details. Maybe she never would be.

"What *are* you?" asked Beni as he sat on the marble floor.

"What?" Scarlett joined him, folding herself into a cross-legged position. The mirror room was resplendent, and she was in no rush to go back through that archway.

"I'm asking Riley," said Beni.

"*I'll answer too,*" said Nori. "*I've been with you since you were born, talking to you in your dreams and planting happy and helpful thoughts in your subconscious. I'm pure divine energy, and I'm here to help you through your life in any way I can.*"

Scarlett glanced over at Beni. He was studying Riley intently, and she assumed he was in a similar mind-to-mind conversation. She focused on Nori.

How does this work? Can you see the future? asked Scarlett.

"*Time isn't linear for me. I see all the possible outcomes you could bring to fruition from this point onward.*"

Scarlett cocked her head to one side. *What, like Manon's oculus ability?*

"*Not exactly. I see more than she does, but I can reveal less, as I'm here to guide you, not to help you cheat at the game of life and personal growth. I'm also most attuned to your timelines, whereas her valor allows her to see the timelines of others.*"

A limited ability to see the future. Scarlett sighed. A desire to think something snarky rose in her, but not wanting to offend Nori, she moved on.

Can you tell me something about my most likely future?

"*In all your timelines, you've got lifelong connections to the Maddox family,*" offered Nori.

Am I going to marry Brayden someday? The embarrassing question had been in her heart since she'd spoken to mirror Brayden.

"*What do you think?*" asked Nori.

I think I'm excited to find out.

"*I'm excited too.*"

Scarlett held out her palm in invitation to the ball of light. Nori obliged, moving to hover directly over it. The light answered her unasked question as Nori moved *through* Scarlett's hand. There was a tiny amount of heat radiating from Nori, but that was it. She was a light without a body.

"What was that voice I heard in the archway?" Scarlett asked.

"The spirit of the Forest Temple speaks through the arch. The spirit is a vessel of the Goddess. Not to worry—you won't be held up on the way out."

She shuddered as she remembered the sensation of being frozen in place. It'd be more than fine if she never encountered that spirit again.

"Did you hear singing in the archway?" Beni asked Scarlett. "That's what I heard."

"No. A voice talked to me about unconditional love," she answered hesitantly.

"That sounds . . . boring. Are you going to be able to help me charge my phone?" was Beni's next question for his light.

Scarlett snorted.

Nori laughed at Beni's question, the sound like small bells tinkling. *"Yes, I can help you charge electronics. The universe is made of energy, and now I'll be able to help you harness it."*

After learning more about you, I can't believe the main reason I wanted to come here was so you could help me charge my cell phone, said Scarlett.

Nori let out her bell-tinkle laugh. *"I can't tell you how happy I am to meet you properly. If charging your electronics was the motivator to get you here, I'm glad of it."*

Scarlett found the courage to ask her most burning question. "Will I ever be alone again?"

"You've never been alone," said Nori. *"I've always been here. We're partners, but I'm also part of you. We don't have to talk all the time. I'm often a silent observer."*

Scarlett sent gratitude toward Nori. *You're so dazzling,* she thought to her light.

"*Thank you,*" Nori replied, and Scarlett heard her gentle laughter.

A thought occurred to her. "Beni, should we head back? Manon might be waiting for us by now."

Beni stood. "Yep. Let's do it."

They slowly began backtracking through the rooms with their lights floating along beside them. As Nori promised, Scarlett didn't hear any voices in the archway. The pictures full of spirits were still there, but she was so focused on Nori that she barely noticed them. She was enamored with her light's presence.

They soon arrived back at the green door, where Gwen was waiting for them. A little blue light bobbed around her head.

"Gwen, we did it!" announced Beni as they walked through the portal. "Riley is my light, and Scarlett has Nori."

"Well done, both of you," said Gwen as she led them out of the catacombs.

Now that Scarlett had Nori, she was much less resentful toward Gwen for being so cryptic. "That was quite the experience."

"Yes, it always is. What questions do you have?" Gwen asked once they'd returned to the statue of the Goddess near the entrance.

"How did this soul-light ceremony come to be? Who created it?" asked Scarlett.

"Excellent question. The Goddess, Cerridwen, visited Hieratia thousands of years ago and left a seed of her divinity in the foundation of this building. She also left a seed inside one other place on the continent, which is now the temple in Zahara. Visitors to the temples are able to connect with her and realize their divine power through that seed, if she allows it."

Divinity seeds. If you say so, Gwen . . .

Deciding to move on from that topic, Scarlett voiced her most burning question. "In the mirror, Beni saw our father, and I saw a friend. Our father died recently, and my relationship with my friend seemed quite different from how it is now—more developed, maybe? He looked older than he is now. Does the mirror show the past for some and the future for others?"

Gwen's look was knowing. "Are you unsettled by who you saw?"

"No. I saw a friend I care for deeply, but I was a little surprised with how . . . emotionally charged the exchange was."

The priestess's eyes twinkled with amusement. Scarlett struggled to hide her annoyance. This had to be something she was ignorant of because she'd grown up in Soleil, and she wished the priestess would just tell her the facts.

"Right," said Gwen with a twinkle still in her eye. "Typically, the mirror shows us someone who is the center of our world, either from the past or the future. For a younger person, it's usually a parent, but as we move into adulthood, it's often a dear friend or a romantic partner. We don't get a lot of adults here for the soul-light ceremony, but I've seen a handful from Soleil, such as you. I think because of the rarity of it, an urban legend has sprung up that you see your true love in the mirror—but rest assured it's not some heavenly decree that you *must* be with the person you see. You still have free will. Anything you saw in the mirror to do with the future is nothing more than a probable outcome, so don't get too fixated on it."

She saw Brayden's face in her mind. How could she *not* fixate on an urban legend about true love in the mirror?

"It's a lot to take in." Gwen studied Scarlett. "Do you have any other questions?"

Scarlett was about to ask about her valor when Brayden appeared in the doorway, followed closely by James. Both of their soul lights were hovering over their heads.

At the sight of Brayden, Scarlett's breath caught. *Goddess help me.* She wasn't prepared for seeing him so soon after that mirror experience.

Brayden looked charmingly disheveled. He hadn't shaved and was wearing his army fatigues. Scarlett wanted to run her fingers over the stubble on his face and feel the heat of him next to her.

What would he say if she told him about her experience in the mirror? He might find it off-putting. Men didn't like having expectations placed on them. Would he see her differently, in a bad way? She was frozen in place as he came closer.

"*Stop worrying. He's going to be happy about it,*" said Nori.

Brayden waved hello to Gwen, then he beamed as he took in Scarlett and Beni and their lights. "Look at you two."

"You're one of us now!" said James as he clapped Beni on the back.

Scarlett's heart warmed at her brother's answering smile. Even Gwen looked delighted.

"Yes, they're one of us now." Brayden swept Scarlett off her feet into a bear hug. When he set her down, he held his hand out to Nori, who obliged by hovering over his palm. "Look—she likes me."

His warmth helped Scarlett to relax a bit, though Brayden's eyes lingered on her, and she suspected he'd picked up on her weird vibe.

"What are you doing here? Where's Manon?" she asked.

"Manon sent us. We ran into her at the castle, and she seemed tired, so James and I offered to come instead. You're staying to get your valor, right?"

Scarlett looked to Gwen, who nodded. "Yes. That's the plan."

"I'm going to stay with you," Brayden said.

James gestured toward the door. "And I'm going to walk Beni back to the castle so he doesn't have to wait."

"Cool, thanks! Bye, Scarlett. Bye, Brayden. Bye, Gwen." Beni dashed off toward the door without a backward glance.

"Good luck." James waved farewell, and then he and Beni were gone.

"Shall we?" asked Gwen.

Brayden and Scarlett trailed behind her as she led them to a new passageway.

"So where's your valor tattoo?" Scarlett asked as they walked. "Manon showed me hers earlier."

"My left quad. I'll show you when we're alone." He gave her a wicked grin.

Trying not to show how much she liked *that* suggestion, Scarlett bit her lip. "Do you like it? The way it looks, I mean."

"I like it, but I keep it invisible most of the time. Most days I like to roll through life without a giant phoenix on my leg." He shrugged.

"Oh yeah, Manon mentioned valor tattoos can be hidden with magic. That does take the pressure off." She imagined the horror of a face tattoo she couldn't hide and chuckled to herself. "I hope my valor is cool though. And useful."

"Getting any valor is sick. I can't wait to find out what yours is."

His enthusiasm was catching, and Scarlett was full of nervous excitement for the ceremony as they followed Gwen. What secret power did she hold? The thrill of the unknown sparked inside her, and a grin tugged at her lips. She almost reached out for Brayden's hand, but she stopped herself, closing her fist. How long till he became the Brayden in the mirror? Five years? Ten? He wasn't hers yet.

She'd wait patiently. As patiently as she could.

And once he was finally hers, she'd never let him go.

CHAPTER (15)

The cozy underground room Gwen had brought them to was so warm Scarlett had to pull her sweater over her head, revealing the black silk camisole underneath. She clocked Brayden's eyes lingering on her chest and cracked a smile. His gaze met hers then, and his cheeks pinked up.

Catching him staring—and his embarrassment at being caught— bolstered her confidence in what she'd seen in the soul-light mirror. Their attraction was definitely mutual.

Oblivious to their silent exchange, Gwen approached a long table against the wall, covered in herbs, tuning forks, and a small set of bells. She lit some incense, and swirls of the musky-smelling smoke slowly filled the room.

"Scarlett, lie down on the table in the middle of the room. Brayden, if you want, you can stand on the other side and hold her hand."

Scarlett climbed onto the table. At least this temple experience

wasn't taking place in the creepy-as-fuck catacombs. Brayden stared down at her, his eyes shining in the dim candlelight.

Gwen moved to Scarlett's other side. "Right. I'm going to start chanting and ringing the bells until your valor comes through. It might take a while to get you in the necessary trance state, so don't fret if it doesn't happen immediately. Are you ready?"

"Yes." Scarlett's heart fluttered as she squeezed Brayden's hand.

Gwen began to hum a haunting, wordless song. Scarlett closed her eyes as she breathed in the incense and tuned in to Brayden's touch grounding her. Gwen rang the bell over her as Scarlett's thoughts started to drift.

Visions of Parliament and snippets of her father's most famous speeches flitted through her mind. Then *she* was the one in front of the podium speaking passionately and watching her colleagues stand and applaud. Scarlett radiated happiness as it played out in her mind's eye: The border issues came to a vote and passed; her colleagues patted her on the back and shook her hand, congratulating her on making her father's dreams come true. A sense of rightness rolled through her, and her father's presence was there with her in her moment of triumph. Soleil's future appeared in snippets as the country slowly opened to the outside world. Magic became more accessible. The world truly became a better place. She was full of bliss as it all unfolded.

Yes, this is what I want.

Lost as she was in her mind, the tingling just under her collarbone barely registered as Gwen continued to hum.

"There's the valor," whispered Brayden. "Below her clavicle. She's a vox."

Scarlett didn't open her eyes—she was too comfortable—but she could hear him, even if he sounded far away.

"It's beautiful," said Brayden into Scarlett's ear.

That's good.

"Hmm," said Gwen after some more time had passed. "I did wonder when you came with her—"

"What is it?" asked Brayden.

"A North Star wants to come through," said Gwen. "Normally, we'd make a little bit more of a to-do about a North Star ceremony, but we could do it today, given she's leaving soon, as I understand. Do you want it now?"

"Goddess above," said Brayden, tightening his grip on her hand. "It's too soon. Scarlett doesn't even know what that is—"

"Say no more. Perhaps the Goddess simply wanted you both to know of the possibility. You can explain it to her and come back another time."

"Could they disappear if we don't take the stars now?" asked Brayden, sounding tense.

"No, of course not," said Gwen with a laugh. "You're North Stars forever whether you manifest the runes or not."

"Yeah, that makes sense," said Brayden, sounding sheepish.

What are they talking about?

"*Relax,*" said Nori. *"He'll explain it later."*

Her light's words soothed her, and Scarlett drifted deeper again—so deep she was on the verge of sleep, Gwen's and Brayden's words already forgotten.

A loud *plunk* cut off the soothing bells.

"We're done. Scarlett, start wiggling your fingers and your toes. Open your eyes whenever you're ready, dear. There's some water and cookies on the table in the corner. Please help yourself." The sound of footsteps was followed by a door closing.

Scarlett did as the priestess suggested and tried to move a little bit. After a moment she opened her eyes to find Brayden hovering over her. She looked up at him, marveling at the intent way he stared back.

He brushed his hand against her cheek, his gaze soft. "That was easy, right? Congratulations. You're a vox."

"The easiest. That was . . . incredible. I had the most amazing dreams." Scarlett didn't move. "I've got the same valor as James?"

Brayden pointed toward a mirror by the door. "Come look."

He offered her his hand, and Scarlett took it, hopping off the table. The effects of the trance hadn't thoroughly worn off, and she moved slowly, her head foggy. She stood looking in the mirror, with Brayden behind her. Below her left clavicle was a delicate-looking sun made of thin lines and dots of golden ink. Little black stars freckled to the left and the right of it.

"It's so small." She traced the tattoo with her fingertip. "Is yours this small?"

"Mine is definitely not small."

She snorted at his joke, glad of the levity.

His fingertips grazed her arm. "But seriously, don't worry about the size. You make the valor special, not the other way around. You're such an incredible person, so you'll be an amazing vox. I have no doubt."

She smiled softly as they stared at each other in the reflection. Brayden's belief in Scarlett moved her even though he thought too highly of her. She wasn't special. All she did was work really hard.

"So you have fire because you're special. The fire doesn't make you special?" she asked.

"Mine's a weird one," he allowed. "I'm the only one in Clair de Lune with the phoenix valor. But still, if I was a dumbass with a phoenix valor, I'd be worthless. The valor is only as good as the one who wields it, is what I'm doing a bad job of explaining."

"No—your explanation makes sense." *Kind of.* There was definitely a hierarchy of some kind that he was at the top of, but she was willing to accept that personal attributes played a part too.

Brayden touched the sun lightly with his fingers, making her heart race. Even in the dim light of the underground room, it sparkled. "That golden ink—it's unique. Yours is much prettier than James's. You being a vox makes sense, you know. Usually, vox are persuasive and charismatic. It's perfect for a peer in Parliament. You'll shine like the sun."

Scarlett remembered what James had said about being good at giving speeches. That would certainly be helpful as she worked to pass the border legislation. The visions she'd had during the valor ceremony boded well if they were any indication of what was in store now that she was a vox.

"I guess I'm a lover, not a fighter, like James said."

Brayden's forehead creased as he worried his lip. Was it her imagination, or did he have something on his mind?

"Are you ready to get out of here?" he asked.

"Yes."

He put his hand on her back as they walked out of the room.

Upstairs, they thanked Gwen and departed from the temple. On the path back to the castle, Brayden and Scarlett walked side by side. The late-afternoon light filtered through the trees, as did the sounds of birds chirping. A sudden breeze made her shiver, and Scarlett was glad she'd worn fitted black pants and her favorite purple sweater, which, in addition to being warm, was covered in sparkly moons and stars.

"What's your light's name?" Brayden asked.

Scarlett looked up at him. "Nori. What's yours called?"

She held out her hand to Brayden's light, and the light came down to hover over her palm. Nori also flew to Scarlett's hand, and the two orbs circled each other as if they were saying hello. Scarlett laughed at the sight.

"His name is Jax." Brayden watched their lights hovering next to each other with a strange expression. "It's a little unusual for them to get so close to each other," he whispered. "This is also the only time I've had a friend meet her light when we've already been friends for over a decade."

"*I met Jax through the mirror,*" said Nori. "*We can talk through the glass just like you.*"

Scarlett repeated Nori's words out loud.

"Jax said the same thing," said Brayden.

"It's so fascinating that the lights are there even if you haven't learned to see them yet." She held her hand out for Nori, and her light came to her. "I want to know everything about them."

"I learn new shit about Jax all the time. The lights do it on purpose—withhold lessons or information until the right moment. Jax knows it frustrates me, but he has my best interests at heart, so I try to be calm."

Jax circled Brayden's head rapidly, forcing him to stop walking.

Scarlett laughed at Jax's antics. "How does Jax feel about you saying he frustrates you?"

Jax hovered over Brayden's shoulder as they resumed walking. "He's not surprised." Brayden grinned. "He usually says something annoying like 'trust divine timing' when I'm impatient."

"In the Forest Temple, I was told time isn't linear."

Nori's bell laugh sounded in her head. "*Are you going to tell him who said that?*"

Quiet! thought Scarlett.

"How *was* the Forest Temple for you? Who did you see in the mirror? Did you meet any ghosts?"

Scarlett's heart jolted. "Who did *you* see?"

He glanced her way before looking down at the path ahead. "My mam. It was incredibly sad, though I was happy to see her."

"I wish I could have met her." Scarlett took Brayden's hand and squeezed it.

"So, who was in the mirror?" he pressed. "Almost everyone I know saw one of their parents or a grandparent, but it's usually different for adults."

"No parents." She toyed with her hair as they walked.

He ran his hand through his hair. "Was it Alastair? Just tell me it wasn't James," he said, his tone full of dread.

Scarlett stopped in her tracks. "James? Why would it be *him*?"

Stopping too, Brayden barked out a relieved laugh. "So it wasn't him—good. I didn't *really* think it would be. James and I were talking about you going to the Forest Temple, and he was all, 'She could see her future husband. Or not. It might be someone she barely knows or doesn't even like, and then it'll be totally weird.' Then he told me how pretty he thinks you are. It rubbed me the wrong way."

He started down the forest path again, but Scarlett grabbed his hand, and he spun around to face her.

"So you don't like the idea of me being with James?" she whispered.

His brown eyes searched hers as he gave her a humorless smile. "I don't."

Still holding his hand, she took a step closer. "I wanted you to kiss me, and you said no."

"I told you, I won't be your rebound," he growled. "You just broke up with Alastair, and you're leaving soon. I don't want you to think I took advantage of your grief or something."

She believed him now, far more than she had the night he'd rejected her, but she wanted more. "That's considerate, but it also sounds like an excuse to let me down easy. Explain to me why you don't like the idea of me and James." She pushed him lightly to emphasize her point.

His grip on her hand tightened, and she squeezed it back. "No more theoretical situations involving my brother. Tell me who you saw in the mirror, and I'll tell you how I feel."

"Tell him the truth," said Nori. *"There's nothing to be afraid of."*

"You sound jealous. Are you jealous?" asked Scarlett. Despite Nori's reassurances, she wanted more from Brayden before she spilled her guts.

The wind picked up, blowing her hair across her face.

His gaze was locked on hers. "Okay, fine. I guess I'm going first. Are you sure you're ready to hear this?"

"Yes." She tensed, fearing he'd destroy her. But if he said what she needed to hear . . .

"I want it to be me. And if, for some Goddess-damned reason, you saw someone else . . ." His voice was rough with longing and jealousy.

Her answering smile felt as bright as the sun. "It wasn't someone else. It was you. No one means more to me than you do. It was always you." She searched his face, willing him to close the distance between them.

Looking like he was exercising every ounce of control he possessed, Brayden stuck his finger through the belt loop of her pants and pulled her closer until they were toe to toe. "Was it really me?" He stood so close his quiet words sent a shiver down her spine.

Scarlett nodded rapidly as she rested her hand on his stomach. His stare seared into her, and her heart raced.

Everything between them hung in the air. Years of wondering what would happen if they met; years of longing locked deep inside her heart. She'd always hoped for a pathway to this, even if she couldn't see how it would happen. She'd been through so much, but it had all led her here, to this moment. Touching him. Being with him. No glass between them. *Everything I've been through was worth it because it led me to you.*

"Scarlett . . ." His long eyelashes lowered as his gaze moved to her mouth. He looked like he wanted to devour her. She gripped the fabric of his shirt as he leaned down, and his mouth was warm as he moved his lips against hers.

Their kiss was soft at first, but as his remaining walls crumbled before her, she eagerly deepened it, burning with need as his tongue brushed against hers. His hot mouth—*Goddess.* She pressed herself to him, unable to pull him close enough. She needed all of him, always, right here.

Brayden's cedar scent enveloped her as she threaded her fingers in his hair with his mouth on hers. His hands gripped her waist, pulling her against him. The taste of him, their bodies pressed together—she was lost for good.

He's it for me. Nothing will ever compare to this. To him. A tingling joy coursed through her chest, and Nori's laugh sounded in response.

After a few long seconds, some rustling in the bushes behind them startled her. Scarlett reluctantly pulled back. She was getting far too worked up for being on a public path. Just as reluctantly, Brayden let her go. His piercing stare told her he was equally smitten.

"I've wanted to kiss you for so long." His cheeks were adorably pink.

"How long?" she said. "It can't be as long as I've wanted you to."

"I think since day one," he said with a laugh.

And with those words, her life's biggest question—did he really feel the same?—was answered.

Scarlett hadn't stopped smiling.

"I have so much to say to you," he told her, "but we can't stand here all day. Should we go back to my room and talk?"

"Yes," said Scarlett with an emphatic nod.

Brayden intertwined his fingers with hers, and they resumed their walk at a brisker pace.

Back at the castle, they were on their way to the privacy of Brayden's room when they spotted Manon and Lachlan in the ground-floor lounge. Scarlett sighed. She wanted to be alone with Brayden, but the excitement in Manon's eyes as she caught sight of Scarlett softened her irritation. Brayden squeezed her hand, and as Scarlett squeezed back, Manon's eyes flicked to their joined hands, and her lips pressed into a satisfied line.

"Your light." Manon beamed as she stood to greet them.

"Don't keep us in suspense," said Lachlan. "What's your valor?"

"I'm a vox." She pulled down the collar of her sweater, and they both peered at Scarlett's tattoo.

"What a gorgeous valor," said Manon. "A vox. I always wondered if Jules would've been a vox. He was such a gifted orator. We'll find you some books on your valor before you return to Soleil." She lowered herself into her seat slowly, like it was a struggle, and Scarlett watched her with concern.

Lachlan raised his bushy eyebrows as he studied Nori. "Congratulations on gaining your light and your valor." Like Brayden, he was dressed in olive-green slacks and a shirt of the same color, with a nameplate sewn into the breast that read "L. Maddox." Five brass stars were affixed below his name. "Please, sit with us for a moment."

"Thank you," said Scarlett, trying not to feel frustrated. All she wanted was to be alone with Brayden. But it would be silly to make an excuse and run off.

She and Brayden sat side by side on the couch across from Manon and Lachlan. Scarlett had to resist reaching out and resting her hand on his thigh.

"Where are James and Beni?" asked Scarlett.

"James is at work. He usually works late. His boss runs him ragged," said Lachlan.

"That sounds familiar," said Scarlett, thinking of her father.

"Beni is with the friends he met at archery practice," said Manon. "He didn't seem interested in hearing about valors when I offered to give him a lesson after he got back from the temple. Said he'd learn about it from those kids." Manon laughed, clearly pleased Beni had made some friends. That pleased Scarlett too.

"What's your valor, Lachlan?" asked Scarlett, realizing his was still unknown to her.

"I'm a specter," he said.

"His power is creepy," Brayden whispered in her ear.

Lachlan scoffed. "It's not creepy—it's extremely useful. I can dematerialize."

"He dissolves until his body is in a billion tiny pieces, like a Lachlan cloud, and then he can slip under closed doors as long as there's a tiny gap," said Brayden.

"Wow," said Scarlett. *That sounds useful for espionage.*

"*Truly,*" replied Nori.

"I'll show you sometime, if you like," said Lachlan. "I'd do it now, but I don't feel like having to put on all my clothes again. They fall off when I shift."

Scarlett forced the image of Lachlan getting dressed out of her mind. "I'd love to see another time."

"Anyway, I'm glad you've got some magic to take back home with you," said Manon. "It'll help you during this difficult time."

"I'm going to need more than a vox valor to help me take down Moira and Laylani. And figure out who killed my dad." Scarlett let out a growl of frustration. "I really believe they had something to do with Dad's death."

"I agree," said Brayden, his presence beside her solid and reassuring even though they weren't touching.

"Walk me through your logic, front to back," said Lachlan, his focus on Scarlett.

"I read a conspiracy theory in the paper that my dad's death was an inside job, and it made so much sense to me." A burst of energy ran through Scarlett as she spoke. Her gut told her it was all true. "The black market in Soleil lines the pockets of the police and Goddess knows who else in the government. That bribe money could easily flow to the bureau—or some of them, anyway. How is it possible they still have *zero leads* on the death of a prime minister? It makes more sense they're taking the dent to their reputation for money and power. What if some of those funds are lining Goldenrod pockets too? What needs to happen for them to keep making that money?" She looked from Manon to Lachlan, gauging their reactions. Manon looked stoic, and interest flickered across Lachlan's face. Scarlett turned to Brayden.

"The borders need to remain closed, and magic needs to stay illegal," said Brayden. His leg pressed against hers as they sat side by side, and his touch grounded her.

"And that's the Goldenrod Party's entire platform," said Scarlett in a quieter voice. "They claim they want to keep our citizens safe from the evils of magic, but it's really all about money and control. My dad thought so. I think so too. It makes perfect sense they'd have my dad killed right before he opened up Soleil. Moira, her party, the bureau, my dad's death . . . I *feel* it in my bones that they're all linked."

Lachlan rubbed his jaw as he stared off into space. "I've had dealings with the Goldenrod Party on occasion, and it's not hard to imagine you're right. If your father's murder was financially incentivized, there'll be a paper trail of some kind."

"Yes," said Scarlett, determination steeling her. "The evidence has to be out there. I just need to find it."

At the very least, the head of the Goldenrod Party had threatened her and worked with her stepmother to kill her. She'd start by proving that. If she was right about her dad's death, the whole thing was so much bigger.

Lachlan continued. "Trust your gut, and by all means look for evidence, but tread carefully. If you end up going up against powerful people who signed off on your father's death, they'll stop at nothing to avoid being exposed. And they'll have virtually unlimited resources at their disposal."

She knew that, but she appreciated his concern. "Yes, of course. I'll be as careful as I can."

"Dearest, don't forget, you are not alone in this," said Manon. "We'll prove it together. If we come up with a plan, I can use the oculus sight to check it."

"I'll help in any way I can," said Lachlan in a gruff voice.

"And me, obviously." Brayden nudged his shoulder against hers.

Gratitude washed over her as she looked at each of them. "Thank you. That means a lot." She couldn't resist leaning into Brayden, briefly resting her cheek on his arm before sitting upright once more. "By the way, I haven't seen the news today. Did anything happen while I was at the temple?"

"I read today's papers, and there's nothing new," said Manon. "Feels a bit like waiting for the axe to drop, but I suppose we should enjoy the calm while we can."

"Elestine will get my letter tomorrow, right?" asked Scarlett.

"Yes," said Brayden. "It'll be there in the morning."

"Then we'll have to wait a day before she can reply, so we might hear from her the day after," said Manon.

"The firewall is a pain in the arse," said Scarlett.

"Indeed." Lachlan gave her a small smile.

Scarlett stood, out of patience and desperate to talk to Brayden alone. "Today was full-on. I'm going to lie down, if that's all right."

"Rest well," said Manon.

"Congratulations again on your valor and your light," said Lachlan warmly.

Brayden rose. "Can I walk you to your room?"

"Yes, that would be great." Scarlett glanced at her grandmother. The older woman was studying her hands with great interest, and a telling smile tugged at her lips.

"Good night," said Scarlett with a parting wave.

Once they were safely out of earshot, she spoke. "I still want to talk. Doesn't have to be in my room though."

She hadn't seen his room yet and was actually dying to. The air was charged with the understanding they wouldn't just be talking as they walked side by side up the staircase to the second floor.

"I've got drinks in my room," he said.

"Lead the way."

He slid his hand into hers, and with a shiver of excitement, she gripped it tightly.

CHAPTER (16)

"Red wine?" Brayden asked once they were alone in his room. "I have that or whiskey."

Scarlett swallowed as she eyed the bed before sitting on the leather couch in front of the crackling fireplace. "Sure. Red wine would be nice." Her palms were sweating as she anticipated what would come next. Part of her wanted to study his bedroom, but she couldn't take her eyes off him for long enough to look at anything else.

He pulled two glasses and a bottle out of a small cabinet next to his desk and set them on top of a trunk serving as his coffee table. Their soul lights flitted around each other as he poured the wine. After handing Scarlett her glass and setting his own on the trunk, he kneeled before her to unlace her boots. "What are you thinking?"

The sweetness of the gesture plucked at her heartstrings. "So many things. It was such an overwhelming day." She took a big sip of her wine, anticipation coursing through her. Their first kiss had

been everything she'd dreamed it would be. But what did it mean? What *could* it mean, with everything happening in her world?

Brayden sat next to her and took his own boots off. Without warning, he picked Scarlett up and slid her into his lap as he stretched his legs along the length of the couch.

She was completely surrounded by his sturdy body. As she leaned against his chest, the contact relaxed her. Things were complicated, but he wouldn't be so affectionate if something were wrong.

"Is there anything specific you want to talk about?" he asked.

"I'm curious what's going to happen between us. Like, in general." She hated how trite the words sounded, but this was Brayden. She could be honest with him.

He dragged his rough fingertips gently over her forearm. "What do you want to happen?"

If she wanted to keep things simple, she'd ask him for another kiss, but that wasn't right. Not after the worries he'd expressed and what she'd seen in the mirror. She wanted to address some of the complexity between them. Her chest tightened as she tried to formulate an answer.

"Before my dad died, when I thought I was going to come for a visit, I hoped it'd be the start of something for us. Then I ended up fleeing here unexpectedly, but I was so damn happy to see you. I immediately started thinking about what might happen between us even though everything was chaotic. Of *course* I want you—you're my favorite person, and *look* at you."

His chest rumbled with quiet laughter against her, and she smiled too.

"You're my favorite person too," he whispered in her ear.

"That's good." She took a deep, shuddering breath. "I guess I'm just saying I get why you were hesitant. The truth is, if my life weren't such a mess, I'd want everything with you. But my life *is* a mess. I . . ." She took another deep breath. "I could come back when things calm down."

He was silent, but his fingers began kneading her tense shoulders. Something tight eased in her chest.

Scarlett went on. "We both know you belong here and I belong there. Lachlan needs you, and I have such a huge responsibility to Soleil."

His fingers moved down her spine. "So you're scared, but you want everything with me?"

She didn't miss the satisfaction in his voice. "You're oversimplifying, but yes."

He pulled her close to his chest once more. "I have something to tell you, but first, will you tell me what it was like when you saw me in the mirror at the Forest Temple? Tell me exactly how it felt."

"All right." Her curiosity piqued, she snuggled into him, reveling in the warmth of his chest against her back and his shoulders encasing hers. Joy filled her as his arms brushed against her and his masculine scent flooded her senses, but the happiness was bittersweet. In another life, this could have been hers every night. But right now, all they had was tonight. "You looked a little bit different. You had a scar on your eyebrow, right here." She twisted around to touch where the scar had been before settling back in his lap.

"What else?" he asked, leaning forward to rest his chin on her shoulder, his hair brushing her cheek.

The mirror room came back to her in a rush, and her voice was laced with longing as she went on. "It felt like you were mine. There was this depth to it . . . I've never experienced anything like it before. I wanted to climb into the mirror with you. I was desperate to touch you."

He placed a soft kiss on her neck, and Scarlett shivered. His lips on her skin . . . She was heartbeats away from turning her face toward his.

"What did you say when you saw me?"

"I asked why I was seeing you. The Brayden in the mirror said it was because we're meant to be."

"That's not intense at all, is it?" he said with a chuckle.

She laughed. "No, it was casual."

"Did it scare you, seeing me like that?"

"No. Does it scare *you*?"

"It excites me," he said without hesitation.

"You don't worry about how hard it could be? There are so many obstacles."

"Forget the obstacles for a moment. Do you want what you saw in the mirror?"

"I want it," she whispered, even as her mind screamed at her that this was a selfish thing to admit.

"Then tell me you'll stay awhile longer. Stay a few weeks at least. Be with me. Don't go running back into danger alone—not until you find a way to stay safe. That's the only thing that really matters." He spoke the words into her ear, and it made her body tingle as her heart pounded rapidly in her chest.

It was almost impossible to say no while she was nestled in his lap. "I'd love to stay. More than anything. But I have to go back eventually," she hedged. If only he could come with her. But she'd never be able to get him a visa. Not unless they got married.

She pursed her lips, chastising herself mentally. While the idea of marriage was less absurd than it had been that morning, it was still too absurd to speak aloud.

"Stay for now, and you'll return when it's safe." His arms were still encasing her, and he squeezed her gently.

"I'll certainly stay for the night." She smiled at her own dumb joke.

Brayden dug his fingers into her rib cage, making her squeal, and when she began to protest, turning in his arms to look at him, he twisted his face into a theatrical scowl, making her laugh.

"What were you going to tell me?" she asked once her laughter had died down. It was an obvious attempt to distract him, but he *had* teased her with something he wanted to say.

He relaxed his grip and pulled her back into his chest once more. "Do you remember Gwen mentioning North Stars?"

A hazy memory from the valor ceremony came back to her. "I'd forgotten, but yes. She said something about a North Star rune wanting to come through, right? What's a North Star?" She put her hands on his thighs, and he placed his palms over hers.

"How do I explain this . . . ?"

"Spit it out." She squirmed in his lap, wanting to see his face.

"No—stay." He circled her waist with his arms and pulled her tight against him.

She relaxed, surrendering.

He made a contented sound in his throat. "That's better. North Star runes appear for two people. Never one person. And as far as I know, they're always a couple. Gwen seeing North Star runes for us means we're twin flames. Goddess-blessed, fated mates. If we get the runes at the temple, we'll be able to hear each other's thoughts and possibly be able to share valor powers."

Scarlett digested this in silence. Was that why he'd kissed her in the woods—because they were fated mates? "Is this like seeing someone in the mirror? Because Gwen said the mirror doesn't always predict your true love."

"No, it's not like that," he rushed to say. "This is real. We're literally *it* for each other. And Scarlett, I told you when we kissed, I've had it bad for you for years."

She flushed with pleasure at his words, but she still didn't totally understand. "I love hearing you say that. But I belong in Soleil, and you belong here. How does the North Star change things?" Desperate to see his face, she turned in his lap. This time he didn't stop her as she repositioned herself so she was facing him directly. She sat back on her heels, still nestled in the V of his thighs.

His dark gaze met hers, and she saw the want in his eyes. Want and zero doubt.

He intertwined his fingers with hers and squeezed her hand. "You belong with *me*. That's what this means. We don't belong anywhere more than we belong with each other."

His words reminded her of Alastair. "*We're forever linked*," he'd said. She hated thinking of him at this moment, but he'd said similar things, and he was so wrong. What if Brayden was wrong too?

"How can you say that when you don't know what it's like to be with me?" she whispered. "What if you spend time with me in real life and you like me less?" It was the first time she'd spoken her deepest fear about Brayden out loud, and her throat grew thick, making it hard to swallow. Scarlett put her fingers to his lips before he could speak. "We're close, but we're not a couple. What if we're not sexually compatible, or you want kids and I don't? What if you can't stand how much I love to eat ice cream in bed?" She smiled, trying to lighten the mood and make him see reason, but he stared at her, his expression defiant. "How can you just accept that we belong together?" she said finally.

He shook his head. "That's not how it works. You don't get a North Star if you're incompatible in a major way. Besides, I already know you want kids, so that isn't a real issue."

Her heart fluttered in spite of herself. Brayden being hers on a cellular level . . . It was too good to be true. How could she make him see how imperfect she was?

Her heart fell as she realized what she could say to push him away. "I had my first orgasm last night with the sex toy Minnie gave me." She searched his face for a reaction, but he stared at her dumbly. "Wouldn't your ideal woman have had an orgasm before age twenty-two?"

His pupils dilated. "You mean after the party, when we said good night?"

"Yes. I went to my room and used a vibrator to get off."

He took his hands off her waist and ran his fingers through his own hair. "That is so fucking hot, thinking of you doing that alone in your room."

Disbelief mixed with relief flooded through her. *Is he serious? That's his reaction to my pathetic sex life?*

Nori's tinkling bell laugh sounded in her head, the only indication her light had been listening to their entire conversation.

Brayden stared at her. "But wait—your first one ever?"

"Ever."

"Wow." His face fell a little.

As she took in his expression, the fearful part of her that had always whispered something was wrong with her flared with recognition. She rushed to name it for him before he could say something that would hurt her more.

"See? It's sad, isn't it, needing a vibrator to figure it out?"

He shook his head. "No, no. It's not sad. I just hate thinking of you going so many years without one." Then he grinned. "If anything, the vibrator thing is a positive for me, because it means you're open to playing with toys." He winked.

She stared at him, dubious that he was completely unflustered by her darkest secret. Then she remembered the lies she'd told.

"Wait though—that's not the worst of it. I lied to Alastair about it for our entire relationship. He assumed I was having orgasms the whole time," said Scarlett.

Brayden's face broke out in a grin as he chuckled.

"You think that's funny?"

His grin faded. "It's not funny you had a hard time figuring it out." He pulled her closer until she was straddling his lap and rested his hands on her waist. "I laughed because I'm stupid-happy your first one with another person could be with me. If you're trying to scare me off, you're doing a terrible job."

"You don't think something's wrong with me for lying about it?" Her stomach turned as their proximity brought a flush to her cheeks. "What if I can't with you either? Wouldn't you be disappointed? Wouldn't you want to leave me?" Defenseless and exposed, she held her breath as she waited for him to reply.

He shook his head, his expression certain. "Alastair wasn't right for you. I *am*. I know you'd never lie to *me*. If you had an orgasm alone, we can have one together. If I watch you use that toy on yourself, that counts." He smirked. "And feel free to let me watch you use a toy on yourself anytime, day or night. That's officially my new favorite fantasy."

Laughing, she blinked away tears of relief. He didn't think she was weird or unattractive.

Brayden went on. "But seriously, I think you should let me try to get you off a few times before you start freaking out about not being able to orgasm with me. I don't mean to sound cocky, but maybe it's a pointless worry." He flashed her a devilish grin.

"And you don't regret kissing me? Are you still worried I'm not ready?" she asked. "Let's not forget, you rejected me only yesterday."

He shook his head, still smiling. "No regrets." His expression softened into seriousness. "The timing isn't ideal, but knowing what I know now . . . I don't think you're trying to escape from your pain with me. Because we're meant to be." His smile returned. "Also, finding out about your vibrator has eased my previous concerns. You seem ready."

All the half-baked points she'd been trying to construct to poke holes in the North Star concept floated out of her mind. She reached up, touching the stubble on his cheek. His gaze was open, full of want, as he searched her face.

Done with words, Scarlett softly pressed her lips to his. He responded eagerly, deepening the kiss with his tongue on hers. His fingers found their way into her hair. She pressed herself as closely to him as she could, and the thick length of him hardened beneath her. Their first kiss had been perfect, but now that she was unburdened, this one was even better. She'd thrown every doubt she had at him, and nothing had fazed him.

As she lost herself in Brayden, she moved against him, seeking friction, until the sound of her own moan startled her enough to make her pull away. His cheeks were flushed, eyes bright. He was so sexy and adorable at the same time.

Nerves fluttered in Scarlett's stomach. She felt so out of control. He was saying all the right things, and she trusted him, but it was so overwhelming.

She gave him a sweet but brief kiss. "I . . . I need time to process all this."

"Totally get it. You're all right though?"

"I'm still worried, but I'm also happy for the first time in a long time." Her lips curved up into a huge smile.

"Good." He swung his legs off the couch and stood with Scarlett still on his lap. Her legs straightened, and he set her down gently onto the ground. Her arms fell from his shoulders and threaded around his waist.

She needed to leave, but she didn't want to. The old feeling of wondering what he'd get up to after they said good night crept into her stomach and made it twist. "I don't want you to think I don't want you. I do."

He brushed his thumb against her cheek. "What are you saying?"

Her cheeks heated. "I don't *think* you're going to go to a bar and hook up with someone after what happened between us today, but I want you to know, if you did, it would hurt me." Even the idea of it made her chest tight. "Would it be unfair of me to ask you to stay away from other girls so I have peace of mind while I'm trying to sleep?"

He gave her a crooked smile. "No, it's not unfair. I'm yours, and do you know what that means?"

She pressed the side of her face to his chest. "What?"

He kissed the top of her head. "You're mine."

She grinned into his chest, elated. They were really doing this. "I'm yours."

Their words hung in the air. With a jolt, she flashed back to Alastair speaking those very same words in the alleyway where they'd broken up, but this couldn't be more different. Alastair had been pressuring her to stay with him as if he thought he was entitled to her. With Brayden, the words were reassurance. She didn't have to worry about his loyalty, because he was hers. It would be so easy to stay with him.

But she couldn't abandon her birthright. Too many people would suffer if she stayed in Clair de Lune and abandoned the Cerulean Party, leaving her father's seat empty for the foreseeable future. She needed space to think about how she could be with Brayden and still tend to the shit show that was her life in Soleil.

Scarlett forced herself to take a couple of steps away from Brayden and toward the door.

"Can I walk you back to your room?" he asked.

"I'll be fine," she said with a small smile. "I'll see you tomorrow."

"All right. Call me if you can't sleep. Or better yet, just come back." He raised his eyebrows suggestively.

She pulled him closer, allowing herself a few more seconds of his sweet lips on hers before she forced herself to walk out of his room and back to her wing of the castle.

After she'd showered, she put on a skimpy pair of pink silk pajamas

Manon had found somewhere on the Clair de Lune high street while Scarlett was at the Forest Temple. The pajamas were oddly fancy for a spontaneous purchase, but they were gorgeous, clinging to her curves in a pleasing way. Scarlett brushed out her hair, brushed her teeth, and washed her face.

As she lay in bed, she stared up at Nori and thought about what kind of a life she could see with Brayden. Present difficulties in Soleil aside, she could visit Clair de Lune during every recess, assuming Brayden was here during those times. He could visit her if the border law changed. But one of them would eventually have to compromise. Would he be willing to do it? She'd love to live in Clair de Lune, especially if she could visit Soleil regularly, but the idea of abdicating her seat in Parliament filled her with shame. She couldn't let everyone down.

"Everyone except you and Brayden," said Nori. *"No one should be a priority above you or him."*

True, thought Scarlett. *But I care about dropping the border.*

Then she thought about Brayden in the mirror and their kiss on the forest path. The way he'd grabbed her and pulled her to him. She was hit so hard with a wave of giddiness that she actually giggled out loud. Brayden was *hers*, after years of longing for him. He'd actually uttered the words "you're mine" about her. What was she *doing* in bed alone on the other side of the castle?

"That's more like it," said Nori. *"Go surprise him!"*

CHAPTER (17)

Scarlett threw back the covers and hurried to cover her pajamas with her trench coat. She stole into the hallway with only a pair of cotton socks on her feet.

Please don't let anyone see me.

"There was no one out earlier," Nori reminded her. *"You won't run into anyone."* The comment eased her anxiety over being seen as she hurried to Brayden's wing.

When she reached his room, she knocked softly. A second later, he opened the door wearing nothing but a pair of black drawstring pants. His eyes lit up as he saw her, and before she could say anything, he had her in his arms. The feel of his bare chest made her breath catch.

"What are you wearing underneath this coat?"

She let out a surprised cry as he picked her up and tossed her onto his bed. "Goddess above, not even a 'hello'?" she asked with a laugh.

He sprawled out on the bed next to her. "I'm glad you came back. I missed you."

She smiled as warmth pooled in her at the sight of him next to her. "I missed you too."

Brayden reached out and touched the collar of her coat. "Are you going to take this off?"

"Yes," she said with as much dignity as she could muster. She peeled off her coat and threw it to the floor.

He stared at her silk pajamas as she climbed into his bed, a low sound of approval rumbling in his throat.

"Now that we're alone, can I see your valor tattoo?" she asked.

He huffed a laugh. "If you want me to take my pants off, all you have to do is ask, Scar."

He wasn't wrong about her motivation. "I just did, Brayden. But I really do want to see the tattoo too."

Brayden chuckled as he sat up and slid off his drawstring pants, revealing a pair of boxer briefs underneath. He flopped back down onto his bed, ready for her inspection.

Scarlett swallowed as her gaze slid to the tattoo on his left thigh. Rising to her knees, she moved to get a closer look. The black-and-white tattoo of a bird made of flames covered his left quad. His muscular legs had a light dusting of hair that tickled her fingers as she traced the valor.

"It's such a badass valor. Do you love being able to make fire?"

"Yep." He held up his palm, and flames sprouted all over his hand. "They can get *really* big." The little flames flared as if they concurred.

She gazed in wonder at his magic, unlike anything she'd ever seen in Soleil. "How big can they get? Have you ever run out of fire?"

"I haven't pushed myself far enough to run out. Hopefully, that'll never happen. I get exhausted if I use it too much though. I'll show you how big they get as soon as there's a chance. There are these gorgeous hidden pools up in Mont Noir. If we go up there, I can heat them up by doing a naked cannonball into the water while I'm on fire."

She laughed. The idea of seeing him naked outside was taking her fantasies to the next level. "That's incredible. I can't wait to see it." She reached for his hand, stopping when she was close enough that the heat from the flames warmed her skin. She tried to touch the fire with a single finger, but Brayden pulled his hand away, and the flames disappeared.

"It'll burn you."

Her face heated. "Guess that was kind of dumb of me."

He grinned. "Yep."

Scarlett stuck her tongue out at the playful jab and then lay back down, this time curling up against Brayden and threading her leg through his. His warmth surrounded her as he began to stroke her hair, and she sighed happily.

"Does a Phoenix have any other cool powers?"

"I told you I'm hard to kill. What I didn't tell you is I can theoretically come back from the dead."

Scarlett stared at him. "Seriously?"

"Freaky, right? I haven't died and come back myself, thank the Goddess, but there are documented instances from the past where firebirds have died of unnatural causes and woken up hours or days later mostly healed. There are hard limits, of course. Please don't cut my head off."

She stiffened as the day of the assassination came back to her. The car, the blood . . . If it had been Brayden who was shot, could he have survived that? The idea of him testing the limits of his magic that way made her stomach clench.

"Will you live longer because of your valor?"

"No. I'll still age and die," said Brayden. "I don't want to live forever. I would hate to outlive everyone I love."

The fireplace was all but extinguished, the dying embers and the faint glow emitted by Jax and Nori the only illumination in the room.

"I'd hate that too. It's nice you can't die suddenly like my parents did," said Scarlett as she trailed her fingertips over his bare chest. "Is it fucked up that was the first thought I had when you told me?"

"No, it's not fucked up." He held her closer. "It's one reason why we should consider getting the North Star runes sooner rather than later. Especially if you insist on going back to Soleil alone. I'm terrified of losing you."

"You won't lose me," she whispered.

"Life is far from safe for you."

"I'll be careful. I'm way too bent on revenge to die," she joked, trying to lighten the mood. It was late, but Scarlett wasn't tired.

"I won't let you die," he said solemnly, and she didn't respond, not wanting to point out that he wouldn't be there.

Brayden spread his calloused fingers over her thigh, gripping Scarlett to him. "Someday you'll open the borders, and then I'll come to Soleil. When I do, what's the first thing you'll show me?"

Scarlett bit her lip as she touched his collarbone with the tips of her fingers. She could happily spend hours examining every inch of his body now that he was close enough to touch. "I'd *love* to take you to Lilac Beach. I could teach you to surf, if you want."

"I'd love that," he whispered.

"Before anything happens, I get a birth control shot every three months," she blurted out. "I got one two months ago, so I'm still covered. And Alastair and I were only ever with each other. But maybe you didn't want to know that." She covered her face with her hands. "Goddess, I'm sorry. Was that an overshare?"

"It's okay," said Brayden. "Intimacy is built on transparency, and I want that with you. And just so *you* know, I *have* been with people other than Alastair."

Scarlett smiled in spite of herself as she slapped his shoulder playfully. He chuckled, grabbing her hand and kissing her palm.

"Okay, in seriousness, I haven't been with anyone since you started talking about coming here to visit a few months ago. As of my summer solstice doctor's appointment, I'm also clean. Although, fun fact—as a phoenix, I can heal from all things, including venereal disease. But I get the checks because we have to see the army doctor biannually anyway."

"So who was the girl from a few months ago? Anyone I know?" She'd meant the words to sound casual, but it came out jealous. "Sorry, I shouldn't ask that." She rolled off his chest and onto her side, facing away from him so she wouldn't have to see his reaction.

Brayden pressed himself into her back as he grasped her chin gently and forced her to look into his eyes. "Hey, no one has ever meant more to me than you do. You were just thousands of miles away. And taken. I stopped seeing other girls the day you came up with a plan to get here. I've been waiting for you, hoping *this* would happen as soon as we met." He gestured to his bed. "And not just this," he said quickly. "I used to fantasize you'd come to visit, fall in love with Clair de Lune—and with me—and never leave."

He wanted her to love him? His fantasy was so similar to hers . . . Scarlett's embarrassment melted away as their gazes met.

"I don't usually get jealous," she said. "It's such an embarrassing emotion."

Brayden slid his arm around her waist and pulled her back into his chest. "Well, it looks adorable on you," he whispered in her ear. He was silent for a moment before he went on. "I'm flattered you're jealous, and for what it's worth, I'd love to travel back in time, punch Alastair in the face, and take his place as your first everything."

"Would you?" Her voice purred with pleasure.

"You have no idea how obsessed I am with you. You want the truth?" he asked.

"Yes."

"I want you so much I can barely act normal around you, and these little scraps of cloth you're wearing to bed?" He tugged at her shorts. "I want to be the only one you've ever worn them for. I'm dying to bury myself inside you so deep you forget there was ever anyone else."

Her breathing became jagged, and a surge of need rose in her. "Jealousy is adorable on you too," she whispered. "And if it makes you feel better, these are brand-new pajamas."

Brayden shifted, something hard pressing against her arse. She ground herself into him and was rewarded with a quiet groan. Brayden tightened his arm around her, brushing the peaks of her breasts through her silk camisole. The heat that had been building since they'd gotten into bed spiked white-hot in her. It was an ache she didn't want to ignore.

Scarlett slipped her hand behind her back and ran it over the thick length of him, covered only by a thin layer of cotton fabric. Brayden groaned as he pressed himself into her palm. Scarlett thrilled at his response. It made her feel powerful, him wanting her so. The heat continued to build. Her breasts were heavy with need.

When Scarlett withdrew her hand, Brayden stilled, but when she pulled the silk camisole over her head, he let out a low, rumbling growl. She moved his hand to her hypersensitive breast and pressed her arse into his erection.

Brayden kissed her throat while he fondled her breasts.

What if I can't finish with him?

Scarlett wanted things with Brayden to be different. She'd had an orgasm; now she wanted to come with him. It would break her heart if she couldn't. But the pleasure was already building, begging her to detach from her racing mind, so she shoved the depressing question aside and let herself be in the moment.

The way he rubbed her nipple . . . He was running his thumb over it so slowly, but the sensation was creating so much heat in her that she let out a moan, surprising herself.

"You like that?" he asked in a throaty voice.

"Yes—it's perfect. But I also want you inside me," she said softly.

He slid away and moved lower on the mattress. Brayden waited for her permission, and once she'd nodded, he slid off her pink shorts and nestled himself between her legs. She ached at the sight of his brown hair tousled from where she'd run her fingers through it. Threading one arm under her leg and resting his hand on her stomach, he used his other hand to graze his fingertips over her inner thigh, toward her entrance, and she gasped as he inserted one finger. It slid in easily, and she shivered with pleasure, gripping his forearm as he increased it to two.

"You're so perfect," he murmured, staring between her legs as he touched her.

Scarlett clenched around him and ground herself into his hand as he moved his fingers in and out of her slickness. Need built up in her body, and she let out another quiet moan.

At first, she watched as he touched her, marveling at how focused he was on her body, in no rush to find his own pleasure. He withdrew his fingers, but before she could protest, his tongue was on her, and she gasped, shocked by how good it felt.

Scarlett closed her eyes as her head fell back on the mattress. With both his arms now threaded beneath her legs, his fingertips found her breasts, and he circled the tips of her nipples as he continued to taste her.

"You're so good at this." She praised him with her eyes still closed. The vibrator had revolutionized her sex life, but it couldn't compare to this beautiful man working her over.

Lifting his head, he dotted kisses over her inner thighs. "I'm glad you like it. Want me to do anything differently?" he asked before licking hard against her hot core. His fingers continued to caress the buds of her nipples, the sensation driving her wild.

"The way you're touching me . . ." she panted. "Keep going. That's incredible."

As his tongue massaged her clit, he drew bursts of pleasure from her nipples. Scarlett rocked against his tongue. It could have been seconds or minutes she was so lost in his touch.

She *needed* him, and knowing it was Brayden licking her—she was so hot—her body tensed, and a sudden wave of pleasure overtook her, surprising her.

Scarlett moaned, gripped his strong forearms, and clamped her thighs to the sides of his face, riding the wave of her orgasm as it crashed over her. It was so different from the vibrator. *How* was it so different? Nothing else would ever satisfy her after this.

She collapsed back, panting.

"Did you just come for me?" Brayden asked.

Opening her eyes, she beamed at him. "I *did*."

His answering smile was delighted.

She held out her arms in an invitation. Brayden crawled toward her until he was next to her on the bed. She grasped him eagerly, pulling him closer. Her fingers wove into his hair as she leaned in for a kiss.

She could taste herself on his warm lips as she slid her tongue over his, and she loved it.

Pulling back, she stared into his eyes. "That was mind-blowing— the hottest experience of my life."

"You're stunning," he murmured, still hard against her thigh as she rubbed herself against him. "Also, that didn't seem especially difficult." There was a wicked glint in his eye.

Her smile grew, and she nodded. "I can't believe I just came. You're . . . very talented."

He chuckled. "I'm happy to go down on you literally anytime you like. Your pussy is paradise to me."

"I'm ready now," breathed Scarlett, pushing at him gently until he was flat on his back.

His eyes lit up. "Ready for another orgasm?"

"I'm ready for the part where you bury yourself so far inside me you forget everyone else."

"Yes, please," he said, his dark eyes full of hunger.

Rising to her knees, she slid her fingers across his stomach and under the waistband of his briefs, pulling his boxers down over his legs. Brayden lifted his hips to aid her. Scarlett bit her lip as she studied his naked body, following the tantalizing trail of hair down his stomach. He was rock-hard, and she touched the soft skin with her fingertips as he stared at her. His eyes blazed with intensity as he met her gaze, and she got the distinct impression he was struggling to wait for her to come to him.

Scarlett straddled him. He pulled her closer and took her nipple in his mouth, licking and sucking her breast greedily, until she pulled back, too desperate with need to wait any longer.

"Can we?" Scarlett asked, looking down at where they were touching but not yet joined.

"Fuck yes."

She hovered over him, and he grasped her by her backside with one hand as he used the other to guide himself into her. Scarlett's breaths quickened as they joined, her body welcoming him as he slid into her fully. At the same time, somewhere in the depths of her soul, her love for him deepened. Brayden was inside her, looking up at her, and she'd never felt so sure about anything as she was about him.

She was drenched, and the gliding sensation, coupled with the feeling of fullness as she began to ride him, built a wave of pleasure in her again. As she ground onto him, chasing that building sensation,

Brayden's breathing became jagged, and Scarlett leaned forward, panting as she bounced up and down.

"You feel so good." With his strong hands on her hips, he thrust into her as she moved on him.

"I love this," she said breathily.

He was hers. Every second he spent inside her made her more certain she was never going to love anyone but him. She wanted him to come. Everything was so perfect—she just wanted him to be satisfied with her too.

Scarlett bent over him, licking his neck as she continued to grind against him. Suddenly, he gripped her hips harder and forced her to still.

"I'm about to come, and I don't want to yet."

She grinned into his neck. "I don't mind if you do." She wanted to give *him* pleasure now.

"*I* mind," he growled.

Before she knew what was happening, Brayden had rolled her onto her back. He hovered over her, holding his upper body up with his forearms, which rested on either side of her. Scarlett wrapped her legs around him, grasping him as closely to her as she could. He kissed her as he drove into her again—slowly at first.

The way he made love to her, so unhurried, had her completely undone. Sex was so different with him. She wanted it to be like this always.

She grasped at him, dragging her nails over his strong back and moaning as she encouraged him. "You're so good, I can't . . . I need it harder now—"

He thrust harder, faster, possessing her as he slammed into her. She clenched on his cock, wanting to keep him and please him.

"Fuck, Scarlett, that's so good. I can feel you—" Brayden pulled out, and she hated the loss of him. But then, as he continued to hold himself above her with one arm, his thumb was at her entrance and on her clit, gently circling as he slid all the way into her again.

Gasping, she melted into the bed. His thumb teased her clit with her own wetness, and she was lost as he moved in her.

"You look like you want to come again, sweetheart. Can you come again for me like a good girl?" he whispered.

His words alone almost drove her over the edge.

"I think so." The words came out in a raspy voice she hardly recognized as her own.

"That's right—come on my cock. Come for me. I don't care how long it takes." He thrust into her again as if to emphasize his point, causing her to cry out. "I love fucking your sweet pussy, and I can't stop till you come for me."

Scarlett had never been more aroused, her whole body begging for release. She wanted to be his good girl and come for him. His deep voice and those words, paired with the unrelenting pleasure of his hand and his cock, his scent—it all pushed her over the edge again. Scarlett moaned his name as she pulsed on his length. A wave of bliss flooded through her core as she came.

Some part of her had sensed—*hoped*—sex would be special with him, but she'd never dreamed it could be this good.

When she opened her eyes, he was staring down at her. "You're gorgeous when you come." He'd pulled his hand away but was still moving in her slowly.

Jax and Nori were above Brayden's shoulders, circling each other in the dark.

"You've ruined me for anyone else."

A wicked smile spread across his face. "That's what I was going for, beautiful."

"I want you to come too," said Scarlett.

"Where do you want me to come?"

"Inside me," she said without hesitation.

Her words seemed to undo him completely; he moved in her like she belonged to him. She wanted to. She wanted him forever.

Brayden pounded into her. Just when she was sure it couldn't get any better, he gripped the headboard behind her and tilted her pelvis up to keep thrusting, reaching a new depth inside her. She let out a low moan as pleasure rolled through her, deep within, and she came again.

"Another orgasm? What *was* that—?"

Brayden went rigid and slammed his mouth against hers as he spilled himself inside of her. He collapsed on top of her, panting hard, and Scarlett grasped him to her, wishing she could hold him in her like this forever.

I'll love you till the day I die.

The sudden and complete certainty of the realization shocked her. Tears spilled from her eyes as she took deep breaths, still underneath his comforting weight.

Brayden leaned back, a cocky grin on his face. But when he saw her expression, his brown eyes searched her face. He slid off, taking her into his arms.

"Are you all right?"

"I've never been better," she sniffled.

"Why the tears?" He tilted her chin up and brushed them away with the tips of his fingers.

"I believed for so long something was wrong with me, but with you, just now, everything was perfect. So perfect. I can't believe I'm crying after sex. I swear I'm not usually like this." She attempted to smile and let out a long sigh.

"That sex was perfect for me too. There's absolutely nothing wrong with you. Trust me, you're a goddess. And it's so different with someone you love, right?"

Is he saying he loves me?

His gaze flew to hers, and she nodded. She did love him.

"I'm afraid I'm feeling too much," she admitted.

"It's not feeling too much, because I'm feeling it too." He squeezed her tighter to him. "I think I've loved you since we were kids—since that first time in the middle of the night when I saw you peering into the mirror looking so curious, with your gorgeous blonde hair wild around you. I think it's safe to say you own my heart and my soul, and you always have," he whispered.

Several more tears spilled down her cheeks, and Brayden kissed them away.

The intimate gesture gave her courage. "I dream about you all the time. When I'm in that place between sleep and awake, it's like I'm always looking for you. It's been that way for years," said Scarlett, her throat thick. "I love you. I know it's too soon, but I do."

His hand moved up and down her back in long, soothing strokes. "Shh," he said, trying to calm her. "It's not too soon. I'm right there with you. I love you too—truly, I do. You saw me in the mirror when you met Nori, and we're North Stars." He leaned in and pressed his lips to hers. "I knew it before, through the mirror. This pull to you was always in the back of my mind, pushing me to speak to you, making me dream about you. I've had so many dreams about you too. I've wondered so many times what we could be. My love for you runs so deep."

Scarlett burst into tears of relief. Her embarrassment melted away, leaving only shining joy as he kissed her languorously for a long time.

Brayden broke away. "I'll be right back," he murmured. He slipped out of bed, and she was instantly chilled without his body next to hers. As he crossed the room to the bathroom, his strong, naked body brought her desire bubbling to the surface again, shocking her with its refusal to subside.

When Brayden reemerged, she took his place in the bathroom. As she gazed in the mirror, she almost didn't recognize herself. This version of Scarlett had a tattoo, her hair was a mess—she *looked* like she'd been thoroughly fucked—and her reflection radiated happiness.

She climbed into his bed, her limbs heavy.

"Let me hold you." Brayden arranged her so her back was to his chest. He draped his arm over her, and their legs intertwined.

She was in a total state of bliss—until she thought ahead to what would happen in the morning. How could she leave him here? She fell asleep thinking about Soleil.

Scarlett awoke in the dim light of Brayden's room. She stretched her naked body and reveled in the delicious sensation of his arms around her.

Brayden stirred. She repositioned herself, threaded her leg through his, and burrowed into his warm chest.

"Good morning, gorgeous," he said into her hair.

"Mmm. Last night was—"

"Everything." His fingers moved along her bare back.

Brayden had just begun sleepily fondling Scarlett's breast when a brisk knock at his door startled her, and his eyes flew open. He leaned down to kiss her before stepping into his boxers. She pulled the blanket up to her chin. Who was about to catch her in his room?

Brayden opened the door a crack.

"Good *morning*," James said cheerily. "It's 8 a.m. No morning run? Any reason why?" His chuckle was audible through the door.

Scarlett's shoulders relaxed. James was preferable to Manon, Lachlan, or Beni.

Brayden blocked the room from view with his body. "I don't have to be on base until midday today. What do you want?"

"So it's a coincidence Manon can't find Scarlett and you're sleeping past six for the first time in months?"

Scarlett sat up. *Shit.* How worried was Manon? Especially after recent events.

"Not a coincidence. Scarlett's here with me." Brayden's voice was edged with warning.

"Can I come in and say good morning?" James's voice rang with false innocence.

"No chance, dipshit," snarled Brayden as Scarlett yelped, "No!" from his bed.

"Nice to see you two are exploring the connection," said James, amusement in his voice.

"Is there something you need, or are you just here to be an asshole?" asked Brayden.

"I'm leaving for work in an hour. Scarlett, I heard you're a vox," he said through the crack in the door. "Do you want to come to work with me today? You could learn more about your valor and do some networking."

"Ooh—yes!" called Scarlett from the bed.

"Dad's looking for you, by the way."

"Thanks. Now fuck off, please," said Brayden as he shut the door.

Scarlett already had her pajamas on. "I'm going to go find Manon."

"Before you go . . ." He reached for her as she pulled the trench coat on over her pajamas.

She threaded her arms around his waist. "Yes?"

He pressed a kiss to her forehead. "After last night . . ."—he kissed her on the mouth—"I hope you'll stay in Clair de Lune longer than you planned. I want you to stay." He searched her face.

She stiffened in his arms and looked up at him, wishing she could do what he wanted in good conscience. It was tempting. Of course she wanted to stay with him. But he *knew* she couldn't. Sure, he'd given her three orgasms last night, bringing her lifetime total up to four, but that didn't give him the right to ask her to stay. He didn't even have the decency to phrase it as a question, and for one unholy moment she was reminded of Alastair and all his pushy opinions about what *he* wanted her future to be.

As Brayden waited for her answer, his gaze dropped to the floor, and he took a step back, folding his arms over his chest.

She took a deep breath, calming herself. Brayden was *not* Alastair. He just believed they were North Stars—whatever that was—and was letting himself get a little too protective. Normally, she'd adore that coming from him. But she had to go back to Soleil. There was no other way, or else she'd be damning her country to a magicless existence, and her stepmother would go free. She wasn't about to let Laylani and whoever she was working with get away with what they'd done. If Scarlett didn't believe her presence could make a difference, she'd pack it all in and stay in Clair de Lune for good. But in her heart of hearts, she knew she could change things. And if her gut was right, she could also get revenge for what Laylani and Moira had done to her and her family.

"I can't," she said finally, her tone firm but her expression pleading. "I love you, but—" She stepped closer to Brayden, but he moved out of reach.

"You won't put your own safety first? For me? It makes me sick, the idea of you going back there."

"I *want* to put you first. I'd marry you to get you into Soleil." The words slipped out of her mouth without hesitation.

His eyes blazed with anger. "You'd marry me to get me into Soleil? The proposal I've always dreamed of. You're only suggesting that because you can't have me *and* revenge, so you're compromising."

He was right, but she hated the way he was throwing it in her face.

Brayden exhaled loudly. "My options are to let you risk your life alone or have a visa wedding neither of us is ready for." He spun away from her. Running his hands over his face, he snapped, "We shouldn't have slept together."

"You regret sleeping with me?" It had been the best night of her life. His regret was like a knife to the heart.

He pulled a T-shirt over his head and then fixed his gaze on her. The hurt in his eyes was a mirror to her own. "I underestimated how hard this would be. Finding out you're my North Star—my *Goddess-blessed* North Star—and having you for a night, just long enough to realize how fucked my life would be without you, and now you're going back without me? You'll be alone in Soleil with your little brother and the stepmother who tried to kill you, and I won't be able to save you when they come for you again. I regret having you for one night only to lose you."

Her heart ached. "It'll kill me to leave you, but I have to do the right thing. If I walk away from Soleil, I'll hate myself." She blinked back her tears, refusing to break down. "You're right—we shouldn't have had sex last night," she said in a tight voice, her stomach in knots. She only regretted it because he did, but it was regret all the same.

Before Brayden could say anything else, she fled. Maybe she'd found the flaw in their so-called fated compatibility after all. If this ended them, he couldn't have been more wrong about what it meant to be North Stars.

But being right wouldn't make losing him hurt any less.

CHAPTER (18)

Scarlett flung open the door to her room. She was eager to change and possibly cry before her grandmother found her. But before she could do any of that, her gaze met Manon's.

Scarlett's face heated as Manon peered at her from her armchair.

"Goodness," said her grandmother. "Do you have anything on under that trench coat, or am I about to get a free show?"

Nori didn't say anything, but she radiated sympathy, and Scarlett's cheeks grew hot. Any other moment and she'd laugh at her grandmother's joke, but right now, no. Right now she wanted to stare into the void in solitude after the fight she'd just had.

"Sorry," said Scarlett as she stepped into the room, closing the door behind her. She faced away from her grandmother until she had her emotions under control. Then she spun around slowly, feigning embarrassment rather than distress. "I can't think of a dignified excuse for my attire." She peeled off the coat and laid it over the back of a chair before wrapping herself in a fuzzy blanket.

A breakfast tray sat on the table in front of Manon with a pot of what was hopefully coffee, and Scarlett sat in the armchair across from her.

"Those pajamas are gorgeous on you. So, you and Brayden?" Manon raised one eyebrow.

Scarlett resigned herself to her grandmother's nosy but well-intentioned questioning. "I saw him in the mirror at the temple. And Gwen said we're North Stars," she said, barely managing to not sound distraught. Last night she'd have been thrilled to tell Manon, but this morning, after their awful fight, the words tasted bitter in her mouth.

Nori darted around Manon's light.

Manon's eyes sparkled as she stood and pulled Scarlett into a hug, her peony perfume enveloping her. "What wonderful news. I'm so happy for you both." She rubbed Scarlett's back for a long moment, making Scarlett suspect she hadn't hidden her feelings as well as she'd thought.

"I'm happy, but I don't know how to handle it with everything going on," Scarlett whispered in her ear.

Manon pulled back and met her gaze. "You're strong enough to handle anything, and the North Star bond is a blessing, so chin up." She beamed at Scarlett encouragingly as they both sat back down, but Scarlett struggled to return her smile. Hearing her grandmother talk about the North Star bond reminded her of Brayden's assuredness, and she was having a hard time with unwavering faith in something she didn't understand. She wanted to believe, but all she had was the faith of others to go by.

Manon picked up a sausage roll and took a small bite.

Scarlett closed her eyes, inhaling the rich smell of the coffee, and took a long, fortifying sip. She needed to know more, but she wasn't sure any answer would satisfy her if it was based on old myths. But she *had* just experienced magic firsthand in the temple. Maybe the North Star bond was real. She had to try to understand.

"Do you really believe all the North Star stuff? Brayden told me this means we're *it* for each other. But then we had a horrible fight this morning over me going back to Soleil. What if the timing is wrong and we don't make it because of my responsibilities back home? I'll be devastated if I lose him." Her throat became thick as she held her breath waiting for Manon's answer.

"The temple mirror wasn't a guarantee of permanence, but a North Star rune is never wrong. Brayden is afraid of losing you. You can't blame him for the angst, given recent events. He loves you too much to lose you. And you love him too. That's the only answer you need."

Scarlett let out a shuddering sigh. "I do love him."

"Of course you do. And that's beautiful. Life is full of the possibility we might all end up devastated. Love makes it worth throwing yourself into the fray. Hang on to Brayden with both hands and don't let go. That's my advice."

"Hang on to him with both hands. I will." They'd get over this fight. Of course they would. But she couldn't bring herself to ask how she was supposed to hold on to him from Soleil.

"*You'll manage. Think of him as a nonnegotiable priority, the same way you would Beni,*" said Nori. The suggestion made Scarlett's heart lighter.

Manon sipped a cup of coffee. "So, do you have any plans for the morning?"

"James offered to take me to work with him so I can learn about being a vox. You?"

"I'm going to enjoy the peace and quiet of my room while I can."

The ominous words gave Scarlett pause. "What do you mean, 'while you can'?"

"Given the circumstances, it's safe to say things will not remain calm. I personally am both nervous and excited to see what Brayden does next, because there's no stopping you from going, and there is also no way that boy is letting you leave alone," Manon said with a pleased chuckle. "A phoenix learns of his North Star right before she's supposed to leave the country to go back to her murderous homeland . . . I couldn't make this up if I tried."

If only Scarlett could be as relaxed about this as her grandmother.

Freshly showered and coat in hand, Scarlett went to the lounge downstairs looking for James and found him reading a book.

James stood as she entered the room, his eyes bright. "You look well. You're practically glowing." Before she could reply, he opened his arms and wrapped her in a hug. "Congratulations on the North Star news. Brayden told me before he left with Lachlan. I'm so chuffed for the two of you."

She hugged him back, her heart skipping a beat at the mention. "Did he seem *happy* about the North Star news?"

"No. He seemed stressed out," James admitted. "But underneath the stress, he's happy, believe me. He's just worried because of your situation. He was always going to be overprotective of you because of your history, but get ready for it to be on a whole new level of obsession now."

To Scarlett's surprise, she grinned. James's cheerful dismissal of Brayden's mood was somehow a comfort.

"You know this means we're basically family now, right?" His dark eyebrows rose inquisitively.

"Erm, I don't know much at all about the North Star other than the basics I learned yesterday."

He chuckled. "Goddess, you being from Soleil is so fun. Did you know that legally, a North Star bond supersedes marriage here? Like, if you wanted to, you could skip getting married, have your North Star ceremony instead, and it would give you all the same legal benefits in Clair de Lune. And get *this*. Let's say you'd married that prick Alastair before you knew about the North Star. If you got the rune after you'd married someone else, under Clair de Lune law, that marriage would become null and void."

Scarlett let out a nervous laugh, trying her best not to think too deeply on the disturbing alternate reality James was describing. She made a mental note to ask Brayden what he'd told him about Alastair. "I didn't know any of that. Thank the Goddess I never got married."

"Yeah, seriously. Anyway, ready to head out? We're going to the guildhall." He wore a button-down shirt with dress pants and nice shoes, and his blazer hung on the back of his chair. It was the most formal she'd ever seen him, and it made her question her own outfit.

"Am I dressed okay? Manon bought this yesterday. I don't have many outfits here with me." She gestured down at her sleeveless black dress. It was a little short, hitting at the middle of her thigh, but the skirt flared out enough that it wasn't hugging her hips. Laylani wouldn't have approved, but she'd seen other peers wear similar things to Soleil's parliament.

"You look great," said James without looking at her. "It's good you brought a jacket. It's a cold morning."

"Good," she said, trying to sound excited. She was excited. But she wouldn't be totally at ease until she and Brayden had worked things out. Sighing, she followed James to the courtyard and climbed into the passenger seat of his SUV.

James drove around the outskirts of Clair de Lune. They passed lots of adorable terraced houses with decorative timbers on the exteriors, the homes painted brown in contrast to the white stucco. Scarlett stared longingly at the quaint-looking city center in the distance. She wanted Brayden to show her more of his country, but they were already running out of time together.

After a quarter of an hour, James parked the car, and they walked up to the guildhall. Scarlett stared up at the intricate stonework of the old building.

"This is gorgeous. What's it used for?"

"Commerce. I'm here most days, although we go to Parliament for the big meetings." He pointed to a white dome visible over the tops of the buildings. "That's Parliament. The prime minister is visiting Evory this week, but if you're still here next week, I'll try to get you a meeting with her."

"Thanks, but I'll be gone by then," said Scarlett regretfully. She'd met Greta Crow, Clair de Lune's PM, at a state dinner the previous year, but their interaction had been brief.

"Shame," said James. "Maybe next time."

They passed through a set of grand wooden doors, and Scarlett stared up at the high ceilings with their exposed wooden beams. Shields painted with family crests adorned the walls.

"Let's sign you in." James stopped at a round desk just to the right of the door. "Now on to the council chamber," he said once she had a visitor's lanyard around her neck. He led her up a grand staircase. "We're discussing tariffs today. I think you should say a few words on the subject, just to try out your valor."

"You want me to give a speech?" Her eyebrows shot up.

"Just a quick one," he said. "You know all about the impact of a restrictive economic border, right?"

"True . . ."

He pointed to a set of double doors. "That's where we're headed, but wait just a second." They stopped a few feet away from the doors. "My boss is the secretary of commerce. He's very much a free-trade guy," James explained.

"Okay," said Scarlett, nodding. She knew Clair de Lune had a market economy, paired with national control of natural resources and extensive—and enviable—social programs like universal healthcare. Their secretary of commerce being pro–free trade made sense.

"The Brightness Isles just instigated tariffs on agriculture imports—which affects us, as agriculture is one of our biggest exports—but my boss doesn't want to retaliate with our own tariffs. He wants to respond to the Isles by signing a free-trade agreement with our allies across Hieratia. Can you address the chamber and tell them about your goals for Soleil's border? If they hear your position, they might be reminded of how important free trade is," said James. "I already called my boss to suggest you say a few words, and he thinks it's a great idea."

Scarlett considered for a second. "If you're sure they'll find it relevant." She looked forward to hearing James's boss discuss tariffs, but she didn't know how much she'd have to add. She had no experience aside from school and observing her dad.

"They'll be fascinated by you," James said with confidence. "And while you're speaking, watch the people listening to you. You'll see your vox powers at work."

"Can you be more specific?" she hissed.

"I could, but that wouldn't be any fun." He gave her a devilish grin as he strode toward the double doors, and she hurried after him.

Hushed voices filled the council chambers, and the sight of all the people was something to behold for Scarlett, who marveled at all the soul lights hovering around the room. She felt eyes on them as she and James sat on a wooden bench near the front with a good view of the speaker's podium. The council chambers were a smaller version of those she'd seen in Soleil's parliament. Old paintings of government officials adorned the walls, and there was a lot of wood paneling. It even smelled like a government building should—like dusty books. The familiarity was comforting.

"How will Soleil receive the news you're eternally bonded to my brother?" asked James as they waited for the meeting to begin.

Scarlett pursed her lips, choosing not to question his use of the phrase "eternally bonded" even though she was still doubtful it was true. She could answer a theoretical question. "If the public's reaction to my father marrying my mother is any indication, me dating someone from Clair de Lune will not be received well. Some said he wouldn't have become prime minister if my mother hadn't died. He became much more popular once he married Laylani, although I disagree with whoever thinks that's because she's from a Goldenrod family. People just liked him being married to a woman from Soleil."

James winced. "They really hated your mam being from Clair de Lune, huh? Do you think it'll be any different now?"

"I do, actually. Over the past couple of decades, people have changed. They're more concerned with the economy and the future we'll give to our children than they are with remaining insular. Studies show relaxing border restrictions will grow the market for our tech industry, and tourism and increased educational immigration should also give our GDP a boost."

"That's perfect fodder for your speech," said James.

Before she could reply, a thin, white-haired man sat down on James's other side.

"He's my boss," whispered James.

"Good morning." The older gentleman stuck a hand out toward Scarlett. "John McNeil, the secretary of commerce."

Scarlett grasped John's hand. "I'm, erm . . . I'm Scarlett Heroux. Pleasure to meet you."

"Not sure of your name, lass?" he said with amusement.

She shrugged. "I'm technically Lady Scarlett Heroux, but I haven't gotten used to the title yet."

His face grew more solemn. "I'm truly sorry for your loss, Lady Heroux."

"Thank you," she said with a dip of her chin.

"So, did James sell you on saying a few words to the council about free trade?" he asked with an excited glint in his eye.

"It would be a privilege," she said.

"Wonderful."

Someone at the front of the room hit a gavel. At the speaker's podium, a woman in pink tweed was ready to begin.

Scarlett listened as the council opened the meeting. They went through some housekeeping business, and when the woman in tweed announced the next item on the agenda was tariffs, a stocky-looking man with wire-rimmed glasses took the podium.

"That's Ian Carmichael. He's a representative for the farmers' union, and he's in favor of retaliatory tariffs," whispered James.

Scarlett listened with a furrowed brow as Ian reviewed the agricultural industry's viewpoint that retaliatory tariffs were only fair given the actions taken by the Brightness Isles. The matter of agriculture tariffs was small in comparison to Soleil's embargo on magic, but countries closing themselves off to each other raised alarm bells in her head. Just like at home, the people, not the politicians, would be the ones to pay for whatever was decided today.

Next, John took the podium. Scarlett thought he spoke very well and didn't need her help, but as he closed his remarks, he introduced her to the room.

"We have someone remarkable with us here today. Lady Scarlett Heroux, daughter of Soleil's late prime minister Lord Jules Heroux and Sabina Bedivere of our own Clair de Lune. Given the rarity of a visitor from Soleil and the unique trade embargoes she lives with, I'd like for her to take the floor to give a few remarks."

"Go get 'em," said James as Scarlett stood.

Scarlett took a deep breath as she made her way to the podium, summoning the manic excitement that usually aided her when she spoke in public. She looked out at all the civil servants. "Thank you, Mr. McNeil, for the kind introduction. It's true—the Cerulean Party is struggling to undo the isolationist economic policies that have handicapped Soleil for so long. Soleil has a lot to offer the world, and likewise, I believe our quality of life would be better if we were more open. I agree with what Mr. McNeil said about tariffs hurting the consumer most of all, because the people are the ones who pay. I've seen extreme iterations of that in my country with our hard borders. Black markets form to offer the restricted goods illegally, and people in need of special services like medical magic are left to suffer needlessly."

As she spoke, she noticed glittery, almost golden tendrils rising in streams above the people listening. She stopped talking and looked across the room, momentarily stunned by the sight. A couple of listeners had black smoke twisting into the air above them, including Ian Carmichael. One man with a thick mustache had both colors above his head.

Refocusing, she relayed what she'd told James about the economic benefits she believed would occur if their border was more open.

"It's wonderful to be in my mother's homeland, and thanks for the opportunity to address the council," she said to finish her remarks.

There was a smattering of surprising applause, which made her face grow hot. She was going to have to get over that reaction before she addressed Soleil's parliament. This had been an excellent practice run at a public address. It was so thoughtful of James and his boss to include her.

James and Scarlett observed in silence through the rest of the meeting, and Scarlett only half listened as she mulled over what the black and gold had meant. Was that all there was to being a vox?

"*There's plenty more to it. James will explain,*" said Nori.

Scarlett was beginning to understand what Brayden had meant when he'd referenced Jax's tendency to withhold information. She got the sense Nori preferred for her to learn by living and was mostly there for emotional support.

"*Exactly,*" said Nori. "*And don't forget, I'm your source of magic.*"

I know. I'm grateful, said Scarlett, feeling guilty for her unappreciative thoughts.

After the meeting, they said goodbye to John, and James took her to the guildhall's canteen. As they entered the bustling café, Scarlett breathed in the smell of coffee and baked goods.

"So, did you see the black and gold smoke while you were speaking?" asked James once she'd slid into the seat across from him.

The canteen buzzed with conversation. Quite a few of the people she'd seen in the meeting had come straight here.

"Yes. What was that?" She took a sip of her coffee and sighed with pleasure.

James waved to a passing colleague before answering. "It's an indication of opinion. Will, even. Golden smoke will appear when you're speaking to someone and they agree with what you're saying."

"And it's black if they don't?" Ian Carmichael came into her mind's eye.

"Precisely. And I'm sure you can see how, when you're speaking to Parliament, this kind of infallible insight could be useful."

Her mind reeled as she imagined seeing black and gold smoke floating above all the peers in Soleil's parliament. "Is it always accurate?"

"People can lie with their words, but not with their hearts." James bit into a blueberry muffin he'd bought along with her coffee.

Brayden. "I didn't see any smoke yesterday, with Brayden."

James shook his head. "You won't. Or at least, I hope you don't. The better you know someone, the less smoke you see. I can't see any when I speak to Brayden and my dad. I'm not seeing anyone right now, but with all my ex-girlfriends, it disappeared as soon as we became close."

"Why?" asked Scarlett.

James shrugged. "It's probably a blessing, to be honest. It would be exhausting to be *on* all the time."

"That's true." She didn't want to use magic every time she talked to Beni, Manon, and Brayden. At work though . . .

"What if someone has both black and gold smoke above them?" she asked, thinking of the man with the mustache. "Mixed feelings?" She took another small sip of her coffee.

"Yep. That's when you know you can persuade them with the right words. Debate with them and question them until you find something they like. Then it's up to you to decide whether or not you can agree to whatever they need to be onside."

"*If someone's undecided, I can help you deduce the right thing to say,*" said Nori.

Scarlett's mouth fell open. "Nori—she's my light."

"Yes, your light can help you navigate conversations to get better outcomes." James's smirk was patronizing.

She ignored his attempt to bait her and cocked her head to one side. "Isn't this manipulative? Immoral?"

"You're not taking away anyone's free will. You just have a leg up at figuring out how to compromise with people. If you want to get into valor morality, is it immoral to use your Goddess-given talents for the greater good? If you're a virtuous politician, this will further the good of Soleil." He took a large bite of his muffin, chewing for a moment before taking a gulp of water.

"I suppose . . ." Scarlett thought of Moira and the lack of virtue in many of her father's ex-colleagues—her soon-to-be colleagues. "I don't want to control anyone's mind."

James gave her an exasperated look and glanced around, probably afraid someone was listening to her embarrassing misconceptions of soul-light magic. "A vox can't do that. None of the soul-light valors can. You're thinking of Sigur Viður in the war?"

"Yes." The most notorious stories from the Great War filled her mind. "People haven't forgotten the awful things that happened. It's why Soleil banned magic, and every time there's a hint of it being legalized, the newspapers rerun stories. The possessed soldiers who came home and murdered their own families . . ."

Years ago, at about age ten, she'd picked up a newspaper and been horrified by an article about the war that described women who'd lived with soul parasites controlling their husbands' or their boyfriends' bodies, not realizing until after they'd suffered tremendous abuse. It made her shudder just thinking about it, even now. She'd die before she'd be controlled that way.

"If the press find out I can influence people with magic, the anti-magic media will draw parallels right away."

"The mind control Sigur Viður is infamous for has nothing to do with soul lights. That's nasty stuff—parasite magic. You'd have to intentionally pursue that. It won't happen by accident just because you're a vox." The look of disgust on his face told her he was as disturbed by soul parasites as she was.

Scarlett's shoulders relaxed. "That's a relief. How do they do magic if not with soul lights?"

"They didn't teach you that in school?"

She scoffed. "No."

"Okay." James drummed his fingers on the table. "I won't get into their religion, because we'll be here all day. In a nutshell, whereas here we tie ourselves to the divine, there they give away a part of themselves to gain power."

"That sounds disturbing." She had a million questions but wasn't sure she had the energy for another lengthy magical lesson, so she held back.

"Agreed. But anyway, to allay your specific concern, they shouldn't find out about your magic unless you tell them. People can't see soul lights unless they have one, and even those with soul lights won't see the vox smoke you're seeing. Just don't tell anyone random what you can do, and you'll be fine."

"I'll definitely keep it quiet as long as magic is illegal in Soleil." She thought back to the speech she'd just given. If the goal was to change black smoke to gold, she still wasn't totally clear on how to achieve that. "Is there anything I should do to practice this stuff?"

"Talk to people. Espouse your opinions and see what happens. You'll learn by doing. You were probably a good orator before, but you can expect to be better now, with a tiny amount of practice."

She grinned. "I can't wait to try using these powers in Parliament."

CHAPTER (19)

After she'd finished asking James every question she could think of about the vox valor, Scarlett called a taxi to take her back while James continued his workday.

Back at the castle, she went looking for Beni, and with some help from the castle staff, she found him in a basement recreation room playing pool with Patrick and Tommy.

"Hey, you!" said Scarlett when Beni noticed her.

"Show us your valor!" he yelled without saying hello.

The two other boys looked at her with interest.

"I'm a vox," said Scarlett. She adjusted the collar of her dress and pointed to her collarbone, and Beni came closer to look.

"Is that a good one?" he asked the other boys.

"It can go either way," said Patrick, who had red hair and a freckled complexion.

"What do you mean, 'it can go either way'?" asked Scarlett.

Tommy, who had dark brown skin and was quick to smile, stepped

in front of Patrick. "It means you could either be a total legend or you could be normal." He said "normal" in a deflated tone, like it was a highly undesirable thing.

Scarlett laughed to herself. Nothing like the brutal honesty of children to bring you down a peg. "And let me guess. The phoenix valor means you're bound for fame and glory?"

"Yeah!" said Tommy and Patrick together.

"Do you two know what a North Star is?" asked Scarlett, keen to get more data points on whether or not the bond really was universally revered in Clair.

"Yep," said Patrick, while Tommy nodded.

Beni looked from Scarlett to them, awaiting an explanation.

"Those hardly ever happen though," said Patrick with a furrowed brow.

"Brayden Maddox and I found out yesterday that we're North Stars," said Scarlett. She watched the Clair de Lune boys for their reaction.

"What? No way," said Tommy. He grabbed her left hand as if he expected to see something there. "Wait, are you hiding it? Where's your tattoo?"

"We found out we're North Stars, but we haven't done the ceremony yet," she clarified.

"Oh," said Tommy. "Psh, you should go back and do that *today*. Why *wouldn't* you?"

"She'll probably get Brayden's fire power when she does," Patrick explained to Beni, who looked confused.

"Goddess, you're so lucky, Beni. Your sister is Brayden Maddox's North Star," said Tommy. "I wish he were part of *my* family."

Scarlett cocked her head to one side as she listened to their chattering. Tommy's reaction was pretty similar to James's. He spoke as if she were already legally joined to Brayden. She wished she could be excited, but it was hard to be when Brayden regretted their first night together.

"Of course his sister is Brayden's North Star. *Look* at her," said Patrick in a low voice.

"Yeah," said Tommy, turning to look her up and down.

"She can hear you," said Scarlett, stifling a laugh.

Beni ignored them. "So Brayden is like my brother now?"

Scarlett shrugged helplessly. "Honestly, I don't know. I'm figuring this out as I go."

Patrick and Tommy stared at her, incredulous.

"Are you guys hungry?" she asked in an attempt to move the conversation along.

"Yeah," came a chorus of agreement.

Scarlett smiled. Was their willingness to spend time with her *completely* due to her new North Star status with Brayden, or only part of it?

Upstairs, she and the boys sat at one of several long dining tables, where a few military staff sat eating their lunches or sipping hot drinks. They were chatting happily over soup and sandwiches when Manon strode up to them and dropped two newspapers on the table next to Scarlett.

"Hello, all," she said to the group.

The boys greeted her and then resumed their conversation about Soleil video games.

"We heard from Elestine and Laylani today." Manon slid into the seat next to Scarlett.

Scarlett put down the Brie-and-fig sandwich she was halfway done with and faced her. "Already?"

"Well, I should say, we heard from them indirectly. Look at these news articles." She stabbed the paper several times with her finger. "Elestine got an answer from the courts and went public with it."

Scarlett skimmed the first article.

Ceruleans Gain Lady Scarlett Heroux

The Soleil Courts released a statement early this morning regarding an approved exception to the age of inheritance, filed by Lady Scarlett Heroux. Lady Elestine Spencer commented, "Lady Heroux is well and staying with family friends, contrary to reports of her being bedridden. I look forward to welcoming her to Parliament now that her age exception has been approved and plan to mentor her closely. With her vote and her influence at work for the Cerulean Party, I'm confident we'll soon resume talks on the border legislation."

"Well, that's positive, I suppose," said Scarlett. She nudged her brother. "You should read this, Beni."

"Okay." He took the paper.

"Read this one next." Manon pointed to another article.

The Abduction of Lord Jules Heroux's Children

Lady Laylani Heroux filed a report this morning with the Soleil Bureau of Investigation regarding the abduction of Lady Scarlett Heroux and Beaufort Heroux. Lady Laylani Heroux, mother to Beaufort and stepmother to Scarlett, believes her children were abducted by Scarlett's grandmother, a Clair de Lune woman by the name of Manon Bedivere. Lady Laylani Heroux commented, "While Scarlett was too infirm to stop her, Manon stole Scarlett and Beaufort from our home in the middle of the night. She's

*always wanted to take Scarlett back to her home country—
for what nefarious purposes, I can't say. I'm devastated by
the loss of them both and pray for their safety."*

Scarlett clenched her fists. "That's all such bullshit. I'll demand they print a retraction."

"She's such a liar," her brother said as he peered over Scarlett's shoulder.

"Indeed," said Manon. "And yes, Scarlett, a retraction is a good idea, but first we need to make contact with the bureau to prevent an international incident. As soon as you're ready, we need to go to Clair de Lune's intelligence offices at Parliament. There's a magic mirror there connected to the Soleil Bureau's headquarters."

"The Soleil Bureau is using mirrors?" asked Scarlett.

"You're surprised?" Manon raised an eyebrow. "There's a lot of magic used in Soleil. It's just a secret."

"I know *that*, but I had no idea the *government* permitted magic." The black market paying off the police was different from the government allowing the bureau to use magic in an official capacity.

"True." Manon nodded. "Outside of some high-ranking members of the government and intelligence agencies, no one knows they use things like magic mirrors for international communication. I know about it because of the work I do for Lachlan."

"So my father was using mirrors all along?"

Manon pursed her lips. "He didn't know about our mirror. We never spoke about magic mirrors, although I'm sure he did use them." She patted Scarlett's knee. "Let's get moving. Lachlan's going to drive us into town as soon as we're ready. Beni, you need to come along, since it involves you too."

When Manon, Beni, and Scarlett arrived at Lachlan's office, Brayden was there with him. Her chest ached as she swept her gaze over him, from his unruly brown hair to his long legs. He stood in front of Lachlan in his civilian clothes: a black T-shirt and jeans.

"If things escalate further in Evory . . ." Lachlan trailed off as they entered the room. He smirked when he saw them. "If it isn't the kidnapper and her prisoners."

"Very funny," grumbled Manon.

Brayden's expression was unreadable as Lachlan closed the distance between them in a couple of strides. To Scarlett's surprise, he hugged her. The spicy scent of his cologne enveloped her as she felt the crisp starch of his uniform under her fingertips, and the warmth of the embrace pierced through the distress she'd been carrying since she left Brayden in his room.

"I'm thrilled about the North Star news, my dear." He pulled back, his dark eyes warm with delight.

"Oh, thank you." A huge smile spread across her face. "I . . . I love your son." She was still pissed at him, but being mad didn't change the fact she loved him. She wasn't that fickle. She stole a glance at Brayden, and his expression softened.

Lachlan beamed as he looked between them.

Scarlett continued. "I understand it means he'll always be in my life, and I couldn't be happier about that."

Gold smoke streamed into the air above Lachlan's head, startling but reassuring. "That's lovely to hear."

Brayden came closer. "I'm still worried about how long that life will be."

Scarlett reached for him. He squeezed her hand for a couple of seconds, the brief contact making her heart leap, but then he released her and crossed his arms.

Lachlan frowned at his son. "We'll make sure she's well looked after, Brayden." He turned to Scarlett. "Now that your age of inheritance exception has been approved, I'm sure you're eager to get back to Soleil."

"Yes. I need to get back as soon as possible," said Scarlett.

"With Manon staying here, we need some kind of protection for you before you return," said Lachlan.

Beni's head whipped to Manon. "Manon is staying here?"

"It's not safe for me in Soleil." Manon put her arm around Beni, ruffling his hair. "*You* have nothing to worry about, because your mother would never hurt you."

Beni's expression became stormy at the mention of his mother, but he stayed silent.

"What are your thoughts on protection?" Scarlett asked Lachlan.

"We're going to get you a first-class bodyguard, and Brayden will accompany you to Soleil and stay until that's arranged. I think it's an excellent time for him to use some much-deserved leave," said Lachlan.

"But—wait. How are you going to get into the country?" asked Beni.

"The only way he can come is if we have a visa wedding." Scarlett's shoulders slumped as she recalled his reaction when she'd brought up marriage.

Brayden took her hand and tried to pull her toward the door. "Scarlett—"

But Lachlan spoke over him. "Exactly. He told me you suggested marriage, and I think it's the best way forward. There's a registrar available later today who can draw up a marriage certificate. We've already booked the appointment. We'll go first to the bureau to clear up this kidnapping nonsense, then we'll go on to the registrar's office."

Beni's mouth fell open, and his eyebrows shot up in surprise. "You're getting married?"

Scarlett looked up at Brayden. "Is he serious?"

"Dad, I told you I wanted to talk to her alone first," Brayden said.

"Nice one, Lachlan." Manon bit her lip and looked at Scarlett with concern.

"Well, what's the point in beating around the bush?" Lachlan said. "If she won't stay here, it's their only realistic option. I can't exactly send a military escort or go along in my specter form. And why *wouldn't* they?"

Brayden sighed and pulled Scarlett toward the door.

"Now, don't get in a tizzy," said Lachlan. "If you two are North Stars, what does it matter if the marriage paperwork is filed?"

"She's still getting acquainted with the North Star concept," muttered Manon.

Brayden glared at Lachlan. "Can you give us a couple of minutes?"

"Of course," said Manon.

Lachlan coughed, and Scarlett caught the look he shot Brayden.

They stood in the hallway outside Lachlan's study, and Brayden took her hands in his. "I'm sorry. I wanted that to be better. And I wanted to talk to you alone. I should have dragged you out of that room as soon as you walked through the door. My dad is so thick sometimes." He let go of her hands and gripped her waist lightly as he stared into her eyes. "I'm sorry I was an idiot this morning. You leaving under these circumstances is my worst nightmare, but I shouldn't have reacted that way."

"Thank you for apologizing." She wanted so badly for things to be well between them that an apology spilled easily off her lips. "I'm sorry too. But what was your dad talking about? You seemed to think a visa marriage was a horrible idea this morning, so what changed?"

They were alone in the quiet hallway as he scanned her face. "I thought about it after you left. In my room earlier, I couldn't see past my desperation in wanting to keep you here, where it's safe, and I was pissed you threw out the idea of a visa marriage so flippantly." He glanced down at his feet as he let out a sigh. "But after you left, I tried to look at the situation logically instead of emotionally, and I realized you were right. I don't want you to give up on Soleil. You can change the world, and I want to support those dreams and help you set things right. But I *have* to protect you. A visa wedding solves our short-term problems. If you won't stay in Clair de Lune, we need to get married so I can go back with you. Let's get married." He squeezed her hands tighter in his, running his thumbs over her wrists.

Scarlett frowned. His apology had softened her, but his proposal left much to be desired. "There has to be a third option. Something other than me staying or us getting married." She loved him, but she didn't want to get married like this. Whenever she'd pictured her wedding, she'd envisioned a beautiful dress, a huge party, and a groom who was unreservedly head over heels for her and eager to get married, not a hastily signed certificate at a courthouse under duress. She planned on only marrying once, and she didn't want to throw that away. And she didn't want that for Brayden either.

He closed his eyes and took a deep breath. "Oh, there's a third option. And a fourth. But I think you'll like them less. Do not underestimate the lengths I will go to for you. If you try to leave Clair de Lune without me, I'll cross the Soleil border illegally to follow you. I'll hire a nocturna to sneak me in, or I'll ride a fucking dragon shifter over the border."

Scarlett stared at him, horrified. "You can't be serious."

Flames danced in his eyes. He looked wilder than she'd ever seen him. "I'm deadly serious. I'd go further, even. I'd kill to keep you alive. If someone has to die for you to live, I'll slaughter them to save you."

His words sent shivers down her spine. They disturbed her but also stirred something deep within. Part of her liked seeing Brayden this worked up over her. But she couldn't let him know that.

"If you do any of those things, you'll get yourself arrested, deported, and banned from the country forever. Then we'll never be able to live together."

Two officers in uniform appeared in the hallway, and Scarlett and Brayden stood in silence as the men passed by, one of them nodding to Brayden. As soon as they'd disappeared, he went on.

"I've given you an option that is legal, and it's up to you whether or not you want to take it. Believe me, I know this isn't ideal. Lachlan was all jolly in there about me taking leave, but the truth is, Evory is on the verge of war with Sigur Viður. I should be here with my dad helping him manage the army. Not to mention I feel like I'm trapping the woman of my dreams into marriage."

They were on opposite sides of this argument, and yet they felt the same: frustrated and somewhat unwanted. Her need for him was indistinguishable from her desire to slap him for being so pushy.

"You shouldn't leave your dad if he needs you—"

"No, I *want* to. You're my North Star. We're not at war yet, and you're worth it a million times over. I'm only highlighting that I'm offering a compromise I can live with, but it's a compromise for me too. Take it. Please." He lifted a hand to her cheek and brushed his knuckles against her skin. "Remember what we talked about last night. *Goddess*, just think about last night. It was the most amazing night of my life. I love you. So much. Please let me do this for you. Please let me protect you. Even if it's just for a couple of weeks."

Her reticence melted away as Brayden expressed feelings as deep as her own. He seemed to genuinely want her to say yes. Marriage was better than him risking his life with an illegal border crossing, and with how riled he was over her safety, she believed he would do something that drastic. He always did what he said he would, and it was usually one of the things she liked best about him. It was strange to see the easygoing Brayden transformed into this nervous wreck. He really was worried about her.

As if he could see her wavering, he continued. "I know it's fast. We might not know how this is going to work yet, but I know we're meant to be together. Let's get married. You don't have to wear a ring if you don't want to. This can be whatever you want it to be. We can keep it a secret if you think it's best, given who I am, or not. I don't mind, but I *need* to go with you."

Scarlett blinked several times. "I want a ring. If you go to Soleil, we'll have to explain it, and I don't want to keep us a secret." If her father, the most career-minded person she'd known, had married his Clair de Lune wife without regret, she certainly wasn't going to hide who she loved to keep other people comfortable. The idea was unbearable. She had to believe enough people would be accepting of her choice. Not everyone, certainly, but there *had* to be enough decent people in Soleil. And if there weren't—damn the consequences anyway.

Relief and joy lit his face. "I'll get you a ring."

Before she could say anything, his hands were on her, and his lips crashed into hers. He kissed her so hard it verged on painful. But she pressed herself to him, eager for it, letting herself feel what she couldn't admit out loud. She was selfishly elated he'd be coming to Soleil with her. Even if it was all madness, in her heart she was relieved. She slid her hand into his shirt, and Brayden pushed her against the wall, his hands braced on either side of her.

"Pardon me." Manon's head poked out of the door to Lachlan's office.

They both startled, and Brayden took a couple of steps backward so Scarlett was no longer pinned to the wall. Nori and Jax spun in circles around them as if they were dancing.

Manon chuckled. "Are you two almost finished out here?"

Scarlett's face blazed with heat. "Almost. Two minutes."

"Okay," said Manon, disappearing as she closed the door.

Brayden ran his fingers through his hair. "I'll get you a ring," he murmured. "Is there anything else you need?"

She leaned back against the wall. "If we get married, what happens when you come back home?"

"We'll do long-distance," he said as if it were the most obvious answer in the world. And maybe it was. "I meant everything I said last night. I want everything with you."

His words from before echoed in her mind. *"You're mine."* They warmed her belly.

"We can talk through the mirror like we always did. And you can come back, and I'll visit too," she added. Having him in Soleil . . . It would be so wonderful.

"Exactly. If we're married, I can come visit you again, and you can come to Clair de Lune the next time Parliament isn't in session. Getting married actually makes more sense than you being forced to stay here and give up everything. We'll have way more time with each other than we've ever had. And I want to be with you in any way I can."

His energetic optimism was infectious. She wanted to believe it would all work out.

But long-distance with no end in sight . . . She suspected this could all end in heartbreak, but Scarlett was tired of fighting him. She didn't want to fight him. She bit her lip as she lost herself in his endless brown eyes. He was so beautiful, and he was hers.

She pushed off the wall and held out her arms, needing to hold him.

"So is that a yes?" he asked, wrapping her in a hug.

Her mouth curved into a smile. "Yes."

"Whee!" Nori continued to float right next to Jax.

Brayden picked Scarlett up and clutched her tightly to his chest for a long moment before setting her back down on the ground.

They opened the door to Lachlan's office and met the expectant stares of their family. Lachlan chortled at whatever he saw on their faces. Beni stared at her, and she gave him a small smile to let him know everything was fine—sort of.

"She said yes," said Beni with confidence.

"She did," confirmed Brayden.

Beni leaped forward and high-fived him. "We're going to be brothers!"

Brayden's answering smile was genuine as he pulled Beni in for a hug. "Yeah, man. That's class."

Manon rushed forward and hugged them both. Then she whispered in Scarlett's ear. "You're doing the right thing, dearest."

"Excellent," said Lachlan with a clap of his hands. "Let's gather up what we need for the ceremony and be off to Parliament."

Scarlett looked down at her simple black dress. "I wish I had a white dress."

"You do," said Manon. "We'll go get your mother's."

CHAPTER 20

Outside the castle in the courtyard driveway, James waited for them next to an SUV, still dressed in his work suit.

"James, what are you doing here?" Scarlett asked. "I thought you were in meetings all day."

"Did she say yes?" he asked Brayden as he approached.

Brayden kissed Scarlett's cheek. "She did."

"Phew. Glad to hear I didn't take the afternoon off for a wedding that isn't going ahead." His grin was mischievous. "Brayden called me right after you left the guildhall and asked if I could skip the rest of the workday for his *wedding*. Of course I said yes."

She smiled at him bashfully. "We're obviously doing this so he can come back to Soleil with me, but thank you for coming. It's nice you'll be there."

"We *are* in love, for the record," grumbled Brayden, and Scarlett bit her lip and sighed.

James slapped him on the back before pulling her into a hug. "Of

course you're in love. Look at you two. So sweet." He let Scarlett go and winked at her before making his way to the driver's seat.

As James drove into Clair de Lune's city center, Scarlett peered out of her window. She wanted to see the city, but she was too distracted to focus on much as they drove down an old-fashioned street. She barely registered the quaint little shops with signs hanging from the twisted metal awnings, her mind consumed as she evaluated every possible way this visa marriage could blow up in her face.

He might hate Soleil. He might tire of long-distance. He could grow to resent me more and more for refusing to stay. He might decide he wants someone who doesn't get harassed by the press every time they step outside . . .

Scarlett blinked as her thoughts returned to the first task at hand—speaking to the bureau. There was so much going on she could hardly keep it all straight. "I don't think we should incriminate Laylani when we speak to the bureau agents. I don't want to accuse her until we have enough to lock her up. Do you all agree?"

"Seems reasonable," said Lachlan.

"Yes, I'm fine with that," said Beni. "I want her to be punished, but it's okay if we have to wait."

Manon spoke up from the back seat. "Makes sense if you want to keep things cordial. You could also tell them I arranged the trip with your consent, given they don't know I was ill. Might be less suspicious than saying Beni whisked us both away. No offense, Beni."

He waved his hand dismissively. "I know how awesome I am. You don't have to tell them."

Scarlett flashed him a grin. "I know how awesome you are too." She turned to Brayden, who was sitting next to her. "Oh, by the way, I know someone in Soleil who might be a good bodyguard." Through his window she caught a glimpse of an enormous fountain, with a celestial-themed set of sculptures stretching high into the sky.

"Who are you thinking of?" asked Lachlan.

"Her name's Cass," said Scarlett. "I really like her, although I'm not sure how I'd contact her. She saved me the night the police raided a black-market boxing match she was running. She seemed strong. Well-connected. And most importantly, she believes in dropping the border, so I know she's pro-magic. Oh, and she's not from Soleil. I couldn't place her accent, but she's definitely not from Clair or Evory either. She might be looking for work. I heard the boxing matches have stopped since they were raided."

"Any idea what kind of magic she has?" asked Lachlan.

Scarlett recalled something Cass had said that night. *"It'll take them a while to get the lights back on."*

"She turned the lights out in the whole place incredibly fast. Not sure if it was magic or not."

"Could be a nocturna," said Brayden, sounding intrigued.

"What's a nocturna?" asked Scarlett. She'd wondered about the meaning of the word when Brayden used it earlier.

"A nocturna can hide themselves and others in the shadows," said Brayden. "Sometimes they can eliminate light. I've read about people with a nocturna valor sucking up candlelight, electricity, anything illuminating. They can also light things up again."

"That sounds incredible," said Scarlett. "Can they hide themselves the same way you disappear, Lachlan?"

"No. Their bodies can't destabilize," he said. "Then again, I can't hide other people the way a nocturna can. There are only a couple of them in Soleil. Cass . . . Could that be short for Cassidy? I know a Cassidy Darwish from Zahara who went to the Soleil Military Academy on one of those rare student visas. Her father is a general in the Zaharan military."

Zahara was a dry desert country on the far eastern side of the continent of Hieratia. Scarlett had read it was hot as hell except for the strip of land nearest to the ocean, but she didn't know a lot beyond that.

"Her full name could be Cassidy," she said.

"Even if they're not the same person, a military-trained nocturna would be a great bodyguard if she's willing. Shall I inquire with her father to see if we can get her contact information?"

"That would be great," said Scarlett.

"Leave it with me," said Lachlan.

Who knew it was that easy to pinpoint someone based on their magical ability?

"*Lachlan is very well-connected*," said Nori.

"Beni, did your friends ever explain valors to you?" asked Manon.

"Yes," said Beni. "I talked to Tommy and Patrick about it for, like, an hour. They both think they're going to get a physica valor, and I think that's what I might be too. They said it means you're usually good at video games."

"What's a physica?"

"Tommy's dad is a physica for the army. That's probably where Beni and his friends got the idea. They're often mechanical engineers or physicists. I can see how they'd be good at video games," said Lachlan, sounding amused.

Everyone fell silent as the white dome of Parliament appeared before them, and James pulled into a parking spot. Scarlett climbed out of the SUV and looked up at the impressive façade of Clair de Lune's parliament. Four enormous white columns framed a massive ornate doorway. Two soldiers stood at attention, guarding the entrance, and they both saluted Lachlan as he led their group through the doors into the lobby.

With a wave of farewell, James and Brayden cut across the lobby toward the registrar's office.

"This way," said Lachlan, leading the rest of them upstairs.

Scarlett read the plaques on the doors as they passed. "Bureau of Veterans Affairs" read one. Another read "Ministry of Education."

Lachlan opened a door with a plaque that read "Clair de Lune Intelligence Agency."

The clerk at the front desk looked up as they entered and stood as soon as he clocked who it was. "Good morning, General Maddox. How can I help?"

"An incident cropped up this morning with Soleil." He gestured to Scarlett and Beni. "These two have been reported as kidnapped, when they're actually just visiting Clair de Lune with their grandmother. Can you please tell whoever is in charge this morning that we need to speak with Soleil law enforcement as soon as possible?"

"Yes, sir. Right away." The clerk disappeared through a door.

A handful of minutes later, he reappeared.

"I'll take you through the veritas now."

Through the doorway, a gray stone archway stood a few feet in front of them. Golden dust with a greenish tint shone under it. The clerk walked straight through the arch without hesitation. Lachlan made to follow him, but Scarlett put her hand on his arm.

"What's a veritas? Is it that archway?" she asked.

"Yes. If you're not telling the truth about why you're here, it won't let you pass through it."

"Will it reject me for being a Soleil peer?" asked Scarlett.

The corner of Lachlan's mouth turned upward. "Not unless all this business was an elaborate ruse to get into our intelligence office and steal Clair de Lune secrets for Soleil."

Scarlett shook her head fervently.

Lachlan put his hand up. "That was a joke. Are either of you spies?"

"No," said Beni and Scarlett in unison.

"Then you'll be fine. Through the veritas you go." He walked through the archway without another word.

Scarlett took several tentative steps forward. Under the archway, the colorful dust swirled around her, but she didn't feel it on her skin. Beni followed after her, smiling slightly at the shimmering dust as he stepped through it. They hurried to catch up with Lachlan and the clerk, who were already halfway down the long hallway.

"There are mirrors to all the countries on the continent in these rooms," said Lachlan as they followed behind the clerk. "These ones are used for law enforcement exclusively. Parliament has their own set downstairs for legislative business. This is common knowledge in Clair de Lune, by the way. Soleil has a similar setup, but I know they aren't open about it. It's probably best not to mention the mirror connecting Clair de Lune to Soleil once you're back home."

Scarlett huffed out a laugh. "I'm no stranger to keeping mirrors a secret. Thanks for explaining."

The clerk knocked on an office door to announce their arrival. A man in a wrinkled black suit came out of the office.

"General Maddox." The two men shook hands, and then he turned to Scarlett and Beni. "I'm Agent McClean."

Lachlan briefed him on the situation, and Agent McClean waved them all inside. His office contained a desk facing the mirror to Soleil and a couple of chairs. In the mirror, there was a woman working at her own desk. She looked up from her computer as they entered, and her eyes widened as she took in Scarlett and Beni.

"That's Agent Thorn in the mirror. You can go ahead and explain your situation to her," said Agent McClean. He took a seat at his desk.

Scarlett approached the mirror, with Beni at her side. "I'm Lady Scarlett Heroux. This is my brother, Beni."

"Of course, Lady Heroux. I know who you are," said the agent. "And Beaufort, isn't it?"

"That's my legal name. I go by Beni."

"No matter. Wait just a minute—I'll go find the agent assigned to your case."

Minutes later, two agents appeared in the Soleil side of the mirror.

"Lady Heroux, Beaufort," said the second agent—a middle-aged man with thinning brown hair. "I'm Agent Ward. Thank you for making contact."

"Of course," said Scarlett. "I came as soon as I saw the news. I had no idea my stepmother was under the impression I was abducted."

"Please tell us what happened from your perspective," said Agent Ward.

Beni and Scarlett stood shoulder to shoulder in front of Agent Ward as Scarlett spoke. "My brother, Beaufort Heroux, and my grandmother, Manon Bedivere, were both concerned for my health. With my consent, Manon arranged for the three of us to travel to Clair de Lune for medical care in the home of our family friends, the Maddoxes." Scarlett looked back at Lachlan, who waved at Agent Ward. "My grandmother was born here, so we're able to travel between countries," said Scarlett. "Admittedly, we left without informing my stepmother of our plans, which I now see was a misstep."

"That's much less nefarious than what your stepmother told me yesterday. Beaufort, you don't have a Clair de Lune visa as far as we're aware. Is that correct?"

"No, I don't," said Beni.

"He's my legal heir," said Scarlett. "I believe I have guardianship rights that extend to shared citizenship. Apologies if I misunderstood the limits of guardianship. The paperwork was filed before I was . . . incapacitated."

Agent Ward's shoulders relaxed. "If that's the case, you're in the clear. I'll contact the courts to ensure everything is in order with your guardianship paperwork. When are you both planning on returning to Soleil?"

"As soon as possible." Scarlett looked questioningly at Lachlan and Manon. "When do you think we can get a train?" She didn't know how long it would take to produce the marriage certificate.

Lachlan stepped forward. "Tomorrow afternoon, I'd wager."

"I'll let Lady Laylani know to expect you tomorrow," said Agent Ward.

One day stood between Scarlett and Laylani. She grinned as she pictured the look she'd see on Laylani's face when she walked through the door. She couldn't wait to make her pay.

But first she had to bind herself to Brayden. She *wanted* to bind herself to him. Her heartbeat became fast and uneven as she considered what was next. Now that the bureau was dealt with, it was time to marry her best friend.

CHAPTER (21)

*I*n the manicured gardens behind the white dome of Clair de Lune's parliament, Scarlett's palms sweated as she stood next to Brayden and their registrar, a sweet older man. Their wedding ceremony was about to begin. A lake bordered the gardens, stretching far into the distance to Mont Noir. Scarlett had always imagined she'd be married on a sunny Soleil day, maybe even on a beach, but a stormy sky hung over the mountains and the lake. Stunning in its own way, but not what she expected.

After they'd finished speaking to the Soleil Bureau, Manon had hustled Scarlett off to her home to get Sabina's dress and a pair of teardrop diamond earrings of her own for Scarlett to borrow. Then they'd gone to a boutique on Clair de Lune's high street, where she'd bought the first shoes she tried on, as well as a blue garter studded with crystals.

It was so strange, wearing her mother's wedding dress. It fit perfectly. Fitted at the waist, its flared skirt came down to mid-thigh. Pearls lined the square neckline, and the long sleeves were perfect for

the cloudy afternoon. Manon had cried when Scarlett put it on, and then Scarlett had cried, both of them missing Sabina. There'd been no time to do anything with her hair, so it hung loose down her back as it would on any other day.

Excitement, worry, and nerves filled Scarlett as she looked at Brayden, who was heartbreakingly handsome in a dark gray suit and a white dress shirt. They stared at each other, and she saw so many things in his expression. Love, need, and maybe a touch of worry. Her heart raced as she wondered what would pour out of them both as soon as they were alone.

She prayed she was doing the right thing, even though her common sense screamed a visa marriage was wrong. She'd always imagined her wedding as a carefully planned affair, not a last-minute rush job. Yet here she stood, in her mother's wedding dress, as if she were acting in a play. But this was the only way to let Brayden help her while still fulfilling her duty to seek justice in Soleil. Duty. Justice. Revenge. Love. This was the only way all those things could fit together, and so it was the right thing to do. The only thing to do. Even though it seemed selfish.

Scarlett cradled a bouquet of sweet-smelling lilies Brayden had handed her when she'd walked out onto the veranda. Beni and Manon beamed at them, looking as happy as if this *were* a long-awaited wedding and not an event planned this morning. Their hope and love for her and Brayden made Scarlett less afraid. She thought of her father, and his absence crashed over her in a wave of grief.

What would Mum and Dad think of this?

At surface level, they'd be horrified, but if they knew everything . . . they'd be pushing her down the aisle just like Manon and Lachlan were. Oh, how she wished they were here to do just that.

"*They're both here with you in spirit,*" said Nori.

Scarlett blinked several times, determined not to cry.

The registrar cleared his throat, and they all turned to him.

"Marriage is a desire by two people to share themselves and their experiences with each other, and their willingness to accept each other for who they are . . ." He went on, but Scarlett was too lost in thoughts of her parents to hear him. The breeze swirled around them as the registrar spoke, and the fresh smell of Scarlett's bouquet mixed with the scent of the lake and the rosebushes framing the edge of the lawn where they stood.

Scarlett's brand-new white heels pressed into the grass as the registrar moved on to the vows. She handed her bouquet to Manon and put her hands in Brayden's, and his touch steadied her.

"I do solemnly declare that I know of no lawful impediment why I, Scarlett Heroux, may not be joined in matrimony to Brayden Maddox. I take him as my husband and give him this ring as a symbol of my love."

Brayden smiled softly at her.

She took the gold band she'd bought an hour before their ceremony and slid it onto Brayden's ring finger as her heart pounded in her chest. Giving him the ring, knowing it meant he was hers, was unlike anything she'd experienced before. It looked so right on his finger, almost like she'd seen it on him before, but she never had.

The registrar led Brayden through his own declaration. Her throat became thick as he spoke.

"I take her as my wife and give her this ring as a symbol of my love." She'd expected no ring or a simple one, given the minimal time they'd had to prepare, but the elegant ring he slid onto her finger was white gold, with a large marquise diamond in the center. Two trinity knots framed the sides of the diamond and flowed seamlessly into the band of the ring.

Her heart melted at the sight. How had he gotten something so perfect on such short notice?

They were pronounced married, and she braced herself for the kiss, not knowing whether it would be frustrated and passionate like their kiss outside Lachlan's office or, worse, an emotionless peck. At first it was a ghost of a kiss as Brayden leaned down and pressed his lips to hers, but the soft kiss lingered, and his fingers slid into her hair. The love inside Scarlett bubbled over, dominating all other emotion as her hands came up to his face. Her lips parted, and the *taste* of him . . .

Beni whooped and James let out a hoot in the background, and Scarlett pulled back hastily. But Brayden still had his fingers in her hair, and he stared at her for a long moment before dropping his hand.

Like Scarlett, he looked like he was feeling many things, but in this moment he seemed . . . satisfied. Yet there was something feral in his eyes, making her wonder if he'd be gentle and sweet or rough on their wedding night. The question sent a shiver down her spine. She'd be fine with either.

"Regretting *this* yet?" she asked, unable to stop herself from baiting him.

A glint of the wicked smile she knew so well flashed across his face. "No. You?"

"No."

Before she could say more, James wrapped Brayden in a bear hug. Manon dabbed at her eyes with a handkerchief, and Scarlett went over to her and Beni.

"That was lovely," whispered Manon. "You look so good together."

Scarlett hugged her grandmother tightly for a long moment. "I think I've always loved him."

"I wish your mother were here. She'd have loved this." Manon stood back, eyes full of tears.

"I wish she were here too," said Scarlett. "But I'm glad I have you." Her life had taught her you never knew when the ones you loved would leave you. In the future, she'd look back on this day and wish to hold this group of people in her arms again, so today she'd do her best to love them with everything she had. The thought was grim, but it made her love fiercer.

Beni grinned at her. "I can't believe I have a brother-in-law." He looked around and then whispered low enough that only Scarlett could hear, "Thank the Goddess it's Brayden and not Alastair."

She cracked a smile. "I'm glad you approve."

Beni threw his arms around her. "Congratulations, Scarlett."

She squeezed her little brother. "I wouldn't be here if it weren't for you. I love you, Beni."

"I love you too," he replied in a gruff voice.

"Come now, let's get your signatures on the certificate," said the registrar. "Then you can celebrate."

Brayden and Scarlett both signed. As Scarlett stood, Lachlan appeared at her elbow and pulled her into his arms.

"Welcome to the family. I'm thrilled to have you as a daughter."

Her heart flooded with warmth at the kind words. Brayden's father could never replace hers, but having another, different, father in her life was such a comfort.

Scarlett laughed as James hugged her and lifted her off the ground. "You're my brother now," she said, her voice bright.

"You know it, sis," he said as he set her down.

The registrar took a few photos of them with their families in front of the lake, with Mont Noir behind them. Then he took some of Scarlett and Brayden on their own. Scarlett's stomach fluttered as she stood next to Brayden. The day had been a surprise, but at least they were *together*, the way they belonged. In another life—one where Soleil's future wasn't in her hands—she'd stay in Clair de Lune with him and sleep next to him every night for the rest of her life. She wanted that badly, more than almost anything. The longing for it broke her heart a little even as she reveled in being his wife. Maybe eventually, they'd find their way to a future where they could live together forever, but how or when, she didn't know.

Please, Goddess above, let it somehow be so. She just needed to stay alive. All of them needed to stay alive.

A few raindrops fell as the last photo was taken, and Scarlett's first thought was that maybe they were Jules and Sabina's happy tears. As if in confirmation, a rainbow appeared in the sky above her as the cool drops of water touched her face. They all headed to shelter—slowly, in Scarlett's case, because of her heels. But then Brayden scooped her up in his arms and carried her to the veranda as the rain began to pour.

Everyone ate dinner at Lachlan's favorite restaurant. After they'd enjoyed a champagne toast, James suggested they head to The Serpent for celebratory drinks. Inside the wood-paneled bar, Scarlett sat next to Brayden, their families surrounding them, and wished she didn't have to leave Manon behind in Clair de Lune. She brushed the thought away, not wanting to cry again. There were plenty of things to worry about, and she'd be dealing with them soon enough.

"*Make the most of the night,*" agreed Nori. "*The time to wait will be over soon enough, and you don't know when you'll be back again. Carpe noctem!*"

Brayden threaded his fingers through hers. He touched the band of her ring with his fingertip, and the diamond glistened in the soft candlelight. Lachlan and Manon were engaged in their own conversation, as were Beni and James.

"This was my mother's engagement ring," said Brayden, sounding hesitant. "My dad gave it to me this morning. We can get you a wedding band to go with it. Or you could pick out something different in Soleil—"

"I love it." She appreciated that he was trying to give her an out if she didn't like it, but the truth was, she loved the ring. It was beautiful and so Clair de Lune, like him.

"You do?" He held her gaze for a long moment before his lips twisted into a one-sided smile.

"Oy, there's the lovebirds!" shouted Minnie from across the bar.

They turned to see her and Keeley walking toward them. Lachlan and Manon glanced Minnie's way but continued their own hushed conversation on the other side of the table.

"I invited them. Hope that's okay," James said to Brayden and Scarlett.

She nodded rapidly. "Of course."

"Minnie, Keeley, hey," said Brayden as he stood to kiss their cheeks. "We . . ." He looked at Scarlett.

"White dress, and you're in a suit for the first time I can remember," said Keeley, gesturing to them. "James wasn't lying—they got married! Where was our invite, eh? Rude!" But she was grinning.

The bar was getting busier, and there were no empty tables left. Scarlett grabbed her gin and tonic to stand next to Keeley, the champagne hitting her more as she got up. "Sorry! If I'd had twenty-four hours' notice, I'd have definitely invited you."

"She's leaving tomorrow, and I'm going with her. I had to threaten her to agree to marry me before she left. If she bursts into tears, that's probably why," Brayden said with a shrug.

Minnie and Keeley laughed.

"I'm happy you're coming with me," whispered Scarlett.

"Are you sure?" Brayden's lips were warm on her ear. "You've been awfully teary today."

"I'm *happy*," she said in a more forceful whisper. *No regrets, right?*

But from the unasked question, fear was born. What if regretting big relationship milestones like sex and marriage immediately after the fact was something Brayden always did in relationships? She'd have no idea, since they'd never really been together.

Ignorant to her inner turmoil, he was already turning back to Keeley and Minnie. "I'm glad I got to see you again before you leave for Evory."

Scarlett thought of the likely war brewing and how it would impact her new friends, but since she didn't know if that information was public, she said nothing.

"You know, I bet Keeley you'd be an official thing by the end of Scarlett's trip," said Minnie. "You've exceeded my already high expectations with this last-minute wedding."

"You didn't think we'd get together?" Scarlett asked.

Keeley scoffed. "I guessed it'd take till winter solstice. I clearly underestimated how horny you'd be after our 'help' the other night. So horny you needed to lock that dick *down*."

Brayden chuckled, looking more like his carefree self, as he took a sip of his whiskey.

Scarlett's cheeks were hot, but Brayden's laugh made her grin. She took a sip of her drink too, swishing the juniper-flavored gin around in her mouth.

James and Beni joined them where they stood, leaving Lachlan and Manon alone at the table.

"James, are you shocked your little brother is married?" asked Minnie. "The untamable Brayden Maddox, locked down in record time by the smoldering siren Scarlett Heroux."

"He's been obsessed with her for years. I'm not surprised at all." Smirking, James took a swig of his beer.

"Obsessed? Come on." Brayden leaned down to whisper, "I'll miss having total control over what you learn about me."

Scarlett looked at him, and his eyes were twinkling. He was probably buzzed too.

James chuckled. "It was always 'Scarlett this' and 'Scarlett that.' He practically lived in Dad's study. Never seen him as happy as he was when she broke up with that boyfriend."

Scarlett laughed, warming at the reminder of their long-standing feelings for each other. She still couldn't believe he'd been pining hard for her too.

But then Beni spoke up.

"When Scarlett was seventeen, she *begged* Manon to take her to Clair de Lune to meet Brayden. She was *so* moody when Manon told her no."

"Beni!" hissed Scarlett. She was surprised he remembered, given he was seven at the time.

Beni cackled so loud the other patrons turned to see what all the ruckus was about.

"Teenage longing! That's sweet," said Keeley, tilting her head to one side.

Brayden pulled her closer. "Is that true?"

She bit her lip, trying not to smile. "Yes."

His arm around her sent a thrill through her. Touching him was still such a novelty.

"Scarlett, are you aware you married the *bad* Maddox brother?" asked Minnie.

"How's he the bad one? I don't think he's the bad one." She leaned into Brayden, her worries disappearing further under the surface with every sip of gin.

"There's a reason James is the one joining Parliament," said Keeley. "James was always the good child—top marks in school, never got in trouble, volunteered, cared about the world. Brayden is successful too, don't get me wrong, but he's always been a bad boy."

"Oy, I care about the world," said Brayden.

"What do you mean, 'bad boy'?" asked Scarlett. Her nerves couldn't handle some big, unpleasant revelation about him the day of their wedding. She chided herself internally. She *knew* Brayden. He was good.

"He started a fight club at our school," said Keeley as Minnie added, "He drinks like a fish."

Scarlett's shoulders slumped with relief. "Is that all? I like a drink too."

"You know, I'm only twenty-two." Brayden sounded disgruntled. "Aren't I allowed to keep evolving and surprising people? Can't I still grow up to be a politician if I want to?"

"Not here," said Minnie. "I think that ship sailed the day you got caught setting the lake on fire."

"You set the lake on fire? That's awesome!" said Beni.

James tapped Beni on the shoulder and pointed to a pool table on the other side of the room. Beni followed him over there, leaving Brayden and Scarlett with Minnie and Keeley. The music became louder and the lights dimmed in preparation for the switch from after-dinner crowd to late-night.

"How did you do that?" Scarlett looked at him in wonder.

The corners of his mouth turned down. "For the record, I was sixteen and immature, and I dumped a *little* gas into the water and lit it just to see what would happen. Nothing dangerous."

"We should have known then he'd be a firebird," said Minnie.

"The flames were high enough that they were licking some of the tree branches hanging over the edge of the lake," said Keeley. "He had to call for help to save the trees, and it took *five* people using their magic to put the fire out."

Scarlett scrunched her nose up. "That's hilarious."

Lachlan cleared his throat behind them. "Sorry to interrupt, but Manon and I are going to head home."

"Should we come with you?" asked Scarlett. An odd mix of trep-idation and anticipation filled her at the idea of being alone with Brayden. There was so much tension between them and—on her side at least—so much attraction it almost hurt.

"No, no," said Manon from Lachlan's side. "Stay and enjoy your-self. The train doesn't leave until late afternoon tomorrow. Stay out with your friends tonight. Beni, you're coming with us!" called Manon as she marched toward the pool table.

"Do I have to?" Beni groaned.

"Yes," said Manon. "I won't be able to sleep if you're out here getting up to Goddess knows what."

Beni sighed. "Congratulations again," he said with a wave to Brayden and Scarlett.

"Night, Beni," said Brayden.

Scarlett wrapped him in a quick hug. "See you in the morning."

"Love you, darling." Manon kissed her cheek and squeezed Brayden's hand.

The three of them headed out into the night.

Once they were gone, Minnie glanced between Scarlett and Brayden. "Now that your relatives are gone . . . Scarlett, did my gift the other night get you all the way down the garden path, as desired?"

The innuendo made Scarlett smile. "Yes, it did."

Keeley and Minnie cheered so loudly people around them stared. They each gave Scarlett an enthusiastic high-five.

"Onward and upward from here on out, hopefully," said Brayden.

Scarlett looked up at him, and he winked at her, his lip curled up in a half-smile. All trepidation left her, and heat pooled in her stomach at the thought of all the things they could be doing back home in his room. It was enough to make her regret not having left with the others. He bit his lip and stared at her, and she reached her hand inside his suit coat to grip his shirt.

"This calls for shots!" said Keeley, snapping Scarlett out of her reverie.

Minutes later, they were raising shots of tequila into the air. "To Scarlett and Brayden!"

"Yeah!" shouted a man at the bar.

Scarlett licked the salt, drank her shot, and sucked on the lime, trying not to grimace. This shot might just push her from buzzed to sloshed, but she was fine with that tonight. It was her *wedding* night after all.

Keeley slammed her empty shot glass down on the nearest table. "To the dance floor!"

"Yes!" said Minnie.

Without waiting for Scarlett or Brayden, the two of them beelined for the open space next to the pool table, where a couple and a group of three friends were already dancing.

"That was adorable to watch," Brayden said into her ear.

"Adorable? What, me doing a shot? I've probably done as many shots of tequila as you have, buddy." Her voice was louder than she'd meant it to be.

"I highly doubt that."

"*I doubt it too*," said Nori. Scarlett's light sounded muffled.

Why do you sound far away? asked Scarlett.

"*Alcohol does that*," Nori replied.

Scarlett grabbed Brayden by his suit jacket and pulled his face to hers, tasting the tequila on his tongue. As they kissed, she ran her hands over his hard stomach, raking her nails against the fabric of his shirt. His breathing grew heavier as her tongue moved against his.

He broke the kiss. "This is getting me too riled up. If we do any more of that, I'll either have to hide in the bathroom till I calm down or call us a cab."

Scarlett bit her lip. All self-restraint had officially left the building, and she was enjoying being tipsy. It was similar to happiness but more distant. It almost made her forget her worries and their fight. She'd probably pay for it all in the morning, but for now, she loved him, she'd married him, and he was looking at her with such hunger.

"I need to tell you something."

"What?"

She whispered in his ear. "I can't wait to consummate our marriage." Then she licked the side of his neck.

Groaning, Brayden pulled her closer, leaning down to nibble her ear. "Are you ready to go? I definitely am."

Scarlett laughed, her heart lighter than it had been for as long as she could remember.

The moment they were alone in Brayden's room, he pressed his body flush against hers and kissed her, her back up against the bedroom door he'd just shut.

Scarlett unzipped his pants, delighting in the heavy breath he let out when her hand touched his soft skin. He hoisted her into his arms. Her legs wrapped around him as he carried her to the closest surface.

Brayden set her on his desk. She pulled her dress over her head, dropping it onto a chair, and Brayden tore off her panties before stepping out of his own underwear.

"Wait," she said as he came closer.

He froze, the only sound in the room coming from the crackling fire.

She grabbed him by the neck, pulling his forehead to hers. "Never use the word 'regret' when you talk about being with me. Never again. Got it?"

He stared at her. "Got it. And you—promise you'll let me keep you safe. Can you do that?" he asked in a throaty voice, his eyes blazing with want and a little bit of anger.

"I promise." Fate might pull them apart regardless of what she wanted, but she'd let him protect her, as long as it was up to her.

Scarlett's thighs parted, and Brayden stepped into them. He slid a finger inside of her, hooking it into the wall of her pussy. She pushed into it, needing more friction.

"I want you. Right now." Pushing his hand away, she reached down and grasped his cock, guiding him inside.

He slid in. "Fuck, Scarlett," he groaned in her ear.

Scarlett sat on the edge of his desk and pulled him closer until he was deep within her. He moved slowly. The edginess she'd been keeping at bay all day was finally gone now that she had his fullness inside of her, and she didn't want slow. She pulled him even closer and kissed him, biting his lip. His breathing was jagged. He was still wearing his dress shirt, and she yanked at the fabric, wanting him as close to her as possible.

"More," whispered Scarlett. "Show me how much you want me."

"Don't be in such a rush. Let me touch you first."

He somehow unhooked her bra single-handedly. She pulled it off, and he flung it aside, exposing her breasts as he continued his torturous slow pace. He cupped them both, running his thumbs over her nipples, and she moaned.

"That's right." He pushed her down onto her back, licked his thumb, and circled her clit as she writhed under him.

An orgasm crested through her seconds later, and her vision went momentarily black as she became a trembling mess on the desk. When she opened her eyes, he was staring down at her.

"Good girl. You still want more?"

"Yes."

He planted his palms on either side of her as she lay with her back on the desk. Scarlett hooked her legs around him, and he thrust into her hard.

"That's what I want," she said breathily.

He slammed into her again and again, and the sheer bliss of it—she felt like she was glowing even as the edge of the desk dug into her back.

He bent over her, and she licked his neck like she had at the bar, loving the taste of his skin and biting his ear as she dragged her nails down his back. His whole body tensed as he spilled himself, and as he rocked into her, she loved knowing part of him would linger inside.

Brayden stared down at her, his expression unreadable as he hovered above her, their bodies still connected. Scarlett reached for him, pulling the nape of his neck and guiding him toward her breast.

Eyes closed, he circled her nipple with his tongue, making her gasp. Inside her, his cock throbbed and hardened again.

Scarlett let out a breathy little moan. "Take me to bed."

He lifted her off the desk and sat upright at the foot of his bed, with her on his lap. She unbuttoned his shirt, and he pulled it off, casting it to the ground.

They were both totally naked as Scarlett got on her knees, wrapped her arms around Brayden's neck, and slid onto his hot cock as he thrust into her. She bounced on him, sliding him in and out of her, loving the control over their speed, and Brayden's grip on her tightened, driving Scarlett down even harder. The need for him—she had to finish again. She stared down at him, his corded muscles gleaming and constricting underneath her in the dim firelight.

The sight of him under her . . . Scarlett rocked against him, desperate for the pleasure that built more and more with every thrust.

"I'm so close," she panted.

He leaned back, bracing himself against the bed with one hand

and grabbing on to her with the other, filling her even deeper as she continued to ride him.

"Oh fuck." She ground her clit into him shamelessly. Then her pussy clenched around him as a wave of endorphins flooded through her.

Scarlett hugged Brayden tight. *I'm so lucky he's mine.*

They fell together onto the bed.

Scarlett leaned over him as he continued pushing into her pliant body. "Come for me," she panted out, dizzy as she breathed in his familiar scent of cedar mixed with clean sweat.

He grabbed her arse, impaling her with his hard-on. Several deep thrusts later, he tensed as he came in her again.

They lay there panting for minutes. Scarlett closed her eyes, letting bliss overcome her.

Some minutes later, she raised herself off his chest. Brayden stared up at her, reverent.

"You make me feel . . ." he whispered. "I just came in you twice, and it wasn't enough." He sounded almost upset.

She ran her fingertips over his chest hair, smiling softly. "I'm glad, especially since we *just* got married. If you didn't want more, our marriage would probably fail." She meant it jokingly, but the words came out sounding more serious than intended.

Brayden's stare was intense. "I'll always want more of you." He held up his left hand, where the gold band glistened in the dim light. "I want this forever. Don't ever leave me."

"I won't leave you," she whispered, all traces of humor gone from her voice.

CHAPTER (22)

When Scarlett awoke, tangled with Brayden's body under his soft flannel sheets, his cedar scent was all over the blankets—and all over her too. Her head throbbed, and her mouth and her lips were dry. As she shifted in the bed, soreness in interesting places evoked salacious memories of Brayden pounding into her on his desk.

Goddess. I am an idiot. Why did I drink so much? No regrets about the desk sex though. Or round two in his bed. She smiled with her eyes still closed. No regrets, she'd made him promise. The moment she'd fallen asleep in his arms was hazy, but that discussion—and the sex that followed it—was crystal clear in her mind.

"Welcome back," said Nori.

Good morning, Nori. She nuzzled against the soft hair on Brayden's broad, muscled chest. The finest chest she'd ever had the pleasure of touching. He had the finest everything.

His arms tightened around her, and he kissed her hair. "Good morning."

"Morning." Scarlett licked her dry lips.

"Big day today." He stroked her back with his fingertips, making her skin tingle.

"It is." Scarlett sighed as she held her left hand above them. She loved the way the diamond ring sparkled as she toyed with the delicate band. "I'm sad to leave. I barely got to spend any time here, but I've fallen in love with it." The cold air made her skin pebble, and she retracted her arm back into the nest of soft blankets.

Brayden was silent for half a minute. Long enough to make her wonder what he was thinking.

"Do you think you could live here?" he asked eventually. His tone was light, but the question was loaded.

His words from last night rang in her head. *"Don't ever leave me."* Brayden's vulnerability was completely new to her, and it made her want to give him everything. Even things she shouldn't. She didn't want to leave him. Thankfully today he was leaving with her. He'd be the one to leave her in Soleil when he eventually returned to Clair de Lune.

He gave her a charming grin, lightening the mood.

She swallowed, gathering her words as she toyed with the hair on his chest. "While I've been here, I've wondered a couple of times what it would have been like if my dad had moved here with my mum instead of her joining him in Soleil. They'd probably both still be alive."

If he noticed her nonanswer, he didn't show it. "Your dad had big dreams though. And an inherited seat in Parliament. He couldn't have lived his life in Clair de Lune," said Brayden. *Are you the same as him?* She could hear his unasked question.

"I think he wanted to use his position for the greater good," she said carefully. She wanted to bind herself to Brayden, not have another fight. "If I pretend duty wasn't a factor, I can see him as a bookseller in Clair de Lune. He'd have been happier doing that than he was as a politician." Under the covers, she rubbed her smooth leg against his hairy one, enjoying the sensation.

"What about you? Would you be happier in another job?"

"Hmm. I've known since I was little I was destined to work in politics. If I had to choose a different career, I might choose teaching."

"You could do *that* almost anywhere." His warm brown eyes looked cautious but hopeful. He reached toward her and brushed some strands of hair out of her face.

"Yes, I could. I could teach politics after a few years in Parliament. It's hard to imagine doing that in the foreseeable future though. The government is so divided. If I gave up my seat to Beni today, it'd be empty for at least six years until he was old enough to get an age exception. The Ceruleans would have a harder time passing any of the legislation my dad believed in." Scarlett raked her nails over Brayden's bicep as she considered it. "If Beni came of age and agreed to take the seat, I could potentially quit."

"What would happen if you gave him the seat and he gave it up too?"

What if Beni would want to live in Clair de Lune with us?

Scarlett sat up, clutching the duvet to her chest. Shivering at the chill in the air, she reached for the water on the nightstand closest to her, taking a long drink before answering. She didn't want to think about both her and Beni abdicating. "They'd give the seat to a distant relative, or if there truly wasn't anyone, the prime minister would award it to someone deserving." Scarlett offered Brayden the glass. His eyes had been glued to her bare back, and he took the glass with a roguish grin.

"Thanks," he said, downing the rest of the water and setting the cup on his nightstand.

Scarlett lost focus for a second at the sight of his bare chest and the curve of his arse, barely visible under the edge of the blanket. Then he scooted closer to her once more, and she was lost in the kiss he placed on her neck, delighting in the sensation of his stubble scraping against her skin.

After a long moment of his lips moving over her body, she laughed breathily and pushed him away. "You're distracting me, and I want to finish this conversation. What about you? Could you be happy doing something else?"

"I want to talk too, but you're so kissable, and in my bed, and so very naked." He bit her earlobe before leaning back against the headboard. "I don't know what else I'd be good at. I've always liked doing physical stuff. I also love this place so much. This may sound cheesy, but there's something fulfilling about it being my job to protect my family and my home. It matters to me, you know? I'd also like to see my dad retire before he gets too old to enjoy it."

She swallowed. "I don't think that's cheesy at all. It's nice. I wish my dad could have enjoyed retirement. I thought we had more time."

"Exactly. That's why I want to take over from Lachlan sooner rather than later."

"What do you mean, you want to take over from him? Do you inherit Lachlan's job because you're his son?" asked Scarlett.

"No. I don't *inherit* it, exactly, but . . ."

"People expect you to take the job?" She ran her fingers through his hair.

Brayden leaned into Scarlett's touch. She gasped as he pulled her onto his lap and wrapped his arms around her shoulders.

"It's because of my valor. I've been the heir apparent since I came out of the Forest Temple with the phoenix valor when I was eighteen." His voice rumbled against her back.

She stiffened. "I can't believe I didn't know that," she whispered. It was another slap in the face, reminding her that while she knew parts of him better than anyone else, much of Brayden was still a mystery to her. Like he'd said last night at the bar, he'd had the ability to control what she knew and what she didn't through the mirror. That was all too apparent now.

He rested his chin on her shoulder. "I didn't mean to keep it a secret. We never spoke about valors, and I don't like to make a big deal about it."

"I wish you'd said something."

"Why does it matter?"

"Because there's no chance you'll ever move to Soleil," she snapped. Before, she'd assumed—arrogantly, she now realized—his position in the Clair de Lune army was less pivotal than hers in Soleil, but it was dawning on Scarlett they were both equally tied to their inherited roles. That could mean never living together full-time, and how could they stand that?

Heavy silence enveloped the room before he replied. "I can't right *now*, with Evory about to go to war. But maybe someday."

She swallowed a remark about conversations they probably should have had before getting married and focused on the politics. "What's the latest on the Evory situation anyway?"

"The latest is they're launching unauthorized, weaponized aircraft into Evory's airspace."

Her chest tightened. Images of what could be flashed through her mind. Brayden, caught up in the horrors of war, while she was thousands of miles away.

"And you'll see combat if there's a war."

"Yes." He still held her caged in his arms, her back to his front, as if the closeness could take away the pain of the thought of him in danger.

She mulled that over in silence. Brayden was powerful, but the idea of him risking his life in combat gutted her to her core.

"Listen," he said as he stroked her skin gently. "Let's not dwell on tomorrow's problems. I'm glad we're talking about the future, but let's get through the next couple of weeks before we worry about long-term plans."

She was about to retort that it was easy for him to be calm when he'd known for longer than five seconds he was going to be the head of the military, but before she could, there was a knock at his door.

"It's Lachlan. Are you two up yet? I'm sorry to interrupt, but Brayden, I want to brief you on Soleil military personnel before you go. We don't have much time today."

"Give me five minutes, and I'll be right out," called Brayden.

Scarlett sighed. Their time together was never enough, even when they were fighting.

"For the first time in my life, I want my own place," grumbled Brayden.

Scarlett thought of Laylani, who was probably having her morning coffee in the Heroux home. The image made her seethe. "Me too." She pried herself out of his lap. "Can I borrow some clothes?"

"Of course." He pulled on his boxers and went to his wardrobe, grabbing a T-shirt and a pair of gym shorts and throwing them onto the bed next to her.

"Look," she said as she pulled the clothes on. "You're right—we should get through the next couple of weeks before we worry about the future. But once we're in Soleil, we have to present a united front. Our marriage is going to be very public very fast. We have to—*have to*—look like a happily married couple with our shit together, not a couple with no idea how we're going to be together. If people think it's not a real marriage, your visa could be denied or revoked. We also don't want the press to pick us apart." She hated the way she sounded. Obsessed with appearances, just like Laylani. The woman was haunting her from another country.

He pulled his pants on and faced her. "Of course."

She stood in front of him, dressed in his clothes, and pressed herself to his chest. "I am so happy you're coming with me."

"Me too," he said gruffly, closing his arms around her.

CHAPTER (23)

The train pulled out of the Clair de Lune station. Less than twenty-four hours after marrying Brayden, Scarlett was on her way back to Soleil. Her throat was thick as her grandmother and Lachlan disappeared from view, but Brayden coming back with her, *as her husband*, distracted her from some of her anguish. His presence next to her was comforting, even if the evolution of their relationship was giving her whiplash. Enjoying their newfound love without rushing into a visa marriage would've been ideal, but there was no question—she'd rather have him like this than not at all. She hoped they could go a few days without unearthing another major roadblock to their long-term happiness.

Beni pulled out a deck of cards and shuffled them on the table in front of them. "Want to play knights and knaves?"

"Sure," said Brayden.

"I'll play later, maybe," said Scarlett. "I have some reading I want to do first."

As they started a game, she reached into her bag, pulling out one of her mother's diaries.

When she'd gone to her room to pack up her minimal belongings, Scarlett had looked at the box of Sabina's journals with regret, wishing she could take them all back with her. She'd spent twenty minutes rifling through it, trying to get a sense of how many years the diaries spanned. Finding one dated the year of Sabina's death, she'd stashed it in her bag along with a journal from the year she was born. Then she'd taken the rest to Brayden's room and set them in his bureau, figuring they'd be safe there while she was away.

Now she opened the older of the two journals she'd taken. Her mother's messy cursive script was familiar from the handful of birthday cards she'd given Scarlett, which she kept safe in a drawer at home.

Scarlett read a couple of entries at the beginning. The mundane was beautiful in her mother's words. Scarlett savored Sabina's observations of social events in Soleil, chuckling to herself at her accounts of lords and ladies, a couple of whom she knew in present day.

Her heart ached as she read entries about herself as a baby. It was obvious her mother loved her so, even through the trials of being a new parent with a spouse who was often absent. Sabina had accepted help from a nanny during the day, but she'd insisted on doing all the nighttime care herself rather than getting a night nanny like most of the Soleil upper class. As a result, many of her entries mentioned sleep deprivation on days when Scarlett had been up in the night several times. She'd never known how her mother had cared for her.

Then her heart skipped a beat as she spotted her stepmother's name.

Laylani Ashworth sat next to me at the state banquet last week, and I think she's my new favorite person. Jules was sitting at the other end of the table when Lord Leon made some idiotic remark about Jules marrying me despite me being from Clair. He was looking down at my chest as he said it, implying in the grossest way possible that Jules had married me for my looks. Laylani overheard the comment and told him he wouldn't get the time of day from any woman on the continent if he wasn't a lord. I've never been so pleasantly surprised. Nor have I had someone from Soleil stand up for me that way. Except for Jules, of course. Laylani and I spent the rest of the dinner talking. She's quite funny. She invited me to attend fashion week with her in a fortnight, and I look forward to seeing her again. I need more friends here. Real friends.

After that came several journal entries detailing Sabina's efforts to publish in a Soleil-based scientific journal. There was no mention of fashion week, nor how it had gone.

Scarlett picked up the newer journal, ready to read some of her mother's last entries. Another mention of Laylani immediately jumped out to Scarlett.

I'm pregnant again, and I couldn't be happier! I wrote to Mam to share the news and to ask if it'll be a boy or a girl. The tests will tell me in a few weeks, but

> *I don't want to wait. I told Laylani, and she offered to come over and help me decide which room to remodel for the baby. Scarlett will love being a sister, although I'm sure she might not like sharing attention!*

Scarlett wanted to scream at her mother to keep Laylani away. Pregnant? She'd never known her mother got pregnant again. She flipped to the last page and nearly stopped breathing.

> *I don't know how to heal. I keep telling myself I was lucky. The car crash could have killed me, and the idea of Scarlett being alone in the world without me . . . I'm grateful to be alive. But losing the baby this way, I feel so heavy. Her whole life was ahead of us in my heart. But she's gone. I only had her for the fourteen weeks she was in my belly. I'll never be the same.*

The idea of a sister filled Scarlett with longing. Glancing at Brayden, she imagined the joy they might one day experience if they got pregnant, and the nightmare of having that joy stolen by a random accident. She took a deep breath and read onward.

> *I've been so sad and in so much pain. I've been oddly lethargic the past couple of days. I'm trying to go through the motions with a smile on my face, because I don't want Scarlett to see how much I'm*

suffering, but it's hard. Laylani has been so kind, staying with me almost constantly and helping me keep my chin up. But she's not family. I can't be totally open with her. Jules is always at work. Thankfully, my mam will be here soon, and she can help me get some space to grieve without frightening Scarlett. I need to get better for Scarlett.

It was bizarre, knowing how close Laylani had been during her mother's darkest hours. What would Sabina think if she could see Jules had married Laylani after she passed? It made Scarlett seethe, and she set the journal down to run her hands over her face.

"What's wrong?" asked Beni from across the table. "Your face is so pale."

She looked up at her brother. Was he old enough to know this? The diary had said nothing and everything. After reading it, Scarlett was certain Laylani had killed her mother. The odd lethargy she'd described had immediately reminded her of her own drug-induced coma. Beni would think the same if she let him read it.

"*He can handle it,*" said Nori.

Scarlett tapped Brayden on the shoulder and pointed to the page she'd just read. He leaned closer to read the journal, and as he read, he let out a loud sigh.

"That's difficult to read." He gripped her hand, his expression filled with sadness. "You should show him."

Without being told, he'd intuited her internal debate.

She handed the journal over to Beni. "This is my mum's last journal entry before she died. You might not know this, but when she died, everyone believed it was sleeping sickness."

The color drained from her brother's face as he scanned the page. "You almost had a sister?" He read onward, his jaw tense. "My mum was there. She did this too. She killed your mum."

"I think so," Scarlett said. "I'm sorry if that's a lot, but you deserve to know the whole truth."

Brayden squeezed her hand under the table, giving her strength and comfort.

Beni's expression was stoic. "There's nothing for you to be sorry for. Is this enough to change your mind about going back home while she's there? Should we go to a hotel or something? I already thought it was weird you want to live with her, but knowing she killed your mum . . ."

Scarlett shook her head. "I want to stay with her, because the closer we are, the easier it'll be to keep an eye on her and get more proof. We have the test results from our urine proving unnecessary drugs were in our systems, but we need more. We need something on Laylani, not just the doctor she hired. I need an opportunity to search her things."

Beni didn't look convinced.

Scarlett continued, more anger in her voice. "Besides, she's in *my* house. *We're* the Heroux heirs, and I'm not going to let her keep us out of our own home. I'll get a bodyguard, and there's no way she can hurt us with Brayden there. I'll sort it as fast as I possibly can. Believe me, she won't be living there long."

Beni's brow furrowed, just like their father's had when he was unhappy about something. "It's ridiculous to go back there when we ran away only a few days ago."

"Everything is different now," said Scarlett. "I'm on my guard, and she won't get the better of me again."

"And you have me," said Brayden. He held his free hand up, and tiny streams of flame flew out of his fingertips as if his hand were a firecracker.

"That's so cool." Beni's expression melted into a grin. "I am glad you're here, man."

Scarlett threaded her arm through Brayden's and leaned into him. "Me too."

After their train had pulled into the Soleil station, warm air blew across Scarlett's face as she disembarked. Her heart pounded as they walked to the passport check with their soul lights hovering over them. She'd believed her grandmother when Manon told her no one without a soul light would see hers, but she still felt an irrational desire to flee as they approached customs.

Beni walked through first with no issues. The officer, a middle-aged man with bags under his eyes, didn't notice Riley. Scarlett's tension eased.

"Lady Heroux, it's good to see you out and about," said the officer as Scarlett approached, with Brayden at her side. "I was sorry to read about your illness in the news." He glanced at her passport before handing it back to her.

"Thank you," said Scarlett, glad to hear that was the first thing that came to the officer's mind rather than her grandmother's alleged kidnapping of her and Beni.

Brayden was up next. The officer's eyebrows narrowed at his green Clair de Lune passport, and his lips pressed into a thin line as he examined the marriage certificate Scarlett held out to him. The abrupt change in his demeanor was a shock after he'd been so warm to her.

"You got married yesterday?" asked the officer.

"Yes," said Brayden and Scarlett together.

The officer cocked his head to the side. "How did you meet?"

"We met when we were children and have been in touch for years," said Scarlett, speaking too fast. Black and gold smoke appeared above the man's head. *Shit.*

"She broke up with her ex a couple of months ago, and I asked her to come visit right away, before she could change her mind and go back to the other guy," said Brayden in a much calmer voice. "She's the love of my life, and when you know, you know. So we got hitched." He leaned down and planted a kiss on her cheek, causing her face to heat.

Why is he saying all this? Bringing up Alastair was weird, wasn't it? Scarlett looked at Brayden, but he just smiled and wrapped his arm around her shoulders. The realization hit her that maybe he was right to reference Alastair. Their relationship *had* been common knowledge in Soleil. Her tension eased slightly.

The officer's eyes slid to her. "Fast work. Smart man, knowing when you're punching. I was the same way with my wife, actually. Married her before she figured out she could do better." He winked at Scarlett. "How'd you two meet as kids, though, being from different countries and all?"

Scarlett took a deep breath. "Oh, I'm a dual citizen. Our families are friends, and I have a Clair de Lune passport as well." Scarlett handed him her second passport, which was Clair de Lune green like Brayden's. "Also, I've got a picture of us at the wedding, if you'd like to see?"

Gold smoke. He believed them, thank the Goddess.

"That's right. I forgot your mother was a foreigner," said the officer, flicking through her passport. He waved Scarlett's phone away. "No need for photos. Head through that door. They'll issue a spouse visa in that office. Congratulations on your nuptials." He waved the next passenger forward for visa inspection as Beni, Scarlett, and Brayden moved on.

Scarlett let out a huge breath and took Brayden's hand.

"I knew you were well-known, but getting recognized by border control—that's the first time I've seen how famous you are for myself," he said. "That officer liked you."

"Yes. Fame is a double-edged sword."

After half an hour's wait, Brayden's spouse visa was in hand, and the three of them went to look for Charlie.

"There he is!" Beni hurried over to the bench where Charlie was waiting. Scarlett halted for a split second as she took in the cast and sling on his left arm. As she and Brayden approached, their aging boat driver wrapped Beni in a one-armed hug.

"You're all a sight for sore eyes."

"Charlie, it's good to see you!" said Scarlett. "What happened to your arm?"

Charlie hugged Scarlett and looked her up and down. "Arm's fine. Just a clumsy accident." He glanced away and then back at her, his eyes gleaming. "I'm more concerned with you. Glad to see you're getting around fine. Are you all right?"

She frowned at the brush-off, sensing there was more to his story. "I'm much better, thank you. They have excellent doctors in Clair de Lune." She wished Dr. Bowen could help with Charlie's arm. Maybe someday that would be possible in Soleil.

Charlie turned to Brayden, a welcoming smile spreading across his face. "Who's this?"

Scarlett waved Brayden forward. "This is Brayden Maddox. Brayden, this is Charlie. He's known me since I was born and is like family." She beamed at Charlie, letting her love for Brayden show. "Brayden and I got married yesterday."

Brayden extended his hand. "Good to meet you." His smile was bright and warm, the carefree smile she'd missed seeing through the past couple of days. *She* wanted to make him smile like that again.

Charlie's eyes were wide as he whistled and clasped Brayden's hand. "Married? Wow, congratulations. I look forward to getting to know you, Brayden. I'm sure you know you've got a good one in Scarlett."

"I certainly do," agreed Brayden, pulling her tight against his side. Between this and that interaction with the customs officer, Brayden was doing a good job of looking like a guy who was happy to be married. He was obviously going to have no problem presenting a united front.

"Now, can you please tell me what really happened to your arm? And how have things been since we left?" asked Scarlett.

Charlie glanced uncertainly at Brayden.

"You can say anything in front of him," said Scarlett, understanding his concerns. "He knows everything."

Charlie nodded quickly. "Understood. Laylani was livid when she figured out you'd gone, but when she asked me about it, I said I wasn't in the business of keeping people in the house who didn't want to be there. That shut her up, but then, the next day, I was on my way to the store for Martin when some thugs jumped me. This was the result." He gestured to his arm.

"And I'm sure that had nothing to do with Laylani," said Scarlett.

Charlie lifted the shoulder that wasn't in the sling in a one-armed shrug. "The cast will be off in a few weeks. Thankfully, it was a clean break. It's all good, Scarlett."

Scarlett disagreed, but it was clear he didn't want to pursue it, so she let the matter drop for the time being.

Charlie gestured to the exit. "Anyway, ready to get out of here?"

"Yes," said Scarlett. "But first, let's stop by the newsagents and get Brayden some sunglasses. He's basically never seen sunlight." She gave him an affectionate smile as she wondered if he could tan or if he'd just burn. Her pale sweetheart.

Inside the small shop, they found a pair of suitable sunglasses. Scarlett was scanning the newspapers when a glossy magazine caught her eye. An old picture of her and Alastair at the diplomat's soirée was on the cover. She pursed her lips as she picked it up and flipped to the article. It was an entire spread of pictures taken earlier that year by paparazzi. She scanned the first couple of sentences: *"When can we expect to see Lady Heroux and the handsome Alastair Spencer out in Soleil? Here's an overview of the season's high-society events!"*

Brayden peered at the page and snorted.

She turned to him. "It's weird they don't know Alastair and I broke up." She'd lived multiple lives since that day at the boxing match.

His lips were pursed, and he was frowning slightly. "Not if he hasn't mentioned it to anyone."

"Maybe we should send our wedding pictures to the newspapers."

He gave her a crooked grin. "More than fine by me."

She glanced at him sideways. "Nice work with the border-control officer, by the way. You're doing a great job of acting like a doting husband."

His grin faded. "You know better than to think that was an act."

"I just meant—"

But he walked away before she could point out that he'd embellished the story somewhat. And maybe he was right. Maybe she needed to take things at face value. Because he was *here*. For her. She kicked herself mentally for not being more sensitive.

"You'll make it up to him," said Nori, comforting her. *"I'd wager he's extra touchy because of that magazine article, but the truth will out."*

Thanks, Nori. It was amazing how much hope Scarlett took from her light's uplifting comments. She imagined the situation in reverse.

If she'd seen a magazine spread featuring Brayden and an ex-girl-friend, she'd probably have had a complete meltdown, especially if he'd gone on to congratulate her on being a great fake wife. She sighed, willing herself to do better.

They made their way out of the shop to the brightness of the Prince's Street Dock and stood on the boat's deck while Charlie pulled the lines in, preparing to cast off. The day was oppressively hot. Already pink-cheeked from the heat, Brayden peeled off his dark green sweater, revealing the black T-shirt underneath. Scarlett, who'd taken her cardigan off back in the station, fished her oversized white-framed sunglasses out of her bag and put them on.

She watched as Brayden took in all the grand buildings surrounding the canal. He wore his new aviator sunglasses as he looked at the statue of Hadrian in the middle of the aquatic roundabout. Today the water smelled fresh, without the taint of sewage that occasionally plagued the city, and as usual, the Soleil sun was making the water sparkle. The familiar sights, the warmth—Scarlett was glad to be home. She hoped Brayden was at least somewhat impressed by what he saw.

He noticed her watching him. "It's so bright here. It's sunnier than the absolute sunniest day in Clair de Lune. Even Evory . . . It gets sunnier there, but nothing like this."

"We do have a winter, but it's mild, and it's still sunny most of the time. This place is basically endless summer." She put her hand into his back pocket and stared up at him, marveling that he was here, in her world, and wanting to make him love it enough to come back again and again.

CHAPTER (24)

When they arrived, Scarlett stood on the dock and stared up at House Heroux. It looked as familiar and grand as it always had, but before, it had simply been home. Now it was where she'd been trapped and sedated. It was the home where her father had lived, but he'd never see it again.

Brayden stepped off the boat behind her, and his hand slid into hers.

The front door opened ahead of them, snapping Scarlett out of her reverie. Laylani appeared. She wore a golden sheath dress, and her brown hair was in perfectly coiled curls.

"Such a pretty face for one with such a black heart."

It was the angriest tone Scarlett had heard from her light.

She probably drinks virgin blood to stay young, thought Scarlett.

The internal conversation quieted as they approached her stepmother. Scarlett had anticipated seeing Laylani, but she still struggled to keep a blank face as she looked at the woman who'd killed

her mother and tried to kill her and her grandmother. She squeezed Brayden's hand as venom bubbled in her stomach. It was sorely tempting to kick off their reunion by pushing Laylani into the canal, but if she began like that, she'd lose what little element of surprise she had.

Beni locked gazes with Scarlett and then Brayden before walking down the dock. She and Brayden trailed behind him. He tried to pass his mother and go straight for the door, but Laylani pulled him back from the threshold and grasped him in her arms. Beni accepted the hug, putting one hand lightly on his mother's back, but his theatrical look of disgust was hidden from her. Scarlett had been full of hate only a second before, but at witnessing this, it took all she had not to burst into laughter.

"Beaufort, I've missed you," said Laylani as she released him.

Scarlett's palms grew damp as Laylani embraced Beni again. She sounded sincere, but it was also such a de minimis reaction after an unplanned trip abroad. She wished—not for the first time—Beni was her full-blooded brother.

"Thanks," said Beni, his voice flat. He stepped around her and headed into the house.

Laylani watched him walk away, pursing her lips as she studied her son. Once he was out of sight, she turned to Scarlett and Brayden, her mask solidifying into a bland smile.

"Hello, Scarlett. I must say, I was disturbed by your dramatic nighttime exodus. Are you well?"

As if she cares. "I'm fine. Apologies for the abrupt departure, but we were concerned for my grandmother. She's recovered, but she's remained in Clair de Lune for personal reasons." None of the rage Scarlett held for this woman came out as she spoke, and she was proud of how level her voice sounded.

Laylani smirked as she scanned Scarlett from head to toe, eyeing the comfortable T-shirt and skirt she'd chosen to wear on the train. "Fair enough. I'm relieved you're all right." Her attention shifted to Brayden. "And who is this?"

"This is Brayden Maddox." Scarlett squeezed his hand, still entwined with hers. His solid presence next to her was comforting in the face of her greatest enemy.

"But *who* is he? And what's he doing here?"

"He's a family friend."

Laylani rolled her eyes. "Then how have I never met him before?"

"He's from Clair de Lune." It was her turn to wear a smug smile as Laylani stared at them for a beat.

As she hesitated, Scarlett guessed she was trying to assess how much of a fake front she needed to put up for him.

"I'm Scarlett's stepmother, Laylani." Her fingers splayed across her chest. She didn't extend a hand for him to shake.

"I know who you are," said Brayden, his voice calm and devoid of any warmth.

"Will you be joining us for dinner, Brayden, or are you just here to help with their bags?" Laylani smiled faintly, her eyes flicking to their clasped hands.

Scarlett saw red. It was *so* tempting to push Laylani in the canal. For her mother, her father, her brother, and herself. But revenge would have to wait. She took a deep breath.

Brayden snorted softly. "All of the above. I'll carry Scarlett's bag anytime she likes." He winked at Scarlett.

His flirting loosened the knot in her chest. "So chivalrous," she said with a sultry stare.

"Excuse me?" Laylani's tone was incredulous. "What exactly is the nature of this? Some sort of rebound fling?" Her eyebrows rose as if she were genuinely surprised, though her cold smile said otherwise.

"Quite the opposite of a rebound. He's moving in. We got married." Scarlett held up her ring finger, and the diamond glinted in the sun. Her lips curved up in a satisfied smile as Laylani's mouth fell open and she assessed Brayden with fresh eyes.

She scoffed as she recovered from the shock. "Married? Goodness me. You didn't waste any time, Scarlett. Poor Alastair won't know what hit him. But where are my manners? Welcome to the family, Brayden. Please, come in." Her thin-lipped smile was icy.

"Thanks." Brayden's tone was quietly sarcastic, making Scarlett smile.

Who is she to welcome anyone to your family? said Nori.

Agreed, thought Scarlett as Laylani strode through the open front door. "I hate that she has my last name," she muttered.

Brayden raised his eyebrow at her. "You could use mine." He stooped to pick up their bags. "If you want to."

The comment gave her butterflies. It was tempting, even if it was unheard of for a head of house in Soleil to take another name. "Scarlett Maddox has a nice ring to it," she agreed as she led him into the foyer. The sunlight streaming through the doorway dimmed as Brayden's form filled the entrance, and the familiar smell of lemon polish and fresh-cut flowers washed over her.

Laylani stood in the foyer waiting for them like she was trying to emphasize that she was their hostess in Scarlett's own home. Scarlett couldn't wait until she'd evicted this evil, murdering witch.

"I'm taking Brayden upstairs to get settled in," she announced before Laylani could say anything.

Laylani's empty smile grew larger. "Of course. Perhaps tomorrow we could all go out for dinner and catch up?"

Scarlett didn't want to eat dinner with Laylani, but maybe her stepmother would get into the wine and say too much. Parliament wasn't in session until the day after next, so she had the time.

"All right," she said after a few seconds. *Let the games begin.*

"Brayden, do you have something nicer to wear, or should I send Charles out to buy some clothes for you?" Laylani asked.

Scarlett narrowed her eyes. *This bitch doesn't quit.*

Brayden remained unfazed. "I'm all set, thanks. I'm sure Scarlett will make sure I'm dressed appropriately—won't you, sweetheart?"

He was so good at managing Laylani.

Her face lit up. "Of course." Scarlett would love to pick his clothes out every day for the rest of his life, if he'd let her. Her eyes raked over him. Even in his rumpled travel clothes, all it took to rile her up was a long glance at his muscular body. Goddess, he looked good in everything he wore.

"Excellent. I'll ring The Twig and Vine. Let's plan for dinner at seven tomorrow evening." Laylani's high heels sounded like hammers on the marble floor as she walked away.

Beni emerged from the hallway that led to his old room carrying his computer and a pile of clothes in his laundry basket. "I'm moving into Manon's room."

"Good idea," said Scarlett, relieved to hear he'd be closer to her. She and Brayden followed him up the marble staircase.

Upstairs, she led Brayden into her bedroom. The bed was made, and the IV stand and other hospital equipment were gone. She let out a sigh and wrung her hands, unsure of what to do now that she was home.

Brayden set their bags down and studied the art in her room with interest. Elaborate hand-painted wallpaper decorated the walls, and a fresco of a dawn sky, complete with frolicking angels, covered her ceiling. He stopped near one of her walls to study a detailed peacock roosting among a cluster of brilliantly blooming flowers, which had always been one of her favorite bits of art in this room.

"This house is something else," he said.

"Do you like it?" she asked, eager to know his thoughts. She'd always loved her family home. It was filled with ancient art kept in timeless perfection. The ceilings were covered in either frescoes or crown molding. There were tapestries and oil paintings on almost every wall. Brayden lived in a working castle, so it wasn't like he was used to a snug family home like Manon's tree house, but would he think this was like living in a museum? His room, while spacious, had been much cozier than hers. To her surprise, the mental comparison made her like her own room just a little less.

"I can't believe this is your room," he said. "Is the whole house like this?"

"Some of the best frescoes are in here, but yes. The whole house is pretty elaborate." She held out her hands, wanting to touch him.

Brayden crossed the space between them in two steps. She wrapped her arms around his waist as he looked down at her. "How are you?" he asked. "After seeing her again."

Scarlett's face fell as she let some of the emotions she'd been battening down below the surface rise. "It took everything I had to remain calm down there. She ruined my life when I was a child, and for what? Did she even love my dad in the end? It's harder than I imagined, being here again." Her voice broke. "I'm glad you're with me. I know it's not convenient for you and the whole visit might be awful." She rubbed her eyes, sniffing. "But I'm so glad you're here. I'd be struggling more if it were just Beni and me." Scarlett leaned into his touch.

As she pressed her face into his chest, his grip tightened around her.

"I'm really glad I'm here too. And Scar?"

She pulled back to look at him. He seemed conflicted. "Yes?"

"I was thinking while we were on the train."

Uh-oh.

"It's not like that," he said hurriedly, seeing her tense. "It's just about the reason I'm here. I'm here to protect you."

She cocked her head. "And?"

He gestured to the couch next to her bookshelves in the corner. "I think I should sleep there."

Scarlett flinched and took a step back. "Why?"

He pulled her closer, refusing to let her back away. "Just for now, okay? Until you get a bodyguard, I need to focus on keeping you safe. I'll probably get up a couple of times a night to do a sweep of the house and check the security footage. I can't do that if I'm getting lost in you for hours every evening, which I know will happen if I don't have some discipline."

She lifted her chin. "So you're not rejecting me because you're mad at me?"

He cupped the nape of her neck. "I'm not rejecting you. I'm putting your safety first. I also don't want to make this week more intense for you than it needs to be. You need rest." He swallowed, searching her face for a reaction. "Goddess knows, neither of us slept much last night."

She stared at the floor. Her thoughts spun as she focused inward, trying to process what he'd just said. How could she not take this as rejection? Did he really think it was necessary to sleep on the couch? She'd probably lie awake later wondering if they were headed for a quick divorce as soon as this was all over.

"*Don't catastrophize,*" chided Nori.

Nori was right. He loved her. He did. This was just his control-freak side coming out again, like it had when she'd threatened to leave him behind. Her chin lifted, and finally, she spoke. "Whatever you think is best," she said in a level voice. It was the best she could do. "Now, come see the mirror from my side. You can put your things in my bureau." She took his hand and led the way.

Inside the dressing room, Brayden set his bag aside and peered through the gilded mirror. "This is surreal."

"I had the same reaction in your dad's office." Scarlett wondered how often she and Manon could continue to use this mirror—then she caught sight of the door to Manon's room. Which was now Beni's room. "I'm going to check on Beni. His room is on the other side of this door. The bathroom's through there, if you want to freshen up or anything."

He stared at her, concern written all over his face. But all he said was "Thanks."

She rapped on Beni's door.

"Come in!"

Manon's peony scent hit her as she walked into her grandmother's old room. Beni was at the desk plugging in his laptop. Manon's floral duvet and sheets lay on the floor in a heap, and Beni's bedding was wadded up on top of the mattress.

Scarlett went to the closest window and opened it, letting in fresh air. "We can fix this room up so it's more you. I'll phone a shipping company tomorrow and have them come get Manon's stuff out of here, and then we can go shopping for some new stuff, if you like."

"Sounds good," he said, not turning toward her.

Scarlett picked up the sheets and started making his bed. After his duvet was spread smoothly over his sheets, she went to stand next to him at his desk. "Are you okay?"

"Like I said on the train, it's *strange* to be back here after everything that happened. I'm afraid of her, and I'm afraid for you. I don't want to pretend everything is fine."

"You and I don't have to pretend anything between us," said Scarlett. "Brayden too. This won't last forever. We just need to keep things calm until we're more in control." She looked him up and down. He'd grown taller this summer. Had it been while she was in bed, asleep? Or was it that Clair de Lune had changed him as much as it had changed her?

He stared up at her, looking reproachful. "I hope she's out of here soon."

"She will be." Scarlett tried to sound confident, but she was remembering how Laylani had watched Beni walk into the house with that calculating look on her face. That expression had made her fear for her brother in a new way, and she couldn't unsee it. "And we'll get live-in security soon. Like, tomorrow, if possible. Is there anything else I can do to put you at ease?"

"Can't we go stay somewhere else?" His breathing quickened.

Scarlett leaned down and gave him a hug, trying to soothe him before he got any more anxious. "If we leave, it'll be harder to take back our home. Plus, Laylani will probably start rumors to try to discredit us if we do anything unusual." She let her hands fall to her sides and straightened.

He studied the desk. "You're probably right." But he clearly didn't agree.

Scarlett continued. "She can't say anything if we're pretending everything's fine. You're my heir and my baby brother—I wouldn't be doing this if I didn't think it was for the best. Soon we'll kick Laylani out and live here by ourselves." She reached down and patted his back. "I love you, Beni."

"I love you too," he said. But he still looked worried.

CHAPTER (25)

The next morning Scarlett woke up to Brayden's muscular form sprawled in an armchair near her bed. The dim light filling her room told her it was early morning, but his brown eyes were alert and fixed on her. Her bed was so empty, and she ached for his body to be curled around hers. Why was he so far away?

Last night, as they'd been getting ready for bed, she'd expressed her exasperation when he'd taken a pillow to the couch. She'd hoped he'd change his mind about sleeping separately, but he hadn't.

"Get in the bed, you idiot" were the exact words she'd uttered. With a wicked smile, he'd obeyed and immediately peppered her with kisses. She'd thought she'd won when he slid her pajama bottoms off, but after giving her a soul-shattering orgasm with his mouth, he'd gone right back to the couch before she could even begin to return the favor.

"That should help you sleep," he'd said smugly. And as she'd closed her eyes, he'd stayed awake, watching her.

Now, in the morning light, she looked at him longingly while he stared back, and the corners of his mouth turned up.

"You *did* sleep, didn't you?" she asked, her voice raspy.

He chuckled. "I got enough. My valor helps me regenerate with less sleep than the average person, so I don't need as much as you."

Interesting. Scarlett was jealous of *that* perk. "Were you watching me sleep?"

"Yep. Watching you sleep and thanking the Goddess you're alive."

"That's sweet." Her lips curved up in a smile as she let herself appreciate the view of him shirtless. He was so fit from his daily workouts and his military training. Speaking of which, he'd usually be out running this time of day. "You know, we have a home gym and a treadmill on the ground floor. You can run in the mornings. There's a television in there too."

His eyes lit with interest. "That's handy."

"I'll show you where it is." Scarlett rose, sitting cross-legged as she faced him. "Oh, and I had an idea while I was falling asleep."

"Tell me," he said.

"I want to take you to the beach today. I've owed Beni a trip for a while now, and I'm dying to take you surfing." Her voice bubbled with excitement.

"I'd love that," he said, his expression warm.

"Good. There's more. If you're up for it, I'm going to tip off a couple of members of the press that we'll be there. If we have pictures of me looking healthy, it'll highlight to the public that Laylani's a liar. Also, we can publicize our relationship quickly and on our terms. Does that sound okay to you?"

"Hell yeah," he muttered. "No more magazines talking about you and Alastair as a couple would be nice. And we can mention Dad and what he does for Clair. Close ties to a military family could put people off hurting you." He stood, pulling his arm over his head to stretch his lat muscles.

"Yes, take notice, ne'er-do-wells—I've got a father-in-law who can turn invisible, and by the way, he has a whole lot of guns." She shivered as she watched Brayden stretch, resisting the urge to pull him into her bed so she could run her hands all over his perfect body. She didn't want to be the one constantly coming on to him while he was in overprotective mode. Hopefully, she'd get a bodyguard fast so he wouldn't have to be constantly on guard.

It was still wonderful to wake up with him here, even if he hadn't slept in her bed. If only he never had to leave.

They arrived at Lilac Beach well in advance of the time Scarlett had given the reporters, so they'd have some time to themselves. She, Beni, and Brayden walked across the warm sand toward the ocean. The beach was busy, as it always was during the summer holidays, but they still managed to find space to dump their surfboards and their bags on the ground.

Scarlett laid their towels out before pulling her white sundress over her head to reveal a dark green swimsuit that matched her eyes. The bikini top was tied together in a knot between her full breasts and left little to the imagination. As soon as the dress was off, Brayden's gaze fixed on her. He came closer and drew her into his arms, leaning down close enough to whisper in her ear.

"You look . . ." He groaned. "If only we weren't in public right now."

Heat pooled in her stomach as she watched his pupils dilate, and Scarlett laughed. Maybe tonight she'd be able to convince him to sleep in her bed. His presence was so reassuring that no part of her believed he wouldn't be able to protect her *and* hold her at night.

"You can take it off later." She winked at him and was rewarded with more of his dark, hungry gaze. "And you look pretty delicious yourself," she added.

They'd stopped at a surf shop near the Lilac Island Dock, and he'd let her pick out some swimwear for him. Scarlett thoroughly enjoyed seeing Brayden shirtless, in form-fitting shorts that cut off at mid-thigh. She reached up to touch the thin silver *necklace* he'd worn today. She'd never seen it before, and she never knew jewelry on a man could be so sexy. Not that he needed it. Her eyes skirted over his broad shoulders, his defined—but not *too* defined—abs and arms. Reaching between them, she ran a fingertip over that sexy space between his belly button and his stomach, making Brayden shiver.

Biting her lip, she looked up. He stared at her, a small smile playing across his lips and his gaze still just as hungry.

"Come on—let's get in." Beni walked past them with his surfboard in hand. Ready to start catching the little waves that dusted this part of Lilac Beach, he rushed toward the water.

Reluctantly, Scarlett pulled away from Brayden, picking up her surfboard too. She waited till Brayden had his board, and then they both set off after Beni.

The sun warming her back was bliss as she walked with Brayden. It was one of those gorgeous Soleil mornings before the peak heat of the day. The pure smell of the sea and the lilac bushes was so much nicer than the sometimes musky smell of the city canals. A group of teenagers were sunbathing nearby, and Scarlett smirked at their faces as they took in Brayden. She reached for his free hand, and they walked the rest of the way to the water with their fingers intertwined.

Scarlett looked out over the waves at Beni where he'd begun to paddle on his surfboard. She released Brayden's hand and faced him. "You've never done this before, right?"

"Never ever," he said as the wind played with his hair. "Is it hard?"

"For a strapping young man like you? Nah. This is a great beach for learning. We'll have you catching waves soon."

Scarlett had Brayden practice getting up on the board on the beach a few times before leading him out into the water. There were a few surfers out there, but they weren't close. Beni sailed past them on a wave, and Brayden grinned at the sight of him, so comfortable and at ease.

"This is a good spot," she said once they were far enough from the shore. "When I tell you, start paddling with your arms toward the beach. When the crest of the wave reaches you, hop up like you did on the sand."

"Easy," said Brayden.

On his third try, he got up and rode a wave all the way into the shallows. Scarlett grinned at the sight. He was a natural.

"Ride one with me!" shouted Beni, who was watching from the beach.

Brayden pushed his wet hair out of his face and then followed behind her little brother out to where Scarlett still sat on her board. Her heart melted as they swam toward her together.

Scarlett paddled into the next wave and hopped up as it began to crest. Her heart soared as the wind blew her hair out of her face while she rode her board all the way in. She hopped off into the shallows and noticed that the group of teenagers had grown. They were all looking toward her.

Do they recognize me? she wondered. *Or maybe they're just watching us surf.* She smiled. *Or they're admiring Brayden.* Being spotted would normally stress her out, but given they wanted publicity, it didn't really matter. She shrugged it off.

They surfed until Beni complained he was hungry. Scarlett gave him money for food, and while they waited for him to return, she stood next to Brayden on the sand and tugged him toward her, eager to taste the ocean on his lips.

Brayden didn't hesitate, pressing his wet mouth to hers. The taste of the saltwater on his lips was delicious.

"Scarlett!" shouted a voice.

Scarlett, who'd been too lost in Brayden's kiss to notice anything else, broke away and turned toward it. Two middle-aged photographers were standing thirty feet away in the sand. Their cameras clicked as she spun around to face them.

She gestured for them to come closer. "Good morning, gentlemen."

"Good morning, Lady Heroux," said Tom Bowles, a heavyset man with gray hair and glasses. She'd met him before at photo shoots for the *Soleil Times* and thought he was a good guy. He'd always respected her privacy when she'd asked him to stand down, and now was her chance to pay him back for that.

"Thanks for coming," said Scarlett, nervous but excited for the photo shoot with Brayden.

"Our pleasure. Appreciate the invite," said the second, a thin blond man she didn't recognize.

"This is my husband, Brayden Maddox. We got married two days ago," said Scarlett. "Please mention that in the article."

"Congratulations," said Tom as he adjusted the lens on his camera.

Scarlett went on. "I've also got some wedding photos. They aren't professional, but it'd be great if you could print at least one of them."

"Be happy to," said the second photographer. He pulled a card out of his pocket and dropped it on Scarlett's towel. "You can send the pictures you want printed to that email address."

"Perfect." A few photos, and proof of her well-being would be all over Soleil, announcing her new relationship status the same week she joined Parliament. "Where do you want us?"

Brayden held Scarlett in his arms, and she was hyperaware of his body next to hers as the photographers' cameras clicked. The group of teenagers Scarlett had spotted on her way into the water had gathered and were eagerly taking pictures with their phones.

Scarlett would never understand why people found her so interesting.

"Can you two look at each other?" asked Tom.

She stared up at Brayden and couldn't help but grin. "Do you find this tedious?"

His lips curved into a smile. "Nothing is tedious when you're in a swimsuit."

"That's great stuff," called Tom. "Now can you two kiss?"

Brayden leaned down, and their lips met as she shut her eyes. His face was rough, but she liked it. His tongue brushed against hers, and her fingertips trailed over his stomach. The kiss was so good she forgot about their audience.

Someone whistled, and Brayden pulled back, glancing at the onlookers. He draped his arms around Scarlett's shoulders. The cameras hadn't stopped clicking.

"Who's your new boyfriend, Scarlett?" called one of the teenagers as Scarlett beamed for the cameras from her comfortable spot in Brayden's arms.

"I'm not her boyfriend," he said. "I'm her husband."

His declaration was met with excited giggles and laughs.

"What about Alastair?" yelled one of the girls.

"We broke up a while ago," said Scarlett.

One of them gasped, and when Scarlett glanced their way, several of them were on their phones, probably texting their friends the huge scoop.

It felt unnatural to expose her private life like this. She'd been trained to be polite but distant to anyone who photographed her or spoke to her in public, but for once, Scarlett's goals were aligned with theirs. This was an announcement she wanted to share with the world. She was more than fine, she was married, and she was here to put things right.

Scarlett couldn't stop looking at Brayden as they moved to the water's edge for one last round of pictures, and he was equally wrapped up in her, watching every step she took.

They posed for one shot with Beni in between them, and another with Scarlett and Brayden kissing at the edge of the ocean.

"Is that enough?" she asked after lots of kissing photos.

"Oh yes, Lady Heroux," said the blond man. "Thank you for the opportunity."

"When will you print these?" asked Brayden.

"As soon as possible," said Tom. "And if you ever want your photo taken again, call me anytime. Day or night."

"You've always been a true professional, ever since I was a kid. Thanks for that," said Scarlett.

With a wave to the reporters, she and Brayden jogged to where Beni was waiting.

By now the news had spread that Lady Heroux was at Lilac Beach, and a crowd was rapidly growing. A handful of teenagers was one thing, but now there were thirty people milling around, staring at her with their phones out, snapping pictures. Her chest tightened and her desire to leave spiked as she pulled her dress on over her swimsuit. Brayden offered her his hand, and she took it.

"Goddess above," muttered Beni. "Let's get out of here."

"On it." Scarlett retrieved her phone and sent Charlie a text asking to be picked up at the Lilac Island Dock.

That evening, after a tense boat ride, they were seated in Laylani's preferred private dining room at The Twig and Vine. A chandelier hovered over a round table in the quiet room, which was so unlike the rest of the bustling restaurant. But that made sense, because Laylani had always preferred the exclusive, sanitized version of whatever the public got. The restaurant wasn't far from where they'd surfed that morning; one of the walls was transparent glass and gave them a phenomenal view of the Lilac Beach boardwalk. The moonlight illuminated the distant waves.

"This place is gorgeous," said Brayden as he sat in the high-backed chair next to Scarlett. *He* looked gorgeous in his midnight-blue dress shirt, with a clean-shaven face.

"It is," she agreed.

Beni sat on her other side, leaving Laylani the chair directly across from her. Scarlett wished they could've come here without her. She straightened the silk skirt of the black dress she'd worn to dinner and took a deep breath. It had been an active day, but she needed to stay alert around Laylani.

The waiter appeared, decanted a bottle of red wine Laylani had preordered, and jotted down their dinner orders. As soon as he'd left, Laylani started in.

"Scarlett, I read in the paper you'll be taking your father's seat soon. What are your plans, exactly? What will Brayden do while you're working?"

Scarlett shifted in her seat. "Yes, I'll go to Parliament in the morning. I'm keen to begin."

"How industrious of you." Laylani's tone was falsely bright.

"I'm going to accompany her to and from Parliament until we can hire a security team," said Brayden.

"Is that necessary?" asked Laylani. "She'll be a junior peer. Jules didn't have security until he was prime minister."

Beni stared at his mother like she was daft. "And look what happened to him *with* security."

Scarlett shot Beni a grateful look. She couldn't have said it better. "Right, and also, we still don't know who killed him. While that question remains unanswered, I'm hiring protection."

"Perhaps you can get someone on a short-term contract until the assassin is caught. I'm sure the Soleil Bureau will have a breakthrough any day now," said Laylani with a small smirk.

Scarlett's eyebrows narrowed. What did that smug smile mean? Nothing good, she was sure.

Laylani sipped her wine as she watched them both. "So, Brayden and Scarlett. Tell me more about your relationship. How did you meet?"

"Through my grandmother," said Scarlett as Brayden grabbed her hand and intertwined their fingers on top of the table, directly in Laylani's line of sight.

"She introduced you? How?" Her dubious expression suggested the idea was absurd.

"Letters." Brayden smiled adoringly at Scarlett. "We've been writing to each other since we were eleven."

Her stepmother's smile was acidic. "Pen pals. Isn't that sweet? But I can't recall ever seeing Scarlett traipsing around with a treasured secret missive from Clair de Lune. Did you write often?"

Unlike Laylani, Brayden was perfectly at ease. "I sent them to her at school."

"I've seen the letters. You never pay attention." Beni's voice was full of irritation.

Scarlett smiled at her brother. "Yes, Beni caught me with the letters. He loves Brayden now that they've met in person. We can't imagine life without him anymore."

Brayden lifted her hand and kissed her knuckles. Her heart fluttered at the touch. He was really laying it on thick for Laylani, but she loved it.

"I see." Laylani looked like she wished she'd poisoned Scarlett's wine.

Scarlett studied her stepmother, considering which levers she should pull.

"*Ask her about your mother*," said Nori.

Scarlett thought of the journals and how Sabina had met Laylani. She hesitated for a split second, but then she asked a question she knew the answer to without knowing the details. And the details would be everything. Even a lie would be revealing—she was sure of it.

"You know, while we're on the subject, I don't think I've ever heard the story of how you met my father. How did you and Jules fall in love?" asked Scarlett.

Something shifted in her stepmother's expression. A flicker of resentment shone through. "Your mother introduced us."

Scarlett's eyebrows rose. "Then she died, and you married him three months later?"

Laylani rolled her eyes. "No, your father didn't cheat on your mother, if that's what you're asking. He may not have waited long before he moved on, but infidelity was only a feature in *our* marriage. Lucky me."

Scarlett tensed. Beni, who'd been taking a sip of water, sputtered and coughed.

"I suppose he could get away with a lot, given the hours he worked," Scarlett said almost to herself. She didn't want it to show on her face, but Laylani's words had immediately damaged her view of her beloved father. She'd believed he was a *good* man, the kind who wouldn't cheat on his wife, even if that wife was Laylani. Her logical mind also understood Laylani was trying to distract her, and it was working. Her sudden resentment toward Jules, her hurt at his behavior—it was visceral.

He should have been better. His expectations for me were so *high—*

"Oh yes, and your hair would curl if you knew with whom." Her stepmother took a huge slug of her wine, holding her chin high as she glared at Scarlett under the dim light of the chandelier.

A wave crashed on the beach outside, but it was as quiet as death in the room.

Scarlett's mind raced. Did she want to know who her father had cheated with? Who would be so bad that Laylani would bait her that way? She could be lying, but why? It was uncharacteristic for her to reveal anything that could make her look less than. Poor Beni, having to listen to this.

Laylani dumped the rest of the wine into her glass. "That's one of the reasons why . . ." She shook her head as if to clear it. "That's one of the reasons why I didn't wear black for long." She gestured toward her elegant white cocktail dress.

"I don't know what to say." Scarlett glanced at Beni. He was staring down at his empty plate, his expression blank, but she was sure there was much more under the surface. He tended to disassociate—like her—but that didn't mean his feelings weren't there. They were just buried deep for now.

"Shocked your father isn't perfect? I know you idolized him. Let this be a lesson to you. If you look hard enough, everyone's shitty. My advice for a newlywed? Don't ever pin your self-worth or your dreams on anyone else."

The waiter arrived with their dinner, and Laylani signaled to him to bring another bottle of the wine. Cutlery clinked as they ate in silence. Scarlett hadn't gotten anything useful out of Laylani, but what a bomb she'd dropped on *them.*

Brayden looked at Scarlett as if waiting for her to make the next move. Laylani was well on her way to getting drunk, and Scarlett could certainly try again, but her heart wasn't in it. She didn't want any more wild revelations in front of her younger brother, and with that in mind, she decided to keep the peace for now and try again another day. Perhaps in a less obvious way.

She looked back at Brayden and shook her head ever so slightly, and he reached underneath the table, resting a comforting hand on her knee.

CHAPTER 26

The next day Parliament was in session. Scarlett rose early, after another night alone in her bed with Brayden watching over her. As she dressed to go into the city center, it felt like the first day of school. On the way in, she and Brayden dropped Beni off at his friend Blake's house and got Brayden a phone that would work in Soleil.

Finally, they stopped at the gym across the road from Parliament. The facilities were only for the use of peers and their families, so they had to reveal their married status to the surprised clerk at the door so Brayden could get a membership.

"This is ten times bigger than our parliament," Brayden said as they entered the peers' wing of the parliamentary chambers hand in hand.

"Yes, it's big, isn't it? I've always loved the decadence and authority of this place. Clair de Lune's parliament is prettier though," offered Scarlett. "We don't have anything like those gardens on the lake."

She took in the familiar building with fresh interest as they made

their way to her father's old office. Soleil's parliament building was hundreds of years old, having served as a courthouse in Hadrian's time, before it was repurposed by the Soleil government after the dissolution of the empire. It was ten times bigger than Clair de Lune's. The marble floors and the dark wood paneling were comfortable in their familiarity, and it smelled old, though not in an unpleasant way, like the University of Soleil's library. It was all bittersweet: the reminders of her father paired with the relief that she was here to solidify his legacy.

They arrived at Jules's office. Scarlett had been here countless times, but she'd thought it wouldn't be hers for years. It still said her father's name on the nameplate. Scarlett pulled out the large key the receptionist had given her and unlocked the door.

She sucked in a sharp breath. A part of her expected to find her dad at his desk. Being in his office was like being with an echo of him. She set her purse down on the desk, opened the globe where Jules kept his whiskey, and stared down at the decanter. The globe blurred as her eyes watered.

Brayden put his arms around her shoulders. "Are you all right?"

His comforting touch meant everything. She breathed in his smell, still like a forest in the rain even though he'd been in Soleil for two days.

"We were in here the last time I spoke to him in private, right before he gave his last speech. We were debating whether or not I should go abroad." Her voice broke. "I had no idea it would be the last private moment I'd ever have with him." She leaned into Brayden and pressed her face into his crisp button-down shirt. His warmth soothed her as he held her, reminding her that while Jules was gone, the present wasn't all bad.

"He'd be so proud of you for all you've overcome the past few weeks," said Brayden into her hair.

"He would be, and he'd also tell me to keep going." She could have stood there for hours, with his body against hers, but Brayden pulled away, taking a step back.

Scarlett sighed, forcing her thoughts to practical matters. "I need to check in with Elestine Spencer. Are you going straight to the gym?"

"Are you sure you don't want me to stay? I'm here to protect you," he said in a low voice.

The corners of her mouth quirked up. His overprotectiveness was equal parts frustrating and a turn-on. "The security here is excellent. You can't stay with me twenty-four hours a day, and I know what you're like if you don't get enough gym time." She smiled, remembering when he was the grumpiest she'd ever seen him through the mirror. He'd been sitting exams and gone a few days without working out, and it had made him so disgruntled.

"All right. The gym it is, then." Brayden cocked his head to one side as he looked down at her, still caged in his arms. "Would you want to work out together sometime? I'd love to teach you some self-defense. Weight training is also surprisingly fun if you have a good teacher." He winked.

Scarlett bit her lip. "I'd love that." Brayden lifting heavy weights and touching her while she lifted heavy weights? Yes, please. "Maybe in a couple of days, once I've settled in."

He squeezed her briefly before letting her go and taking a step back. "Sounds good. Oh, and before I work out, I'll give Cass a call."

Lachlan had managed to get her contact details before they'd left Clair de Lune, but it was still unclear if Cassidy from Zahara and Scarlett's Cass were one and the same. She hoped they were.

"Fingers crossed she's open to meeting. Will you come here afterward?" she asked. "There's a canteen, and you can use my computer if you want to get on the internet."

"Actually, if you're really sure you don't need me, I thought I'd head down to the military headquarters. Lachlan gave me the name of a Soleil general he's friendly with and wrote me a letter of introduction." He patted his pocket. "If Cass doesn't work out, maybe he'll know of some muscle for hire."

"That's great. Thank you. I should be fine here. I promise not to leave the building until you're back."

He pressed a kiss to her cheek. "Good luck with your first day. I can't wait to hear about it later."

Scarlett knocked on Elestine's door.

"Come in."

As soon as Scarlett appeared, Elestine rose from her seat behind a large wooden desk, strode toward her, and wrapped her in a tight hug. After a moment of holding her, she pulled back to look at Scarlett's face.

"My dear, I'm so deeply happy to see you." Elestine's eyes gleamed with emotion. "I've been so *worried*." She pulled Scarlett close again, and Scarlett closed her eyes and breathed Elestine in.

Through Jules, Elestine had been in Scarlett's life since she was a little girl, and for some of the years she'd been with Alastair, she'd imagined the woman might become her mother-in-law. The comfort of being with her again was poignant yet complicated.

"I'm so happy to see you too." Scarlett's brow furrowed as she tried to keep her face from crumpling. "Congratulations on being named prime minister."

Elestine pulled back a bit but still held Scarlett's arms. "That's very kind, Scarlett. I can't imagine a worse way to come into the role. I want you to know, I sent Alastair over several times during the weeks you were ill—or being kept asleep, rather. I visited once, but your stepmother insisted you weren't well enough for visitors."

The reminder the Spencers had visited her caused a wave of something bittersweet to rise in Scarlett's chest. "My brother told me. Thank you for coming even if you weren't admitted. I wasn't conscious anyway, so a visit probably wouldn't have helped, unless you'd pulled out my IV while you were there. That's how Beni woke me up."

"Good heavens," said Elestine. "How'd he know to do that?"

"Lucky guess." It was still ingrained in her not to reveal the mirror. "Thank you for trying to visit. I do appreciate it."

"I feel *terrible* that I didn't do more, especially given the truth. Your letter shocked me to my core." Her gaze bore into Scarlett's.

Scarlett hadn't known what to think about Beni being left to save her on his own. She *had* wondered why the Spencers, who knew her so well, did nothing to intervene. However, as she looked at Elestine's pinched face, some of her resentment faded. "Truly, Elestine, all's well that ends well. I'm grateful it's over with. I'm ready to move on. Let's focus on how I'll help the Cerulean Party now that I'm back."

Elestine gestured to the chair opposite her. "Please, have a seat. I should have known Jules's daughter would be ready to hit the ground running. But before we talk about Cerulean business, in your letter you alluded that the danger you were in wasn't solely to do with Laylani. Can you tell me more about what happened?"

How much do you think I can trust her? Scarlett asked Nori.

"I think you have to be honest. Otherwise you'll have no help from the Soleil government. Perhaps leave your mother's death out of it for now."

Scarlett sat in the uncomfortable wooden chair across from Elestine and told her almost everything, starting with her encounter with Lady Moira Ashworth at her father's funeral. To Scarlett's pleasure, gold smoke streamed out of Elestine's head and into the air above her. There wasn't a hint of black as Scarlett detailed what Beni had overheard Laylani saying to the doctor about keeping Scarlett and Manon asleep. Elestine listened with rapt attention, her eyes wide as Scarlett described their terrifying escape.

"Do you agree Laylani and Moira could've been behind it all?" Scarlett asked when she'd finished.

"I can see why you're coming to that conclusion, but we need ironclad proof before we make any moves."

Scarlett's jaw tensed. "I have my and my grandmother's urine test results, which prove the doctor employed by Laylani committed malpractice. Paired with Moira's threat, isn't that enough to start an internal investigation?"

Elestine's expression shifted from concerned to calculating as she leaned back in her chair. "Let's start with the doctor. Did he interact with anyone other than Laylani? How was he paid, and from which accounts? Now that you've inherited your father's finances, you should check your family banking records yourself. Also, I'd suggest stripping Laylani of account access if you haven't done so." Elestine was suddenly more assertive than she'd been the whole time Scarlett was unconscious.

Scarlett paused for a beat before answering. "I'll check the bank records. I do know Laylani had her own accounts, and it'd be unusual if she hadn't used those for the doctor, given the circumstances. It's worth a double check though. And I appreciate the suggestion to strip her account access, although I'm sure she'd see that as me declaring war."

Elestine nodded thoughtfully. "You want to keep things neutral until it serves you. Fair. At least adjust so she requires a cosigner on purchases over a certain threshold. I think Jules had that in place already, but it's worth double-checking."

This knowledge struck Scarlett as odd. "Thanks." She paused before asking, "How do you know he had a cosigner requirement?"

Elestine blinked several times, then her face brightened. "I overheard a bit of a lads' chat in the canteen. They were discussing their wives' allowances." She rolled her eyes.

"I see." Except it didn't sound like any "canteen chat" her father would've engaged in. She'd known him to be highly private about his finances.

"Anyhow," continued Elestine, "while you start with that, I'll bring some colleagues I trust into the conversation. Lord Navarre and Lord Garfield to start. They're quite influential, and getting them onside will be key if we're to launch a formal investigation."

Scarlett's tension eased. Elestine was taking her worries seriously. "Thank you. Oh, and what about Lord Mayweather? I interned for him last year and consider him a friend."

"Mayweather is a good shout. I'll include him."

Scarlett shifted in her seat. "Thank you. And can I ask, please, that you speak of this to no one else? The last thing we need is Moira Ashworth catching wind of it. We're taking precautions, but I'm concerned for my family's safety."

"Of course."

A knock at the door interrupted them.

"Come in," called Elestine.

Alastair strode through the door. He stumbled, nearly falling as he clocked Scarlett. "You're back." He looked her up and down as if searching for injuries.

She froze. Only a month or so apart, and how her attachment to him had changed. The invisible cord that had once connected them was gone, severed by their breakup, leaving behind only nostalgia for the time they'd shared. Some of her anger had faded too in the time since their last fight.

Her heart was also forever changed. She belonged to Brayden, and no one else. Alastair might not yet know it, but any possibility between them had withered and died in Clair de Lune.

"Scarlett." He said her name reverently, approaching like he wanted to hug her, but she stayed seated in the chair across from his mother. "I'm so sorry for everything, and I'm so glad you're here and all right. Is your grandmother well? And Beni?"

"They're both fine. Thank you." Scarlett didn't trust herself to say much more.

Alastair held his arms open, offering her a hug. At first she went to decline, but was that really how she wanted to behave? Didn't she want to someday be his friend? She gave in to his expectant hovering and stood. He embraced her without hesitation. The scent of the neroli-and-bergamot cologne he'd always worn washed over her like a breathy kiss from the past, reminding her of their old closeness.

Then she stepped back, and the smell faded.

Alastair grabbed her left hand. Brayden's ring sparkled even in the dim office light. "That's pretty. Did you get it in Clair de Lune?"

Scarlett swallowed. "Yes."

He raised an eyebrow. "You should wear it on another finger. People will think we got engaged." He said the words reproachfully, but there was hope in his expression.

"*She's not pretending to be engaged to* you, *spoiled man-child*," said Nori with venom.

Scarlett glanced at Elestine, whose attention flitted nervously between Scarlett and her son. "I got married in Clair de Lune," she said.

"*What?* Married? You can't be serious." Alastair's face blanched.

Elestine covered her lips with one hand.

Scarlett raised her hands palms-up. "We fell for each other in Clair de Lune, and it wasn't safe for me to return to Soleil alone, so we decided to marry." Her gut twisted at having to minimize her relationship with Brayden, but she ignored it. She didn't owe Alastair the entire explanation.

"Tell me it isn't so." He grabbed her by the shoulders, his fingers digging into her skin. "You *married* that forest trash you were always blathering to through that godforsaken mirror?"

Scarlett froze, shocked by his cruel words. She never should have told him about the mirror, but they'd been so close he'd known everything about her.

"Alastair." Elestine's voice was full of reproach. "You were raised better than that. And must you have this conversation now?"

Pressure bloomed behind Scarlett's eyes, indicating the start of a headache. "He's not forest trash, you bigot. Don't forget, I'm from Clair de Lune too. If you want to be on speaking terms with me, don't ever insult us like that again." She tried to jerk out of his grasp, but he continued to grip her shoulders, making her wince. She couldn't believe he was behaving like this.

"Are you sure he didn't compel you with magic?" Alastair's eyes were wild.

"Let me go!" She finally wrenched herself out of his grip and pushed him away. "And of course he didn't *force* me. I didn't want to rub this in your face, but if you must know, he loves me, and I love him. More than anything."

"How can you love him? You barely know him," growled Alastair.

"You said it yourself. I was always *blathering to him through my godforsaken mirror*. Things were obvious to us once I arrived in Clair de Lune."

"So you married him after, what, a week?" Alastair turned from her and dug his hands in his hair, staring at the ceiling. "I can't believe you don't see he *must* have compelled you. We were together for three years and you still weren't ready to get engaged, and now you've permanently tied yourself to *him*? Please tell me you plan to get it annulled."

"I was afraid for my life, and he wanted to be there for me. I *won't*—"

"You could have come to *me*." Alastair interrupted her, his eyes flashing. "Despite our fight, my family would have protected you. Surely, you knew that."

"Then where were you when my little brother needed you?" she hissed. "When *I* needed you? Maybe if you'd been there for him, I wouldn't have been in a coma for weeks while Beni was sitting there alone thinking I was about to die!"

He recoiled as if she'd slapped him.

Elestine rose to stand between them. "Let's pause for now, shall we? This won't be productive with emotions running so high." She looked between them both. "Scarlett, there's a budget-committee meeting in half an hour that we should attend together, and if you'd like to have a working lunch together later—"

"They caught the shooter," said Alastair, folding his arms across his chest.

Scarlett's lips parted in shock, and Elestine gasped.

"Your father's assassin—they caught him. I came in here to tell you, Mother. The bureau called to let Parliament know before they speak to the press. It'll be public knowledge soon."

Alastair paused for a beat, and it was Scarlett's turn to recoil as she froze, waiting for him to go on as her heart raced.

"Soleil counterintelligence decoded some electronic communications between Sigur Viður agents and discovered detailed records of their assassination plans, as well as confirmation after he was shot."

Scarlett sank into her chair, the shock of it making her unsteady on her feet. "Why would Sigur Viður do that?" It didn't make any sense. She'd been so sure, deep in her gut, that everything was connected. Her mother's death, her abduction, and her father's murder. The news about Sigur Viður felt all wrong.

"*Follow your intuition*," said Nori. "*Push for more information until you're satisfied.*"

Alastair's blue-eyed gaze locked with hers. "The motive hasn't been discovered yet, but the agent I spoke to from the bureau thought Sigur Viður didn't like the idea of an alliance between everyone but them, which may have occurred had your father lived. If the economic union eventually became a military alliance, for example, that group of countries would be a formidable player on the world stage."

"Did they give you a copy of the communications between the Sigur Viður agents?" Were all her suspicions wrong?

"No. I spoke to them over the phone, but I'm sure they'll supply the comms if we ask."

Elestine turned to Scarlett, her gaze piercing. "Given what we've discussed, I'll call John Bates and insist the bureau release all the evidence to Parliament. And of course, we'll speak to the Sigur Viður ambassador." John Bates was in charge of the Soleil Bureau.

Scarlett's features were wooden as she tried to process this confusing development. "Yes, let's insist. Thank you."

When Scarlett, Alastair, and Elestine arrived at the budget-committee meeting, one of the lords lingering in the standing area at the back of the room made a beeline for Scarlett.

"Welcome to Parliament, my dear," said the elderly, white-haired man with tiny round spectacles. His name popped into Scarlett's head: Lord Otis Garfield. They'd met a few times at state dinners.

"Thank you," said Scarlett warmly.

"Looking forward to working with you. I heard they caught your father's assassin. I can't believe we lost him to those devils in the north."

Scarlett took his offered hand. "Yes, it's quite a shock. I'm keen to hear more from the bureau. Lord Garfield—"

"Otis," he interjected. "No need to stand on ceremony when it's just us peers."

He'd casually called her a peer. How long would it take to get used to that?

"Thank you, Otis."

Several more members of Parliament greeted her before she managed to sit. Many peers blatantly stared at her.

Moira Ashworth approached Scarlett right as the meeting was due to begin. Goose bumps covered Scarlett at the sight of the woman who looked so much like Laylani.

"Lady Heroux, wonderful to see you well. Would you like to say a few words when we begin?" Her face was a polite mask.

"Of course," said Scarlett with a bland smile.

Moira narrowed her eyes, apparently surprised by her lack of fluster.

Scarlett's new vox powers gave her heightened confidence. Without them, she'd probably be nervous about giving an unrehearsed speech right after this strange news about Sigur Viður. First impressions were important, and lords and ladies were notoriously vicious about poor public speaking. These were much higher stakes than all the public speaking she'd done for her politics degree. But she'd outshine Moira, today and always, until she managed to take her down.

"You're going to be wonderful," said Nori. *"I'm right here with you."*

"Perfect." Moira's smile was acerbic as she turned to the podium to start the session. As head of the Goldenrods, she flourished in the spotlight. Her voice carried clear and steady across the room as she addressed the peers. "Before we begin, it has become public knowledge that Lord Jules Heroux, our dear friend and colleague, was murdered because Sigur Viður didn't like his politics."

Outrage echoed around the room as the peers cursed Sigur Viður.

"Jules and I didn't always see eye to eye—"

Grumblings of assent from Elestine and others confirmed that. Moira's voice grew louder to cover the noise.

"But I believe in the right of the government of Soleil to operate without foreign influence. We must discuss our response to the news Sigur Viður is responsible for the death of a Soleil prime minister, and as such, the budget meeting is canceled."

Scarlett studied the faces of the peers. Everyone, Ceruleans and Goldenrods alike, was nodding. She wished her vox abilities would allow her to see how other speakers were being received, but to her disappointment, she saw nothing.

"You may have noticed we have a new peer in our midst. Scarlett Heroux is here today, ready to fill the House Heroux seat. How fitting that she joins us on the day we'll be discussing retribution for her family tragedy. Lady Heroux, the floor is yours."

"You've got this!" cheered Nori. *"Let the rise of Scarlett Heroux begin!"*

The back of Scarlett's neck prickled at her light's encouragement as she made her way to the front of the room. Although she was confident, her palms were sweating, and her heart raced as she stared out at the vast room filled with almost two hundred of her colleagues.

This is for you, Dad.

When she spoke, her voice was strong. "It's an honor and a privilege to join the leaders of Soleil, and I'm relieved to be here to speak on my father's behalf. If he were here, he'd tell us to put the citizens of Soleil first."

Peers in the audience spoke in barely lowered voices, as was common during a speech, but streams of gold dust rose into the air above them.

Relieved, she continued. "I'm optimistic we'll be able to realize many of his dreams. My deepest desire is to open the economic borders in order to raise the standard of living for those in Soleil, as well as those abroad."

Enthusiastic clapping and foot-stomping sounded from the Cerulean side of the room.

"Not *again*," said a loud voice. A few laughed in response.

Scarlett's eyes darted toward the man who'd spoken—a handsome and impeccably groomed Goldenrod sitting near the front. She didn't need her powers to know his opinion. As expected, black smoke was dominant above his head. She smiled at him, but he didn't meet her gaze.

On the broader Goldenrod side, there was a considerable amount of black smoke, but also more gold than she expected. Scarlett tried her best to memorize the faces of the opposition who might be open to working with her as she pivoted back to Soleil's well-being. As expected of the hundred peers sitting on the Cerulean side of the room, gold smoke rose above the majority, with only a few wisps of black.

Scarlett went on. "In regard to the news about Sigur Viður, I look forward to seeing the evidence. I'm particularly interested in learning why it took weeks to have this breakthrough."

She looked around the room and found all eyes on her. The murmurs had died down. Scarlett hesitated. Would what she wanted to say get Brayden in trouble? No—she'd seen in the news this morning that the situation in Evory was public knowledge now.

She continued. "I just returned from Clair de Lune, where their attention is on the escalation between Evory and Sigur Viður. Why would Sigur Viður want to make enemies of two powerful countries simultaneously? Separatism and warmongering are not how I wish to avenge my father."

"It's disgusting to hear you make excuses for your father's killers," said the same lord who'd spoken dismissively about her comments on the border. This time she didn't even glance his way.

Her words were bold, she knew. She was far from the best briefed in the room—or was she? No one else had heard about the likelihood of war from the future head of the Clair de Lune military. The other peers stared back at her with shock and what looked like respect. A mix of black and gold rose above them, but to her satisfaction, the gold was more prominent. Not bad considering she'd just slagged off the Soleil Bureau.

"As I said, I look forward to seeing the bureau's evidence. I'm still grieving my father's death, but in spite of recent events, I believe in Soleil's bright future. Lady Ashworth, thank you for the warm welcome. To all my peers, I look forward to working together."

As she finished, the gold smoke overtook even more of the black. *Most of them liked my speech!*

There was a round of applause and the thunderous noise of feet stamping the ground from the Ceruleans as she made her way back to her seat. All the tension left Scarlett's body. She'd dominated her first parliamentary address. As she passed Moira, the woman lifted her chin, her lips pressed tight into a thin line.

"Exceptionally well-done speech for an off-the-cuff introduction," Elestine whispered to her, looking pleased. "I don't think Moira expected you to rebuttal her politicking. I'll say, you've got all the charisma Jules had and maybe a touch more, if that was any indication."

The compliment made Scarlett warm with pleasure. She loved being compared to her dad.

"Thanks, although I still had a heckler. Who was he?"

"That's Lord Federsin. You can give up on winning him over. He's as dogmatic as they come."

"Seemed that way," said Scarlett. He'd probably be annoying her every day from now on. *Welcome to Parliament.*

"Well done, Scarlett," said Alastair from her other side. Scarlett ignored him.

CHAPTER (27)

Thank you, Lady Heroux. Let's get into the evidence," said Moira as she shuffled some papers at the podium. "Operatives from Sigur Viður orchestrated the assassination on Lord Heroux. There are at least seven Sigur Viður agents implicated, and they snuck into the country via magical means."

There were rumbles of anger from several peers. Scarlett listened to Moira's rhetoric with rapt attention, dissecting each word.

"At first I thought they might have been terrorists acting alone," she continued. "But the evidence described by the bureau shows the murder was premeditated, politically motivated, and sanctioned by their government. They don't want Soleil allying with other countries. The appropriate response to such flagrant interference in our democracy is to declare war."

The lords and ladies of Parliament listened as she went on to outline a detailed proposal for military action.

War? Oh no. She's moving way too fast. We need to stop this. Scarlett

clenched her fists as Elestine gave the Ceruleans' rebuttal. Her stomach churned. If her father were alive, he'd be horrified to hear that bombs might be dropped in his name.

"Lady Ashworth is right. We should respond with strength, but we must also act with one hundred percent irreproachable certainty. We *must* be sure, and how can we be, when we haven't yet taken the time to view the evidence? I'm all for swift and decisive action, but we simply must shelve any vote to declare war until we've heard testimony from the bureau."

"When will that happen?" shouted Lord Buckland.

"I shall arrange it for this afternoon," said Elestine.

"Why aren't they here *now*?" demanded Lord Buckland. "We need *immediate* evidence and *immediate* retaliation."

Several shouts of agreement and thunderous foot-stomping came from around the room, and Scarlett's eyes widened. The war hawks in the Goldenrod Party would *love* this excuse to drop bombs on Soleil's old enemy. Even if they had killed her dad, he wouldn't want this. Would Elestine be able to stop them from motioning to declare war?

"I'm suggesting a delay of no more than a day," protested Elestine.

As she spoke, a young staff member burst through the doors and approached her. She stepped down from the podium, and he spoke to her in a low voice. When he'd finished, he left as quickly as he'd come.

Elestine faced the peers looking confident. "We've had a message from Soleil's ambassador in Sigur Viður. They're denying any involvement in Lord Jules Heroux's death and are offering to cooperate with an investigation. We must delay action until we've seen *evidence*," said Elestine emphatically.

The room was a flurry of foot-stomping, clapping, and grumbles.

"Delay for evidence!" shouted Scarlett as she shot to her feet.

Seconds later, many of her peers joined her, wisps of gold smoke above the heads of all those nearest to her.

Elestine shot her a grateful look from the podium. "All those in favor of tabling this discussion until after we see what the bureau has?"

"Aye," bellowed Scarlett. Enough of the opposition agreed with the Ceruleans—they had a majority.

Thank the Goddess.

She returned to her seat, hoping the meeting would contain no more crises.

"*Well done, Scarlett. Your presence here meant everything today,*" said Nori.

Scarlett let out a sigh of relief as she realized her soul light was right. Jules Heroux's daughter had been here to say no to a hasty revenge war. She was overcome with a wave of gratitude that she hadn't waited another day to return.

From her place at the podium, Elestine asked the budget committee to proceed with the originally scheduled overview. Scarlett stared at the back of Moira's head wishing she could see the disappointment on her face. Her heart raced through the first fifteen minutes of the dull fiscal discussion as she struggled to relax after the barely avoided vote for a war. She couldn't wait to tell Brayden everything and get his thoughts.

Unsurprisingly, the budget meeting ran over. Afterward, Scarlett followed the herd of her colleagues to the peers' dining room. She sat in an empty seat next to Otis, who gave her a tired but kind smile and congratulated her on a well-made speech, but she smiled blankly, barely hearing him, as she spied Alastair and Elestine in conversation across the room. Elestine had intercepted him on the way to get his lunch and was now pointing vehemently toward the door. He walked off looking unhappy.

Minutes later, Elestine sat next to Scarlett, a cup of coffee in her hand. "I told Alastair he wasn't eating until he'd arranged a time for the bureau to give testimony. I wish those bastards at the bureau hadn't blown their load so quickly—they could have given us more than a couple of hours' notice. They're clearly kissing Moira's arse."

"Too right," said Otis. "Scarlett, how are you doing? You know, you can take the day if you need to. Everyone would understand."

Scarlett stared down at her lunch, her hunger gone. "This is too important for me to miss. I meant what I said to all the peers—why would Sigur Viður act against us when they've been escalating their presence on Evory's northern border? Are they trying to start a war with two fronts? I don't think their leaders are stupid."

Otis let out a throaty grumble of agreement. "That's right, Scarlett. Not rational, is it? What you said about the timing of the news, only a month before elections? We were supposed to have the border legislation in hand by now, and instead, there'll be mounting public pressure to send troops to Sigur Viður. It's an absolute disaster."

Half of the two hundred seats in Parliament, including Otis's, faced an election in a month. Losing their majority would mean handing over power to the Goldenrods—likely Moira Ashworth. It was enough to make Scarlett want to scream.

Elestine looked at her. "Several Goldenrods who supported your father's border legislation have withdrawn since his death. I hope you can bridge the gap. They might be more sympathetic to you. Perhaps we wait until this situation with Sigur Viður is resolved, but once it is, would you be interested in helping with that?"

"Of course. That's exactly what I'm here to do. Tell me more about who withdrew support," said Scarlett.

Elestine went on to break down the conversations she'd had with the four lords and the lady who'd stalled the vote. When she'd finished, Scarlett considered for a moment.

"When the time is right, we should start with Lady La Rue. I've met her several times, and we got on."

Elestine brightened. "Excellent. Glad to hear you have a good history with her."

"Are you free to come to my office? We could go over talking points so I'm prepared when the time comes. Fingers crossed the Sigur Viður situation resolves quickly." Scarlett pushed her chair back, ready to get right to it.

Otis turned to her. "You're such a natural at this, Scarlett. It's like your father is here with us."

Scarlett's face softened as she looked at him. "Thank you. That means more to me than words can say."

He grinned. "You're welcome. Oh, and before you go, in four days, there's a charity night at the National Theater to support disabled veterans. I'm on the planning committee, and we still have tickets for sale, if you'd be interested?"

"I'd love to attend," said Scarlett. She'd always think of Brayden when she thought of the army. Of course she'd support the vets. Brayden would be up for attending with her. "Put me down for a box, and I'd also be happy to make a donation."

"Thank you, my dear." The skin around Otis's eyes crinkled, and his expression was warm as he rested his hand on hers.

"We'll be there too, of course," said Elestine with a tired smile.

She must have so much on her shoulders, thought Scarlett.

"*Much like you*," said Nori.

The rest of the day went by at breakneck speed. The chamber questioned John Bates, the head of the Soleil Bureau, for hours. He repeated claims about decoded electronic communications and had a list of names of those supposedly involved. At one point, Elestine got the Sigur Viður ambassador on the phone, and Bates read him the names of those who'd supposedly carried out Jules's murder. The ambassador cross-checked the names and told the chamber those people didn't exist in the Sigur Viður citizens registry. John Bates had looked shocked, making Scarlett think he was either ignorant to the truth or an exceptional actor. After the exchange with the ambassador, the contingent pushing for war knew they'd lost, and there was no argument when Elestine moved to adjourn the session.

When Scarlett left the peers' chambers, it was dark outside, and her body ached from the stress of the long day. She walked slowly back to her office and found Brayden waiting for her inside.

"There she is." He stood as she entered and gave her a peck on the cheek. "How did it go?"

She grabbed his shirt, holding him close. "We came close to declaring war on Sigur Viður, but we avoided it in the end."

His eyes filled with worry. "War?"

"Yes. Have you seen the news?"

He shook his head, so she filled him in on the alleged evidence.

Brayden's face darkened as he learned how close they'd come to war. "What a first day."

"In the end, Elestine released a statement to the press to say we're still reviewing the evidence. We'll have to give the public something more significant as soon as possible." She let out a loud sigh and pulled Brayden toward the chairs beside her father's globe of whiskey. After one day on the job, she understood better why he drank so much.

Scarlett poured them each a small glass and sat next to Brayden with her drink in hand. "How was *your* day?"

"Good. Successfully met with the general my father wanted me to meet. We had lunch and he showed me around army headquarters. He was surprised to hear we got married." He laughed to himself.

"Seems like he'll be a helpful contact in the future. And I had a chat with Cassidy. It *was* her at the boxing match, so Lachlan was right—she's a nocturna. Cass was cryptic at first when I asked about the night she met you, but when I made it clear I'm only trying to hire a bodyguard on your behalf, she relaxed. She seems great, and she's free to meet tomorrow morning."

Scarlett's face lit up. "That's so perfect. I'd love to meet her tomorrow, and I'm thrilled she's the same Cass I met. I really trust her after what she did for me that night. Thank you for getting in touch with her." She squeezed Brayden's hand. "Shall we grab some dinner and head home? Beni sent me a text to tell me he's invited his buddy Blake over, and he asked me to order them pizza, if you're up for that."

"Sure."

Scarlett was locking her door in the hallway when she heard footsteps behind her. She turned around to find Alastair and Brayden staring at each other. Elestine was nowhere in sight.

"Alastair, what are you doing here? I don't want to speak to you," said Scarlett. She wanted to tell him to fuck off after their earlier conversation, but she was bone-tired and didn't want another blowup.

"I came to see him. Mother mentioned he might be with you." He was eyeing Brayden up and down, and the angry glint in his eye had Scarlett's hackles up. The contrast between the two was stark. Brayden looked, if not happy, calm, while Alastair was on the verge of a temper tantrum. Brayden was muscular, and Alastair was fit but lean. Most importantly, she was madly in love with one and couldn't remember what she'd ever seen in the other.

Brayden folded his arms across his chest. "Alastair. I've heard a lot about you." Clearly, he hadn't heard good things.

Alastair looked like he wanted to physically assault him. "She might not see you for what you are, but don't think you've fooled me. I *know* you've compelled her somehow, and I'll have you arrested."

Scarlett's fingertips went to her lips. She nearly died of embarrassment. What would Brayden think, knowing *this* was the man she'd loved before him?

Brayden shifted his stance, placing himself more squarely in front of her. "How little you know about the world. We don't do compulsion where I'm from. You're a fool if you think that's why she left you."

Scarlett grimaced. Only days ago she'd asked James if her vox power was a form of compulsion . . . but she was still different from Alastair. She *wanted* to be a part of the outside world. To know it better.

"Then why did she, if you know so much?" scoffed Alastair.

Scarlett wanted to save Brayden from this, but he took a step forward, looking more than happy to answer. "Where to begin? How about this—you only care about yourself. She was suffering under the surface, and you either had no idea or didn't care." He took another step closer as Alastair took one step back.

Scarlett was as riveted by Brayden's words as she was anxious to get him away from Alastair's poison.

"*Or maybe she broke up with you because you didn't know what to do with her in bed,*" said Nori, as if Alastair could hear her.

Scarlett's eyebrows flew up. *Did you really just say that?*

"*Yes.*" Nori laughed.

Her light's laugh made Scarlett crack a smile, even though that was completely inappropriate, given what was happening in front of her. Thankfully, neither Brayden nor Alastair could see her face.

Brayden took another step forward, and Alastair had to pivot to keep from being backed against a wall. "Then there's my personal favorite reason—she's *my* North Star. Not that you'd know what that means. Let me rephrase. She's my soul mate. No one could ever love her better than I do," said Brayden.

The bond between them was all she could feel, and Brayden's words meant everything to Scarlett. Hearing him speak such truths like he knew her as well as he knew himself—he was right about all of it. She wanted nothing more than to leave with him.

Scarlett moved in between them and took Brayden's hand. "Thank you, my love." She tried to imbue her gratitude for his words into her expression as she met his gaze. "Let's go home."

She turned to leave, but Alastair reached out and grabbed her by the arm. "Don't you see I'm trying to help you?" His voice broke. "I care about you."

His words and obvious distress on her behalf would usually move her, but the way he was grabbing her erased any sympathy she might have felt. Scarlett tried to yank her arm away. Alastair held on, but Brayden's hand came down over it and squeezed until Alastair released her with a shout of pain.

"Listen to her, and let us go," said Brayden, his voice low and threatening.

Alastair slammed his body into Brayden's, but Brayden didn't budge. "This isn't over," he yelled over his shoulder as he stormed off.

"Keep telling yourself that, mate. Try not to trip over your own ego on the way out," Brayden called after him, earning a growl from Alastair.

"I'm so sorry," said Scarlett when he was gone. They started down the hallway hand in hand.

"You have nothing to be sorry for," he said, but he was smiling.

Why was he smiling?

"What's funny?" she asked.

"It's not really that funny," he said, sobering. "It's just, I've always been a little bit jealous of him. He got to be here, with you, and it seemed serious. It might be petty of me, but I'm enjoying our role reversal."

"You were right about everything you said back there," she said. "And I'm enjoying our life together too."

His hand slid to the small of her back as he let her go first through the exit. Happiness flooded through her as she replayed his words again and again in her mind.

"*She's* my *soul mate.*"

Scarlett would never tire of hearing those words.

CHAPTER 28

The next morning, Scarlett and Brayden walked into Wake Up, Darling, a coffee shop near Parliament. They bought coffees and took them to one of the high-backed booths—the only seating available in the oddly long, thin shop.

Cass walked in minutes after them. Scarlett rushed to the front of the shop to greet her, with Brayden trailing behind.

Beaming, Scarlett held out her hand. "We meet again. Thank you for coming. I couldn't believe it when I mentioned you and my father-in-law knew exactly who you were."

Cass returned her friendly smile as they shook. "Good to see you again, Scarlett. And yes, how fortunate he could put us in touch." She wore a white T-shirt that emphasized the bronze of her skin, and her brown hair was pulled back in the same practical braid she'd sported the last time they met.

"This is Brayden, who you spoke to on the phone," said Scarlett, gesturing to where he stood behind her. "We just got married."

Cass's gaze darted to Brayden and back to Scarlett, following Nori's path as she buzzed around Scarlett's head. "He mentioned that when we spoke, and I could hardly believe it. You have your soul light, and you've upgraded to a better man. So many changes in a short time."

"Oh, yes. Lots of changes." Scarlett sighed and her cheeks grew hot as she remembered the breakup fight Cass had witnessed.

Brayden, on the other hand, grinned. "Good to meet you in person, Cass. And thanks for that endorsement."

"To be fair, it wouldn't have been hard to come across better than that guy," said Cass with a crooked smile.

Brayden chuckled. "Still, I'll take it."

Wanting to move the conversation on from Alastair, Scarlett gestured to the counter. "We just ordered. Tell me what you want, and I'll add it to our order."

"Thank you," said Cass, turning toward the menu.

A few minutes later, she was seated across from Brayden and Scarlett. Scarlett placed her phone on the booth's dock and activated her noise-canceling app. The sounds of the coffee shop faded around them as white noise streamed out of the booth's speakers. The air hummed, barely noticeable but enough to reassure them the technology was indeed working.

Brayden stared at the phone curiously.

"These booths were designed with this technology in mind," explained Scarlett. "No one will be able to overhear us."

"That's neat," he said, looking impressed.

"Soleil has some things right," said Cass with a nod.

Scarlett took a sip of her iced coffee before pulling a folder from her handbag. "Now that we have privacy, would you be open to signing a nondisclosure agreement before I get into the details of why I need a bodyguard? To explain the job, I'll need to tell you sensitive information." She took a piece of paper out of the folder and set it on the table in front of Cass, along with a pen she'd pilfered from her father's desk that morning. He'd always had a pen to hand.

"Of course," said Cass as she signed. "That's no problem. I'm good with secrets." She sounded genuine.

Can I trust her with the whole truth? Scarlett asked Nori.

"*Yes,*" replied her light.

Scarlett told Cass everything. She didn't seem surprised at all and listened carefully, interjecting only with clarifying questions.

"Last night I checked my family's bank accounts. There weren't any direct payments to Dr. Turner, the man who helped my step-mother keep me and my grandmother in a medically induced coma. I could meet with him, but without anything linking him to Laylani, it's a dead end. And it would definitely show our hand." Scarlett sighed.

"I can certainly see why you need protection and why *you* were eager to come back to Soleil with her," Cass said, looking at Brayden.

"Right. I'm living with her currently, but I'll have to go back to Clair de Lune soon," he said. "Especially given the Evory situation. I want round-the-clock protection in place for Scarlett before I get called back."

"Makes sense," said Cass.

"And what about you?" asked Scarlett. "What happened after the police raid? Have you been permanently shut down, or would you need time off to work the boxing matches?"

"We decided to shut down for the summer, so no, I won't need nights off right now," said Cass.

"Can I ask why?" asked Brayden.

Cass's lips pressed into a thin line. "We can't trust the cops we were bribing. We'd never been raided before because of the small fortune we were paying the police. They swear the raid was a one-off mistake, but I'm not willing to risk opening until we have further assurance it won't happen again."

Scarlett shifted in her seat. "Does that mean the police have lost all their bribery revenue from the black market?"

Cass shook her head. "No. There's far more than the boxing matches happening. They'll still be taking in heaps of bribes for all the magic that's bought and sold in the rest of the black market."

Then that motivator for the cover-up of her dad's death was still in play.

"It's possible we'll open the border by the end of the year, and then perhaps legal magical boxing matches won't be off the table." She had such a good feeling about Cass and was already praying she'd accept the offer Scarlett knew she wanted to make.

"It would be nice to run a legit business." Cass's eyebrows rose. "Meanwhile, it would be my pleasure to guard you while you work on that legislation. You said round-the-clock—that means live-in. For how long?"

"Moving in would be ideal, but in the future, if things stabilize, you could easily move out again if you'd prefer. My dad's security team lived with us on and off," said Scarlett.

"I'm open to moving in, and we can reassess at any point if that's not working for either party," said Cass. "I have one request."

"Yes?"

"I'm married. He's why I'm still in Soleil, and we're a package deal. My husband, Tyler, works with surveillance technology, among other things. I'd highly recommend letting him review your home security and perhaps making improvements if he suggests any."

Sounds ideal.

"*Completely,*" agreed Nori.

Scarlett glanced at Brayden, and at seeing he was amenable, she agreed. "Tyler coming along isn't a problem. We have plenty of space, and I'd love for him to audit our security. When can you start, and when can you move in?"

Cass's easy smile grew. "I can start tomorrow, and I'll have to speak to Tyler about the move, but we should be able to move in a few days."

"Excellent," said Brayden.

"Tyler can sign an NDA as well so you can fill him in on what we've discussed today," added Scarlett. "I don't expect you to keep secrets where he's concerned."

"Thank you," said Cass.

"And here's our standard employment contract." She pulled another document out of her handbag. "I believe the offer is above the market rate, but don't hesitate to let me know if you have any needs that aren't met here."

Cass took the contract, glancing at it briefly before tucking it into her bag.

"One last thing," said Scarlett. "Would you be willing to share how you made bribery payments to the police? Is there a bank account number? Do you have any names?"

Cass's eyes narrowed ever so slightly.

"I'm looking for ways to link my dad's death to the police," said Scarlett quickly. "I don't want to cause trouble for anyone involved in the matches."

Cass's face softened. "Ah, I see. Sadly, no. The drops were all cash left in a lockbox under the Elysian Street Dock. No paper trail that I know of. All the communication was faceless and established before my time, when the police did a raid years ago and made the offer to stay away for a price. We'd receive letters in the mail occasionally, usually when they were upping their rates, but that's it."

Another dead end. Scarlett's shoulders slumped. She wasn't getting anywhere.

"It was worth a try."

Brayden's hand covered hers where it rested on the table.

"Sorry I can't be of more assistance." Cass sounded like she meant it. "You know, my husband might be able to help you. If there's an online footprint of that bribery chain, he'd find it. He's a great hacker."

"Sure," said Scarlett, though she doubted most hackers could crack a government conspiracy. "Once you two are settled, I'd love to talk to him about it."

After they'd sorted out the essential details, Brayden and Scarlett parted from Cass outside the coffee shop. Their walk to Parliament was hot and uneventful, but when they arrived at the peers' entrance, a horde of people was crowding the security checkpoint.

Scarlett tensed, uncertain whether they should find another entrance. Before she could decide what to do, someone yelled her name.

"Scarlett! And Brayden! Congratulations on your marriage!"

Numerous voices exclaimed as people spotted them. Cameras clicked around them, but to Scarlett's surprise, many of those gathered around the security entrance weren't photographers. Well-wishers quickly surrounded the two of them, blocking their path.

Brayden's arms formed a protective cage around Scarlett. "We need to get you inside."

"Look at that." Scarlett pointed to a handmade sign featuring sloppily drawn wedding rings and their wedding date surrounded by hearts. "They're here to congratulate us!" She should probably be worried about danger lurking in the unruly little crowd, but she was too thrilled by their enthusiasm to worry. They were *happy* she'd married Brayden.

A middle-aged woman shoved a bouquet of roses into her arms. "Your mother would be overjoyed."

"Thank you," said Scarlett as the woman faded into the crowd.

Several people held out copies of the *Soleil Times*, hoping to get an autograph on their wedding issue. Scarlett and Brayden signed a couple before a determined teenage girl elbowed her way to them holding out an elaborate-looking decorative box displaying two dolls.

"Scarlett, Brayden—I made this for you when I heard the news."

Awestruck, Scarlett handed Brayden the flowers and took the box, looking at it as a security guard grabbed her by the elbow, ready to haul her away from the beaming teenager.

"Give her a second," said Brayden gruffly.

The guard let go but hovered nearby, yelling at the bystanders to back up.

Two little dolls that looked like her and Brayden stared up at Scarlett, their painted faces smiling and happy. The dolls wore macramé wedding clothes, and the background of the box had been painted to look like a heart that was half the Soleil flag and half the Clair de Lune flag. "Love Transcends Borders" was written on the outside of the box, along with Scarlett and Brayden's wedding date.

Scarlett's eyes teared up. She handed Brayden the box and turned back to the girl, who looked at her expectantly. She wrapped the teenager in her arms. "Thank you. I needed this today," she said into her ear.

"You're welcome," said the girl in a shaky voice.

Several security guards formed a perimeter around them as the crowd grew louder. More well-wishers shoved teddy bears and bouquets into Brayden's and Scarlett's arms until security forced everyone back.

With a wave, Scarlett blew a kiss to the crowd and walked through the metal detector, with Brayden right behind her carrying several bouquets. They shared a glance as they walked into the much quieter marble entrance hall.

"That article worked better than I'd hoped," she said with a soft smile. She was still holding the box of dolls.

Brayden wrapped his arm around her shoulders as he peered into the box. "That gift is very sweet, but those little dolls are kinda creepy."

Scarlett laughed and clutched the box tighter. "I love them, and I'll keep them forever."

Scarlett's first week as a peer flew by as she immersed herself in her new world. Diplomatic talks between Sigur Viður and Soleil began. When the bureau failed to present further hard evidence, enough doubt was shed on their claims that they escaped further escalation, although not for lack of effort from the Goldenrods.

As Scarlett had requested on her first day, several of the lords and ladies approached her for help with the legislation her dad had been cosponsoring, including a bill for free lunch for schoolchildren, one for government-funded preschool, and a third for an environmental law regarding the water quality of the canals.

Less than one week in and the workload was already enormous. Brayden had been near her almost constantly, supporting her after their awful encounter with Alastair. Although, to Scarlett's growing disappointment, he continued to sleep on her couch rather than in her bed. Brayden was happy to hold her or go down on her before she went to sleep, as he'd done so every night, but he wasn't letting himself come undone with her the way he had when they'd slept together in Clair. She prayed he'd be able to relax more once Cass started work. He was right to put her safety first, but they might only have days together. And she wanted all of him. Badly.

Because of her long hours, they also hadn't made any progress digging up evidence against Laylani.

Scarlett had several flashbacks to her father answering emails on the weekends and late-night as she tried her best to keep up. She'd always looked down on him for doing that, thinking it was a flaw in his personal organization, but to her chagrin, she was at risk of living with no boundaries too. She'd already offered up several prayers of regret for her harsh treatment of Jules at various moments during her teenage years.

The worst part by far was how easy it was to spend the whole day orbiting Brayden without having any time to really *be* with him.

As the week drew to a close, Scarlett sat in her office sending out a few emails she'd been neglecting. Her muscles ached, and her left eye kept twitching, probably due to overwork. She paused and glanced over at Brayden, who was sitting in a nearby chair reading one of her father's books—something extremely dry by a long-dead philosopher. He was focused enough that he didn't notice her looking.

He'll probably never move here if I'm always working this much.

She quickly shoved the thought aside. This crisis wouldn't last forever. She promised herself things would be different soon. Scarlett would move heaven and earth for Brayden, and she'd love him better than anyone else.

CHAPTER (29)

That weekend, Cass and Tyler moved into House Heroux. Laylani had disappeared, with a flippant mention of a garden party across town, twenty minutes before they arrived. It was the first time she'd been out of the house while Scarlett and Brayden were home, and Scarlett was itching to use the opportunity to search her space. With Cass and Tyler around, she hoped to have many more opportunities to look for evidence.

"Do you play the game *Allbright*?" Cass asked after they were introduced to Beni.

"Oh yeah," Beni said enthusiastically. "All the time."

Tyler, who was tall, skinny, and pale, with bright eyes and blue hair, grinned. "That's a relief. Do you have a hard LAN line?"

"Yeah, and fiber internet. My parents put it in a couple years ago. Wait—do you stream *Allbright*?"

"Yep. I'm Katana," said Tyler.

"You *are* him!" Beni looked up at the streamer with wide eyes.

Scarlett grinned, amused by her brother's awe.

"You'll need to set up your computers right away, and I can move a second desk in so you have more space for your screens. Scarlett, what room are they in?"

"The room with the harp at the end of the hall upstairs," said Scarlett. "It's the closest to our bedrooms," she said to Cass.

"There's an Ethernet port there. I'll help you move your stuff," said Beni. He took a suitcase from the small cluster of bags and boxes they'd brought with them and ran upstairs.

Scarlett and Brayden stood in the upstairs hallway while Beni showed Cass and Tyler where to hook up Tyler's computer.

"I'm going to search Laylani's study," Scarlett told Brayden.

"Yeah, let's," he said.

"Tyler?" called Scarlett.

Tyler spun around. "Yeah?"

"If we needed help getting into my evil stepmother's laptop, is that something you'd be comfortable doing?"

His answering smile was serpentine. "For sure. Cass told me everything, and I'm totally on Team Scarlett's Revenge."

"Aww, we have a team name," said Beni.

"Thank you," said Scarlett, with a grateful look at both Cass and Tyler. "It means a lot to have you on my side."

"Here to help. And on that note, where's your security setup?" asked Tyler.

"It's in my father's study."

Scarlett led him to the downstairs study, which was filled with Jules's books. Brayden watched from the doorway as she opened the cabinet where the security system was kept.

"There are some cameras on the outside of the house, although no one checks them unless there's an issue," she said to Tyler as she pulled out the old laptop they used to view the feeds.

"Great." Tyler took it from Scarlett.

"My stepmother's study is next door. I'm not sure if her computer is in there or not. I'll go check while you get started here."

Tyler sat down in front of the laptop. "Cool."

Scarlett's nerves spiked. She prayed Laylani would stay away long enough that she didn't get caught in the act. She half expected the door to be booby-trapped or locked, but the room was still as she pushed it open. She noted right away that Laylani's laptop was missing from her desk.

"I'll check the desk." Scarlett was hyperaware of every sound around them as she moved into the room.

"I'll look in there." Brayden moved to a decorative white trunk sitting under the large garden-facing window.

All of Laylani's desk drawers were unlocked. Scarlett methodically searched each one, her palms sweating as she did, but all she found were old receipts for clothing and jewelry purchases.

"The trunk has nothing important," said Brayden as he kneeled next to her and ran his hands along the underside of the desk.

"What was in it?" asked Scarlett.

"Her wedding dress and a few photo albums."

"Ugh," said Scarlett. She lost hope as every drawer revealed only the mundane. There were no bank statements, birth certificates, or anything of the like. She finished looking through the final desk drawer—unused greeting cards—and sat on her heels. "It makes sense she'd remove anything I could've used against her." She looked around for anything else that could hold Laylani's secrets. Just for good measure, she took the cushions off the small love seat, but she found nothing. Not even a pack of Laylani's menthol cigarettes.

Brayden ran his hands through his hair. "Should we look in her bedroom?"

"Yes, but something tells me there's no point. She must be keeping things somewhere else, like at Moira's house."

"Let's try anyway," said Brayden.

They did a similar sweep in the bedroom Laylani had shared with Jules until his death. This time, they did find cigarettes in the night-stand. And disturbing artifacts Scarlett wanted to forget, including Laylani's extensive lingerie drawer. Aside from the clothes that still hung in his section of the closet, there was little evidence of her father in the room.

In the bathroom, Scarlett stilled when she noticed a bottle of his cologne. She took the cap off the bottle and inhaled. The familiar smell of vanilla and leather reminded her of visiting her dad in his study. Laughing with him. Talking with him. Tears spilled over her cheeks as her breath caught. She missed him so.

Brayden appeared in the doorway. When he saw her, he slid his arms around her waist.

"That must be your dad's."

"Yes, it's his. The smell brings back so many memories." She leaned into him. The comfort of his arms around her meant every-thing. As the ache in her heart lessened slightly, she replaced the cap on the bottle and placed it back where she'd found it. "I'm so tempted to take it even though I know she'd notice."

"She would notice," said a voice behind them.

Scarlett looked in the bathroom mirror and let out a yelp, her heart hammering against her ribs. Laylani stood behind them, her expression mocking, like she'd found them exactly where she expected them to be. "But you can keep it. I don't want it."

Scarlett spit out the excuse she'd concocted in case this very thing happened. "I want to give Beni Dad's watch. I was wondering if you had it in here somewhere."

"Of course. That makes sense, to come in here to find it on your own instead of asking me," said Laylani with a smirk. "I do agree, though, and I've sent the watch to the jeweler to get it resized and cleaned for Beaufort."

"Thanks for the cologne." Scarlett took Brayden by the hand and left the room as quickly as she could.

"She must have done that on purpose. Told us she was going across town so she could catch us searching her shit," said Scarlett as they made their way back to Jules's study.

"We lost nothing by her catching us," said Brayden. "The civility between you is clearly wafer-thin."

Scarlett huffed out a laugh. "True."

Back in Jules's study, they found Tyler showing Beni and Cass how to use the new surveillance app on their phones. Scarlett and Brayden eagerly pulled out their phones to join in.

Scarlett studied her phone. She could flick between feeds to view the exterior of her home from several angles, and she could set up a million different kinds of alerts. "This is so much better than having to go into the study to check the feed."

"We'll all sleep better tonight," said Cass.

She looked at Brayden, her unspoken question obvious. He gave her a quick nod and crooked smile.

Yes! The self-imposed exile from my bed is over! Her smile was over-bright, earning an odd look from Cass and a chuckle from Brayden.

"*Congratulations*," said Nori, sounding amused.

Behind the closed door of the study, Scarlett relayed what she and Brayden had discovered before Laylani surprised them.

"No laptop, and a whole lot of nothing," finished Scarlett.

"You don't need her laptop necessarily," said Tyler. "Get me a list of companies she's affiliated with and any personal information you have—everything you can think of. Where she gets her cosmetic surgery, her gym, everything—and we can try to get her that way."

"I can do that." She sat down at her dad's desk and picked up a pen.

CHAPTER (30)

That evening was Otis Garfield's charity event at the National Theater. Brayden emerged from the dressing room in a black tuxedo with satin lapels. Scarlett stared at him, clean-shaven and pink-cheeked from the shower, with his hair in artful disarray, and had to remind herself to breathe.

"Look at you. So handsome." She rose from her desk and ran her hands up his chest, letting him see plainly on her face how much she wanted him.

Brayden's gaze raked over her red satin dress. He brushed his fingers over the glossy waves of her hair, arranged that afternoon by a stylist just for the event. He let his hands rest lightly on her hips. "You're so gorgeous I'm speechless."

"I wish we had more time tonight." All she wanted was to spend the evening in bed with him, but they were due to depart for the charity event any minute.

He pulled her into his arms, holding her to him. "Me too. But we

have tomorrow. No Parliament tomorrow."

"And now that Cass is here, do you feel better?"

His face was so close to hers their noses touched. "Much better. Especially with the new security setup."

Her smile became devious. "Maybe we could—"

A knock at the door cut her off.

"Come in," called Scarlett as she disentangled herself from Brayden's arms.

Charlie appeared in the doorway. "The boat's ready."

"Thanks," she said, trying her best to look grateful.

Charlie disappeared, and she turned back to Brayden. "All I want to do right now is undress you. I think you've had a much easier time this week than I have. I'm *addicted* to you." Scarlett said the words like they were nothing, but deep down, insecurity had crept in. They were still so new, and she didn't know what their normal was. She made to leave, expecting him to make some lighthearted joke, but he overtook her, slamming the door and planting himself firmly in front of it.

He put his hands on either side of her face. "You think this has been easy for me?"

"You made it look easy."

Gripping her wrists in his large hands, he leaned down and whispered in her ear. "Eating you out was the only thing that kept me going this week. Being this close to you . . ." He let out a groan that was half-growl. "I saw that lace thong you left sitting out. Are you wearing it now?"

"Yes," she whispered. Of course she'd left it out to tease him. To make him imagine her in it, like he was right now.

"I want to take it off with my teeth and spend the rest of the night finding new ways to make you come."

Lightness filled her chest, and her heart raced as she tried to break his grasp to touch him. "Good—"

"I'm pretty wound up, Scarlett," he interjected, holding her firmly in place. "If you push me now, I'm going to ruin your hair and this ravishing dress before we even make it to the event." He leaned closer, and his tongue traced her earlobe. "Still think I've had an easy time this week?"

She gasped as he licked her, the last of her frustration melting into pure need.

"I'm tempted to do the wrong thing right now, but I think you'll regret it if you don't show tonight. So let's go to the event, and when we get home, I'll show you exactly what the inside of my mind looked like this week. Can you wait until then, or do you want it now?"

He sounded so on edge. Had this been lurking beneath his control all week? Her cheeks flushed thinking of it.

She took a shuddering breath and forced herself to think clearly; to remember why tonight mattered. The heat in her dropped away as she pictured the box reserved for her and what a letdown it would be for Otis Garfield and his charity if they didn't show. She wanted Brayden, needed him, but she could wait a few hours. Then, tonight, they could be together, and all day tomorrow.

She bit her lip and then smiled. "I can wait till tonight."

He kissed her briefly but forcefully. "Good."

Scarlett practically floated as they walked arm in arm through the marble lobby of the National Theater. She couldn't have been prouder to be on Brayden's arm as they made their way to the bar. She was also grateful Cass was trailing behind them. She did have a mental countdown till the time they could graciously leave, but she was still happy to be here. With him.

Many of the peers of Parliament loitered nearby in the lobby.

Otis Garfield had done his part to fill the theater's seats. As she looked around the room, Scarlett bumped into someone while she was looking the other way.

"Oh, I'm so sorry," she said, turning to offer her apologies.

It was Moira Ashworth, looking devastating in a floor-length, long-sleeve black dress.

"It's quite all right, Lady Heroux." Moira looked Brayden up and down, and inwardly Scarlett seethed at the way she studied him. "Lord Maddox. We haven't met, but I've seen you in the papers this week. I'm Lady Ashworth, Scarlett's aunt by marriage."

The words "aunt by marriage" irked Scarlett. She wished she could reject the connection.

"Good evening." Brayden's expression was inscrutable.

Moira crossed her arms. "How have you been finding Soleil? It must be tough for someone like *you* to get by without magic."

Brayden looked amused by the obvious insult and answered calmly. "The people of Soleil are friendly. When I'm on the street, I swear someone stops me at least once a day to tell me they think it's great Scarlett married someone from Clair de Lune." He looked down at Scarlett, his adoring gaze giving her butterflies. Then he looked up at Moira. "Some say magic will be legal here in our lifetimes, so maybe I won't have to live without it forever."

Moira's eyes flashed. "I don't know what part of town you've been hanging out in, but I assure you, the majority don't see it that way."

Brayden shrugged. "I guess we'll see."

"The medical healing alone would sway a lot of people," added Scarlett.

Moira pursed her lips. "Perhaps. Please excuse me." She strode off without another word.

"I refuse to believe most of the country thinks like her," said Scarlett as they watched her go.

"Every day one of them dies and another young person becomes a voter who disagrees with her," said Cass from behind them.

Scarlett snorted. "True. It's just a matter of time."

From the bar, they purchased champagne for Scarlett, a coffee for Cass, and a glass of red wine for Brayden, then they made their way up to their box. The view from the upper tier was breathtaking even to Scarlett, who'd seen it many times before. Brayden and Cass looked around in awe. It all dazzled—the red velvet seats, the gilded gold filigree covering the decorative molding, the chandelier that dangled from the end of an ornate globe in the center of the ceiling.

They settled in as Lord Buckland and Lord Garfield took the stage to give a quick speech about the veterans charity benefiting from the event, and then the performance began. It was the famous opera inspired by the Great War, *The Sorrowful*. With Brayden's hand in hers, Scarlett sat attentive as the lead soprano strode onto the stage in period dress from two hundred years ago and belted out the famous opening number. Scarlett half listened to the familiar music while she daydreamed about what would happen *after* the performance.

At intermission, they exited their box and headed for the lobby. Lord and Lady Spencer emerged from a box a few doors down from theirs, followed by Alastair and a friend of his that Scarlett knew well: Rufus Hill, son of Lord Hill, a Goldenrod.

"Here we go," Brayden whispered, tightening his grip on her hand.

Scarlett's stomach clenched. *Please, Goddess, let Alastair not act like an absolute cake tonight.*

"*Not likely,*" said Nori.

"Oy, Scarlett." Rufus waved.

"Hello, Rufus," she said, willing herself to look friendly and relaxed.

"It's Lady Heroux now, Rufus. You'd think your own father

wasn't a lord," Elestine admonished. "Good evening, Lady Heroux and Lord Maddox."

"Rufus, this is my husband, Lord Brayden Maddox, and my bodyguard, Cass."

"Good evening." Brayden shook hands with Edward Spencer and Rufus. Alastair was buried in his phone. Cass remained standing just behind them, her eyes scanning the theatergoers around them.

"Will either of you be changing your names?" asked Elestine.

Scarlett narrowed her eyes, surprised Elestine would ask them about that in public. But then she glanced at Brayden, who gave her a one-sided smirk as he waited for her reply, and she relaxed. If he was amused by the question, she had nothing to worry about and might as well have fun with it.

"I'm tempted to take Maddox as my name. But maybe we'll hyphenate." Scarlett shrugged and was rewarded with comically shocked stares from both Edward and Elestine, black smoke above their heads.

"Maybe I should become Brayden Heroux," added Brayden.

Scarlett looked up at him adoringly.

Edward's brow furrowed. "No rush to figure it out until a child's on the way."

Scarlett stared at Edward. Was he *trying* to make them all as uncomfortable as possible?

"Shall we make our way to the lobby bar?" asked Alastair in a bored tone.

"Up for another drink?" Scarlett asked Brayden.

He murmured his agreement.

They followed Rufus and the Spencers downstairs. At the foot of the stairs, Elestine and Edward started toward the closest bar, next to an enormous marble statue of the three muses—the mythical patronesses of the arts in Soleil.

"Mother, Father," called Alastair, bringing them to a halt. "The bartender at the bar near the entrance told me earlier they've got a thirty-year-old whiskey only at that particular bar."

"Oh, excellent." Edward went after Alastair.

"Well, I guess we're off that way, dear." Elestine grasped Scarlett's hand before trailing after her family.

Scarlett's shoulders relaxed as the Spencers disappeared to the other side of the lobby. "I don't think Alastair even clocked who you were, Cass," she said to her bodyguard.

"He's not the most observant," said Cass, earning a chuckle from Brayden.

"Seeing them was awkward." Brayden put his arm around Scarlett as they got in the line for drinks.

"Yes, and I don't know why Elestine brought up name changes in front of Alastair," agreed Scarlett. "The bad news is, we'll see them frequently at things like this, but the good news is, it can't possibly be that awkward every time."

"I hate to think of you attending these events alone once I go back. I can just hear them. 'All alone tonight, Scarlett? Such a shame.'" Brayden ran a hand through his hair as he searched her face. "You know I'd stay if I could."

She'd been afraid to ask when he'd be going. The way he was talking made his departure sound imminent. But she put on a brave face. They'd always known it would be this way.

"I won't be *alone*. I can bribe Beni to be my date."

Brayden gave her a pointed stare. "Is that supposed to make me feel better?"

She leaned into him. "I guess not. I get your point."

As they waited for drinks, several gasps and a small shriek cut through the murmuring that filled the lobby, causing Scarlett and Brayden to turn toward the noise. Five men wearing balaclavas emerged from the far end of the lobby. The men headed straight toward them.

Pulling out her gun, Cass stepped in front of Scarlett. "Stop!" she shouted. "I'll shoot you in the kneecap if you don't stop! Brayden, get her out of here!"

Brayden took Scarlett's hand, and they hurried toward the theater entrance. They'd only gone a few feet when a gun fired, followed by a loud *thump*. Scarlett's chest tightened to the point of pain. She saw Cass on the ground, her legs bound in rope weighted with balls the masked men must have thrown. One of them was hunched over, rubbing his upper quad, but he didn't look like someone who'd just been shot. Cass fired again, but the men overtook her, and Scarlett's jaw went slack as one of them tasered Cass and took her gun.

"Cass!" she cried. "Someone help her!"

Cass went limp on the ground.

The rest of the men were upon them too quickly. Brayden shoved Scarlett behind him, raising his fists and knocking one of them down with a right hook to his jaw. Brayden kicked out, dropping another to the ground, but two of the men grabbed his forearms and pulled them behind his back, while a third approached, pulling cuffs from his belt. Each of them carried a handgun strapped to a utility belt.

Brayden splayed his hands, and Scarlett's whole body tensed, knowing the fire he could call if he wanted to. But what would the consequences be if he did? His fists clenched as if his thoughts were mirroring hers.

Instead he slammed his left elbow into the gut of one of the men trying to restrain him, freeing his arm, but before he could disentangle himself, another man grabbed it and pulled it back again.

"Run, Scar!" yelled Brayden. "I'll be—"

He was cut off as one of the men kneed him in the gut.

"Brayden!" screamed Scarlett. She turned frantically to the crowd for help. Many of the people closest to them were either hurrying away or staring with wide eyes, but Lord Buckland rushed toward them, his wife just behind him.

Scarlett spun around in time to see Brayden elbow one of the men in the face, freeing his arm again as the man's blood sprayed across the floor. The third man jumped on him before Brayden could fully free himself.

"See here, unhand that young man!" shouted Lord Buckland.

"Go get security," Scarlett called to his wife, who scurried toward the door.

Lord Buckland kneed one of the men holding Brayden in the stomach, and the man let out a loud groan but didn't let go. The one who'd taken an elbow to the face ran at the lord with murder in his gaze. He hit him in the jaw, and Lord Buckland crumpled to the floor.

"What are you doing?" screamed Scarlett. "Who are you?"

One of the men holding Brayden spoke. "Time to grab her."

The self-defense lessons she'd taken as a teenager came back to her, and Scarlett ran at the man closest to her and slammed the heel of her hand into his nose.

"Fucking bitch," he said. He flung her to the floor, pulling his own set of handcuffs from his belt.

Scarlett scrambled away, her eyes darting around the lobby as she racked her brain for her next move. She hid behind the large statue, trying to keep out of sight of the man as he followed her around the base. Death was a heartbeat away.

I can't lose Brayden. I can't leave Beni. Those thoughts played over and over in her head as she stayed just out of the man's reach.

"I've called the police!"

The words of the woman on the staircase distracted her, and Scarlett missed it when the masked man doubled back around the statue, only realizing her mistake when he hooked his arm around her waist.

"No!" Her shrieks filled the air as he threw her over his shoulder. Reaching for his head, she tried to smack him, but his hold on her was too tight. She screamed and hit his back as hard as she could with her fists. He didn't even react.

The theater guards were rushing toward them, but they were still too far away to help her.

The man started to walk, with her over his shoulder, toward the staff entrance from which they'd come. He'd have her outside in a van in minutes if no one intervened.

"Brayden!" Her voice reached a new octave as true panic set in. She twisted, trying to see what was happening, as blood rushed to her head. Seeing Brayden on his knees, she let out a sob, sure she was losing him and unable to do anything to stop it. She was being carried away.

No. This can't be the end.

"Scarlett!" bellowed Brayden, his gaze locking onto her. *"Scarlett!"*

The lights flickered and went out.

Cass?

A second later, a brilliant inferno erupted.

Screams filled the room. Scarlett gasped at the heat of Brayden's flames. The men holding him collapsed with cries of pain as his flames climbed the bloodred drapes lining all the walls of the lobby.

The man holding Scarlett whirled toward the fire and was consequently taken by surprise as security guards tackled him. A shot, and her captor screamed and collapsed to the floor, still holding on to her. Scarlett cried out as her body slammed into the marble, the man's weight crushing her legs.

The lights flickered back on—not that it made much difference with the flames growing around them.

Cass stumbled toward Scarlett, free of her bindings. "Are you all right?" Her face was full of concern.

"Help Brayden," Scarlett yelled as one of the guards helped her off the ground while the other cuffed her assailant.

Before Cass could, Brayden rushed toward them. He'd freed both his hands. The cuffs and part of the tuxedo's sleeves had been burned off, but to her relief, he appeared unharmed. Small flames danced across his skin—the aftermath of whatever he'd done. She gaped at all the assailants he'd laid out with his fire, their masks and their clothes burning away as they writhed and moaned in pain.

Brayden took her face in his hands and looked her up and down. "Are you hurt?"

She shook her head, coughing as she inhaled smoke. "I'm fine." But a sudden wave of nausea said otherwise. She willed her stomach to cooperate as she grasped his hand, pulling him toward the exit.

He used magic. What should I do? Nori, help me. We can't run, can we?

"There's nowhere to run," said her light. *"What's done is done. You both survived—that's all that matters. Keep breathing."*

A fire alarm sounded, and the sprinkler system went off above them. Scarlett shivered as water rained down. The flames had spread up the fabric along the walls and were licking the ceiling, but the sprinklers halted their progress.

The alarm was still blaring in Scarlett's ears as she and Brayden emerged onto the rainy street, followed closely by Cass. Three police cars pulled up, along with a fire truck and an ambulance. Brayden held Scarlett as she breathed in the fresh night air. Knowing they probably only had seconds, she grasped him tightly, pressing herself into his chest.

"I almost lost you," he whispered in her ear. "We should have gotten the North Star runes. You'd be so much safer."

She coughed. "I'm just glad we're both alive."

"Me too, but the smoke wouldn't be making you cough right now if you had my powers." His voice shook as she held on to him.

"Thank you for saving me," she said. "I'm sorry you had to. I don't know what the police will do. Maybe under the circumstances they'll minimize the charges." But a fresh wave of nausea rose as if to contradict her. She knew they wouldn't be lenient.

"Don't be sorry. I'm glad I was here tonight. No matter what happens next."

Firemen rushed past them with a large hose. Cass pulled out her phone, and Scarlett heard her speaking to Tyler.

"There," said a woman. "The one holding the lady in red. He started the fire."

Two officers rushed toward them, guns in hand.

"You—hands off her! Put them up in the air!"

"No!" shrieked Scarlett. "He isn't the one who caused this."

Releasing Scarlett, Brayden put his hands up. "It'll be okay, sweetheart," he said. "They're only doing their jobs."

"You're under arrest for assault with deadly magic," said one of the officers. "Face down on the ground *now*."

The pavement was wet from the rain, but Brayden did as they said. The officers wrenched his hands behind his back and pushed his face into the concrete as they cuffed him.

"This is outrageous," said Scarlett. "We were attacked in the lobby. My bodyguard was tasered, and they were trying to abduct us. My husband saved us. Don't *arrest* him." She kneeled next to Brayden, hovering over him. Hearing him scream her name just before he burst into flames—he'd have killed them all for her. He was hers, and she was his, and they couldn't take him from her.

"Detectives will be along shortly to bring in witnesses for statements. Get *out* of the way, unless you want us to arrest you too," said an officer. He took her roughly by the arm and pulled her away from

Brayden. Cass caught her and helped her stand.

"You're supposed to protect people, not arrest the victim!" she yelled, but they ignored her, hauling Brayden upright and walking him toward a police car.

Scarlett and Cass followed.

"I'll hire a lawyer! I promise." Scarlett's voice shook as she tried to force her way closer to Brayden. A photographer's camera flashed, but she ignored it.

"Get in touch with my father," said Brayden over his shoulder. "Don't leave Cass's side."

"Quiet," said one of the officers as they pushed his head down into the back of the car.

"We'll follow you to the station. I love you!"

Scarlett's words were cut off as the officer slammed the door shut. She stood on the curb staring at the car carrying Brayden away as the rain poured.

People were talking, but she stared straight ahead, unhearing.

He fought for me, and I'll fight for him until he's free.

CHAPTER (31)

At the station, an officer took Scarlett and Cass to a window-less room that held nothing but a table and a few chairs, and after asking if they had any immediate needs, he left her and Cass alone.

Who had been behind the attack? Could it have been a new enemy or were Moira and Laylani behind it all? Forcing herself not to jump to conclusions, Scarlett tried to imagine why Moira might have had her attacked in public. Or why someone else might have. All she could think was that doing it at the theater exposed Brayden. Otherwise, why wouldn't the person responsible have ordered the hit in a more private location? She prayed the men who attacked her wouldn't turn out to be from Sigur Viður. She hadn't clocked an accent, but things had been moving so quickly it was hard to be sure.

Scarlett was sure of one thing: She would obliterate everyone involved. She'd rain legal and physical pain down on all of them with all the means available to her. Visions of Lachlan using his

specter powers to slip into their cells and end them spiked a dark excitement.

"I don't know what you're thinking, but you look freaking terrifying right now," murmured Cass. "If you'd like my resignation, I understand. I can't believe how quickly they incapacitated me."

Fantasies of revenge faded from her mind, and Scarlett grasped Cass's hand. No part of her resented or doubted her. "I was thinking I want to find who's responsible for tonight and make them pay. You took a Taser for me—I'm not mad at *you*. *Please* don't resign. I need you more than ever right now. As for what happened, it was five men, completely out of the blue, and they had that rope with the balls they threw at you."

"Yeah, that was a new one for me. I assumed shooting one would be enough, but . . ." Cass shook her head. "He was up so fast—they must've had bulletproof gear on."

Scarlett flashed back to the sight of Cass passed out on the floor. "Are you okay? They tased you till you passed out, didn't they?"

"I'll be fine. I'll see a doctor tomorrow." Cass rubbed her abdomen in the spot where the Taser prongs had touched her.

Scarlett started to shake—from shock or cold or both. "Goddess knows how long Brayden will be locked away. I need to contact his father." She craved Lachlan's solid, capable presence, but she also feared what he'd do. If he extradited Brayden, what would that mean for them?

"Call Beni when you get your phone back. He can get in touch—"

The door opened, and a plainclothes officer stepped into the room. "Sorry to keep you waiting. I'm Officer Geruda. I'm the lead on the investigation involving your husband."

"I'm Lady Scarlett Heroux."

"Lady Heroux—of course I'm familiar," said Officer Geruda.

"Cassidy Darwish." Cass held out her hand.

The officer shook it as he noted her empty holster. "The front desk told me they checked your gun. You have a permit for that weapon?"

"Of course, Officer. I've been a professional bodyguard for several years. I fired shots to incapacitate, not to kill, but I didn't succeed in stopping anyone."

He sat at the small table. "Noted. Who wants to go first? What's your recollection of events from start to finish?" He was ready, with a pen hovering over his notepad.

"I'll go first, but can you tell me, where's the prime minister? Is she safe?" The thought had belatedly occurred to Scarlett that she and Brayden might not have been the attackers' sole targets.

"I heard over the dispatch radio that she was gone as soon as the incident started," he said. "Now, please proceed."

Scarlett cleared her throat and rested her elbows on the table in front of them. "My husband Brayden and I were in the lobby waiting in line for drinks when five or so masked men came for us. Cass shouted a warning and shot one of them when they didn't listen, but they threw something at her to incapacitate her and tased her. Then they grabbed my husband, and three of them worked together to handcuff him. I believe they meant to abduct both of us."

Gold smoke. He agreed so far.

"I see. What happened when the men restrained your husband?"

Scarlett paused, choosing her words with care. "He fought them. I hit one of them in the face. He came for me, and I ran. He caught me and picked me up. The others had managed to handcuff Brayden. That was when he used magic to overcome them—when it was clear we weren't escaping them without it."

Black and gold smoke.

The officer's eyes flashed. "Which is still illegal. Can you be more specific about the magic he used?"

"He's from Clair de Lune. He has fire magic. If he hadn't used his magic, we would've been kidnapped and probably killed," she protested.

"And did you know he had these abilities?"

"Of course I did—we're married," Scarlett snapped.

"I saw in the papers you were only recently married, so please forgive the intrusive question. Cass, do you have anything to add?"

"No," she said. "Lady Heroux gave an accurate account."

He made a note. "Are you aware that two of the men he burned are in critical condition?"

"I've been in here since the incident, so no, I was not aware," said Scarlett.

"Additionally, the smoke damage to the property was considerable, and there's water damage from the sprinkler system. Luckily, the fire department arrived before it could spread beyond the lobby."

"But if he hadn't, we might be *dead* right now. Those men had guns. Maybe you recall my father was recently assassinated, and also, I've just taken up the work that got him killed." Scarlett locked eyes with the officer. "Doesn't that change how he's charged? In a typical self-defense case, wouldn't it be warranted to incapacitate your assailants? I'm happy to pay for the damages to the theater—"

"He used deadly magic," interrupted Geruda, his expression guarded. "We haven't had a case quite like this one before, so it's hard to say how this will pan out."

Scarlett let out a growl as she glared at the officer. "I'll change that law if it's the last thing I do."

He shrugged in a way that said, *Go ahead, but it's not changing shit tonight, lady.*

Cass cleared her throat. "What happens now?"

"Lord Maddox will be charged for Class A magic use. Further charges depend on witness statements and security footage." He paused for a moment. "Unless you have further questions, leave your number with reception, and we'll be in touch."

"What about bail? Can't Brayden come home tonight? Can I see him?" He'd told her he regretted not getting the North Star runes. She'd meant to tell him she felt the same, but the moment had passed too quickly. Now he was gone. She *needed* to see him.

"There's no bail for a Class A offense. He's currently being processed, and visitation won't be possible until tomorrow."

Scarlett stood. "Don't think for *one* minute I won't use all my vast resources to come down on this precinct with the fire of a thousand suns if you don't do everything by the book. If I catch one *whiff* of bias in how you handle this investigation, you won't be able to get a job as a security guard."

Officer Geruda's face flushed red, his jaw working for a moment before he spoke. "I assure you, everything will be by the book, although threatening me won't make me any more charitable toward your case. I'll see you out."

He escorted them to the lobby and walked off without a backward glance. They got their stuff back from reception, but when Scarlett pulled her phone out to call Beni, the screen was black. She sighed and stuffed it back into her clutch.

Cass and Scarlett stepped out onto the street. It was close to midnight. The rain had stopped, but the streets were still shining.

"What a fucking mess." Scarlett burst into tears. "I'm going to get him back," she added.

Cass put her arm around her shoulders. "You will, and I'll help."

CHAPTER 32

As Scarlett and Cass walked into House Heroux, Beni appeared at the top of the staircase, with Tyler behind him. Beni's eyebrows shot up as he took in her gown, wrecked from when she'd been kneeling in the street and still wet from the rain.

"Scarlett! I was so worried. Mum came up and told us you were on the news, and you didn't answer your phone. Where's Brayden?"

"I'm sorry, Beni. Tonight was a nightmare." Scarlett's voice was wooden. She couldn't afford to melt down yet—not until she was alone. "We were attacked and almost abducted. Brayden was arrested."

Beni's mouth fell open as Scarlett and Cass reached the top of the staircase, his eyes darting between her ruined dress and their stoic expressions.

Scarlett held out her arms, hoping for a hug from her brother. "I'm sorry I didn't call. The police took me to the station and had my phone checked at the front desk while I was being questioned. When I got it back, the battery was dead."

Tyler opened his arms to Cass as Scarlett hugged her brother. Then the four of them made their way down the hallway and stopped outside Scarlett's door.

"That fire looked gnarly," said Tyler. "Is everyone okay?"

"Cass should see a doctor tomorrow," said Scarlett. "The attackers got burned, and a couple of them are in critical condition, but I believe everyone else is fine."

"I'm fine," said Cass as Tyler's hands cradled her face. "Have you seen the news? What are they saying?"

"It's pretty bad," said Tyler. "They're saying Brayden used magic to start the fire. They mentioned an altercation, but not in any detail."

"Never mind that Brayden and I were almost killed," said Scarlett.

"They keep showing the pictures of you two at the beach . . ." Beni trailed off.

Scarlett waited for him to continue, but then she followed his line of sight.

Laylani was standing at the top of the staircase, her eyes gleaming with interest as she listened. "Rough night, by the sound of it?"

A tidal wave of rage built in Scarlett. It had been the worst night of her life—that didn't involve an actual death—and she had to come home to this shit from her stepmother. The weight of the evening, of her entire Goddess-damned tragic life, bore down on her. Like a levy breaking, it all spilled out.

"You know what?" She rushed toward Laylani, who, alarmed, backed several steps down the staircase. "Get the fuck out of my house. Leave. Tonight."

Laylani gasped as she paused her descent, clutching the banister to steady herself. "I understand your husband just got arrested, but don't take it out on me!"

Heat blazed through Scarlett's body. The fire inside her burned away her tears, her sorrow, her pity, leaving her with nothing but rage and vengeance. "You *knew* we'd get attacked tonight. Why else didn't you attend such a high-profile event? Just like you knew Dad would get shot in the motorcade. That's why you stayed home that day, isn't it? Because you fucking *knew*."

Scarlett wasn't a phoenix, yet, but right now she wished she could burn Laylani till she was nothing but ash. For her father and for him. For Brayden.

Laylani's eyes were wide as she tried to compose herself. "What a *wild* accusation. How can you believe something so mad?" Her voice wobbled at first but grew stronger. Then her face flushed deep red with anger. "You sound paranoid, Scarlett. Are you sure you're all right? Do we need to call the doctor, perhaps?" She started back toward Scarlett, daring to come closer.

Scarlett let out an inhuman shriek as she lunged for her step-mother, but Cass grabbed her arms as Laylani retreated once more.

"Scarlett!" Beni rushed to Scarlett's side, panic etched across his features. His fear pierced through her rage. She couldn't do anything to jeopardize him.

"Get out!" Scarlett yelled, but she didn't struggle against Cass's firm grip. She hated Laylani, but she didn't want to scare Beni any more than she already had. She needed to protect her brother. And the last thing she needed was for Laylani to fall down the stairs and die before Scarlett could send her to jail.

Laylani angled her chin up as she stayed where she was. "I didn't have anything to do with what happened tonight. You're making a mistake—"

"Funny your first reaction wasn't to say that about my dad's death," hissed Scarlett. She grabbed Beni's hand, needing the physical reminder of why she couldn't get violent. "I don't care what you say. I don't care! I don't *care*. It's *your* fault my parents are dead, and I want you fucking out of here. This is my house. I'll give you half an hour to pack your essentials. The rest of your things will be shipped to your sister's house within the week. Just get out!"

The color drained from Laylani's face. She glanced at her son, who still held Scarlett's hand firmly in his. "Beni, let's go. You're coming with me."

Beni's grip on Scarlett's hand tightened. "Scar said you're leaving. Not me. I'm staying."

Scarlett squeezed back. "There's no way I'm letting you take my brother."

For the first time in Scarlett's memory, Laylani's face crumpled for a brief second before her mask returned. She pointed a finger at Scarlett. "You'll regret turning my son against me."

Baffled, Scarlett nearly laughed. "You have no one to blame for that but yourself. You think I wanted it this way? I'm just like Beni. All I wanted was a loving family, and you ruined any possibility of that for me *and* your son. Now do as I said and get *out*."

Laylani glared at her but was silent as she turned and hurried down the stairs.

"Cass, watch her pack and make sure she gets a taxi without coming back up here," said Scarlett. "Don't let her take anything other than her own clothing—nothing of my dad's."

Cass rushed after Laylani.

Scarlett faced her brother and Tyler. "I'm sorry you had to hear that."

Tyler's eyes were wide, but he looked impressed. "Don't apologize. I do suggest we sage the house once she's gone."

Beni let out a long breath, his shoulders collapsing inward. "She's leaving? For good?"

Scarlett looked at her brother with concern. "I had to get rid of her. I know I said I wanted to keep her close, but now that Brayden's in jail, I just can't risk it anymore. Are you okay?"

Beni scooted closer and wrapped his arms around Scarlett. "I'm glad she's gone. Now we don't have to pretend anymore."

She held her brother close. "Things will be a lot easier at home from now on. We can build the loving home she never gave us."

He let out a sigh that was almost a sob, and she squeezed him tighter.

"They'll be keen to make him the poster child for magical abuse," said Manon. She and Lachlan were sitting in Lachlan's office in the castle, looking at Scarlett through the mirror.

"We could extradite him back to Clair de Lune," said Lachlan.

Scarlett shook her head, her exhaustion weighing her down. The fight with Laylani had drained her body of any energy reserves she'd had left after the National Theater, but she didn't want Manon to worry, so she tried to sit up and keep her eyes open. "They won't allow that, given how high-profile this is." She leaned in closer to the mirror. "I know you could get him out, but he'd never be able to come back. Please, Lachlan, let me work on this from my side. If I fail, you can do what needs to be done, but at least let me see what my lawyer can do for him first."

Lachlan's expression was pinched. "We'll wait a few days. But I hate the idea of him sitting in a Soleil jail cell."

She met his gaze but had to quickly look away, rubbing her eyes to hide the tears forming. "I know. It kills me too. All he did was protect us. Whoever sent those men is probably overjoyed he's locked up right now."

"You're both alive and unharmed," said Manon. "That's the important thing. You'll find a way to free him."

It was true. Earlier, she'd believed death had come for her. As long as they were alive, there was still hope.

Elestine called Scarlett early the next morning. "I wanted to check if you're all right."

Scarlett rose from her bed, where she'd been lying awake for some time, and moved to sit at her desk. "I'm glad you called. We have a lot to discuss."

"We do, unfortunately. I assume you've been watching the news."

"Of course. Some of it is totally off base, but I'm relieved there are some neutral and sympathetic perspectives." As the police had released more information, the account had shifted from focusing on the fire to the masked men who'd infiltrated the National Theater. "Today I'll call the reporters I know to help push the narrative even further our way."

"Excellent. The public adores the star-crossed lovers story. Make sure they know Brayden was defending you," said Elestine. "Which reporters do you know?"

"One at the *Soleil Times* and one at *Citizen*. If you have any others, send them my way."

"I'll send you a list. I have contacts at every paper."

Scarlett blinked. But of course the prime minister would have those contacts.

Elestine sighed. "Before last night, you two had so much public support, and that counts for something. Let's get the young progressives riled up on your behalf. If we play our cards right, we could use this awful incident to help bolster the case for legalizing magic."

Scarlett had been so focused on Brayden and Laylani she hadn't calculated that far ahead, but she was once again impressed by Elestine's dedication to the cause. "That's a good point. And imagine if the incident last night turns out to be linked to my dad's death."

Elestine whimpered softly. As Scarlett took in her distress, her fondness for the prime minister deepened. They sat silently for several seconds, both thinking of Jules. Laylani and all that had transpired yesterday flashed through Scarlett's mind.

"There's something I should mention. I kicked my stepmother out of my house last night."

Elestine's voice rumbled with satisfaction. "It's about time you got rid of her. The woman can't be trusted. We'll find more evidence without her under your roof. We need something, though, if we're ever going to get a subpoena to search the Goldenrods' headquarters or the bureau."

Scarlett stared out her window at a boat passing by on the canal as she voiced the daring idea she'd been mulling over. "What if we act without evidence? What if *I* act? That Goldenrod fundraiser—the Golden Gala—is tomorrow night at the St. Germain Hotel. They'll all be there. I could personally send someone undercover into the Goldenrod Party headquarters to search for evidence while it's empty. Records of payment, employment—anything to incriminate them."

Worst-case, she lost her seat in Parliament and had to flee the country with Brayden to escape arrest. As long as Beni came with her, that didn't sound so bad. It sounded much better than meeting a violent end in Soleil.

"If I were acting alone, rather than as one of the Ceruleans, it wouldn't be as disastrous for the party—for you—if we were caught. Would the court allow evidence obtained that way?"

"That seems rather bold," said Elestine, but to Scarlett's surprise, she didn't sound horrified. "Given the suspicions we have about the bureau, it could make room for me to issue an executive order for a retroactive subpoena. But only if it were *real* evidence. The ends would justify the means."

Scarlett tapped a pen on her desktop. "I'll try it. I'm desperate. Brayden is in jail. I have a capable bodyguard, but that doesn't mean

I'm safe. I've never been happier that Beni is Laylani's son, because that will keep him safe, but the last thing I want is to die and leave him alone with her." After last night, her already intense desire to keep Beni out of Laylani's grasp had multiplied exponentially.

"We won't let that happen," said Elestine. "One thing at a time. Let's spend the rest of the weekend doing damage control with the press."

"I'll line up as many interviews as I can," said Scarlett. "Garner more public sympathy and stop my father's legislative dreams from bleeding out. And could you revisit your conversations with some of the Cerulean lords to convey the uptick in urgency? Perhaps we should make them aware."

"Of course. So far, I've been vague with the lords I've spoken to about the need to investigate key Goldenrods. I think it's time to be more direct. I'll contact our allies and arrange a strategy meeting at my office at 7 a.m. tomorrow. If you're sure about the break-in, come with a plan. If there are any further developments in the meantime, call me."

"Perfect, thank you," said Scarlett, grateful Elestine was convening a meeting. "By the way, I'm glad you weren't hurt last night. At least I assume you weren't. The police said you left right away."

Elestine hummed in agreement. "Hmm, yes. It was lucky we were quite close to the exit when it all kicked off."

Scarlett pursed her lips. "Yes, you might have easily been right next to us in line if it weren't for that thirty-year-old whiskey."

"It's funny how the tiniest things can make such a difference." Elestine sounded pensive.

After she hung up, Scarlett took a deep breath. She didn't want to deal with any of this. For a brief moment she fantasized about screaming into the mirror, until Lachlan appeared. She could tell him to break Brayden out of jail today so they could both run off to

Clair de Lune and forget Soleil entirely, but that wasn't really what she wanted. Steeling herself, she picked up her phone once more and called the police station where Brayden was being held.

She was on hold for five minutes before a voice asked, "Lady Heroux?"

"Yes, this is she."

"Officer Geruda here. I know you'd like to speak to your husband. Unfortunately, given the high-profile nature of the case and the severity of the charges, we're restricting him from speaking to anyone except his lawyer."

Scarlett swallowed her desire to scream. "Our family lawyer will be at the station shortly. I expect to hear from him that my husband is being treated with respect while he's in custody, sir."

Next on her list were mercenaries, so Scarlett went looking for Cass. She found her bodyguard in the gym using the weights bench. Even seeing the gym caused a pang in her chest—everything reminded her of Brayden. They hadn't worked out together yet, and who knew when they would? Even her surfboard racked against the far wall reminded her of teaching him to surf.

Cass was watching live surveillance footage of the house up on the small mounted television while chest-pressing a heavy barbell. Sweat gleamed on her skin. She racked her weight and sat up as soon as she noticed Scarlett.

"Hey. You need me?"

"Sorry to bother you," said Scarlett, impressed by the multi-tasking. "*Should* you be working out after last night?"

"I heal quickly. It's a nocturna thing." Cass wiped the sweat off her brow with a small towel.

"Oh, cool." A small weight lifted off Scarlett, knowing she needn't worry about Cass's health. Then she remembered why she came down here, and her jaw tensed. "I came down because I need your help. I need to find the sort of people who can help me break into Goldenrod headquarters and possibly the Soleil Bureau."

Cass's eyebrows shot up.

Scarlett grimaced. "I was wondering if you might know anyone."

Cass's surprise melted into a serpentine grin. "I happen to know a hydra and a dire wolf who'd love some work. A few others come to mind. Want me to make some calls?"

For the first time that day, a genuine smile tugged at Scarlett's lips. "Yes, please."

"Any issues if I head up the team?" asked Cass.

"You'd do that? It'll be dangerous." Scarlett vividly recalled the helplessness of seeing her friend drop to the floor.

Cass scoffed, looking unconcerned. "First of all, yes. This is completely aligned with my values. I also had my ass handed to me at the National Theater, and I want to redeem myself."

Scarlett shook her head, frowning. "I don't think you let me down."

Cass looked up at her earnestly. "*I* think I did though. And to me, that's more important."

"Okay, then. I'd be grateful if you headed up the team."

"Great. It's a plan," said Cass.

Scarlett shivered even though it wasn't cold. This wild plan was all her idea, and it was really happening. Soon. Taking control like this was heady, exciting, and scary as hell. She just hoped she could pull it all off in the end.

CHAPTER (33)

The rest of the day was a fever dream of preparations, phone calls, and emails. Scarlett heard from the family lawyer, who was optimistic that the uniqueness of Brayden's case had its advantages, but he saw no path to getting him released before his trial, which would be weeks away, if not months.

"When can I talk to him?" she asked after the lawyer had finished.

"I'm sorry, Lady Heroux. They were very adamant I'm to be his only point of contact," he said apologetically. "Is there a message you'd like me to pass on?"

Scarlett debated asking him to tell Brayden she loved him but decided against it. "Just tell him I'm doing everything I can to get him out and that I miss him."

By dinnertime, Scarlett had given several interviews to the papers. The *Soleil Times* had confirmed the interview would be on the front page tomorrow alongside a feature about the attack. Cass had lined up several candidates interested in helping with a break-in,

and she and Scarlett had outlined a timeline and a plan for the night of the gala. Elestine had called back to say they were on for the 7 a.m. meeting.

Scarlett was relieved by all the progress but exhausted to her core. In an attempt to boost her energy, she ate her first meal of the day with Beni, Cass, and Tyler—fries and a chicken burger from a nearby burger joint Tyler had found.

Beni bit into his burger with enthusiasm, making the corners of Scarlett's eyes crinkle with amusement as she chewed.

"It's interesting there's disagreement about whether or not the evidence against Sigur Viður is legit," said Tyler after Scarlett had told them more than an NDA could cover. She needed to share the burden with someone, and she trusted them.

"Right. The Soleil Bureau claims to have more evidence, but they say the information is too sensitive to share publicly, because it could expose undercover agents. It's so fishy. The Ceruleans think the evidence is a ploy to get us to go to war against magic, and the Goldenrods think we should mindlessly trust the bureau for national security reasons." The fries tasted so good. She reached for her chicken burger. The food was helping push back a low headache that had been irritating her all afternoon.

"Did you know some people can hack into the bureau's systems?" Tyler's eyes sparkled. He looked around nonchalantly, then he pointed to his chest as he mouthed, "Me."

The corners of Scarlett's lips turned up as hope lifted her heart. "Could you actually?"

"That's next-level hacking." Beni sounded awestruck.

Tyler glanced from Beni back to Scarlett as he chewed and swallowed, looking like an eager deviant. "Yes, it's more difficult, and yes, I could easily tell you where those emails really came from."

"No way." Beni's delight mirrored Tyler's.

"How?" asked Scarlett. She was excited too, but also worried about the legality and whether this would hinder their already laid plans for the break-in. Were two huge risks at once really a good idea?

"Last I checked, the bureau has terrible cybersecurity. I could hack into their system tonight, if you'd like," said Tyler with a relaxed shrug, as if it were as easy as buying the fast food he'd picked up for their dinner.

"You'd do that? I'd compensate you, of course," said Scarlett. "What if you get caught?"

He snorted. "I'm not getting caught. And yeah, I'd do that for you. For free. Sounds like fun, and I'm curious."

"Yeah!" Beni punched the air, and Scarlett couldn't help but laugh.

Cass grinned at her husband. "You love this revolutionary shit."

"I love you, my subversive beauty," he said, blowing her a kiss. His phone pinged, and his eyes lit up as he took in the message.

"What?" asked Cass.

"Remember how I said I'd try with your stepmother?" he asked, eyes on Scarlett. He burst into laughter. "I may have just gotten the passwords to her email and her bank accounts."

Scarlett shot up. "That's amazing! How?"

He showed Scarlett his phone. "The dumbest way. This morning I sent her an offer for half-price youth-enhancing injectables if she purchased an entire year's worth of injections at once. She filled out the form five minutes ago."

Beni hovered behind Scarlett as she read the very realistic email Tyler had sent from an address that would've fooled even her. It looked just like something Laylani's aesthetic spa would've sent.

"Ha!" Beni high-fived Tyler.

It was the lightest Scarlett had been since Brayden's arrest. "Incredible work," she said.

"Well done, babe," said Cass, who'd joined them. She leaned over Tyler's shoulder. "Shall we see what she's packing?"

"We'll look while we work on the bureau's system." He laughed maniacally.

Scarlett wrapped her arms around him. "Thank you."

"I haven't done anything yet," he said, still chuckling.

"Thank you for trying," she said, straightening. Finally, she was getting the upper hand on Laylani and Moira. She was gaining control. Leveling the playing field. If only Brayden were with her, she'd be on the cusp of total triumph.

With Cass and Beni behind them, Scarlett sat next to Tyler while he worked his magic. He put a bot to work on the bureau's intranet and opened up Laylani's accounts on two different screens.

"What are we looking for here?" asked Tyler.

"Anything to do with my dad's death, my abduction, bribe-sized payments to Dr. Turner, or—and this one's a long shot—the murder of my mother thirteen years ago," rattled off Scarlett. She'd lived through it all, but she could hardly believe the list as she summed it up for Tyler.

"Nothing major, then." He frowned at the screen as he did a couple of quick searches. There were too many mentions of Jules for her dad's name to work. Nothing came up when he tried searching for "Turner."

Tyler's attention was on the bank account, while Scarlett scanned Laylani's inbox for anything particularly damning, but all she saw was a bunch of online shopping receipts, RSVPs for social functions, and dinner reservation confirmations.

A ping came from Tyler's computer. "We're into the bureau's system."

"Damn, that was quick," muttered Scarlett, making a mental note to propose security upgrades for the government websites. For now, it was a good thing security was lax.

Finding exactly what they needed proved more difficult than simply gaining access. After the first thirty minutes, Beni and Cass sat on the floor playing cards. Scarlett remained next to Tyler, scouring the screens in front of her for anything she could use.

An hour passed.

"It's a matter of figuring out where the files might be stored," murmured Tyler. He had a script running on his computer searching the bureau's files one by one for mentions of Sigur Viður. He and Scarlett opened promising-looking folders together. There were many mentions of the country across the bureau's internal system, but so far, they'd seen a lot of irrelevant top-secret documents.

The script stopped, blinking an alert.

"Another hit—looks promising." Tyler's eyes lit with excitement.

Cass and Beni got up off the floor to see what he'd found.

"Code— Where is the—? Oh, you fools." Tyler's voice notched up an octave with excitement.

Scarlett stared at him, her hopes rising.

Tyler pointed to his screen. "It's written in code. Look—in this file? The coded version. Now look at the decoded version. There's your dad's name in the decoded file—Lord Jules Heroux." He pulled up the translator app he'd been using to check anything remotely relevant and read the first message out loud.

> Kjartan Holm approved. Eliminate Lord Jules Heroux
> at the first opportunity. Report with confirmation.

Scarlett's lips parted. Kjartan Holm was the chancellor of Sigur Viður.

Tyler clicked into the reply.

> Confirmed. The target, Lord Jules Heroux, will be eliminated by the end of day. Exit assistance will be needed by five o'clock latest.

"Then there's a third and final message that just says 'done,'" said Tyler.

"Are the messages real?" A painful lump formed in her throat. If they were, it would cast doubt on everything she'd been believing in so fiercely.

"No." With a laugh, Tyler pointed to the screen again. "These IP addresses are both native to Soleil. Hang on. I'll look in the police database to see the exact address they came from."

"I know you're helping me, but it's kind of scary you can do this," said Scarlett.

"Right?" said Cass.

Tyler smirked. "Don't worry, I use my powers for good and gaming. Here we go. The IP addresses on these messages point to two computers owned by people in Soleil. Goddess above, these are some stupid criminals. One of them lives at an address on the downtown side of the Sapphire Canal. The other one is from the outskirts of Soleil, out toward the marshlands."

Scarlett tensed. "Who lives at the home on the Sapphire Canal?"

"Hold, please." Tyler quickly searched a database of Soleil landowners. He pulled up the address, and Scarlett read in shock as he said aloud, "Lord Lyle Federsin."

Scarlett stood so fast she knocked her chair over. It was the prick who kept heckling her whenever she took the podium in Parliament. He was part of Moira's inner circle.

"This is fucking amazing, Tyler. I can't wait to expose him. How can I take this to the prime minister?"

"I'll put the bureau's files on a thumb drive. Just don't tell them where you got it." Tyler winked.

"Of *course*. I'm so grateful." She threw her arms around his shoulders. "Thank you! If we can't get a subpoena with this, I'll quit my job." Unable to contain her exuberance, she hugged Cass and then Beni too. Her smile faded as, once again, she wished Brayden were here to share this moment. She wasn't sure how any of these breakthroughs would help him, but she'd keep trying until something led to the truth behind the attack at the National Theater.

Cass laughed. "No quitting until you pass the border legislation. I want my father to be able to come see *us* for the winter solstice."

"I want that for you," said Scarlett. "Now, I'd better go call the prime minister."

Tyler swiveled around to face her. "I'll look at your stepmother's accounts and let you know if I piece anything together. Before you go, write down everything you know about the people you suspect of taking bribe money—their names and where they bank, for example. You suspect the bureau, but do you know specifically who? I can hack into the account of whoever you say. If they have any unrecognizable payments, it could be a lead."

"Sure." Scarlett recalled the conspiracy theory articles she'd read. "The second-in-command of the bureau. What's his name?"

Turning back to the computer, Tyler did a quick search. "Aaron Fox."

"Yes!" exclaimed Scarlett. "His involvement was a random theory from some online message board, but that's the best lead I have. Also, I know Moira banks at Barings, just like Laylani." She had hazy memories of Moira and Laylani bitching about how their branch locations were so inconvenient at some long-ago dinner party. "If you could start with the three of them, that would be amazing."

"It'd be my pleasure," said Tyler, cracking his knuckles.

She smiled as she wrote down everything she could think of. *I'm coming for you, Laylani. And you, Moira.*

CHAPTER (34)

Scarlett's sleep was fitful, and she rose the next morning feeling worse than she had before going to bed. While Charlie drove her and Cass into the city via speedboat, she was notified that the morning session, earmarked for a debate on education spending, had been postponed in favor of an open-forum discussion of the incident at the National Theater.

Scarlett stared out the window of the boat's cabin trying to imagine how the day would unfold. She dreaded listening to the peers debate whether Brayden was a dangerous criminal or deserving of clemency. Maybe people would surprise her though. She hoped they would.

"Everything okay?" Cass asked.

"The session this morning has been switched to a discussion of the National Theater incident." She shared a look with Cass as she patted her handbag, which held the thumb drive full of evidence. "But this might derail plans. We'll see, anyway."

When they arrived at Elestine's office, several prominent Cerulean lords were already there, including Lord Garfield, Lord Navarre, and Lord Bombardier. Cass found a spot by the door and stood with her arms folded. Alastair was sitting in the far corner, his computer on his lap. His gaze caught on Scarlett, and he studied her intently.

What's he looking at me like that for? Her stare was icy, and he looked away, frowning.

"*Probably looking for signs of weakness that he won't find,*" said Nori.

Scarlett certainly hadn't softened toward him, if that's what he was hoping for.

Otis Garfield shuffled toward her, snapping her out of her thoughts. "Are you all right, my dear? What Elestine mentioned over the phone—ghastly stuff."

"It was horrible. Thanks for your concern. I appreciate your support."

Otis patted her shoulder. "We'll see what we can do." His kindness and optimism bolstered Scarlett.

Lord Mayweather slipped into the office. The small space was now crowded with the most influential members of the Cerulean Party. It still hadn't fully sunk in that she was now undoubtedly one of them. She wondered when it would.

"Right," said Elestine. "We have everyone I expected. Let's begin. There's been a new development. Last night, Lady Heroux obtained evidence that the Soleil Bureau worked with Lord Federsin to frame Sigur Viður for the assassination of Lord Heroux. We believe this was done at the behest of Lady Ashworth."

Lord Navarre gasped.

"What's the evidence?" Lord Mayweather sounded more quizzical than shocked, and he leaned forward in his seat eagerly.

Scarlett faced her colleagues. "Files pulled directly from the bureau show that the IP addresses of the alleged messages between

Sigur Viður operatives are actually both native to Soleil. Police databases were used to match the IP addresses to the homes they're registered to. They pointed to Lord Federsin's home and a residence out in the marshlands registered to an unknown name. Whoever they are, we'll come for them too, but they aren't a peer."

There were murmurs of shock in response amidst the swirls of black and gold smoke—mostly gold—floating in the air.

"How reliable is this information?" demanded Lord Bombardier.

"Unless the bureau planted this in their own systems as a misdirection, it's extremely reliable," replied Scarlett.

"We must take this to the police," said Lord Mayweather. "And the head of the bureau? Perhaps he wasn't aware of the cover-up."

Scarlett shared a glance with Elestine. "Given we have a dangerous conspiracy on our hands, Lady Spencer and I would like to propose something more . . . clandestine," said Scarlett. "Right now, we have the element of surprise. If we take this to the police, there's a chance they manage to dismiss the evidence. We need *more* proof, both of the cover-up by the bureau and the violence against me and my family." Speaking about the plot against her family out loud was strange, but it was refreshing to be able to tell the truth now that Elestine had told the lords everything.

The smoke above them was almost exclusively gold, bolstering Scarlett's confidence.

"You're right," said Lord Bombardier. "We don't know which parts of law enforcement to trust. We need a case so solid it can't be ignored."

The other lords nodded.

"Are we all in agreement?" asked Elestine, scanning their faces for tacit consent. "Good. Scarlett, go ahead and tell them your plan."

Scarlett cleared her throat. "I've got a team assembled that includes a couple of ex–intelligence agents and some talented individuals who are used to operating in secret." She didn't turn to look at Cass. The less the lords knew the better, in case it all went sideways. "I propose we send them tonight to raid Lord Federsin's home, as well as the Goldenrod headquarters, in search of evidence."

"Any questions?" asked Elestine.

Otis's brow pinched. "You realize if this goes badly, it'll be traced back to you?"

"It's a risk I'm willing to take. If we get caught, I'll own it," said Scarlett.

"That could mean jail time," said Lord Navarre.

Scarlett shrugged. Maybe she could have the cell next to Brayden's if it came to that. But she also had the same exit opportunity he did. "I'm a dual citizen and could ask to be extradited."

Lord Navarre's eyes lit up. "That does help somewhat."

"Anyone else?" asked Elestine.

The room was silent.

"All in favor, say aye."

Every person in the room, aside from Alastair, murmured, "Aye."

"Thank you all so much," said Scarlett, her shoulders relaxing. If they'd all been against the idea, she didn't know what she would have done.

"There's no thanks necessary," said Lord Bombardier. "If this is all true—and I believe what you've told us—the integrity of the senate and the future of Soleil are at risk, and we must act accordingly. We should be thanking you for taking this risk."

There were murmurs of agreement from the rest of the room.

"Before we disperse," said Elestine, "let's discuss how to handle the National Theater situation."

Lord Navarre frowned. "Lady Ashworth will be trying to resurrect her old proposal to make violent magic a capital offense."

Scarlett's stomach clenched.

"Exactly," said Elestine. "She'll want to use this to her advantage, and she might have some votes swing her way, given it's an election year. However, the damage control Scarlett did with the press yesterday will shift public opinion, so today's strategy is to prevent a vote."

"May I ask a question?"

Heads swiveled to Alastair in the corner. Scarlett narrowed her eyes, and several lords looked like they'd only just noticed he was there.

Elestine's mouth was drawn in a tight line. "Go ahead."

"Forgive me, but are you *all* condoning what Lord Maddox did?" asked Alastair.

Elestine sighed. "The Cerulean platform is against outsized punishments for magic. The punishment should be tied to the crime—assault, murder, damage to property. All of those have wildly different categories within the law, particularly if there's a case for self-defense. Lord Maddox believed he was fighting for Lady Heroux's life, as well as his own."

"But he burned down the entire lobby—"

"Is my life less important than a lobby?" Scarlett's voice overrode Alastair's. "Property can be replaced, and I've offered to fund the repairs."

Alastair opened his mouth to reply, but Elestine put up a hand to silence him. "Because he had no other choice. Wouldn't any of us have done the same if our family were at risk?"

"I would've done the same, I reckon," said Otis.

"Absolutely," agreed Lord Mayweather. "If I had fire magic and balls as big as Lord Maddox's, I'd do the same." His elegant diction made the brash comment sound somehow refined.

Scarlett smiled in surprise as the men around her chuckled. Alastair's expression was stony as he stared at his computer.

Elestine suppressed a smile. "Glad to know we're all onside. Alastair, to bring this full circle for you, the Goldenrod desire to label violent magic a capital offense is political grandstanding to their base. They'd put Lord Maddox away for using fire magic to light a candle. It's unreasonable. Does that answer your question?" Her authoritative tone said he'd better be done asking questions.

"Yes." Alastair's cheeks were tinged pink.

Scarlett wrinkled her nose, certain that if she'd spoken those words instead of Elestine, she'd be seeing black smoke above Alastair's head.

"*He looks like a reprimanded child,*" said Nori.

The meeting ended, and the peers left Elestine's office. When it was just her, Scarlett, and Cass left, Scarlett gestured for Cass to come closer. They sat opposite Elestine at her desk.

"My bodyguard, Cass, is going to head up the break-in tonight," said Scarlett. "Do you have any questions for her?"

Elestine's eyebrows drew together. "Why in the world would you go without protection? Wasn't there anyone else available to help?"

Scarlett's shoulders kept tensing up, and she had to force herself to relax. "We need this to be a success, and she has special abilities."

"Special abilities?" Elestine's eyes flashed with interest.

"That's right," said Cass. "I'm from Zahara, and I have magic that prevents detection."

Scarlett felt confident in their odds of success as she thought of the darkness Cass wielded. "If Cass is leading them, they're much less likely to be caught."

"Understood," said Elestine. "We need to head to the meeting, but let's regroup later and firm up the plan for the evening. I'm still concerned about your safety tonight, but we can worry about that later."

Scarlett spent the bulk of her morning reviewing the incident at the National Theater. She was called to the podium multiple times, first to tell the chamber what happened, and then again, after an initial debate, to take questions from her peers.

"It was a matter of life and death," Scarlett said, trying not to let her annoyance shine through at being asked—for the second time—to go through the exact sequence of events. "My husband used his abilities to save us. To save *me*. Given my father's recent death—"

"Your father's killers are free due to this chamber's refusal to pursue justice in the north," bellowed Lady Ashworth from her seat. "It's hardly an excuse for illegal, violent behavior in Soleil. Three Soleil citizens are in intensive care due to Brayden Maddox's actions, and—"

Scarlett gripped the sides of the podium in front of her so hard her hands hurt, but her voice was clear and level. "Yes, they're in intensive care because they *attacked* us. We know from the report in the *Times* this morning that those men work as mercenaries for hire. I don't understand why you're victim-blaming instead of questioning who hired them."

"Because it seems I care more about avenging your father's death than you do, Lady Heroux," spat Lady Ashworth.

Scarlett's eyebrows shot up. Moira's venom was getting overt enough that it reminded her of their encounter at her father's funeral.

"Out of order," bellowed Lord Buckland. He was officially Scarlett's favorite Goldenrod ever since he'd tried to help at the theater, and he'd been reinforcing her opinion all through the questioning. It bolstered Scarlett that not all of Moira's party were behind her.

"That's *quite* out of order," agreed Elestine as she stood from her seat. "If the discussion is back to Lord Heroux and Sigur Viður, we're clearly done discussing the National Theater. I motion to disband the discussion."

"I'm not finished." Moira's loud voice echoed across the chamber.

"I second the motion," said Lord Garfield. "Thank you, Lady Heroux, for your multiple rounds of testimony."

"All those in favor of disbanding?" Scarlett called to the chamber.

The "ayes" were clearly in the majority.

"We are adjourned," said Scarlett.

As she made for the exit, Elestine and Lord Bombardier filed out next to her.

"Well done," said Lord Bombardier with a wink.

"Thanks." Scarlett smiled weakly as a wave of exhaustion came over her. They weren't out of the woods yet, but she'd managed to keep Moira from turning sentiment against Brayden. For now that would have to be enough.

Back in her office, Scarlett was at her desk trying to force down a cucumber sandwich she'd grabbed from the dining hall when a knock sounded at her door.

"Come in," she called.

Elestine entered and closed the door behind her before approaching Scarlett and Cass. "I'm here to firm up the timeline for tonight. Cass, are you all set?"

"I am, but we should discuss where Scarlett and Beni will be while I'm working. I don't like the idea of leaving them home alone with nothing but a security system to look after them." Cass had already warned Scarlett that Tyler was no good in a fight and that she wasn't comfortable leaving Scarlett alone with him during the break-in.

"What about this," said Elestine. "Scarlett, you and Beni could come to my home for the evening. We have in-home security, gates, and surveillance. Anyone coming after you wouldn't think to look there."

Cass's gaze met Scarlett's, and her expression said, *Don't fucking do that.*

Agreed, thought Scarlett. Then something occurred to her. There was nothing stopping her from going along to the headquarters. Instead of twiddling her thumbs at some second location, she could be there, with Cass. Maybe she'd even be useful. If there was even a chance she could help bring down Moira and Laylani and free Brayden, there was no question she'd take the risk.

Scarlett looked at Cass. "I'm coming with you tonight."

"What?" gasped Elestine. "That's too great of a risk, Scarlett."

"So it's okay for me to ask Cass to take risks but not okay to join her?" asked Scarlett, unwilling to give in. "I might know something that could help. I'm not military-trained, but they're breaking into a lord's house. I could help distract the staff, or I can talk to Tyler while you're busy, Cass."

Cass's expression was contemplative. "I could use you for that. It would free me up to oversee."

Elestine sputtered, "That's—that's not what I meant. What if you're recognized? Everyone knows your face."

"I imagine the entire team will be wearing balaclavas or similar."

"Masks on the lot of us," said Cass.

"Would I be a liability to you?" Scarlett asked.

Cass shrugged. "A bit. It's a shame we don't have time to train you up."

Scarlett looked down at the floor. "Yes, that's a shame." Then she looked up at Cass and smiled. "You did say you felt guilty about the National Theater. If you take me with you, we'd be more than even."

Cass smirked. "You don't have to beg. If you want to come, boss, then come."

"That settles it," said Scarlett. "I'm coming."

Elestine looked aghast. "At least let Beni stay with us."

Scarlett gave her a grateful look. "That'd be great. Thanks. Cass, will Tyler be okay in our house? Charlie will be there too, so he won't be alone."

"Oh, for sure," said Cass. "He'll be online like any other night." She locked gazes with Scarlett, probably thinking of the incriminating money trail Tyler was still searching for. "I'll ask him to stay available in case we need any tech support."

"All right, then. Elestine, thanks again for offering to host. I think we're all set."

Elestine's features were tight. "Of course, dear. It's the least I can do when you're taking such a risk."

Scarlett stood, and Cass and Elestine stood with her.

"I'm leaving early to try to visit Brayden," said Scarlett. "I called the police yesterday, and again today, and they refused to let me speak to him. Isn't that unusual? He's only been allowed to see our lawyer." The lack of contact with him was eating away at her. She'd been catastrophizing, imagining him regretting the day he set foot in Soleil.

At least she hoped she was catastrophizing.

Elestine winced. "I'm afraid I don't know what's typical in a case like this. Do you want me to call them?"

Some of the tension in Scarlett's shoulders eased. "I'd appreciate it. I don't want him to think I've abandoned him."

Elestine came close enough to put her hand on Scarlett's shoulder. "I'm sure he doesn't think that. He's lucky to have you, Scarlett."

The kindness of her comment took Scarlett by surprise, but she shouldn't have been surprised at all. Elestine was so many things: wife, mother, prime minister, and someone who'd known her for years.

"That's very kind. I'm lucky to have him too," said Scarlett.

Elestine gave her a small smile. "Wait here. I'll step outside to call the police."

A short while later she was back, setting her phone in front of Scarlett. "I spoke to the chief of the precinct, and he's got an officer waiting to patch you through to Brayden. He apologized for the lack of flexibility and said as long as you're comfortable with an officer listening in on Brayden's end, they'll let you speak to him."

"Thank you so much." Scarlett rose and squeezed her tightly. Being able to speak to Brayden meant everything to her.

"Let's grab a coffee, eh, Cass?" asked Elestine once Scarlett had released her.

Scarlett picked up the phone with shaking hands as Cass and Elestine filed out of her office. "This is Lady Scarlett Heroux. I understand the call will be listened to. Can I speak to my husband?"

"Here he is, Lady Heroux," said the officer.

"Scarlett?" Brayden asked, sounding surprised.

Tears sprung into her eyes at the sound of his voice. "Brayden. Yes, it's me. I'm so sorry I haven't been able to see you. I've been asking, but it took Elestine's help to get this phone call. How are you?"

"I'm fine. I mean, it's jail, so it obviously sucks, but I'm fine. I know you'd be here if you could. It's so good to hear your voice. Is Cass with you? I've been worried sick."

He sounded so calm, like this wasn't the first time they'd spoken in days. To be fair, he was probably highly aware of the officer listening in. Hearing his voice was both a comfort and a torture, the way it made her miss him so badly. She hadn't thought she could miss him more.

Scarlett tried her best to sound as calm as he did even as a tempest of emotions rushed through her. "Cass stepped out for a moment, but she's in the building, yes. She's been with me constantly since your arrest."

He sighed. "That's a relief. Did you talk to my dad?"

"Yes. He's waiting for more news from the lawyer. We all are."

"Good," said Brayden. "I saw the lawyer earlier. He seems competent."

"Good." She bit her lip, deciding in a split second to let everything out regardless of the cop listening in. "Brayden, I love you," she said, her voice cracking with emotion. "I've been thinking about you constantly. I can't sleep because I'm worried about you, wondering if you're cold or sad . . ." She trailed off, taking a gasping breath.

"Sweetheart, I know you do. I love you too."

There it was—the way he spoke only to *her*. She was relieved to hear the warmth in his voice. "I'm sorry I've caused so much trouble for you."

"Don't apologize. I came here to defend you. I've missed you *so* fucking much." His voice was low and full of longing.

Her breathing became shallow as she thought back to the night he got arrested and how she'd wanted to spend it. "I wish we'd stayed home that night. I was so excited to be alone with you when we got back, to sleep in the same bed—"

"Excuse me," interjected the officer on the line. "Just a reminder, this is a recorded call. Please cease the bedroom talk."

"Of course, Officer," Scarlett said, panicking. "Apologies. Please don't end the call."

"Go ahead, then," the officer said after a moment.

"How's work?" Brayden asked.

"There have been some positive developments." Her mind raced as she tried to think of ways to tell him what was happening so that only he would understand.

"Oh?"

"Our biggest priorities are getting a lot of attention," said Scarlett, wishing she could tell him everything.

"Hmm," said Brayden. "That sounds positive."

What would he say if he knew what I'd planned?

"He'd be happy you're not going to stay at Alastair's house," said Nori.

Scarlett snorted. *True, but what would he think about everything else?*

"Just promise me you'll stay with Cass," said Brayden. "If I lose you while I'm stuck here . . ."

Scarlett's heart pounded. "I'm going to work with her tonight, actually. She got a one-time gig she didn't want to turn down. It should be fun." She sounded awkward and she knew it, but she wanted to give him as much of the truth as she could.

He was silent for several seconds. "That sounds interesting. And Beni?"

"He'll be with Elestine."

He let out a loud sigh. "I see."

Scarlett sighed in frustration. She was probably giving him enough information to make him worry *more*. "With Elestine's security, her home is probably the safest place in the city while Cass is working. Alastair isn't involved at all."

"Sure," he said. "As long as you're both safe." He sounded distant and calm again, and she hated it even though she understood.

"Pardon me," said the officer. "Your time is up. Please wrap up the call."

"Thanks," said Brayden brusquely. "Be careful, Scarlett."

"I'll call again first thing in the morning," she said. "I love you so much."

"Love you too."

The call ended with a click.

CHAPTER 35

As Beni, Cass, and Scarlett rode in a rented enclosed speedboat to the Spencer house, Scarlett prayed. *Please, Goddess above, watch over us tonight. And help me find a way to free Brayden.*

Security admitted them through the front gate, and after parking the boat, Cass and Scarlett walked Beni to the front door.

"Good evening." Elestine beckoned them into the elegant foyer. "Beni, we're having drinks in the garden, if you'd like to join us for dessert. Or I can also show you to your room if you'd like."

Beni threw Scarlett a grateful look. "I'll come out to the garden, but do you mind showing me my room first?"

"Of course," said Elestine. "I'll be back momentarily."

Beni hugged Scarlett tight. "Be careful."

"I will. Promise."

Elestine walked away, and Beni waved to Scarlett as he followed after her, with his overnight bag slung over his shoulder. He'd also packed clothes for Scarlett to change into when she was done. She

hoped she'd make it back to use them.

Alastair came into the foyer from the back garden, and Scarlett had to try hard not to let her irritation show on her face.

He looked her up and down. "Scarlett. You're dressed like a thief. I couldn't believe it when Mother told me you're participating tonight—" He stopped, noticing Cass by the door. "Oh, you're not alone."

"She never is," said Cass, with a disdainful look.

Since Cass had become Scarlett's bodyguard, Alastair had seen her several times in passing and had yet to acknowledge he'd met her that night at the boxing match. Scarlett was sure he remembered, but she suspected he was too embarrassed at what Cass had overheard so was choosing to ignore her rather than acknowledge it. Or maybe he was just forgetful. Or an asshole. Or both.

Alastair faced Scarlett. "Why risk this? It's too dangerous. Stay here tonight, where it's safe. You trust me with Beni—why not stay here yourself?"

He reached out for her, but Scarlett shrugged him off. "I trust your mother, not you, and I'll do whatever it takes to get justice and free *him*."

His eyes narrowed, and he glared down at her left hand. "I'm surprised you're still wearing his ring. When will you realize you made a mistake?"

She snatched her hand away. "What mistake?"

"I thought when he went away, whatever he did to you would wear off." He grabbed her by both shoulders, forcing her to look at him. "When are you going to wake up?"

"Stop," she said, pulling away.

Cass stepped forward, but Scarlett signaled for her to stand down. She could handle Alastair. She pointed her finger at him. "You're acting like he stole me from you. Do you not remember breaking up *before* I left for Clair de Lune?" Her eyes were locked on his. "Listen closely, because I'm tired of explaining this. I *love* him. I'd marry him again tomorrow. He hasn't compelled me. There's nothing to wake up from. You just didn't know me as well as you thought you did, and I certainly didn't know you."

Thick black smoke appeared above him, surprising her. But it was just a confirmation of her words. They weren't close. Not anymore.

Alastair's hands clenched and unclenched as his jaw ticked.

Elestine reappeared. "Right, I offered to have a soda brought to Beni in his room, and he took me up on it. It seems he's got what he needs for the time being." She frowned as she took in Alastair's stormy expression, but he walked away, leaving the room before she could say anything.

"Thank you," said Scarlett, relieved he was gone. "I appreciate you being so accommodating."

Elestine waved a hand. "I had a twelve-year-old boy once. I know what they're like." She glanced through the doorway Alastair had left through. "I wish he were still easy to understand."

Cass tapped her watch. "If Beni's all set, we'd better be off."

Scarlett took a deep breath. "Yes, let's be off."

Elestine took Scarlett's hand. "You're sure I can't convince you to stay?"

"Thank you, but no," she said, squeezing her hand. "I've got to do this."

Scarlett chugged an energy drink as Cass drove the speedboat to the Prince's Street Dock to pick up the rest of the crew. She was on the precipice of risking everything, but for now, she was just riding on a boat, drinking a fizzy drink. Living in the moment would get her through this evening.

At the docks, Scarlett spotted Mace and Brixton, the hydra and the dire wolf she'd seen in the boxing ring months ago. Mace was so huge it was impossible to miss him. Brixton, short and lean but no less tough, looked the same as ever. Their soul lights zoomed around them, bringing Scarlett a small amount of comfort as she glimpsed the little lights.

They each nodded in greeting as they stepped into the speedboat's enclosed cabin. They were followed by two men of average height and weight: one dark-skinned with a shaved head, and the other pale and freckled with auburn hair. These two didn't have soul lights. All four were dressed in all black, just like Cass and Scarlett.

"Good evening, gents," said Cass from the driver's seat as they pulled away from the dock. In the enclosed cabin her voice was easy enough to hear over the boat's engine. "Masks and earpieces in the box on the floor. Did you all bring your guns?"

Sounds of affirmation came from all the men. Scarlett didn't have a gun, but she knew Cass did. She had her under strict orders to stay by her side.

"Great. Hope for the best and plan for the worst, right?" Cass sounded cheerful, not at all like she was about to do something extremely risky. "Heads-up, I'm masking us from view now."

A shimmer passed over them, and every light on the boat darkened. Unless they ran right into someone, no one would be able to spot them coming or going. Most importantly, they wouldn't be caught on surveillance cameras. It was why they'd waited for nightfall instead of beginning earlier in the evening. The delay meant they had a time crunch, but the stealth Cass's power lent them made it worth it.

Mace picked up the box and took a mask and an earpiece before passing it on to Brixton.

"Quick intros," called Cass as she drove. "Code names, please.

I'm Cobra for tonight. Team lead and driver, and I'm a nocturna, in case any of you were too thick to notice."

Mace cracked a smile. "I'm Ace. Hydra shifter, muscle, and miscellaneous."

Scarlett waved to the four men. "I'm Crimson. Financier and tech communications. I'm a vox. Thanks for coming tonight."

The man with the shaved head gave her a small smile. "We all know who you are. Thanks for the job. I'm Rex. Reconnaissance and chemistry." He patted the black bag he'd brought on board.

"Lock," said the man with the auburn hair. "Recon, and as the name implies, I pick locks."

"Brix," said Brixton as he cracked his knuckles. "Dire-wolf shifter. Muscle and miscellaneous."

"Now that we're all friends, here's the schedule," barked Cass. "We're hitting two locations, and we need to be quick. The Golden Gala finishes in ninety minutes, and every minute we linger increases our odds of getting caught. We're using a fake warrant on any staff at the Federsin residence, and Lock will be getting us into the Goldenrod headquarters. We've had our tech support arrange for the phone lines and security cameras in Goldie HQ to go down when we arrive, so the alarm system won't be able to call out when we trigger it. Any questions?"

Everyone was silent.

"Good," said Cass. "Also, we're aiming for no fatalities tonight. Disarm as needed, but try not to kill anyone."

Scarlett's heart hammered in her chest. She looked around, but the statement fazed no one. No one except her.

Their first stop was the Federsin home.

Cass parked the boat in a narrow canal near the enormous home on the Sapphire Canal. She killed the engine and swiveled in her chair to face them. "Right. Let's do the damn thing. Rex, Lock, you have your badges?"

They'd discussed using Cass's powers to get into the Federsin home unseen but decided that doors opening of their own accord were more likely to cause trouble with the staff than pretending to be the Soleil Bureau.

Rex pulled a badge out of his pocket and flashed it to the group. It looked as real as any Soleil Bureau badge Scarlett had ever seen.

How many fake badges are out there?

Given she needed Rex's help, she wasn't in a place to question what else he did with that badge, but she'd be asking Cass about it when everything calmed down. Cass *had* assured her the men were trustworthy, and that was enough for tonight. They were doing the right thing, trying to expose these people.

"Masks and earpieces on, please," said Cass.

Scarlett made sure her sleek earpiece was inserted correctly.

"Crimson," said Cass, pulling her aside as the others disembarked onto the dock. "You mentioned your vox powers, but I want you to stay quiet in front of anyone we come across tonight. Given your role in the public eye, there's a chance someone could recognize your voice."

Scarlett thought of Brayden, forced to use his power at the National Theater, and asked, "But what if it's a life-and-death situation?"

Cass cocked her head to one side. "Use your discretion. That's what we all do. Just don't forget the risk."

"I won't."

Together, they made their way in the darkness to the house's back entrance. Cass took the lead, banging on the door with authority.

An older man opened the door a minute later. "What—?"

Cass flashed a badge, as did Rex and Lock, who stood just behind her. "We have a warrant to search the premises on behalf of the Soleil Bureau."

"He—he's not home," the man stuttered.

A stab of guilt coursed through Scarlett. The man looked like he was Manon's age.

"He doesn't need to be," barked Cass. "Take us to Lord Federsin's office."

"Why are you masked?" The man twisted his hands as he shrank back, but he didn't step aside.

"Sir, impeding bureau officers is a jailable offense. Take us to his office."

"I don't want any trouble," said the man as he let them in. "I'm just the cook."

"Is there anyone else in the house?" asked Cass.

The cook looked up at her with wide eyes. "They're all at the gala. The study is the second door on the left upstairs."

"Thank you for your cooperation. Ace, stay downstairs, please," said Cass.

Mace nodded and gestured for the cook to lead the way into the nearby kitchen.

Scarlett tensed as they followed the old man's directions to Lord Federsin's study. Brixton stood by the door while Rex, Lock, Cass, and Scarlett went inside.

An enormous map of Soleil dominated the back wall, and Lord Federsin's shelves were filled with model ships and other nautical-themed ornaments. Unlike her father's study, there were no books, and the room was as neat as a pin. Federsin either didn't read or did all his policy reviews at Parliament.

Adrenaline rushed through Scarlett as they approached his desk and she spotted his laptop. Lock went straight for the closet, while Rex pulled open desk drawers.

Cass handed a burner phone to Scarlett. "Here—tell him you have a laptop."

"Yes?" answered Tyler after one ring.

"I've got a laptop," said Scarlett without preamble.

He cackled. "Hell yeah. Here's what you do."

Scarlett was too focused to laugh with him as she followed his instructions. Once Tyler had access, he began to transfer the contents of the laptop to his cloud. As her heart pounded, Scarlett kept an eye on the others moving about the room while she waited next to the laptop in case Tyler needed her.

"Bank statement with account numbers," Lock said in a low voice. He placed several papers on top of the desk in front of Cass, who was searching the desk.

Scarlett glanced toward the closet, noticing an open safe. Lock got into a safe? *Yes*. That was something.

Cass took the bank statements and began photographing them with her phone.

"Okay, the laptop's done," said Tyler a minute later.

"Wonderful." Hope filled Scarlett at the thought of all the incriminating evidence that could be on it.

"Tell him bank statements are in his inbox," whispered Cass as she shoved her phone into her pocket.

But before Scarlett could, a *thump* shook the floor, causing a golden stapler to topple off the edge of Federsin's desk. Scarlett whipped her head to the office door.

Brixton stood over a body in the hallway. "The cook lied. There was someone else here. He came down from the third floor holding this, so I had to knock him out." He plucked a gun out of the unconscious man's hand.

"Nice work. Guess we've got to arrest him for messing with bureau business." Cass winked at Scarlett. "Cuff him, and let's get out of here."

Scarlett remembered her task and told Tyler about the bank statements. Brixton produced a pair of handcuffs, cuffed the man, and threw him over his shoulder, ready to carry him downstairs like a sack of potatoes.

Scarlett stopped Cass by the door. "What are we going to do with him? Won't it be a problem when he wakes up?"

Rex came closer. "That's my shift. I've got plenty of injectable anesthetic. We'll keep him unconscious on the boat till the job is done."

"Then we'll dump him on the dock by the hospital," added Cass.

Scarlett's brow pinched. "What if he dies from the blow to the head?"

Rex waved his hand in dismissal. "He's going to be fine."

Seeing her worried expression, Cass gripped her hand. "Brix is a trained fighter. He knows how to knock someone out without doing permanent damage. Now, come on. Rex, the cook is going to have to come along now that his buddy is down."

They hurried downstairs. The cook whimpered at the sight of Brixton carrying his unconscious colleague.

Rex stalked over to him. "Hold him for us, Ace."

Mace's large arms circled the small man tightly as Rex shoved a needle into his neck and pushed the plunger down. Mace caught the old man as he fell.

Scarlett's gut twisted. Was that what it had looked like when she'd been kidnapped? She shook her head, dismissing the thought. This man would be back on his feet later tonight no worse for wear. She had to believe Cass and Rex, or she'd be unable to go on.

"Nice one," said Cass.

Before Scarlett could blink, the cook was over Mace's shoulder, and Mace was on his way back to the boat.

They'd gotten in and out of the Federsin house in twenty minutes. They had to go across town to get to the Goldenrod headquarters, which would leave them a short time before the gala was scheduled to end.

Scarlett stared down at the two unconscious men on the floor of the boat. Assault, drugging, and kidnapping. Impersonating bureau officers. She'd known the night would be high-risk, and here it was, right in front of her eyes. She swallowed thickly. The rest of her life might be ruined if they failed.

As they pulled away from the house in the concealed speedboat, she was still on the phone with Tyler, waiting while he searched.

"Oh wow," said Tyler eagerly. "He's got a bunch of extremely damning deleted emails he probably thought no one would be able to find. They didn't even use code names, the idiots."

"What is it? What do you see?" Scarlett couldn't breathe as she waited.

Everyone in the boat sat in silence. The engine was the only sound as it propelled them along the canal.

"Emails between Federsin and Ashworth confirming the timeline for the day your dad died. They're referencing the date and time and confirming Federsin sent the payment to the designated account. I got into his bank account, and there's a record of two hundred and fifty thousand marcs going out that same day. I'll look at his banking contacts and see who exactly that went to."

She sat in stunned silence. *Two hundred and fifty thousand marcs to murder my dad.* Federsin and Moira had done it, and they had *evidence.* Real, irrefutable evidence that pointed directly to not only Federsin, but also Moira. Scarlett saw red. Federsin had paid someone to kill her dad, his colleague, whom he'd known for years. The son of a bitch. She almost wished he'd been home when they arrived so she could have seen Brixton tear him apart in his wolf form.

"Justice will be served, Scarlett. He'll have to live through worse than a dire wolf attack once this is all exposed," said Nori. *"Remember, you didn't like seeing those men harmed."*

True. Scarlett let out a huge sigh of relief. Nori was right. Prison would be a worse punishment.

Tyler went on, oblivious to Scarlett's emotional roller coaster. "I'm scanning all the large payments. There are also several payments of fifty thousand leaving his account in May—a total of one hundred and fifty thousand marcs. Those have a name on them. Dr. Mel Turner. Was he your doctor?"

"Yes, that's him!" Scarlett whooped in triumph, and Cass looked at her, both curious and admonishing. "Sorry," she said in a lower voice. She approached Cass, who was driving. "He found payments from Federsin to Dr. Turner. I thought Laylani had acted alone, maybe with Moira's help, but it was a full-blown Goldenrod conspiracy against *me* too. And now I can prove it." She beamed at Cass.

Cass's answering smile was dazzling. "Excellent. Now let's see what we can find in Goldie HQ."

The Goldenrod headquarters was located in a nondescript high-rise downtown in the financial district. Cass led them to the back of the building, covered in her nocturna darkness.

Lock slid a thin black case out of his bag and kneeled in front of the door. Less than a minute later, he pulled it open. The alarm system immediately started to beep. He bashed the alarm with a hammer until it ceased. When he turned around, he was grinning.

"I know it can't dial out, but we couldn't leave it beeping, right?"

Cass snorted. "Glad you enjoyed that."

The lights went out one at a time as they walked to the elevator still cloaked in her nocturna darkness. Nori and the three other soul lights lit the way for Scarlett. She wondered if Lock and Rex were nervous at all as they walked in the dark.

The elevator dinged, and they exited on the floor where Moira Ashworth's office was located. They walked past the rows of cubicles, heading toward the large offices along the far wall. Cass left the lights on this time, presumably because they'd have an easier time searching if they could see.

In Moira's bland office, they did the same meticulous, fast-paced search they'd done in Federsin's study. Mace and Brixton stood by the door, keeping watch, while Scarlett facilitated Tyler's plundering of the desktop computer. Cass, Rex, and Lock searched every drawer, closet, and box in the office.

This time there were no noteworthy paper records.

They'd just left Moira's office when an elevator dinged.

The overhead lights were still on, and before Cass could put them out, a young man appeared by the elevator bay, fifty feet away. He wore a white button-down shirt and slacks—definitely a junior staff member working late. He stumbled at the far end of the floor as he stared at them.

Brixton sprang forward faster than lightning, and the movement jolted the young man out of his shock. He ran for the elevator bay, his hand outstretched.

Brixton reached him seconds later, kicking out and dropping him to the floor, but it was too late. The fire alarm began to sound through the building.

"Fuck. Let's go!" shouted Cass.

Scarlett had to force herself to breathe as they rode the elevator to the ground floor. Flashlights danced in the lobby, but Cass immediately snuffed them out.

"What the hell?" said a male voice.

Cass led the way as they ran across the lobby to the back door they'd come in through, their footsteps echoing across the marble floor.

"Hey!"

How can they see us?

But then Scarlett heard two gunshots, and she stopped thinking. All that remained in her mind was one word.

Run.

She sprinted through the exit right behind Lock. The dock wasn't far. Ahead of her, Lock, Rex, and Cass were halfway there. She started after them, but shouting behind her made her turn. She caught a glimpse of Brixton and Mace bursting through the door.

And then she fell.

Scrambling to her feet as the shifters reached her, Scarlett tried to run, but Cass appeared, pushing her down to the ground again as two more shots were fired. With her face against the pavement, Scarlett couldn't see anything but the dock.

A strange ripping sound filled her ears, then the growls of a wolf.

A dire wolf.

Cass helped her up just in time for Scarlett to see the dire wolf snarling as it ran straight for the two cops. They fired their guns but hit nothing, because the wolf was too fast. Mace followed behind him, shielding himself by crouching behind the giant wolf as it ran.

One of the men shrieked as the wolf's jaws locked around his hand. The gun clattered to the ground, and the cop clutched his mangled hand, the bones bent at odd angles. Mace darted for the weapon, scooping it up off the ground.

"Get on the boat!" Cass shouted, pulling at Scarlett.

Scarlett looked back as she ran to the dock with Cass.

The second cop raised his gun, but Brixton was on him. He dropped the gun as he hit the ground, pinned by the giant wolf. Mace snatched it up, and Brixton leaped off the man, bounding toward Cass and Scarlett and quickly overtaking them.

The dire wolf dove into the boat's cabin. Scarlett boarded, with Cass right behind her. Finally, Mace was inside. Cass started the engine, and they were off into the night.

Scarlett tried to catch her breath as she watched Brixton shift back. Then she looked away, face hot, when she realized he was totally naked.

Mace pulled some clothes out of a bag and threw them at Brixton.

"Thanks," said the dire-wolf shifter.

"Everyone all right?" Cass asked from the driver's seat.

"Yes." Scarlett looked at each of the men around her. They all appeared whole and more or less fine. Unlike that cop with the injured hand. Scarlett rubbed her face with her hands, wondering what long-term impact the dire wolf's crushing bite would have on the man's life. She'd do what she could to make it right once this was all out in the open.

The burner phone in her pocket buzzed, and Scarlett picked it up.

"We're back in the boat."

"Good to hear, since there's a call out on the police radio for rein-forcements at the Goldenrod headquarters," said Tyler. "I'm already into Moira's emails—and holy shitballs. This is the mother lode."

Scarlett's smile spread across her face as he read email after email to her. There was one between Laylani and Moira where Laylani said she was ready for Moira to end her marriage. Then there were drafts of the falsified emails the bureau had used to frame Sigur Viður for her father's murder. There were even monthly emails between Aaron Fox and Moira Ashworth discussing payment amounts.

"Those could be linked to the bribes Cass was paying the police," said Tyler. "This should be enough to subpoena their bank accounts."

"Is there anything about the National Theater?" asked Scarlett. Would all her wishes be granted tonight?

Tyler was silent for a long minute. "Nothing obvious, but I'll keep looking."

Her heart fell. She was beyond grateful their mission had been successful in so many ways, but she couldn't be happy until Brayden was freed. She'd hoped for evidence that would make it impossible for the courts not to pardon him, but unless Tyler dug something up, she'd have to think of another plan—fast.

As they approached the drop-off point in a small alcove off Cobalt Canal, Scarlett thanked each of the men for their help with the mission. "This wouldn't have succeeded without all of you," she said as she shook Brixton's hand. "I'll have Cass send double the agreed amount to each of your accounts."

Rex and Lock both dipped their chins in acknowledgment before disembarking. They strode off in different directions.

"We're rooting for you. Get justice for your pops and then open the damn border." Mace patted her shoulder, and then he was off.

"I'll do my best," said Scarlett as he departed into the night.

"I'm a believer in the cause too," said Brixton. "If you need any help, you know where to find me."

She thanked him and waved as Brixton followed Mace into the night. Now it was just her and Cass. She stared out into the water, taking it all in. Tonight had changed everything, and it was only 11 p.m. Then she looked down at the two unconscious men lying on the floor of the boat. The night wasn't *quite* over.

As promised, Cass and Scarlett took the men and dumped them on the dock by the nearest hospital. To Scarlett's relief, someone was approaching them before the dock had disappeared from view.

She put Tyler on speakerphone as they headed toward the Spencer house, and they listened in silence as he continued to search through the wealth of information they'd found. The list of incriminated government officials grew longer by the minute.

"*A lot of people are going to get arrested tomorrow,*" said Nori.

Fuck yes, they are.

CHAPTER (36)

Thank the Goddess!" shrieked Elestine when they were shown into the Spencer home. The three Spencers had waited up in the sitting room. She hugged first Scarlett, then her husband.

"Scarlett, tell us everything!" Edward stumbled toward her like he'd had quite a few drinks, and Cass caught him, helping him onto the sofa. "I'm so chuffed you made it back unscathed," he said from his lowered vantage point.

Scarlett's judgment of him softened at the heartfelt sentiment, and as her shock subsided, she found she wanted to tell Elestine and Edward everything. So she did, including a recount of the police shoot-out. She even mentioned the stapler that had fallen to the floor in Lord Federsin's office.

Alastair, who'd stood near a bookshelf through Scarlett's tale, came to sit next to her on the sofa and threw back the rest of his drink. His eyes were as glassy as his father's. "This is the best news.

Everything's going to be fine now. You'll be safe once Laylani is arrested. You'll be free."

"We still don't know who was behind the National Theater." Tears formed, and Scarlett blinked them away. She was trying to focus on the good, but she wanted Brayden in her arms. All she wanted was to tell him how ready she was to get their North Stars. She never wanted this distance between them again, for any reason. But he was sitting in a jail cell somewhere with no idea how much things had changed for Soleil—and for her.

"That doesn't matter. You're safe, I swear." Alastair's words slurred. He tried to rub her back, but she moved away from him, scooting farther down the couch.

"Don't touch me."

He stared at her, thoroughly confused by her behavior. "But my darling S-Scarlett—"

"I am not your darling, and I never will be again," she hissed. "The sooner you get that through your head, the easier your life will be."

He reached for her again, but he recoiled, as Cass was suddenly hovering over him.

"Alastair, you're drunk. Go to bed," ordered Elestine, watching her son closely.

Alastair let out an exasperated sigh. "As you wish, my liege."

To Scarlett's relief, he stumbled off in the direction of his bedroom.

"I'm so sorry about him. You must be so tired of it," Elestine apologized once he was gone.

Scarlett only had the energy for a thin-lipped smile. She *was* tired of it. Not to mention exhausted from the night. She hoped to the Goddess she never had a son like Alastair.

"You're sure there's nothing related to the National Theater?" asked Elestine.

Scarlett rubbed her eyes, gathering her composure. "No, we're not sure. At least not yet."

"There's a lot of information to go through," said Cass from her seat in the chair across from Scarlett. "It'll take some time to know for sure."

"Well, let's do what we can with what we have," said the prime minister with a visible burst of energy. "Scarlett, let's get some coffee going and make our game plan for tomorrow. We have a lot to do."

For the next few hours, with Tyler on the phone, they combed through the evidence they'd obtained, prepping a to-do list for the following day. It was nearly morning by the time Cass and Scarlett were trudging upstairs behind Elestine.

"Beni's in the room across from Edward's office," said Elestine as she paused on the landing. "The room across from his is empty, as is the one at the end of the hall, if you two want to catch a few winks." Then, with a wave, she was gone, off to her own bedroom on the other end of the floor.

Scarlett halted in front of Beni's room and pointed to his door. "I'll be here." She could have had her own room, but what she didn't want to admit out loud was that she didn't want to sleep alone in this house. But Cass would be fine. Alastair wouldn't bother her.

Cass pointed to the door opposite. "I'll take that one. What time are you setting your alarm for?" She yawned.

Scarlett pulled her phone out. "Six." *In two hours.* "Elestine wants to work from here in the morning, so there's no need for you to get up. Sleep in as long as you can."

"Thanks." With a wave, Cass disappeared into the room across from Beni's.

Scarlett slipped into Beni's room. He didn't wake as she lay down fully clothed on top of the unoccupied side of the bed. She doubted she'd be able to sleep after the pot of coffee she'd drunk, but as soon as her eyes closed, she heard Nori.

"Sleep."

Scarlett's exhausted body welcomed unconsciousness.

Scarlett startled awake when her alarm went off. At first, she couldn't remember where she was, but then it came back to her. The break-in. The evidence. It wasn't all a dream. She glanced at Beni, who was still sound asleep despite the alarm. Then she stumbled into the en suite to shower, trying in vain to rinse the tiredness out of her eyes with the stream of hot water. Once she was as presentable as she could be in the change of clothes she'd packed in Beni's bag, she opened the bathroom door to find him awake.

"How did it go?" he asked, sitting up in bed.

She told him everything. Beni listened with rapt attention, and when she got to the evidence they'd found, his green eyes became glassy with tears.

Scarlett pulled her brother into her arms and hugged him tight. "Are you okay?"

He sighed deeply. "I will be. Eventually. Do you reckon they'll be arrested soon?"

Scarlett held him at arm's length for a moment before dropping her hands and stepping back. "Moira and Laylani will probably be arrested later today."

"Goddess, what a relief," Beni said, running his hand through his hair. "Now we can really move on."

"That's true." Once justice was served, they'd finally have real closure. Scarlett had been so lost in the weeds she hadn't taken a moment to process that yet. It'd probably take her ages to really work through all her bottled-up feelings about both her parents.

But for now she'd keep going.

"We'll work from here this morning," she said. "Are you good to stay here for a while?"

"Sure. All I need is food and my laptop."

Scarlett made her way to Elestine's study, where they'd worked the previous night. There she found Elestine already up and at her computer, with a breakfast tray full of coffee, toast, and hard-boiled eggs sitting at one end of the expansive mahogany desk.

"Good morning, dear." She gave Scarlett a once-over. "Grab an espresso—it's going to be one hell of a day. You just missed Alastair. I sent him to Parliament to man the phones with some of the other staff, but key Ceruleans will be meeting here shortly."

"Thank you," Scarlett said. Her voice sounded rough to her own ears, and she had serious brain fog. She forced down a few bites of egg in the hope some protein might help. "Do you mind if I take some of this food to Beni?"

"Oh, don't go to the trouble. We're moving to the dining room to set up a war room. I'll ask Liz to take him a breakfast tray on our way," said Elestine. "Shall we head down now?"

"Sure." Scarlett stood. "By the way, how do you look so fresh? You hardly slept too."

"Underneath my makeup I look absolutely rough," said Elestine as she led the way downstairs.

Scarlett grinned. "You look lovely to me."

"Thank you." Elestine whispered conspiratorially, "My secret is the most *expensive* concealer in Soleil. I'll send you some when this is all over. But don't worry, dear. You look marvelous. You're as fresh as a daisy if you ask me." She squeezed Scarlett's hand briefly and then beelined for the kitchen.

The conversation reminded Scarlett of the many times Elestine had acted as a mother to her over the years, and it made her glad their friendship, as well as their professional relationship, had survived the utter destruction of her love for Alastair.

Over the next hour, the lords who'd been at their meeting yesterday trickled into the Spencer home, along with their staff. The house buzzed with excitement. As Scarlett and Elestine walked them through the damning evidence they'd spent all night poring over, Scarlett caught a second wind, energized by it all despite her poor sleep.

After reviewing the findings, she released the information to the police, and together, the Cerulean Party announced an evening press conference at Parliament. Elestine had a series of whiteboards brought into her dining room, and they made a list of expected arrests.

Around midmorning, Cass emerged in Elestine's dining room carrying a cup of coffee. Her eyes were bright, though they were lined with shadows. Scarlett gave her an enthusiastic hug.

"Thank you for last night. You've helped me change the world."

"Happy to." Cass leaned closer to Scarlett and spoke into her ear. "Everyone made it home fine. According to the news, the two men from Federsin's house paid a visit to an ER and filed a police report, but they were both sent home hours ago. They'll be fine."

"Good to hear. Anything on the officers from Goldie HQ?"

Cass grimaced. "Yes. The hand injury is bad. He's got tendon damage and several broken bones, but he won't lose his hand."

Scarlett's face crumpled. "I feel terrible. I need to reach out and see what I can do to help."

"Hey, don't beat yourself up. It's all for the greater good. And speak to your lawyer before you do anything hasty. Send all inquiries through him."

Scarlett's shoulders slumped. Cass was right. "I will. Thanks. I'm just praying the public will think the ends justify the means. I know that sounds terrible. But I hope people don't think I acted selfishly, going all rogue the way I did."

Cass chuckled. "We'll be fine. We've unearthed the biggest conspiracy in Soleil history."

"I hope so. Let me know if you need anything. I'm going to step away while there's a lull and try to call Brayden."

Cass gave her a knowing smile. "Good idea. While you do that, I'll grab a bite to eat and head back to bed, if that's all right."

"Of course," said Scarlett. "It'd be good for you to rest up before we have to leave for Parliament."

"Come get me if you need me," said Cass.

Scarlett stepped into Elestine's empty study and dialed the police station.

"Apologies, Lady Heroux," the officer on the phone replied after listening to her request. "As you know, this is an unprecedented day in Soleil, and there are no spare officers to supervise a call."

Scarlett closed her eyes, trying to dispel her frustration so she could speak calmly. "Of course. Apologies for asking, but can you at least tell him about the arrests? And tell him I'm fine." Brayden felt so far away. Her thoughts ran in circles when she tried to imagine what he could be thinking or feeling.

"Yes, Lady Heroux," said the officer before ending the call.

By the afternoon, they'd finished all of Elestine and Scarlett's planned comms and had prepared remarks for the press conference. Now all that was left to do was wait to hear from the courts on warrants for arrest.

"All right," said Elestine. "*Soleil Times*, check. *The Observer*, check. *The Daily Soleil*, check. *The Financier*, check. *The Journal*, check. We've got all the majors covered." It was the third time she'd confirmed this aloud, but Scarlett didn't mind. Sleep deprivation meant her brain wasn't fully functional.

"The warrants have been issued by the court," called out Lord Garfield. He hurried to the whiteboard and held his phone to one ear as he wrote out a list of names.

Scarlett's heart thudded. She knew half the names, but not all of them. She stared as he misspelled her stepmother's name—"Lady Leilani Heroux"—just after "Lady Moira Ashworth."

The moment she'd been waiting for since Beni woke her from her coma was finally here. Under the exhaustion, Scarlett's soul was suddenly lighter, as if the burden of seeking revenge had left her body. She wasn't triumphant—yet. There was still so much to do. But now she wasn't alone. Now everyone would know the biggest truths. She was hit with a wave of deep relief—so deep her body relaxed into her chair. It was almost tempting to put her head on the table and sleep where she sat, so soothing was this newfound peace.

"Who is Leonard Orsino?" asked Lord Navarre, who was sitting next to her at the table.

"Third from the top in the bureau, I believe," said Edward. "That's his boss, Aaron Fox."

"Please tell me Bates isn't on the list," murmured Lord Navarre. Bates was the head of the bureau. "I don't want to be responsible for repairing the wreckage at the bureau after this."

Scarlett was in a dreamlike state as she watched the news in the living room alongside her colleagues while they waited for the arrests to take place. She glanced at a security guard who came in and went straight to Elestine, whispering something in her ear.

A frown creased Elestine's forehead, and the prime minister's gaze locked with Scarlett's. Scarlett's stomach plummeted.

What now?

Elestine gestured toward the hallway, and Scarlett followed her.

"Laylani's here," she said once they were alone.

"What?" Scarlett's hand flew to her chest. How had she known where to find Scarlett? Or was she here for Beni? Scarlett had expected to see Laylani next in court, weeks from now, not *today*.

"The arrests have started. She knows she's going down, and she probably came here to . . . I don't know, humiliate me? My security team is holding her out back. The police are on their way, but I wanted to offer you the chance to speak to her before they arrive. You might not have another opportunity to approach her off the record, and you deserve that—if you want it."

The demon herself was here. A mess of pain and other uncomfortable emotions Scarlett couldn't even name passed through her. Had she come to humiliate Elestine? An itch at the back of her mind told her why. But Scarlett didn't want to even think it.

"She didn't ask to see me, did she?"

"No. She has no idea you're here."

Scarlett considered Elestine's offer and found she was oddly tempted. Better to confront your demons whenever possible.

"All right. Take me to her."

"One thing before I do. She'll likely be spilling secrets to anyone who'll listen from here on out. If she says anything about me that particularly upsets you, promise you'll give me the opportunity to discuss it with you."

"I know better than to take what she says at face value. She's one of the biggest liars I've ever met," said Scarlett.

"But Elestine isn't a liar," said Nori. *"Listen to what she's telling you and prepare yourself."*

"Even liars tell the truth sometimes," said Elestine, looking away. "We'd better get you out there. You won't have long."

Scarlett's chest was tight as she walked into the back garden. Her proud, elegant stepmother was seated on a bench next to the high wisteria-covered wall that separated the garden from the small canal at the rear of the house. Laylani was already handcuffed, and two guards hovered close by.

The sight of her in cuffs lightened Scarlett's mood a touch.

"So this is where you've been hiding." Her words were coated in disdain. "I went looking for you first."

"Here I am," said Scarlett, spreading her hands wide before letting them drop back to her sides.

"You must feel pretty proud of yourself."

She seated herself across from Laylani. "Why'd you do it? My mother, my father, me. Why'd you want us all dead?"

Laylani stared at her for a long moment. "How'd you know about . . . ?" Then she let out an angry sigh, realizing she'd given something away.

How'd you know about Sabina? That was what she'd been about to say. The evidence already proved she'd acted against Scarlett and Jules.

It surprised Scarlett how much the admission satisfied her. The journal, the gut feeling—none of it had been absolute confirmation until now. Now that she knew the truth for sure and Laylani's arrest was imminent, a strange sense of calm came over her.

"*That's right. You've won,*" said Nori. "*She'll lose everything now.*"

"Would you believe I did it for love?" Laylani's eyes were dull, absent of the usual haughty confidence, and her shoulders were slumped. This version of her was new to Scarlett.

"For love? That doesn't make sense."

She shrugged half-heartedly. "Imagine you met Brayden today but he'd already married someone else. What would you do?"

Scarlett narrowed her eyes. Was Laylani trying to say Jules was her Brayden? She couldn't believe it. She'd never seen anything that looked like her love for Brayden between her dad and Laylani. "We'd never be in that situation." At least according to James, a marriage couldn't have come between them, but she wasn't about to explain Clair de Lune's North Star law to Laylani.

Laylani shook her head. "But you can imagine, can't you? If he'd gotten married while you were with Alastair, and then you woke up one day and realized he should've been with you, what would you have done?"

"What are you talking about?"

"I loved him, and my sister helped me get him because she believed it was better for Soleil. Back then she hoped Jules might be swayed if Sabina wasn't in his ear whispering about her ridiculous, magic-worshipping beliefs. Your mother was his greatest *handicap*, Scarlett. I got rid of her for him, and he became prime minister because of *me*."

Scarlett closed off the part of her that wanted to rage at this woman. "You killed my mum because she stood between you and my dad, but what about Dad? Why'd you let him die?"

Laylani brought her cuffed hands to her face, brushing a tear off her cheek. "I loved him more than anything, and all I wanted was for him to love me back. I thought he did for a time, but then he made it clear he didn't want a *real* marriage anymore. Why do you think I came here today, Scarlett?" She lifted her joined hands together once more, gesturing to the house.

Scarlett flashed back to Elestine's comment about humiliation, and then to the dinner at the Twig and Vine when Laylani alluded to an affair. What she'd guessed that night but hadn't wanted to acknowledge came rearing into her consciousness again.

"My dad loved Elestine."

"Your dad definitely fucked Elestine," said Laylani, her nostrils flaring. "They were at it for over a *year*. Can you hear that, Edward?" she yelled at the back of the house.

The guards moved toward her, and she put her hand up.

"Back the fuck up. I'll be quiet," she said in a more level tone.

The two guards did not back up, but they didn't come closer.

"What the fuck, Dad?" muttered Scarlett, too quiet for Laylani to hear. She turned her back on her stepmother.

Elestine and Jules had gotten together while she'd been dating Elestine's *son*. All the times her dad had pushed her toward Alastair—had Elestine been telling him to do it? That was fucking weird if so. It was weird either way. She closed her eyes, massaging her temples as she tried to grapple with what it all meant. Then an image of her father between Elestine's legs appeared in her mind, making her nauseous. She made a sound of disgust. Pushing the image out, she replaced her disgust with her old friend, anger.

Anger she wouldn't let Laylani transpose onto Elestine. Because while what Elestine had done was wrong—and gross to imagine—it was nothing compared to Laylani's crimes. The delusional bitch had killed both her parents.

Scarlett turned around to face Laylani, scowling at her.

"You don't have anything to say?" asked Laylani, her voice quiet but laced with poison. "Can't your little rule-follower heart understand? I did everything for Jules, and he shit all over me. I gave him a child. A boy. He married me for it, but he still made you his heir. You'll probably end up abdicating and moving to Clair de Lune. Beaufort should've been his heir all along." Her head drooped. "What a waste."

Scarlett stared at her stepmother, stunned by the venom she spewed. Had she baby-trapped Jules? Either way, Beni didn't deserve this any more than Scarlett. She'd make sure he was never Laylani's pawn again.

"What is there to say? Nothing comes to mind except that I look forward to watching your trial."

Laylani continued as if Scarlett hadn't said anything. "You know, if Jules had lived, maybe Elestine would have left Edward, you might have married Alastair, and then you could have double-dated with your parents." She stood and started to shriek. "If she weren't so old, she could have had his *baby*, and then that baby would be related to you *and* Alastair—"

The guards moved toward her, but as they did, police officers flooded the garden.

Satisfaction coursed through Scarlett as an officer recuffed Laylani so her hands were behind her back.

"Let's go, Lady Heroux. Lots of arrests today."

"She came in through the back," said one of Elestine's guards, pointing to the gate that opened up to a small side canal. He was probably assuming—correctly, Scarlett thought—Elestine wouldn't want Laylani paraded through the house.

"Our boat's in the front. It'll be faster to walk her out that way," huffed the officer.

Laylani's eyes were wild as she was hauled through the garden and into the house. "You think you're better than me? All of you are so high and mighty," she shouted as they led her through the dining room, where all the Cerulean lords sat in stunned silence. "But Elestine's as morally bankrupt as— Oh, Edward, lovely to see you! Did you know about El and Jules? I always wondered if you were a cuck or if the relationship was actually open." She cackled at Edward's stormy expression.

Everyone in the dining room gaped as Scarlett followed Laylani and the officers out onto the dock. Her family's pain was out in the open for all to see. It was worth it to watch evil brought to her knees.

"One last thing, Laylani," called Scarlett as her stepmother was led to the police speedboat. "Elestine was a better mother to me than you ever were. And she'll continue to be, in spite of what you just pulled."

"Like I care," called Laylani.

"Well, maybe you care more about Beni. He's upstairs—did you know that? I knew he'd be safe here. With Elestine Spencer. Safer than he'd ever be with you. And we're going to live a *good* life without you."

Laylani looked over her shoulder, her expression twisted in pure hatred. The cop didn't miss a beat, though, hauling her into the boat before she could say another word.

Scarlett watched the police boat drive off into the distance before heading back inside.

In the dining room, Lord Spencer stood stone-faced next to his wife. He bellowed across the room, "No one leaves the premises without signing an NDA. I'll ruin anyone who doesn't comply. That woman is a liar, and anyone who corroborates her story will have me to answer to." He stomped off without another word. Elestine hurried to follow him.

Lord Navarre gave her a sympathetic grimace before returning to hushed conversation with Lord Mayweather. Otis Garfield was the first to approach Scarlett, a kindly look of concern on his wrinkled face.

"What a nasty display," he said as he patted Scarlett on the back. "Don't worry, Scarlett. No one will listen to that snake of a woman." He opened his arms to her, and Scarlett leaned into the hug, taking what comfort from it she could.

"It's all right, Otis. Whether they believe her or not, she's gone. That's all that matters to me right now."

CHAPTER (37)

At Parliament that evening, reporters, lords, and ladies packed into the same large room where her father had given his Remembrance Day speech.

"Ready?" Elestine asked Scarlett. She'd graciously offered her the job of speaking for the Ceruleans in the press conference, given that all the revelations were Scarlett's doing.

"I'm ready," she said. She'd napped for an hour before coming to Parliament, but she was still exhausted. Everything that had happened had culminated in a strange sense of calm.

Reporters were noisy as they took pictures and talked among themselves while waiting for the press conference to begin.

They walked to the podium together, and Elestine stood to Scarlett's left as Scarlett spoke about the chain of events leading up to the arrests. "Insidious conspirators, including Lady Moira Ashworth, many of her inner circle, and several senior agents in the Soleil Bureau, were arrested today and will be charged with my

father's murder, among other things. Evidence indicates they were also behind the kidnapping and attempted murder of my grandmother, Manon Bedivere, and myself. If it weren't for my brother, Beni Heroux, I wouldn't be alive today."

Mostly gold smoke streamed from the heads of everyone in the room. Many pairs of eyes were on Beni, who sat next to Cass in the front row. Scarlett met her brother's pained gaze. His jaw was set, his back straight. She'd given him a pass on the conference, but he'd wanted to come and show his support. And she was glad he was here. Flashes went off as the press tried to capture their eye contact, and Scarlett looked out at the crowd once more.

"In light of the findings," she continued, "a retroactive subpoena was granted by a judge for the investigations conducted last night."

This caused a stir among the press, as well as a slight uptick in black smoke, but Scarlett silenced them.

"A retroactive subpoena is unusual, but the depth of the corruption warranted it. My father was murdered by his colleagues." She paused as a hush came over the room, but she was determined to convince them. "The prime minister and senior members of the Cerulean Party validated my plan to break into Lord Federsin's house and the Goldenrod Party headquarters, which was based on preliminary evidence proving corruption at the bureau. If we weren't dealing with high treason, such invasions of privacy would never have been considered. I believe we saved Soleil from real corruption. If the citizens disagree, it's an election year, and they can stack the house with Goldenrods to put me in my place."

Amidst a mix of black and gold smoke, reporters shouted, and dozens of hands flew up when she called for questions. Scarlett pointed to a woman with exclusively gold smoke above her head.

"Your question, please."

"Sarah Leeward, *The Daily Missive*. Your stepmother, Lady

Laylani Heroux, was on the list of those arrested. Can you comment on her ties to the conspiracy against your father?"

"There was evidence she approved her sister's plans to have my father killed," said Scarlett. "One day, Hell will welcome her with open arms."

There were murmurs across the room at that, but Scarlett didn't care.

"One more question please," Sarah said. "The press release mentioned that cash payments were received by Aaron Fox and Lady Ashworth. How are these mysterious cash payments linked to the murder of Lord Heroux?"

Scarlett had anticipated this question. "Unfortunately, we don't have all the facts yet, as the cash payments used for these payouts are difficult to trace. However, we believe they received regular bribes from third parties and that the desire to keep receiving that income was a motivation for having Lord Heroux killed. The police will share more as they continue the investigation."

Do you think they'll ever be able to tie that money to the black market? Scarlett asked Nori. Moira had been vanquished, but Scarlett wanted the whole world to know she'd done it all for greed, not just for some self-righteous belief in her party's doctrine. She wanted her to be remembered by history as the complete piece of shit she was.

"*It may take a while, but the truth will come out,*" said her light.

Scarlett's heart raced as the questions continued, but to her great relief, no one asked her about an affair between Elestine and her father. They did, however, ask about Brayden.

"Maeve Sharp, *Soleil Times*. Two questions, if I may. First, will pardons be issued for those who assisted with the break-in to Goldenrod HQ?"

The news had reported a wolf shifter, so Scarlett was ready for this question. "Yes, given the findings, we've been able to secure pardons for those who assisted the investigation, though their identities are being protected for their safety."

She nodded, looking unsurprised. "Has there been any link formed between the events at the National Theater and what's been revealed today?"

"We're looking for ties, but so far, we've found none." Scarlett forgot where she was for a second as she pictured Brayden still sitting in jail. He might not even be aware of all that had transpired today.

Elestine came closer, brushing against Scarlett's elbow. "Can I make a comment, Scarlett?" the prime minister whispered in her ear.

Scarlett moved out of the way, grateful for a momentary reprieve.

Elestine said into the microphone, "I'd like it known that I'm well aware Lady Heroux has lost her father to a Soleil-based conspiracy and her husband to an outdated, bigoted anti-magic law. I'd like nothing more than to see Lord Maddox set free. I can't promise anything yet, but it's possible he'll be pardoned." She stepped aside.

Scarlett grasped Elestine's shoulder as she passed in a brief show of gratitude. Her words meant a lot, even if a pardon would depend on the courts. She wasn't sure a pardon for Brayden would get the necessary support, even with public sympathy at an all-time high, and she couldn't let herself hope too much when disappointment might follow.

"Next question," she said, pointing to another reporter.

"Ben Johnson, *The Financier*. You're in the midst of a remarkable first month in office, Lady Heroux. You've shocked the country with your choice to not only plan but be present at the raids for evidence, but many Soleil citizens will admire the risks you took for yourself and your country. Any plans to follow in your father's footsteps and run for prime minister?"

Scarlett raised her eyebrows. She hadn't expected *that* question, nor a string of compliments from a traditionally Goldenrod-leaning publication. "While I appreciate the compliment, we're only taking questions about the arrests at this time." She gave him the smallest of smiles.

After the press conference had finally drawn to a close, Scarlett, Cass, and Beni rode to House Heroux in silence. Boats filled with press followed them all the way.

"Please give the Heroux family some space," Cass shouted as they disembarked.

Scarlett put her arm around Beni in an attempt to shield him from view as they walked up the dock to her home. "This press feeding frenzy is painful," she said as she followed him into the house.

"It'll probably be like this for a while," said Cass from behind her.

Inside they found Tyler watching an action movie on the film projector in the living room.

"I had to take a break from the computer after the past twenty-four hours," Tyler explained as he paused the movie. "And it takes *a lot* for me to say that."

Scarlett nudged Beni. "He's been on the computer for most of the past twenty-four hours too. It's probably a good thing school is starting soon. Since I'm your guardian now, it's my job to keep you from staring at a screen all day."

Beni made a comically disgusted face.

"Meh," said Tyler. "I used to game all the time as a kid, and it worked out for me."

"See?" said Beni.

"If you're hungry, Martin made chicken and raviolo," said Tyler. "I already ate. It's in the warmer on top of the oven."

Beni headed for the kitchen.

"You go ahead," Scarlett said to Cass, who was waiting for her reply. "I'm going to call Brayden again."

This time the officer patched her though to Brayden without

argument. She melted at the sound of his deep voice. Scarlett walked upstairs as she told him everything she could with an officer listening.

"Scarlett, that's incredible. You're incredible. I can't believe what you've achieved. But the risks you took—Goddess, I should have been there. Why did you go with Cass? She's got military training you don't have." His voice held a touch of reproach.

Scarlett flopped onto her bed, staring up at her painted ceiling. "You're right," she admitted. "I was a liability. But I couldn't sit at home while others took these massive risks for me. Besides, with Cass out, I would've had no security. Beni had to stay with Elestine, and I didn't want to wait there all night."

He sighed. "You know, I would have done the same thing in your shoes, if I'm honest. You were really brave. I'm relieved you're safe. And Beni was at Elestine's the entire time? Like, all night? Did he hate being left there?"

She smiled softly at his concern for her brother. "Yes, that's right. Beni was fine. He gamed in their guest room all night."

"And so, what, you picked him up afterward and went home with Cass last night?" he pressed.

Scarlett's smile faded as she took in the frown in his voice. "Well, no. We stayed up almost all night at Elestine's reviewing everything we found. Beni slept while we worked. I napped briefly in his room."

"So there weren't any more nasty encounters?" he asked, somewhat appeased. "You slept in the room with Beni, and he left you alone?"

Brayden didn't have to clarify who "he" was.

Scarlett let out a huff as she rolled onto her side and hugged one of her pillows. "No, there *was* a nasty encounter. He tried to get me to snap out of the spell he thinks you put me under. He was definitely a dick."

"And that's it?" asked Brayden. "He didn't do anything else to hurt you?"

Her brow pinched. She understood his concern, but she hated wasting their valuable phone time on Alastair. "What do you mean, 'that's it'? *It* was really annoying. And I did put him in his place for it, just for the record."

Brayden was silent for a long moment. Then he let out a loud sigh. "Sorry. I was just worried."

"On that note, your time is up," said the officer.

They said their goodbyes and hung up.

As Scarlett lay in bed without Brayden, the day's victories felt hollow.

I miss him so much, she thought to Nori. *The phone isn't enough. I can't see his face. I only get little snippets of how he's really feeling.*

"I know, dear one. You'll find a way to free him. I know it," said Nori soothingly.

The next day, Scarlett rubbed her eyes as she sat in her office at Parliament. Most of her parliamentary sessions and meetings for the day had been canceled due to the entire Goldenrod Party—at least the ones not in jail—having to meet at their headquarters to elect a new leader and begin damage control. She was alone, having sent Cass to the peers' dining room for a long lunch. Exhausted from the events of the past few days, she spent the downtime emailing her lawyer about the four people hurt in the break-ins. Three had already agreed to settle out of court. The fourth—the cop with the injured hand—was the only holdout and had asked to meet Scarlett personally. She typed a quick reply telling the lawyer she'd be free to meet with him over the following week.

After that, Scarlett attempted to scour the news, but all the articles were starting to sound the same, and she couldn't focus. She refreshed the screen, and a new headline screamed up at her: "EVORY DECLARES WAR ON SIGUR VIÐUR!"

No. Her breaths became shallow. She tensed, unsure what to do. *What will this mean for Clair de Lune?*

"*Nothing good,*" said Nori.

Lachlan will want to extradite Brayden right away. He'll never be able to come back.

A knock sounded at the office door.

"Come in."

Elestine appeared. It was the first time she and Scarlett had been alone since Laylani's unhinged display in the garden. Scarlett hadn't spent any time worrying about the prime minister's private life, wrapped up as she was in the bigger issues, but she wondered now what things had been like between her and Edward since yesterday afternoon.

Elestine hesitated at the door. "May I sit?"

"Please." Scarlett gestured to the chair in front of her desk.

"I know I'm probably not on your list of favorite people right now," the prime minister began. "Edward and I have always had an arrangement, but I still want to apologize to you—"

Shaking her head, Scarlett held up her hand. "Please. That's not necessary."

"But I don't want you to think—"

"Elestine, I don't care."

"Why not?"

Scarlett sighed. "Maybe it's more accurate to say I'd prefer to move on *not* knowing the specifics. I do care. What you did is gross. I wish my dad had divorced Laylani rather than cheat on her. Doing it with my boyfriend's mother—again, gross—but Alastair and I aren't together anymore, so I'll do my best to let that go and not let it harm our working relationship."

Elestine's shoulders slumped. "That's more grace than I deserve from you. I hope you still feel that way when I tell you what I've learned."

Scarlett recoiled, unable to fathom taking on more stress right now. "And that is?"

"I'm sorry. I'll start with the good news. I've issued a full pardon for Brayden. It took until now to arrange it because of the magic use, but the senior court's approval came through today. He's being discharged from jail as we speak."

Scarlett stood. "Right now?" *Thank the Goddess. If that's true, he won't end up exiled from Soleil.*

"Yes, but I have some bad news as well."

Scarlett's heart screamed for Brayden, but she sat. "Go on."

"Last night, after the press conference, something wasn't sitting right with me. I was as shocked as you that we didn't find anything about the National Theater incident in the raid. Then I was thinking about Lord Federsin. He's claiming he had no knowledge of the money that went out of his bank account. Blamed it on his son, the coward."

"That's pathetic." Scarlett couldn't imagine trying to pin something she'd done on Beni.

"Agreed, but as I was listening to his sad explanation, I thought to myself, what kind of a ninny would miss such an astronomical sum being withdrawn from his household account?" She took a deep breath and continued. "So I looked through our accounts. And I noticed fifty thousand marcs were withdrawn last week from Alastair's trust fund."

A shiver ran down Scarlett's spine as she stared at Elestine. Her fingers found her lips. "He didn't," she whispered.

"At first he acted like it was a down payment for a flat, but when I threatened to trace the payment with the bank, he admitted he hired the men to attack Brayden and you at the National Theater."

The shock stunned Scarlett momentarily. Of all the possibilities she'd considered, she hadn't even *dreamed* of this. Her whole body tensed as her worldview realigned around the new information. "Was he trying to get us killed?"

"He got what he wanted—Brayden in jail. He said he did it to free you, but obviously, that's absolute nonsense."

"That bastard," growled Scarlett.

"I *completely* agree."

"He deserves to be arrested. *He* deserves to be sitting in jail for sending those men after us."

Elestine hid her face in her hands for a second, and then she looked Scarlett in the eye. "Scarlett, I'm so sorry. Words can't convey—"

Scarlett held up her hand. "Please. It's his mistake to apologize for. I just want to see him brought to justice for what he's done."

"That's true, and if that's what you want, we can see it done together. But I do ask you to take a moment to look at the big picture."

"What's the big picture? He paid people to assault us, several people were seriously injured, and it led to Brayden burning down the lobby of the theater!" Scarlett's voice echoed off the walls of her office.

Elestine put her hands up. "Please—if someone overhears you, the choice will be made for us. I want you to consider the big picture. The border legislation." Elestine's eyes pleaded with her. "Right now we have complete public sympathy, both for you and our party. If we expose Alastair, I'll be obliged to resign, which would be a disaster for the party. And while I'm willing to take responsibility, it gives me pause to give up your father's dream when we're so *close*, Scarlett. I was up all night thinking about the greater good and justice, and I don't think there's a perfect way to resolve this. So I want to know what *you* think we should do. Do we punish Alastair publicly, or do we do it privately for the sake of the legislation we both believe is for the greater good?"

A splitting headache assaulted Scarlett. She massaged her temples with her fingertips as tears pricked at her eyes. "Is this some kind of quid pro quo?" she asked, her body tensing. "If I don't agree, Brayden's pardon gets revoked?" She was too tired to read between the lines.

Elestine's eyes widened, and she shook her head. "Certainly not. I can show you the emails. His release is happening regardless of what you decide."

Scarlett steeled herself as she racked her brain for the right answer. Either way, she was letting people down. Elestine or herself, either via a lie that birthed a new corrupt cover-up or via the truth that forced Elestine to resign.

It's not fair, she cried to Nori. *Nothing is fair.* Justice for her and Brayden or the fate of Soleil's border? She couldn't put her private grievances above the greater good, could she?

"*Make it fair*," said Nori.

Fair meant transparency and putting a stop to the lies. Scarlett wanted to be better than those who'd come before her. *That* was what Soleil needed from her.

"I won't do the right thing the wrong way," she said. "I want to see him punished."

"Punished how though?" asked Elestine.

"*You know what to do. Follow your heart*," said Nori.

But the border?

"*There's always another way. She's wrong.*"

She locked eyes with Elestine, finding the strength to sit up straighter and stare her down. "We need to be better than the peers we just had arrested. I want to tell the truth. I want Alastair to face justice for what he did. He should be banned from Parliament."

The words set her free. She was unchained, acting for herself *and* for Soleil, because the people wouldn't want her to lie to save them from themselves. She trusted them, and she'd tell the truth.

Black smoke with a small tendril of gold appeared above Elestine, but Scarlett barely glanced at it. Her opinion didn't matter. This was up to Scarlett to decide.

"We can arrange that without exposing him, you know." Elestine's blue eyes—Alastair's eyes—searched her face.

Scarlett let out a breath. "I'm sorry, but no. I'm going to press charges. If that leads to the border legislation stalling, that's a shame, but I believe in my heart it will pass eventually. I won't lie to the country because Alastair committed a crime that would be inconvenient to expose."

Elestine sat there as if hoping Scarlett would say more. When she stayed silent, she tapped the desk once and stood. The hope had drained from her expression, her face now set in resolve. "Do you mind if I wait a day to turn him in? It's been one hell of a week. I'm still severely underwater."

Scarlett trusted her enough to give her that. "Sure. What's one night? Get some sleep." Brayden was getting out. That was all she cared about.

Elestine smiled with gratitude, but all Scarlett saw was the darkest shadows she'd ever seen under her eyes. "Thank you for that." She turned to leave.

"Will you resign?" asked Scarlett.

Elestine stopped in her tracks. "Should I?"

Scarlett considered for a moment. "I doubt Moira Ashworth would, if she were in your shoes. If we can still salvage the legislation . . ."

"Perhaps I'll take it a day at a time." Elestine stared into space. "Who knows what the full repercussions will be?"

Scarlett studied Elestine's wan face. Her son was an awful human being, but this woman had just held her hand and walked through hell to free Scarlett and Soleil from a terrible conspiracy. She wasn't sure if many others would have been as bold as her.

"I hope you won't resign," she said quietly. "I'd be happy to give a statement of support for you once the news is out."

Elestine's eyes were bright with tears. "That's very gracious of you, given everything that's just come to light."

"I know you're not a bad person. Your son, however, is beyond the point of redemption as far as I'm concerned. The Alastair I knew would never have done this." Scarlett shook her head, ready to forget Alastair. "If that's all, is it all right if I go? I want to be there when Brayden is released." She needed to find Cass and call Charlie.

Elestine cracked open Scarlett's door. "Yes, of course. Go. I'll give you a heads-up before I go to the police tomorrow."

Scarlett grabbed her handbag and sped down the hallway past Elestine. Her mind was already far away from Parliament and fixed on the man she loved. She had to get to Brayden.

CHAPTER 38

Scarlett made it to the police station before Brayden was released. She ran at him as soon as he came through the door, unshaven and wearing gray sweatpants and a matching sweatshirt. He could have been dressed in a garbage bag for all she cared. He dropped the bag he was holding and caught her in his arms.

She couldn't squeeze him tight enough. "Goddess, I'm so happy you're free. I love you."

His grip on her tightened. "I love you too."

There was so much she wanted to say as he set her down carefully and held her face in his hands, his gaze boring into her soul. Then all the words left her mind as he kissed her deeply. She clutched at him, and he ran his hands over her as if assuring himself she was truly all right. Scarlett never wanted to let him go again. The outside world faded away, and there was just him in her arms. His lips on hers. She wanted him with her every day for the rest of her life.

Someone whistled, bringing Scarlett back to reality. She

reluctantly pulled away to find several people filming them or taking pictures with their phones. Brayden turned his body to try to block some of the cameras, but it was impossible to hide. Cass was having to actively work to keep some space between them and the onlookers.

Good for our public image, but bad for my life.

"Let's go," she said, taking his hand.

He picked up his bag. "Yeah, I want to get the fuck out of here."

Hand in hand, they rushed outside to where Charlie was waiting in the Heroux speedboat, and soon they were on their way toward the Sapphire Canal as the midday sun sparkled on the water around them. Brayden yanked his sweatshirt over his head, revealing a white T-shirt underneath, and Scarlett brushed her fingertips over the short beard he'd grown in the several days he'd spent in jail.

As she drank in the man she adored, reality flooded back into her mind. "There's so much I have to tell you about the past few days, but first, there's something big you need to know. Evory declared war on Sigur Viður today."

The light dimmed in his eyes. They both knew what it meant. He'd have to go home, and soon.

He pulled her into his lap. "Tell me some good news. Moira Ashworth was arrested, right?"

Grinning, Scarlett rested her head on his shoulder. "Yes, and Laylani. She's gone. Probably for a long, long time, and if she ever gets out of prison, everyone she meets will know what she did."

"Thank fuck for that." He pressed his lips to hers as he held her.

"There's more," said Scarlett, running her hand over his warm chest and breathing in the scent of him for the first time in days. Even after a stint in jail, he still smelled like fir trees in the rain. "Elestine discovered Alastair hired the men who assaulted us at the National Theater."

Brayden's grip on her tightened. "You could have *died*. I'll fucking kill him."

With a quick glance toward the front of the boat to confirm Charlie and Cass were still both facing away from the enclosed cabin, Scarlett rose to her knees, straddling Brayden so she could look him dead in the eye as she threaded her fingers through his hair. "You won't. I just got you back, and he's not worth it. I'm pressing charges. He'll pay with his freedom and his reputation. And he'll be banned from Parliament."

He relaxed slightly, and Scarlett settled back in his lap as she relayed the full conversation with Elestine.

"Did I make the right decision?" she asked once she was finished.

"Undoubtedly. He deserves it. I can't wait to see that prick get flogged publicly."

"No more seeing him at work." She gave him a small grin. "Do you think the public will turn on the border legislation because of this? Elestine is worried it'll hurt our cause."

"Even if it does, you'll work through it. I'd bet on you every single time." He sighed. "I wish I could be here to see him locked up." He shifted Scarlett in his lap and ran a hand through his hair.

"Will you have to leave right away?" she asked.

"Soon," he said. "I wish it weren't so, but Lachlan will need me."

"I know. And now I'm safe here. You won't have to worry about me." Images of Brayden in an active war zone burst into her thoughts. "But what if something happens to you? I can't lose you again," she whispered, her voice catching.

"I'm invincible, remember?" He stroked her back, soothing her.

"You're hard to kill, not impossible to kill." She met his gaze. "While you were in jail, I realized some things."

"Like what?" He stared back at her, something that looked like uncertainty flickering across his face.

Her heart raced as she searched for the right words. Their marriage had been hasty, but she wanted all of him, forever. Scratch that—forever wasn't enough. She needed the North Star runes *and* forever.

She swallowed. "Like, I can't live without you. The North Star stuff was a lot when you first told me about it, but now I wish we'd gotten the runes when we had the chance."

Light filled his eyes, and everything tumbled out of her in a rush.

"I hated not knowing what you were thinking and feeling, like maybe you were sitting there slowly growing to hate me for bringing you here—"

He put a finger to her lips to silence her. "That could never happen. I was only afraid of *losing* you. I don't resent you for anything that's happened. Watching you get attacked and grabbed at the theater— it was the worst moment of my life. I was cursing myself for not begging you to go through the North Star ceremony, because I can't live without you either, Scarlett. I'd marry you all over again today. And not for a visa."

She started to laugh as her eyes filled with tears. "I wish we had more time. You'll be shipping out to Evory—" Her voice cracked.

"Come back to Clair de Lune with me." He threaded his fingers into her hair and brought his face so close to hers their noses were touching. "I'll have to stop there before I deploy. Let's go to the Forest Temple for our North Star ceremony. If we do that, we'll be able to talk to each other whenever we want, and if you have the phoenix valor afterward, you can protect yourself and Beni while I'm gone."

"You want that? Really? You think we're ready?" Longing for him was all she could feel. She didn't doubt she'd want him always.

"I feel the same way you do. The worst part about being locked up was not being able to communicate with you. While I was in there, I wished we'd already done it, because then I could have talked to you all night when I was in jail not sleeping, or at least until you had to go to bed—"

"I wasn't sleeping either," said Scarlett with a shaky laugh. "I was too worried about you, and I hated being separated."

"So does that mean you're open to going through with the ceremony? I know it's fast, but with the war breaking out . . . I already told you I regretted waiting as soon as we were attacked. It would give me a lot of peace while I'm gone."

"I want to," she said. "I want every part of me to belong to you."

He loosened his hold on her, but all his attention was on her. "Scarlett, my soul will belong to you until I stop breathing, and probably even after that."

Their lights circled each other rapidly.

"Say you'll come with me. We could go to Clair tomorrow, do the ceremony at night. You'd be back the next day."

A sudden lightness filled her. "I'll come with you."

His lips found hers, and they kissed until Cass coughed at the door of the cabin to let them know they'd arrived at the house.

Scarlett pulled back, glancing at Cass, who looked like she was holding back a smile. With a wave, she disappeared, and Scarlett turned back to Brayden. His flushed cheeks sent a shiver down her spine.

He stared back at her. "Your room. Now."

CHAPTER (39)

Scarlett and Brayden rushed through the quiet foyer and up the stairs. She thanked the Goddess no one got in their way to delay them with exclamations over Brayden's return. She'd be happy to entertain that kind of chat later, but right now, no.

Inside her room, Brayden shut and locked the door behind them. When he turned around, Scarlett was already on the bed, pulling her boots off and flinging them to the floor. He was on her in seconds, and she clutched him to her, their lips crashing together in a bruising kiss as his body pressed into hers, pushing her down onto the bed.

An ache was already building in her.

She broke their kiss, her breaths jagged as she slid her hand down between them to grasp his stiff cock through his sweatpants. "I need you so badly right now."

Her husband. Her North Star. Her everything. The man she'd chased through her dreams.

She'd been without him for so long. It had only been a few days, but it had seemed like forever.

The pain of their separation sat heavy in her gut, and she needed him to fuck that pain out to prove to her he was really here; really ready to be with her completely. Her need was echoed in his gaze as he pressed himself into her hand.

"I need you too. Goddess, I do," he groaned. Hiking up the skirt of her dress while she lay beneath him, he slid her panties to the side, exposing her.

Brayden inserted a finger, letting out a growl of pleasure. "So wet for me already," he murmured.

She ground onto his finger, whimpering when one finger became two and protesting when they slid out of her, leaving her unsatisfied.

"Take these off," he ordered, tugging at her underwear.

Scarlett slid her panties off and tossed them aside. Then she stood, intending to pull off her dress, but before she could, Brayden had spun her around so his hips were behind hers, her thighs pressed into the edge of the bed. He pushed her skirt up, his hand splaying across her stomach as his hard length rubbed against her backside. He lifted one of her knees onto the mattress.

Scarlett fell forward onto her forearms, her arse hovering in the air near the edge of the bed. She looked over her shoulder in anticipation, expecting to see him about to enter her, but instead he fell to his knees behind her.

"I just want to taste you first," he said, almost to himself.

She let out a gasp as he gripped her thighs with both hands, his tongue sliding first into her wet pussy and then over her clit. She pushed against him, grinding on his tongue as he ate her out from behind, somehow finding her most sensitive spot even with his face buried in her.

As he massaged her sensitive bundle of nerves, Scarlett moaned, the heat in her quickly building. A low hum of pleasure spread throughout her hips. His tongue and his hands on her were all there was.

Barely any time had passed when she gasped, "I'm coming." She throbbed against his tongue, feeling the pleasure everywhere, from the tips of her breasts to her curled toes.

He licked her for a few seconds longer before pulling back slightly, his face still between her legs. "I think I spent half my time in jail worrying, and the other half thinking about this."

"Brayden." His name came out as a breathy whisper. Closing her eyes, she reveled in her post-orgasm glow, her body ready to melt into a puddle.

"Scarlett, my love. My sweetheart." He rose, standing behind her. "I can't wait for you to be mine completely."

"I can't wait to be yours," she murmured, her eyes still closed. Her body was weightless, her soul consumed with joy at the thought of realizing their North Star bond the very next day.

He dragged his fingertips up her thigh and then kneaded her arse. Her eyes flew open, the touch making her want him again. Still on her knees, resting on her forearms with her backside in the air, Scarlett looked back at him. Brayden's eyes were dark with need as he stared down at her. She grinned at the sight. He'd stepped out of his pants, but he was still wearing his sweatshirt. They'd been in too much of a rush to undress properly.

As if reading her mind already, he yanked the sweatshirt over his head, flinging it to the floor next to his pants. She raked her gaze appreciatively over the view of his naked body before her. The solid curves of his muscles, how big he was, the knowing that he was hers, body and soul. She was so fucking lucky.

He tugged impatiently at her dress, and Scarlett snapped out of her worshipful stare to help him pull it over her head. Now totally naked, she lay on her side and waited expectantly for him.

Brayden slid onto the bed behind her and pulled her back against him so their bodies fit perfectly together. Nudging her legs apart, he gripped her to him as the head of his cock found her entrance, sliding back and forth. With several small thrusts, the thickness of him filled her, making her cry out. Scarlett adjusted to him with a sharp intake of breath, and his fingers explored her body.

He slid out of her slowly and pushed into her again, until he was fully inside her once more. She wiggled her hips, wanting him to give it to her hard, but instead of picking up the pace, he only chuckled softly as he reached an arm around to her front and rubbed one of her peaked nipples with the rough pad of his thumb.

Scarlett panted, no longer impatient as he stroked her heavy breast and continued to push in and out of her in an unhurried fashion.

"I . . ."

"You love me?" he whispered in her ear, sounding out of breath despite his slow pace.

"I love you. Forever."

She throbbed as he moved in her, touched her, and as if sensing her on the edge, his fingertip found her clit. Scarlett rocked on his shaft as a surprising second orgasm coursed through her.

"That's right, sweetheart. Are you satisfied now?" he asked.

"No." She managed to make the one-word answer sound petulant as she pressed herself into him. He was still inside her, and she wanted him undone. She needed him to come with her.

Brayden rolled her onto her stomach, threading his fingers through hers as he used his hands and his body to pin her to the bed, pushing into her harder and picking up the pace. "You want it like that?"

She moaned her answer, her voice husky and pleading.

White-hot fire seared through her as he began to move with urgency. Brayden inside her was all there was as he drove into her hard and fast. She couldn't move much with his body covering hers, but she rocked into him as best she could, her body still flush with desire.

"More." She wanted him to stay inside her until she couldn't remember what it was like to live without him. "I need it hard, Brayden."

He slowed, and she growled in frustration.

"Shh," he said. "Let me . . ."

Her aggravated need turned to curiosity as he hooked his arm around her waist and hauled her onto her hands and knees. Then his hands circled her wrists. She stilled for a second, not knowing what he wanted, but she let him gently guide her hands behind her back, with her hips still in the air. Turning her face to one side, she let her head and her shoulders fall to the mattress. He held her wrists, her arms taut by her sides, and she cried out in pleasure as he used the leverage of the hold to drive into her even harder.

Brayden had her moaning with every deep thrust. The dominance of the position made her writhe under him, the surrender of it bringing her to the brink of climax yet again. He was actually here, and after tomorrow, they'd never *really* be apart again.

As he pounded into her, she tightened the walls of her pussy on his cock, coming again, and was rewarded as he jerked, spilling himself inside of her. He groaned, releasing his hold on her wrists and stroking her lower back as he pumped in and out of her slowly.

"That was, without a doubt, the best orgasm I've ever had."

She flushed hot, pleased she'd been the one to give him that. They were finally together, the way they should be.

They cleaned up and got back into bed. The familiar sound of birds over the water outside reached Scarlett through her window. A golden glow from the fading sun lit up her bedroom as she glanced around at all her familiar things. Brayden encased Scarlett's body with his, her back to his chest and their legs threaded together.

"I should probably get up," murmured Scarlett. "Beni might be wondering about dinner."

"I'm sure he's fine, but why don't you text him and see if he needs anything?" said Brayden.

"Good idea." Scarlett reached for her phone.

His reply came through a minute later. Scarlett smirked and showed Brayden.

Beni: I'm fine. Cass said you needed some "alone time" with Brayden, so we're out at dinner. Tell Brayden I say hi! I'm glad he's home.

Brayden chuckled softly. "You'll bring him to the North Star ceremony, right?"

"Of course," said Scarlett. She wouldn't have it any other way.

"Good." He rested his chin on her shoulder, his warm breath tickling her as he nuzzled into her neck.

While they lay in each other's arms, Scarlett recalled the last time they'd been in bed together and the arguments that had ensued. She'd been so unyielding, worrying about her duty over everything else, and for what? A job she wasn't even sure she wanted? A promise rose within her, begging to be spoken aloud.

"There's something I want you to know," she said.

He stiffened. "What?"

Her grip tightened on the forearm he'd draped over her. "I'll move to Clair de Lune."

He was silent for several seconds. "But . . ."

"Not right away," she clarified before he could go on. "I want to give Parliament my best shot for a while and see if I can get the border legislation passed. But let's say we're three years down the line and nothing has changed—if by then I haven't succeeded, I'll start making a succession plan. Beni could prepare to take it if he wants, or I can try to name a nonfamilial heir."

His hold on her tightened. "You'd do that? Your family's legacy—you wouldn't regret giving it up?" His voice was soft, tentative. "I could be the one to move too. I'd do it eventually."

She turned in his arms so they were face-to-face. "I know you would. But I love Clair. I could be happy there. And being with you means more to me than the seat in Parliament. I want to leave the world a better place than I found it, but there's more than one way to do that. Ways that involve us living together, not apart."

Brayden's gaze was tender and filled with joy as he searched her face. He closed his eyes and pressed his forehead to hers. "I love the idea of you and me together in Clair de Lune."

She grinned as she reached up and threaded her fingers through his hair. "Me too."

"*Me three*," added Nori, who was floating together with Jax at the foot of the bed, looking peaceful too.

"Until the war is over, it does make sense for you to keep pursuing your goals in Soleil. And three years . . . I pray we're at peace by then."

Scarlett's smile faded slightly. "I'll pray for that too."

"Either way," he said, sounding happy once more. "Thank you. I love knowing we'll be together in Clair de Lune someday. After the war."

A sense of foreboding fell over her at the thought of Brayden at war. She forced it away by nuzzling into him. He was here with her, in her arms, right now. And for now, that was more than enough.

CHAPTER (40)

The next day, they left for Clair de Lune.

As night fell in the forest around them, Scarlett kneeled next to Brayden in the main chamber of the Forest Temple in front of the statue of the Goddess Cerridwen. An array of priestesses stood around them, along with Brayden's friends and family, Manon, Cass, Tyler, and Beni, who'd all come to see the once-in-a-lifetime North Star ceremony take place.

Gwen stood at an altar lighting incense for the ceremony. Scarlett ran her fingertips over the pearl lining of her mother's white dress—the same one she'd worn for their wedding. Brayden kneeled next to her in his suit, ready to make his unbreakable lifetime commitment. She reached for his hand, and his fingers interlaced with hers as he smiled at her, joy, light, and love plain on his face. It was a marked contrast from their wedding day—for both of them. Love had been there that day, but now all the doubt and fear was gone from their hearts.

They were ready.

"Let's begin," said Gwen as she turned to the altar where they were kneeling. "You can keep holding hands, if you like, but please close your eyes."

Scarlett shut her eyes, and the priestess started chanting, her melodic voice echoing across the large room as Scarlett kept Brayden's warm hand in hers. The scent of the incense surrounded her, the smell more vivid without the distraction of her sight. Her body thrummed with excitement for what was to come next.

Even upright as she was, Scarlett dropped into a trance. Her head fell forward as the chanting quieted her thoughts. Her parents appeared in her mind's eye, reunited and beaming at her, as if giving their blessing. Then came a carousel of memories of her and Brayden through the years, until finally, the image of Brayden in the mirror— older, and all hers—was all she could see.

Was that children laughing, or was it Nori and . . . ?

The familiar prickle of the valor manifesting arose on her left ring finger. Gwen continued to chant, and an itchy heat spread over Scarlett's shoulder. It hurt for just a moment, causing Scarlett to twitch and her conscious mind to awaken, but then the heat became gentle.

"Congratulations to the world's newest North Stars," said Gwen, her voice bright. "You can kiss, if you like!"

Scarlett opened her heavy eyes to the sound of enthusiastic cheers and clapping around them. Brayden beamed at her and pulled her into an embrace. The cheering around them grew louder as his lips moved against hers, but they didn't break the kiss. Scarlett threaded her fingers into Brayden's hair, heat building in her as his soft lips caressed hers. Her mouth grew hotter. The blaze spread across her face and over her neck, but she didn't want to stop kissing him to see what was making her so feverish.

Gasps of surprise filled the temple. Brayden pulled away and stared at her in shock and then wonder.

"You're not hurt?"

She laughed. "Why would I be hurt?"

"You were just on fire," cackled Manon from her seat behind the altar.

Beni laughed. "That was amazing."

Brayden held out his hand. His fire danced on his fingertips like always, but this time he didn't pull away when Scarlett reached out and intertwined her fingers with his. Her hand burst into merry flames, and she stared in wonder as the flames grew larger. Then her dress began to burn. She shook her hand, trying to put the fire out, as the smell of burning fabric filled the air.

Brayden chuckled and smothered the flames with his hands. "We need to teach you how to control your fire." He patted the sleeves of her dress, where the fire had burned the fabric.

"Please don't incinerate the castle tonight," called James from next to Lachlan. Lachlan shushed him.

"Look at the valor," whispered Brayden, grabbing her hand.

A cross-like star, etched out of the finest lines, had appeared on the ring finger of Scarlett's left hand. The vertical line extended downward and was just visible beneath her wedding ring. Scarlett seized Brayden's hand and was delighted to find a matching rune in the same place on his left ring finger.

You're so beautiful.

Scarlett startled, and then a smile spread across her face. It was Brayden's voice in her mind. She threw herself at him so hard he had to grab on to the altar to keep both of them from toppling to the floor.

Brayden, I love you so much. I'll love you till the end of time. It's us against the world now.

His laugh lit her up. *Always and forever, and even after that. I love you too, Scarlett, my beautiful firebird.*

Author's Note

From the bottom of my heart, thank you for reading *The Rise of Scarlett Heroux*!

If you enjoyed this book, I would be grateful if you'd leave a review on Amazon and/or Goodreads! Reviews mean the world to authors. If you want more of Brayden and Scarlett, consider visiting my website (elizabethwatsonbooks.com) to sign up for my newsletter. As a thank-you for subscribing, I'll send you a bonus scene where Scarlett and Brayden explore their new North Star bond in the hidden pools of Mont Noir. It's a steamy one, literally and figuratively.

If you're into social media, I'd love it if you found me on Instagram or TikTok! I'm @elizabeth_j_watson on both platforms. Come by and say hello. :)

Cast of Characters

MAJOR PLAYERS

(the Herouxes, the Bediveres, the Maddoxes, and the Spencers)

Lord Jules Heroux — Prime minister of Soleil. Father of Scarlett and Beaufort Heroux. Married to Lady Laylani Heroux.

> **BIRTHPLACE:** Soleil.
> **POLITICAL PARTY:** Cerulean.

Scarlett Heroux — Daughter of Lord Jules Heroux and Lady Sabina Bedivere Heroux. Heir to House Heroux.

> **BIRTHPLACE:** Soleil.
> **POLITICAL PARTY:** Cerulean.

Beaufort "Beni" Heroux — Son of Lord Jules Heroux and Lady Laylani Ashworth Heroux.

> **BIRTHPLACE:** Soleil.

Sabina Bedivere Heroux (deceased) — Mother of Scarlett Heroux. Daughter of Manon Bedivere. First wife of Lord Jules Heroux.
    BIRTHPLACE: Clair de Lune.

Manon Bedivere — Grandmother of Scarlett Heroux. Mother of Sabina Bedivere Heroux (deceased).
    BIRTHPLACE: Clair de Lune.

Lady Laylani Ashworth Heroux — Second wife of Lord Jules Heroux. Mother of Beaufort Heroux.
    BIRTHPLACE: Soleil.
    POLITICAL PARTY: Goldenrod.

General Lachlan Maddox — Head of the Clair de Lune military. Father of Brayden and James Maddox. Widower of Alyssa Maddox.

Brayden Maddox — Son of General Lachlan Maddox and Alyssa Maddox (deceased). Brother to James Maddox.
    BIRTHPLACE: Clair de Lune.

James Maddox — Son of General Lachlan Maddox and Alyssa Maddox (deceased). Brother to Brayden Maddox.
    BIRTHPLACE: Clair de Lune.

Lady Elestine Spencer — Married to Lord Edward Spencer. Mother of Alastair Spencer.
    BIRTHPLACE: Soleil.
    POLITICAL PARTY: Cerulean.

Lord Edward Spencer — Married to Lady Elestine Spencer. Father of Alastair Spencer.

BIRTHPLACE: Soleil.

POLITICAL PARTY: Unknown.

Alastair Spencer — Son of Lady Elestine Spencer and Lord Edward Spencer.

BIRTHPLACE: Soleil.

POLITICAL PARTY: Cerulean.

GOVERNMENT AND LAW ENFORCEMENT

Lady Moira Ashworth — Leader of the Goldenrod Party. Sister to Lady Laylani Ashworth Heroux.

Lord Otis Garfield — Senior Cerulean peer (elected seat).

Lord Navarre — Senior Cerulean peer (elected seat).

Lord Bombardier — Senior Cerulean peer (inherited seat).

Lord Mayweather — Senior Cerulean peer (inherited seat).

Lord Buckland — Senior Goldenrod peer (inherited seat).

Lord Lyle Federsin — Senior Goldenrod peer (inherited seat).

Lord Hill — Goldenrod peer (elected seat).

Lady La Rue — Goldenrod peer (elected seat).

John Bates — Head of the Soleil Bureau.

Aaron Fox — Second-in-command of the Soleil Bureau.

Leonard Orsino — Third-in-command of the Soleil Bureau.

Officer Geruda — Soleil police officer.

Agent Ward — Soleil Bureau agent.

Agent McClean — Clair de Lune Intelligence agent.

Shannen — An officer of the Soleil courts.

Kjartan Holm — Chancellor of Sigur Viður.

Greta Crow — Prime Minister of Clair de Lune.

SUPPORTING CAST

Minnie — Brayden's friend from school. Doctor.

Keeley — Brayden's friend from school. Veterinarian.

Gwen — Forest Temple priestess.

Cassidy "Cass" Darwish — Bodyguard and more.
>   **BIRTHPLACE:** Zahara.

Tyler Darwish — Streamer and more.
>   **BIRTHPLACE:** Soleil.

Charlie — Heroux family boat driver and friend.

Dr. Mel Turner — Heroux family doctor.

Blake — Beni's best friend.

Martin — Heroux family chef.

Liz — Spencer family chef.

Flora — Castle staff in Clair de Lune.

Dr. Bowen — Energy healer in Clair de Lune.

Tommy and Patrick — Beni's Clair de Lune friends.

Mace the Menace — Hydra shifter and more.

Brixton the Beast — Dire-wolf shifter and more.

Rex — And more.

Lock — And more.

Rufus Hill — Son of Lord Hill. Friend of Alastair.

Tom Bowles — Photographer.

Sarah Leeward — Reporter.

Maeve Sharp — Reporter.

Ben Johnson — Reporter.

MAGIC SYSTEM

Soul lights — Small balls of blue-white light that serve as a connection to divine energy. Anyone is eligible to meet their soul light from the age of ten. All that is required is to travel to one of two temples on the continent of Hieratia (one in Clair de Lune and one in Zahara).

Valors — Magical abilities granted in one of the two temples, valors manifest in the form of a tattoo. Each person is able to receive their valor from the age of eighteen. There are as many different kinds of valors as there are different kinds of people. Manipulation of the elements, psychic abilities, and aptitude for various vocations such as medicine, energy healing, and engineering are all well-documented valors.

The North Star bond — Occurring between two people with their soul lights, this extremely rare bond between soul mates allows for power sharing and telepathy.

SOUL LIGHTS

Nori — Scarlett's soul light.
Jax — Brayden's soul light.
Riley — Beni's soul light.

ACKNOWLEDGMENTS

Thank you to my husband, Marcus. Without the support you've given me the last couple of years, this book would never have been written. I love you to pieces, and I'm so grateful for you.

To Ella and Eric, thank you for choosing me as your mom. I love you more than life itself. I'm looking forward to reading your bedtime stories tonight and every night until you won't let me anymore.

To my parents, Steve and Carolyn. Dad, you used to report Harry Potter news to me when I was a kid, and you never said no at the bookstore. Mom, you read to me many nights before bed. You're the only one who has read all three of my books, and I'm so appreciative of that. I'm grateful you both made our household a literary one. Thanks for always being so supportive!

To my brother Miles, who paid for the final round of developmental edits on this book in exchange for a Shark Tank–style deal to receive 10 percent of my profits (up to $50K). Thank you for gifting me that dev edit. We both know the deal was so that I felt okay taking the money, but hey, let's shoot for the stars and hope you one day max out that $50K. Your lack of risk aversion is both appalling and mesmerizing to me, and if I could live my life over again, I'd try to be more like you.

To my critique partners Christina Boyd and Sarah Doulman, it was a gift to be paired with you in the Beta Reader Matchup—shout-out to the *Shit No One Tells You About Writing* podcast for my pairing with these amazing ladies! It's been a joy spending time exchanging feedback with you both!!! Thank you for all the hours we've spent together.

Dena Berg, thank you for encouraging me, reading my drafts, and helping me expand my writer community! You're a wonderful friend, and I'm so glad we're on this writing journey together. I still laugh about you telling me everyone probably gets diarrhea the week of their book release. I know someday you'll publish, and I look forward to hearing what your bowel experience is like when you debut.

Stephanie Boda, thanks for telling me to put everything I have into this book. You've always been an amazing cheerleader for me. Thanks for all the times you've done my hair and makeup and for encouraging me to experiment. <3 The laughs we share are sometimes so unhinged (the logo you made me), and that is priceless to me. OMIT! Lol.

Megan Czajka Alford, you're a real one! Thank you for being so awesome that you inspired a character in *Love & Malice*. Thank you for reading that book and for being so supportive all these years! And thank you for all the good times. Yankee Doodle Dandies for life.

David Dodds, your support has been unwavering. We're *so* aligned, it sometimes freaks me out how similar our minds are. Your friendship is the best thing I took away from the London trading desk. Thank you for encouraging me to put myself first and for being enthusiastic about my life after finance, even though it was so different. Thank you for reading *Love & Malice*, and for starring in it!

Karen Olson, thank you for always being there for me and for telling me that you're a guaranteed buyer of multiple copies of the book when I self-consciously asked if you'd buy *one*. I love our times drinking Wildflower iced tea and watching Chris Corsini astrology videos. Our friendship has aged like one of Kevin Olson's fine wines, and when I look to the future, I know you'll be there.

Sarah M. Anderson, I was going through a wee dark night of the soul when I met you in 2024. I wasn't super transparent about that, but you sensed it anyway. Then you proceeded to give me SO MUCH tremendous encouragement and support. You made me laugh *so fucking much.* And I really respect your writing chops. Thank you for helping me learn more about first kisses, action scenes, and all the other stuff. You rule!! *cue guitar solo*

Ema Barnes, you're awesome at what you do, and I really appreciate the developmental edits you gave me. You were the first contact my books had with the outside world, and you treated me with such professionalism and expert care. A million thank-yous for that. I feel so grateful and lucky that you were my first editor!

K. D. Guthauser of Story Wrappers, thank you so much for the beautiful cover. I'll never forget the day I saw the first sketch. It gave me chills. You are truly gifted.

Travis Hasenour of To the Moon and Back Design, thank you for designing my book's beautiful interior. It's so freaking pretty! I really appreciate the hand-holding you gave me given this was my first rodeo, and you are a joy to work with.

Bryony Leah, you are the reason I do not have Elestine and Cèlestine in my book! (Lol, I cannot believe I did not see that.) Thank you for that and for all your expert editing. Your thoughtful questions and suggestions helped me elevate this book to the next level, and you're an absolute pleasure to work with.

Crystal Shelley, a.k.a. the Rabbit with a Red Pen, thank you for proofreading my book. You are incredibly skilled, thoughtful, and detail oriented, and I'm lucky to have found you.

Jeanne De Vita, I'm so thankful we met when we did! You're a total boss. Thank you for all your advice on everything from commissioning a cover to website copy.

Thank you to my beta readers! Dena Berg, Crystal Riches, Purvi Roe, Bree Hagberg, Meg Alexander, Kelly Faulkner, Nicolas William Harper, Mayela Arbona, Maja Brickey, Anna Rolandelli, Alyssa Huck, Matt Washkowiak, Kayla Al-Shamma-Jones, Allyson Whitlow, Jen Grosman, Stephanie Toner, and Catherine Cooley: Your insights and opinions helped shape this book, and I shudder to think what this book might have been if I hadn't gotten your input. Thank you for taking the time to read an unpublished manuscript and for providing such valuable feedback!

Morgan Butler and Dom Fox Santos Sa, thank you both for beta reading my first book. You're both legends for making it through that thing!

Finally, I have to thank God. I don't know what to call my religion, but I pray every day. So many of my prayers and dreams have come true—it makes me feel like magic is real. For the magic that is my actual life, I want to thank God, the universe, my ancestors, my spirit guides, and all the angels watching over me and my family. I'm so deeply grateful that I'm not alone as I walk through this life on Earth.

ABOUT THE AUTHOR

Elizabeth Watson lives in her home state of Arizona with her husband and two tiny overlords. Before turning to writing full time, she spent more than a decade in the world of finance, living in Edinburgh, San Francisco, and London. When she's not writing or spending time with her family, Elizabeth enjoys astrology, tarot, and reading badass fantasy romance. *The Rise of Scarlett Heroux* is her debut novel.

www.ingramcontent.com/pod-product-compliance
Lightning Source LLC
Chambersburg PA
CBHW022017300726
48970CB00003B/923